''Ware rats, 'ware rats,' the cry went up.

The rodents began swarming along the ladder towards the weasel vessel. This vanguard were the terrible berserkers everyone feared, high as kites on the smell of blood and tar. Mawk gave a screech of terror, but was rooted to the spot, unable to run because his legs had seized up.

The doughty Scirf jumped forward onto the ladder, and ran out along it. There he stood, between the ships, ready to defend the *Scudding Cloud* on his own. The rats would have to pass him to board her and he looked determined to stay where he was. 'Come up behind me,' he yelled to his friend Mawk, 'and when I fall, you take my place!'

Mawk was so used to following Scirf's suggestions that he jumped up on the ladder without thinking. He soon realized his mistake, however, and would have turned and gone back, except that Alysoun had jumped up behind him. He could not move forward or back . . .

Windjammer Run is the final triumphant conclusion of a thrilling and very imaginative fantasy, the *Welkin Weasels* trilogy.

GARRY KILWORTH

WINDJAMMER RUN

Book Three of
The Welkin Weasels

CORGI BOOKS

THE WELKIN WEASELS:
WINDJAMMER RUN
A CORGI BOOK : 0 552 54548 1

First publication in Great Britain

PRINTING HISTORY
Corgi edition published 1999

3 5 7 9 10 8 6 4 2

Copyright © 1999 by Garry Kilworth

Set in 11/12pt Palatino
by Phoenix Typesetting, Ilkley, West Yorkshire

Corgi Books are published by Transworld Publishers,
61–63 Uxbridge Road, London W5 5SA,
a division of The Random House Group Ltd,
in Australia by Random House Australia (Pty) Ltd,
20 Alfred Street, Milsons Point, Sydney, NSW 2061, Australia,
in New Zealand by Random House New Zealand Ltd,
18 Poland Road, Glenfield, Auckland 10, New Zealand
and in South Africa by Random House (Pty) Ltd,
Endulini, 5a Jubilee Road, Parktown 2193, South Africa.

Made and printed in Great Britain by
Cox & Wyman Ltd, Reading, Berkshire

TO JENNIFER KETTLE

FROM 'THE HISTORY OF WELKIN'

In the Year of the Egg the woodland weasel Sylver's band was down to seven: there was the monk Luke, Wodehed the magician, the reliable Bryony, Alysoun-the-fleet, Mawk-the-doubter, the redoubtable Scirf and Miniver, the finger-weasel.

All around Welkin the sea walls and river dykes were crumbling fast and Lord Haukin, one of the few good noblestoats, was assisting the weasels to discover the whereabouts of the humans. The weasels wished to encourage the humans to come home. It was hoped that once the humans were back they would then work on the sea defences and save Welkin from the terrible floods which threatened the land.

Prince Poynt and his stoats had no wish to see the return of the humans. The prince was doing very nicely, thank you, and he and his courtiers would rather be washed away by the sea than give up their status as rulers of Welkin. Prince Poynt and his henchstoat, Sheriff Falshed, were committed to doing all in their power to turn the weasels from their task.

At that time there were still a few statues, which had come to life when the humans left, and now bumbled around the countryside. The animals had given the statues nicknames: stone figures were known as 'blocks'; hollow metal statues were called 'gongs'; wooden figures went by the name of 'stumpers'; plaster statues 'puddings'; and finally busts and heads without bodies were termed 'chunks'. These walking statues, the chunks being carried by legged friends, were harmless creatures looking for their First and Last Resting Place – the place where their metal or stone had been mined – where they would lie down and melt back into the earth. Occasionally one of these statues unwittingly hampered the weasels in their quest.

Two clues as to the whereabouts of the humans had now been found: the carving of a dormouse at Thunder Oak and the name of an island at Castle Storm. Sylver's small band of rebellious weasels from Halfmoon Wood now knew where to go to find the lost humans. However, they needed all their weasel courage, for it involved a long sea voyage.

They had no experience of journeying on water and they knew it was a venture from which they might never return. There would be sea monsters with which to contend. There would be wild storms with giant waves. They knew also that there was a chance of encounters with strange tribes on islands where they would have to stop to make repairs and take on provisions. If that was not enough, Flaggatis, the stoat ruler of the rat hordes, was also out for their blood.

Sylver and others of his band, including the more elderly Wodehed, had never seen a live human. The humans had left Welkin before Sylver and his friends were born. It was true that there were some long-living creatures – toads for example – who numbered their lives in years, and these amphibians may have met a human or two in their time. But weasels are more inclined to count the seasons, even the months, rather than years. Their lifespans are somewhat shorter than those of humans or toads, and lengthy time is confusing to a woodland mammal.

Since helping to save Prince Poynt from being overrun by Flaggatis and his rats, Sylver had reluctantly been made Thane of County Elleswhere and Lord of Thistle Hall. Falshed, the High Sheriff, was still determined to get him and the other weasels if he could, but Sylver had so far kept within the law.

Thus Sylver was preparing to go to sea, in search of Dorma Island, where the humans were locked in sleep. He and his weasels knew Prince Poynt would regard this as treason. Their mission had to remain a secret until they had left Welkin. Lord Haukin and myself helped them prepare for the dangerous times ahead, with the only weapon at our disposal: knowledge. When a weasel is armed thus he is a match for any stoat, whether his name be Poynt, Falshed – or Flaggatis.

From the pen of –
CULVER THE WEASEL

9

Chapter One

It was March, the time of the Twirling Hervishes, when hares would come spinning down the country lanes. They would stand on tiptoe and twirl as daintily as any dust devil, hardly stirring the dirt at their feet. When they danced thus, the hares' tar-tipped ears would twist around each other, forming a rope which stood up straight above their heads. Sometimes they would further twist this ear-rope into a top-knot on their scalps, so that they looked like exotic creatures from an oriental land.

The dance was an insane whirling movement, which the dancer performed with wild eyes and wild fur. Often the hares would tie ribbons to their waists and shoulders, which flared when they twirled, entrancing not only themselves but their watchers.

The weasel Scirf, one of Sylver's merry band of ex-outlaws, had taken a winter job. He was a milk-mammal, delivering churns of volemilk to the outlying districts of County Elleswhere.

'I has to keep busy,' he told the rest of the band, who lived in Halfmoon Wood. 'I can't just sit on my bottom the whole winter, like Mawk here.'

Scirf, that redoubtable weasel who had once

watched rhubarb dung for a living, was not an idle creature by nature, except when it came to improving his appearance. There was no vanity or pretension in Scirf: what you saw, you got. And what you saw was a patchy, flea-bitten weasel, with matted fur and scruffy whiskers. He took no pride whatsoever in his appearance. It came, he said, from being companion to dung flies for so many years. Yet his mind was always alert and ready to question the unusual.

'Why do you do that?' he asked the Twirling Hervish hares. 'All that spinnin' stuff?'

'Because it's March,' came the enigmatic reply.

'Mad lot!' clicked Scirf as the hares went swooshing by. 'Must be the wind, gets in their ears and turns their brains funny. Don't like the wind much meself, not when it blows down your lugholes. Enough to make anyone daft.'

It was the time of year, too, for the traditional boxing matches between the hares. Prince Poynt opened up Castle Rayn to the hares and their audiences, coining huge sums in entrance fees. These days you could only reach the castle by boat, since it stood in the middle of a great lake of sea water. Still, that did not prevent the contest from going ahead, and Scirf had begged Sylver to take them all to see this great event in the sporting calendar. The weasels were lounging around amongst the early daffodils on the edge of Halfmoon Wood, when Scirf repeated his request to visit the castle.

'You know, now that spring has arrived, we shall need to look for a ship!' Sylver had replied sternly. He decided this was the moment to

12

make the speech he had been preparing for his weasel band. 'We have to make a voyage to seek the island called Dorma. As you all know, Dorma Island is a place where creatures fall asleep the moment they step ashore.

'Wodehed, our brave magician, has made a deep study of this strange phenomenon and believes it is to do with the lotus flowers which are said to grow on that island. These particularly heavy blooms give out a perfume – a gas – which when one sniffs it causes one to fall into a deep sleep.

'Further study of the flower's effect has caused Lord Haukin, who worked on this project with Wodehed, to put forward the theory that creatures who fall asleep on Dorma Island do not age while under its care. They may sleep for a hundred years and still remain as old as the day they arrived . . .'

There was a buzz of interest amongst the audience. This was a new piece of information. It meant that Alice and Tom, the children who had left clues for the animals, would still be almost as young as they were when they left Welkin. The weasels felt it would be easier to talk to these two than adult humans, who were reputedly warlike, irascible creatures, hard to convince of anything which they did not think of themselves. If the weasels could get the children on their side first, they might stand a chance of winning over the adults.

'Wodehed and Lord Haukin,' continued Sylver, 'have found a herb, a leaf, which when dried and broken up can be stuffed up our nostrils. This will filter out the sleep-inducing fumes from the lotus

13

flowers. We shall hopefully be able to visit the island without falling into its trap.'

Sylver went on to emphasize how important it was to persuade the humans to return to Welkin, even though it was said they spent much of their time at war with one another. The sea walls were crumbling and there would be disastrous floods if they were not properly repaired. Animals could patch the places where the sea walls let in water, using stones and clay, but not as effectively as humans. Great stone blocks were required for the foundations, which only the humans could cut out of the granite hills. These blocks had to be hauled across country and winched into place, before mortar could be applied to seal the cracks.

Mawk was still not convinced. 'You sure we need humans, Sylver? I mean, look what trouble they can cause. I think if we called together all the coypu and badgers – creatures who can dig – why, we'll surely be able to do something.'

Sylver shook his head sadly. He privately agreed with Mawk about the trouble humans could cause. Most four-legged creatures distrusted those who walked on two legs. But humans had hands with thumbs, and could use tools quickly and efficiently.

And they had the trust of larger animals such as horses. A horse would never work for a weasel or a stoat. Already the sea was seeping through in places, forming great salt lakes in low-lying areas. Houses had been washed away. Villages had been flooded. The tips of steeples revealed the whereabouts of towns, but their streets were under water. Animals were skilled at using wood and iron, but huge engineering projects like roads, castles or sea walls were beyond their capabilities.

'We could call in to the castle on our way to look for a ship,' suggested Scirf, not at all put out by Sylver's serious tone. 'We could just drop off at the castle, then make our way up to the north-west, where there's a harbour full of ships. It won't take but a day or two longer, will it?

'I've never seen the hares box. We couldn't do it in the old days, when we was outlaws and Sheriff Falshed was after our necks. Now Prince Poynt has said we're not to be hunted no more and we can go where we like—'

'Don't know why you should want to watch boxing,' interrupted Alysoun sniffily. 'I think it's a barbaric sport.'

'More people get injured at croquet than doin' boxing,' replied Scirf hotly. 'It's a known fact.'

Bryony intervened: 'It is not. I think you made that up. I think you make up a lot of these "known facts" you keep coming out with.'

Scirf shook his head vigorously. 'Croquet and deck quoits – worst sports there is for injuries. You should see some of the lumps and bruises I've seen. Them croquet mallets is deadly in the wrong paws. And them rings at quoits gives you nasty rope burns if you ain't careful how you throw 'em.'

'What a load of rubbish you talk, Scirf.'

However, Luke, Mawk and Wodehed supported Scirf's bid and eventually Sylver gave in and promised they would pay a visit to see the competition on their way north-west.

They set off one morning in April, calling in on

Lord Haukin, now Thane of Fearsomeshire. The stoatlord was busy mooching amongst his books, while his servant Culver polished his collection of bottles. He looked up when Sylver and the rest of the band entered his library. There was always a befuddled look to Lord Haukin as he greeted his unexpected guests.

'Ah, Lord Whatsit. So nice, so nice. You've come to call on your neighbour, have you? Well, as you see, I am at home. Big draughty fortress, not like my dear old Thistle Hall, but one has to make sacrifices if one wants a bigger library.'

Lord Haukin had been the previous occupant of Thistle Hall. One of the more kindly stoats in the kingdom, he treated everyone as equals. It was he who had persuaded Prince Poynt to promote Sylver to the gentry.

'We are just on our way to find a ship, Lord Haukin, by way of Castle Rayn.'

The old stoat frowned. 'By way of the castle? Why is that?'

'I have some rebels in my band who refuse to go to sea without first having witnessed the boxing matches between the hares. You know that at this time of year there are bouts at the castle?'

The three jills waited smugly for Lord Haukin to condemn the sport of boxing out of paw. The bumbling aristocrat was bookish and disliked violence; he was more likely to grow prize geraniums and take pride in his herd of pedigree water voles. And when all was said and done, finding a good ship and setting sail was far more important than watching two male hares slug it out on their hind legs. Bryony, Miniver and

Alysoun were confident of his support against the fraternity of boxing.

'Ah, the ancient art of fisticuffs? Splendid, splendid. Nothing like a good boxing match to set you up for your heroic voyage into the unknown. I heartily approve.'

The female weasels were not only astonished; they were disgusted. 'Come on, Bryony,' said Alysoun, 'let's go for a walk around the box garden while they talk about left hooks and straight rights.'

'Box garden? Not a good choice of words, Alysoun, but I know what you mean,' said Miniver.

The jills went out into the fresh air while the jacks did indeed chatter on about the finer points of barepaw fighting. A little while later, however, they came in again, very breathless.

'There's a group of travelling players in the courtyard, requesting entrance,' said Bryony excitedly. 'They say they wish to put on a play tonight, here at your fortress.'

'Do they now? Well, well. What do you say, Culver? Shall we give them entrance?'

His lordship's servant was the one who actually ran the place and he nodded. 'No reason why not, your lordship. What are they? Weasels or stoats?'

'Both,' replied Alysoun. 'There are seven weasels and three stoats. The stoats appear to be tradesmammals by their speech and manners. One of them wears the apron of a cobbler; another a tanner; a third is a candlemaker.'

'Ah, yes, yes,' murmured Lord Haukin, 'I remember now. The rude mechanicals. They

17

promised me a treat now that I am installed in Lord Ragnar's fortress. He couldn't abide amateur players, you know. Said they were the dregs of the kingdom. Quite enjoy a good play, myself. Send 'em in, Culver.'

'I don't think we can stay,' Sylver said hastily. 'Perhaps we'd better be on our way—'

'If we've got time for boxing matches,' interrupted Bryony, with a dark look at her leader, 'we've got time for a play.'

'Not a *rude* one,' said Mawk. 'I don't think that's right.'

'He doesn't mean "rude" in that sense,' Alysoun replied. 'Rude mechanicals means your rustic tradesmammals, basic workmammals who make things for a living.'

Sylver and Mawk might have argued further with the two jills had not Scirf let out a long, lingering sigh. They all, including Lord Haukin, turned to stare at him in surprise. What they saw was a weasel whose eyes were dreamy, with a faraway look, as if he were in some sort of different place. His mouth opened as he made a flourishing gesture to a suit of armour.

'"Two bees, or not two bees? Perchance they are wasps then, Horatio? What thinkest thou, my philosophical friend?"'

Mawk, Wodehed, Luke and the rest of the weasels groaned.

'I might have guessed it,' Mawk said. 'Scirf is a ham!'

There was now no question of leaving before the play took place. In came the players, full of self-importance and a little too pompous, in the view of the Halfmoon Wood weasels. It turned out that the stoats were a separate group who just happened to arrive at the same time. They were tumblers and acrobats, which posed a problem for Scirf. He thought he was good at that sort of thing, too. He did not like having to choose between asking to be in the play and asking to take part in the more robust entertainment which was to follow.

'Maybe they'll let me be in both,' he whispered to Mawk.

The players wished to do their acting immediately, since they had to get back to their shops, and Lord Haukin agreed to sit his guests down in the big West Hall. Culver set about this task straight away and herded the weasel band into the hall. Scirf hung back a bit, but then decided he would tackle the problem when they were all set to go.

Once they were settled, the players came in wearing a variety of costumes.

'The play we are about to perform for you,' said the leader of the rude mechanicals, 'is called *Pyramouse and Thisbee*. I have to warn the jills that there is a rather ferocious water rat in the play – the villain of the piece – but we have asked our carpenter here not to snarl too loudly. We have told him to speak his part in a small voice—'

Scirf jumped up. 'I can speak in a small voice. Listen –' Scirf's voice rose to a grating squeak – '"Thisbee, Thisbee, wherefore art thou, my little cockleshell? Hidin' in the cupboard under the stairs?"'

The leader of the rude mechanicals frowned. 'Sir, we are well endowed with players and need

19

no members of the audience to swell our ranks. I am certain your acting is of the highest calibre, but actually the word "wherefore", in the context of this play, means "why" and does not refer to anyone hiding away from anyone else. May we proceed?'

'You mean, you don't want to use me?' said an astonished Scirf. 'Even with my background in actin'?'

'I am certain our play will be the poorer for your absence, sire, but we must learn by our own mistakes.'

'Suit yerself, squire,' replied Scirf, folding his forelegs and assuming the pose of one who was about to become the fiercest of critics.

The play actually went quite smoothly, considering it had been rehearsed but a single time before the live performance, and the jills clicked their teeth loudly in appreciation. Lord Haukin murmured his congratulations to the leader. The jacks of the ex-outlaw band nodded and said quietly to each other that it was not as bad as they had expected. Scirf simply sat there and scowled.

After the players had left the tumblers somersaulted into the room, with a 'Hup!' and a 'Hey!' as they span head over heels and landed back on their feet with their forepaws raised.

This time Scirf was not going to ask. He leapt to his feet and went somersaulting into the middle of the hall with the tumblers. He, too, could do his 'Hups!' and his 'Heys!' with just as much flourish as the visiting stoats. Ignoring their black looks, he continued to copy their tricks. When they made a pyramid of three, with the top stoat balancing on the shoulders of the other two doing a paw-stand, Scirf did a magnificent leap over the top of them, narrowly missing the jill at the top and causing the whole animal structure to topple.

The stoats were not pleased with Scirf, but he had made his point, and sat down after that to enjoy the show.

Shortly after midnight, when it was all over, the weasels took their leave of Lord Haukin and set off in the direction of Castle Rayn. Scirf was explaining to Mawk (and anyone else who would listen) that he had practised acrobatics while he was watching the dung heap in his early years. Mawk asked if there was no end to Scirf's talents and was not surprised to receive the answer in the form of a modest shrug.

Each weasel now carried a haversack. Lord Haukin had suggested that since they would eventually have to pass through Glubba's kingdom of frogs, they should take gifts with them for the massive king. Each haversack was packed with fly cakes which Lord Haukin had had prepared before the weasels had arrived. These were cakes made of packed and compressed dead flies. Each weasel carried about thirty black cakes with runny red fillings and a kind of yellowy-green topping. They would be counted a great delicacy by the frog king.

Chapter Two

In Castle Rayn Prince Poynt was preparing for the annual hare boxing event. He loved times like these, when he could hurry from room to room amid the bustle of servants and slaves. His face would reveal his feelings within a second, showing satisfaction or displeasure with the arrangements. He did not even have to use his brain. All he had to do was look at a hall decked with red bunting and frown.

'No good, wrong colour, change it,' would be his only command.

Then he would sweep away, leaving the weasels and stoats halfway up ladders or hanging from dusty beams, looking at each other with helpless expressions. If only the prince would indicate what *might be* a good colour, their looks said, then they would have something to go by. Instead they had to clamber up the pillars and remove the red bunting and replace it with blue, or yellow, or pink.

Then they would stand by again and hope for the best.

Prince Poynt was, of course, still in his winter coat of ermine, even though it was spring. He never changed out of it. In consequence of this, he thought it was still cold outside. In consequence of this, the castle always had fires roaring in its hearths. In consequence of this, everyone else in the castle, especially the manual workers, sweated buckets.

'We don't like this ruddy hue, change it for another do,' sang a gaily-attired weasel to the workers in the hall. 'Pink or green or white or blue, black or orange – something new.' This individual would then rush from one worker to another beating them all about the head and backside with a mouse's bladder on the end of a stick.

They took this humiliating treatment with gritted teeth, for the clowning weasel was the prince's jester, Pompom, and he basked in reflected authority.

The rest of the noblestoats, such as Jessex, Wilisen and Lord Elphet, wandered around making dry comments and picking up on detail. This pleased the servants and slaves no end. There is nothing like hanging dangerously from a chandelier by your forepaw, trying to hook a piece of bunting over a beam, while advice comes from the mouths of idle watchers below.

'Bit more to your left. No, that's no good. It won't stay up there a minute like that. You need to hoick yourself up onto that beam and crawl to the middle. What are you frightened of? A bit of dust? Spiders? They won't hurt you. Lord Elphet here used to scoot up there when we were kittens playing hide and seek, didn't you, my lord? Oh, heavens above, now you've dropped the whole ribbon. Butterfingers! No, I won't paw it up to you, you lazy dolt. You come down here and get it.

Serve you right for not paying attention to what you're doing . . .'

Down in the kitchens, one level above the dungeons which were now flooded and unusable, Sibiline was supervising preparations for the banquet. The prince's sister wanted this to be a really grand affair, since the castle had been under siege for most of the previous year and its occupants starved.

Haunches of hickory-smoked mouse meat hung from hooks, ready for slicing. Roasting sparrows basted with frog fat sizzled in the ovens. Freshwater prawns stuffed with water boatmen stood on platters ready to be served cold.

For starters there was slug soup or worm consommé served with bread peppered with wild earwigs; followed by newts' tongues in volecream sauce; cuckoo spit and snail-slime dips; toad-spawn jelly with salty biscuit; and finally, the caviare of Welkin, stickleback roe on little strips of crunchy toast. However, Sibiline could not obtain many of the foodstuffs which she would have loved to have on her table. The floods had unfortunately ruined many crops: grain and vegetables had rotted in the fields and much of the populace was without nourishment.

Sibiline was not too concerned about starving magpies in the south, or hungry moles in the north. Sad to say, castle life had given her a rather blinkered view of such things. Her intention was to put on a feast, come Otherworld or high water, and finish it off with Crudder Valley cheese.

There was nothing much in the way of afters. Stoats and their kind are not fond of sweet things;

a little bees' honey here, a little wasps' honey there, but merely as an ingredient. Sibiline was famous for savoury dishes, garnished with fluffy dandelion seeds, the silver threads of old man's beard or, if she was feeling really adventurous, pink campion petals dusted with pollen from lords-and-ladies.

She busied herself around the cooks and chefs, humming a special springtime tune, happy to be in charge.

When Prince Poynt tired of wafting around the halls and staircases, changing things, he called for Sheriff Falshed to meet him on the battlements. Falshed was enjoying a bath at the time. His servant Spinfer was pouring scented oils into the water when the messenger arrived to summon the good sheriff topside. With a testy look which the sheriff would never have used in front of the prince, Falshed got out of his hot tub and allowed himself to be towelled by his servant.

'Here, not so rough,' he told Spinfer, who looked on towelling his master as an opportunity for revenge for all sorts of put-upons. 'Steady with that tail – it's delicate.'

'Yes, sir,' murmured Spinfer silkily, but rubbing harder still, knowing that the sheriff was in a hurry and could not afford to remonstrate too much. 'I just thought you ought to dry quickly, so as not to keep the prince waiting.'

Fluffy-furred but sore-tailed and smarting, Falshed eventually hurried up a spiral staircase to the battlements. He found the prince looking out over the salt lake which now surrounded his castle. An invasion of rat hordes had recently been repelled, but only at the cost of dry land. Lord Haukin and Sylver had supervised the breaching of certain sea walls to cause a flood, thus driving the rats back to the unnamed marshes in the north. Prince Poynt, now a prisoner in his own home, with half his kingdom lying under salt water, wondered whether it had been worth it.

'Ah, Falshed,' said the prince as the sheriff approached, 'I want a word with you about the boxers.'

Falshed's fur tingled. He knew what was coming. 'Yes, my liege?'

'That big bruiser who knocked everybody out last year – what is his name? The one with the wide shoulders.'

'I think you mean Bludger Brassnose, my prince.'

'That's the fellah. I want you to get him to lose.'

Falshed gulped. 'You mean, take a fall, take a dive, throw the fight—'

'Any one of those will do, so long as he makes it look good. I've put a thousand groats on Kipper, that lean and hungry-looking hare who was last year's runner-up. He has to win, of course. I can't afford to lose a thousand groats, now can I? I'm not made of money, even though I am a prince. Besides, I don't *like* losing. It hurts me in here.' The prince tapped his white furry chest.

'No, my liege. I mean, yes, I see that Kipper has to win, only – it's very difficult, my prince.'

Falshed's problem was that hares were all very honourable creatures. They refused any offers of bribes. And you could not threaten them. In theory, stoats were the masters of hares, but hares

26

were big rough creatures with savage back feet. Even when the humans were around, hares did not fear carnivores in the same way as rabbits did. Hares were extremely fast on their feet; they could outrun foxes, let alone stoats. And if cornered they put up one dickens of a fight. Their claws could rake a dog and send it whining home.

'I don't see what's difficult about it, Falshed,' the prince responded sweetly. 'Either you make sure Kipper wins or you end up hanging on the gibbet, with the wind blowing the rain . . .'

'. . . through the holes in my pelt. Yes, my liege. I understand perfectly. Leave it to me.'

Falshed hurried away in a deep funk. He knew where he was going: straight to his stoatservant, Spinfer, whose skull was like an eagle's egg, full of thick gooey yolky brains. The kind that counts when it comes to thinking. There have been masters and servants like Falshed and Spinfer all through history. The masters got the double-chins and funny noses, and the servants got two help-ings of brains.

'Spinfer?' cried Falshed, hurrying into his quarters. 'I need you.'

'Yes, sir?' Spinfer came out of the shadows like a phantom, making Falshed jump.

'How do you do that? Never mind, I need your help. The prince has asked me to make sure that lean and hungry-looking hare, Kipper, wins the boxing tournament.'

'Kipper is a very good boxer, sir.'

'He is?' cried Falshed, his hopes rising.

'Unfortunately, not quite as good as Bludger Brassnose.'

Flashed's hopes came crashing down to earth again. 'That's what I thought. That's why I need your help.'

'And the Brassnose has never yet taken a bribe or succumbed to a threat.'

'Yes, yes, that's why . . .'

'. . . you need my help. I understand, sir. I shall put my best mind to the job.'

'I thought we might put a few iron mouseshoes in Kipper's gloves.'

Spinfer gave his master a withering look. 'Please, sir, do leave it to me. I would prefer not to have your assistance if I am going to do the thinking. This is barepaw boxing. They do not wear gloves.'

'Oh, yes, I forgot. All right, you go ahead and think away, Spinfer. I'll just sit here and watch you.'

'I would prefer to do it in the quiet ambience of the kitchen, if you would not mind, sir.'

With that the redoubtable servant left the room. Falshed paced impatiently up and down, staring out of the arrowloop windows gloomily, watching the fish break surface after flies. He hated to wait for results, especially when someone else was doing the work. His inclination was to rush into the kitchen after two minutes and ask how it was going. He managed to stifle this desire, though it welled strong inside him. A very long time later Spinfer came smooling (this is not a real word but describes the action perfectly) into the room.

'Yes, yes?' cried Falshed.

'It is my opinion, sir, that the Brassnose should not be at the boxing tournament at all.'

The worried sheriff considered this statement, since Spinfer did not elaborate on it. Was the fellow mad? Bludger Brassnose was clearly on the list of boxers, which meant he would certainly be at the tournament. What did the fool mean? Falshed was willing to admit he often missed nuances, subtle little details, but he could see none of those here. He gritted his teeth and said the words he hated to say in front of Spinfer: 'I'm afraid I don't quite understand.'

Spinfer clicked his teeth in amusement, having registered the score. 'I mean, sir, we have to stop him arriving. You need two good stout fellows with cudgels to waylay the Brassnose and put him in cold storage for a few weeks.'

A light went on in the dark recesses of Falshed's mind. 'Ah! Now I'm with you. Two scoundrels, you say? Like those ferrets, Rosencrass and Guildenswine?'

'As you well know, Rosencrass and Guildenswine are dead, sir. I was thinking rather more on the lines of bigger chaps, since the Brassnose is no half-pint. What about the badgers, Herk and Bare? They're unmitigated rogues to be sure, sir. And they're big enough to put away a fully-grown wolf, if required. Would you like me to contact them? I have a cousin who lives at the bottom of the lane where Herk and Bare inter most of their victims' bodies. They dig them up again later, of course, and sell the rotten bits to sorcerers for use in spells. All it would take is a message to my cousin.'

A chill went through the sheriff. 'Yes, yes. I suppose so. Are they expensive? To hire, I mean.'

'They're not cheap, sir.'

'No, no, they wouldn't be. All right, yes please, Spinfer. Get them to come to the castle.'

Spinfer bowed and left the room.

Three nights later the gentle splash of oars could be heard below Falshed's windows. The sheriff peeked out to see two badgers in a rowing boat. One of them was a huge fellow with half his right ear missing and a bite scar on his shoulder the shape and size of leaping salmon. The other was bigger and rougher looking. They both glanced up at Falshed's windows together, as if they had sensed him looking out. A shudder trickled down Falshed's back, making his fur rise like a hedgehog's spines. He noticed that in the bottom of the boat there were two thick cudgels with knobbly bits.

Somehow Spinfer managed to spirit the two villains into Falshed's quarters without the prince being aware they were in the castle. Falshed gave them each a mugful of cheap honey dew and then got down to business.

'It's the hare, Brassnose. I want him prevented from coming to the boxing tournament. Think you can do it?'

Herk was sitting on a stool, his feet up on the sheriff's card table. He was filling the chamber with noxious fumes from his home-made chokey, which to Falshed's annoyance he had lit without so much as a by-your-leave. This particular badger also had an enormous belly hanging over his leather belt. Sheriff Falshed, coughing in the fug the badger was producing, could not help staring at this enormous gut.

Herk caught his eye and showed his yellow teeth, patting the expanse of flesh. 'Too much cheap honey dew,' he growled, not without a touch of annoyance. 'Puts on the lard.'

Bare was thinner, a nervous creature, pacing the floor in front of the inglenook fireplace. Occasionally he snatched Herk's chokey and took a puff, giving it back to his companion afterwards. He had narrow eyes and kept picking objects from the mantelpiece, inspecting them, then putting them back, but he was not really looking at the things. He was just doing something to occupy his paws while the business was transacted.

'Think we can do it?' said Bare, after a long time.

'Course we can *do* it. But what about the payment? We're not cheap.'

Falshed sighed and began to haggle with the pair until finally a price was agreed.

'Now, what do you want us to do with him?' asked Herk. 'I mean, do you want him a gone hare? Or shall we just tap his skull and leave him to wake up a few days later? Either will do. It doesn't matter to us. Mind you, if we put him away for good, there's extra for getting rid of the body. It'll have to be buried somewhere secret and digging a grave is hard work.'

Somewhere secret, thought Falshed, like at the bottom of Spinfer's cousin's lane. 'Just make sure he doesn't turn up at the boxing. That's all that's necessary. You've already had a purse full of money out of me. There's no more.'

'No problem, sheriff. Don't get yourself excited,' said Herk. 'You won't see hide nor hare of the fellow.'

31

With that, the big badger clicked his teeth in a show of amusement at his own joke, while his friend stared moodily at the carving of a damselfly which Princess Sibiline had given Falshed very recently. Falshed being a commoner and the princess being royalty, there was no question of a *serious* romance. However, her previous disregard for him had gradually changed to mild affection, since he was the one castle bachelor who was not saddled with an established mate or an addled brain.

Like certain spoiled royalty Sibiline fed on flattery and attention. These needs were kept amply supplied by Falshed who, as the prince's right-paw stoat, was a brilliant sycophant. One had to be to survive in the prince's service. Sibiline had always dreamed of a knight in shining armour coming for her, a bunch of marigolds in his mail-gloved claw.

However, she now realized that this scenario was very unlikely, since most of the nobles lived in the castle and were rather boring. Those who did not had become either old and dithery, like Lord Haukin, or alarmingly eccentric recluses like Earl Batherspoone-Richly-Phelps. Only Falshed was even remotely available and Sibiline had let him pour adulation on her head at every opportunity.

Falshed had promised on his mother's grave that he would never part with the carving: Sibiline had told him he had better not because it symbolized their spiritual devotion to one another.

The two badgers left at midnight, rowing back to the shore in the dark. Falshed could see the burning red tips of their chokies long after their forms had melted into the night. He hoped he had done the right thing in hiring these creatures. He ordered Spinfer to light a fire and then sat in front of it until two in the morning, rubbing his paws together, praying that all went well with his plan. It was not until he was ready to go to bed that he noticed that half his ornaments were missing from the mantelpiece.

Falshed sat up with a start and let out a cry like a seagull in pain.

The carving of the damselfly had gone.

Chapter Three

Sylver and the ex-outlaws were passing through lonely country. They had just crossed moorland studded with small clumps of trees, fording a fast stream that cut a winding path through the rocky peat, when they came upon a large wood. A dry-stone wall abutted the wood on the near side. There was no gate so they climbed over the wedged stones to enter the relative gloom of the forest. Each of the weasels was immersed in his or her own thoughts. A lot had happened to them over the last few seasons. Two of their band had lost their lives and now their leader was suddenly elevated to lordship. These were momentous events in the life of any weasel.

Although he had fought for the right to bring back the humans, Sylver was still not sure he was doing the correct thing. Perhaps the humans did not want to return. Perhaps they would refuse, outright, to come home. Perhaps they were not even masters or mistresses of their own fate. Perhaps a higher order had ordained that they leave Welkin for ever. These were all un-answered questions and the young weasel wondered whether he would ever get the answers to them.

As the band approached a clearing in the middle of the wood Sylver began to think about finding a place to bivouac for the night. It was at that moment he held up his paw for silence amongst the weasels. There were sounds of a struggle coming from a circle of rocks ahead.

'Help! Ho!' came an urgent voice. 'I am beset by thieves!'

Then there was a thumping sound and the world fell silent.

Sylver, Bryony and Scirf, who were at the front, rushed forward. Around a big boulder they came across a clump of pines. In the dimness were two bulky shapes hovering over a lump on the ground. One of them had a smoking chokey in the corner of his mouth. He was in the act of striking the mound with a cudgel when Sylver shouted a command.

'Hold! Stay your paw, whoever you are, or it will be the worse for you.'

Bryony and Scirf were already fitting pebbles into their slings. The two shapes with cudgels in their paws stared out at the three weasels. Their eyes glinted in the dark interior. They were huge beasts – Sylver could see that – and they seemed ready to attack the three weasels, until they saw the rest of the band running round the big boulder.

Bryony immediately loosed a stone, which struck the bigger of the two beasts on the snout. The creature let out a growl which immediately told the weasels that these pawpads were badgers, no doubt robbing a wayfarer. Like any other beast, there were good and bad amongst them. These were definitely two *bad* badgers, intent on robbery with violence.

'Badgers or no, we'll bring you down with a hail of pebbles if you don't step away from your victim,' cried Sylver, now whirling his own sling-shot.

The two figures began to edge away into the darker shadows of the pinewood. They were growling threats at the weasels in some foul and ancient tongue, known only to subterranean creatures like themselves. Moles might have understood them, or perhaps even rabbits, but weasels had no knowledge of such dialects. Then one of the badgers suddenly stepped forward and threw his cudgel. It came spinning through the air with a whistling sound.

'Look out!' cried Scirf, and brought Mawk down with a tackle at the waist, just as the club went whirring over the spot where he had been standing.

Then the two badgers were gone. The weasels could hear them crashing through the forest on the other side, but it was useless to chase them, for the night was closing in. Instead, the ex-outlaws hurried into the trees to see if they could do anything for the lump of fur and bone which lay still on a mossy bank.

'Make a light, someone,' ordered Sylver. 'Let's see what we've got here.'

Alysoun took out a tinder-box from the pouch on her belt and soon had a little pile of dry pine needles blazing away. She made a brand of some bracken and stood near while Sylver inspected the badgers' victim.

'It's a hare,' said Sylver, looking down at the silent form. 'Anyone know him?'

Scirf pushed his way to the front of the circle. 'Bludger Brassnose,' he said immediately. 'He'll be on his way to the boxing at the castle.'

'Bludger Brassnose?' repeated Wodehed. 'He's supposed to be quite good, isn't he?'

'The best,' confirmed Mawk.

'Well, he's all lumps and bumps at the moment,' Alysoun said. 'I think he's dead. He's taken quite a beating from those pawpads. I wonder if they got his money.'

Miniver nodded. 'Yes, look, his purse has been cut from his belt. There's just a little bit of leather left. What a great pity it is a lone animal can't walk the woods of Welkin without being attacked by animals.'

Mawk said, 'Shall we bury him?'

Wodehed, who acted as physician amongst the group, put his ear to the hare's chest and listened hard. It seemed to him that he could still hear a faint beat there, but it was softer than the pulse of a bee. 'Still alive – just. Build a fire and try to keep him warm for the night. If he manages to make it through until morning he might stand a chance. Otherwise I think he's had it. I'll mix up something from the healing herbs in my pouch.'

Sylver said, 'Those savages really laid into him with their clubs. Mawk and Scirf, you go and find firewood. Bryony, make a bed of pine needles, nice and soft. He might as well have a comfortable night, even if it is his last. Miniver and Alysoun, you stand guard – one on the north side of the wood, the other on the south. There's a deep gorge to the west and a fast-running torrent to the east, so we need not worry about attack from those directions . . .'

The weasels busied themselves with their given tasks. They built a large fire in the middle of a clearing. Wodehed applied a balm to the hare's cuts, lumps and bruises, then forced some medicine down his throat.

As for the badgers, Sylver thought the firelight would probably deter them if they tried to return; nevertheless guards were posted throughout the night. Nothing untoward happened, however, and morning eventually came, sneaking over the moors like a grey cat. Alysoun went down to a rushy beck for some water; then they inspected the hare.

'He's still breathing,' said Bryony. 'I think he's going to live.'

'It was touch and go, though,' Mawk commented. 'Those rogues nearly did for him.'

Bryony dipped a piece of rag in the cool water from the stream and dabbed the hare's bruised face with it. A little while later, as the breakfast porridge reached the boil, he opened his eyes. He stared into the faces of Bryony, Mawk and Alysoun, who were leaning over him.

'Bad-gers,' he croaked.

'*Very* bad gers,' Mawk agreed.

Bryony remonstrated with him. 'This is no time for joking, Mawk.'

'Why not? It might cheer up Brassnose.'

'Brass-nose, yes,' murmured the hare. 'I am – Brassnose.'

'More like Spongenose at the moment, squire,'

said Scirf, coming over to the group. 'You're all squished up. Never mind, we'll get you to the castle. Sylver and Wodehed are fixing up a litter to carry you on. You're in safe paws now.'

Brassnose seemed satisfied and closed his eyes.

After breakfast they heaved the hare onto the litter and carried him, a weasel to each corner. His eyes remained closed and he seemed to be resting. He was a very heavy hare and they were glad when the water hove into view. They could see the castle on an island in the middle of the lake.

'Now we need a rowing boat or some such craft,' Sylver said. 'Scirf, will you walk along the bank and see if you can find one? There's bound to be a jetty near by. Ferries spring up like mushrooms when there's a new stretch of water to cross.'

They did indeed find a quay where ferries were doing good business, especially with the boxing tournament coming up. A grouchy old stoat with a raft agreed to take them across. He made no comment when they carried the stiff and seemingly lifeless hare on board. It seemed curiosity was not part of his make-up. He looked as if he had seen everything in his lifetime and would not have raised an eyebrow at the moon falling from the sky and landing in the water.

When the group reached the castle there were other boats arriving and departing. A set of wooden steps had been built on the outer wall to cope with the passengers. Idle nobles were hanging over the battlements watching the to-ing and fro-ing. It was a new interest for those who were easily bored.

Among these aristocrats stood Sheriff Falshed. His eyes fell on the ex-outlaws and then on the figure lying on the litter. He stiffened visibly, his white bib with the burn mark bristling.

'Up the steps with him now,' said Wodehed. 'Careful, weasels, don't let him slip off.'

Falshed came huffing and puffing to meet them at the top.

''Ello, 'ello, it's our old friend, Sheriff Falshed,' said Scirf. 'Come to greet us, 'ave you?'

'Certainly not,' replied Falshed, scowling. Then his voice changed a note. 'I – I say, is that Bludger Brassnose?'

Sylver glanced down at the figure on the stretcher. 'Yes, it is. He was set upon by pawpads on the mainland.'

'Is he – dead?'

'No,' answered Bryony, 'he's very much alive, thank goodness. The poor hare has been beaten black and blue by those devils with cudgels.'

'Is he – is he in any condition to fight?'

'You must be joking, squire,' replied Scirf. 'He can hardly move an eyelid, let alone a paw. This is one hare who'll be out of the competition. Why, did you have a wager on him?'

A look of relief flooded across the features of the stoat sheriff. 'Wager? No – that is, yes, but I don't mind losing it. I mean, it's only money, isn't it? This poor creature can't help not being fit for the fight, can he? Fancy being set upon by badgers. You can't trust them, these days. They are apt to go bad, you know. I once knew a badger . . .' Falshed stopped because the weasels were looking at him through narrowed eyes.

40

'Who said anythink about *badgers*?' Scirf demanded.

Sylver said, 'Yes – what do you know about this, Sheriff Falshed?'

'Wha— didn't you say badgers?'

'He said *pawpads*,' answered Bryony, with tight lips.

'Yes, I did,' added Sylver.

'Well,' Falshed let out a tinkling click of the teeth, 'you know, most pawpads these days *are* badgers. It's an honest assumption to make. I just naturally assumed they were badgers.' His voice hardened a little when he realized to whom he was speaking. 'Anyway, what's it to you, Sylver?'

'That's Lord Sylver, to you. I think I outrank you, Sheriff Falshed, and I would be obliged if you would call me by my proper title.'

Falshed went purple-faced and looked as if he were about to explode. 'Listen . . .' he said in a taut voice.

'Lord Sylver,' Bryony urged.

'Listen – Lord Sylver –' the words choked in Falshed's throat – 'I know nothing about this affair. It was an honest mistake. There have been a lot of reports about two rogue badgers on the mainland, attacking pilgrims and wayfarers. I shall send a band of armed stoats over there today, to see what can be done about them. In the meantime I should be obliged if you would not accuse me of – whatever it is that you *are* accusing me of – in front of my subordinates and friends.' He made a sweeping gesture towards the soldiers – his subordinates – and the noblestoats – his friends.

'What's going on here?' asked Jessex, coming over to where the group was standing. 'What are you weasels doing here, crowding our battlements? Who's that fellow – good gosh, I say, it's Bludger Brassnose. Is he dead? I've wagered a thousand groats that he'll flatten the Kipper.'

Sylver replied, 'No, he's not dead, but he's close to it. He certainly won't be fit enough to box. Might I ask who you have the wager with?'

'Why, Prince Poynt,' replied Jessex, his head coming up. He scowled. 'Not that it's any business of yours, weasel. And don't look at me like that, or I'll knock your eyes out. I don't care whether you've been puffed up to a lord or not. You're still a nasty little weasel as far as I'm concerned. For two pins I'd call you out, but I haven't got the time.' With that, Jessex stared at Bludger Brassnose in disgust, then turned on his four paws and left them.

Scirf stared at Falshed. 'Prince Poynt, eh? I reckon every noble in the castle has probably got a bet on with Prince Poynt for Brassnose to win. It would suit the prince very well if Brassnose was not able to fight, wouldn't it, eh?'

'Don't you go making assumptions about the prince too,' growled Falshed. 'I am quite happy to let personal insults fly above my head, being contemptuous of oaths from the mouths of babes and weasels, but I would have to arrest anyone bringing accusations against my prince.'

'Would you mind directing us to the hospital ward?' asked Bryony coldly. 'This hare needs attention.'

'Take him to the nuns in the west tower,' replied

the sheriff airily. 'But before you go, I should like to inspect those packs on your backs. We are becoming too lax at the castle, allowing all sorts of riff-raff to enter without checking them for weapons which might be used to harm the prince.'

'We carry no weapons but our slingshots,' said Sylver testily, 'and we need those to protect ourselves when crossing open country.'

'Just the same, I should like to see in the packs.'

Scirf stepped forward, took off his haversack and opened the top. 'Help yourself, squire.'

'That's *sheriff* to you.'

Falshed reached into the pack and extracted one of the fly cakes. 'What's this?' he asked, holding it up. 'It looks like a bun.'

'It's a cake. Present for someone,' said Sylver.

'Present for *me*,' Falshed said, opening his mouth and taking a huge bite. 'Hmmmmm.' He began chewing. Suddenly his expression changed. He stared at the cake in his paw. 'Wha— what's this made of?'

'Dead flies,' Bryony said with a click of her teeth.

Falshed dropped the cake and spat out what was still in his mouth. He retched violently, staggering to the edge of the battlements. When he had finished heaving he came back to the amused weasels looking pale-eyed and ill. 'That's horrible,' he said. 'I ought to have you arrested for dealing in poisonous foodstuffs. Read that notice over there on the tower.'

Scirf stared at the notice and intoned, 'FOR I EG NGOOD SMU STNOT BEIM POR TEDIN TOTHI SCAST LE.' Having read the notice he turned to the sheriff. 'Don't understand it,' he said. 'What is it, Latin?'

'You oaf,' growled Falshed, 'it reads, FOREIGN GOODS MUST NOT BE IMPORTED INTO THIS CASTLE.'

'These ain't foreign, they're home-bred, these flies. They're fine clegs, they are. I collected most of 'em myself, the live ones from the cesspit at the bottom of Thistle Hall garden, and the dead ones from Mother Quin's kitchen windowsill.'

'They're not poisonous, as such,' Bryony said, tying up the top of the pack again, 'they're just disgusting. We're thinking of opening up a restaurant to sell them. "Zoonoos", we'll call it, after a cousin of mine . . .'

The bitter sheriff glared, then began to retch again, finally walking away and leaving the ex-outlaws to themselves.

'Serve 'im right,' Scirf said. 'Hope he gets the runs.'

They hoisted Brassnose back onto their shoulders and then set off in search of the west tower. Wodehed began sorting through some herbs he had gathered early that morning. He was not a particularly good magician, but he knew his medicine. He had been known to revive an animal close to death with a pinch of this and a sprig of that. Certainly he felt that once Brassnose was comfortably ensconced in a proper bed, with facilities to simmer a concoction or two, he could set about improving the hare's condition.

Chapter Four

The weasels deposited their load in the west tower, leaving Brassnose in the care of weasel nuns. Wodehed remained with him. The wizard was already boiling up some strange-looking leaves and roots in an iron pot. The rest of the band made their way to the great hall, where a boxing ring had been erected. Unlike human boxing rings, which are square in shape, those used by hares are circular. Hares invented the boxing ring, which is where the term actually came from in the first place. Humans took the name but changed the shape for some peculiar reason known only to those contrary two-legged creatures.

Here they found hares sparring with one another, just as they do out on some grassy hillock in the fields.

Watching them, from a large chair, was Prince Poynt. He was accompanied by his sister, Sibiline, and his jester, Pompom.

On seeing the weasels, Pompom came dancing over with his inflated mouse's bladder on a stick. He seemed full of the joys of spring and was about to batter the ex-outlaws with his balloon. Then he caught the look in Scirf's eye and stopped dead.

'Touch me with that thing,' said Scirf, 'an' I'll take you into that ring over there and give you a pasting.'

Pompom blinked, as if he were about to cry, then turned and pranced back to the prince's side, shouting, 'Spoilsport,' over his shoulder.

On hearing this the prince glanced over at the weasels and then scowled. He whispered something to his sister and they both clicked their teeth in amusement. A little while later the prince rose languidly and went through a doorway at the far end of the hall, followed by his retinue.

'Good riddance,' muttered Sylver. Then, to a nearby hare, he called, 'Aren't you the Kipper?'

The lean, wiry-looking hare stopped in the middle of a sparring bout. 'That's me. Who's asking?'

'Sylver – Lord Sylver of Thistle Hall, County Elleswhere. We picked up a friend of yours on the road here. Bludger Brassnose.'

'He's no friend of mine. Good boxer, but you can't afford to be sentimental in this business. I'm going to knock his block off when the time comes.'

'No, you're not. He was beaten up with cudgels. He's lying in the hospital now.'

Kipper frowned and came over to the weasels. 'Beaten up, you say? That's bad. He may be a rival but I wouldn't wish him that sort of harm. Know who's responsible?'

'Two rogue badgers. They were standing over him when we arrived on the scene. I think they would have killed him if we hadn't turned up.'

Kipper nodded. 'I bet there's some nasty work going on. I've heard the stakes are high this year.

46

Don't approve of gambling, myself. I wish we could keep the sport clean of such things. But there you go. Even if there was a law against it, they would still do it, those foolish enough to part with their hard-earned money.'

'So you know nothing about it?' asked Scirf.

'Not a thing and I kind of resent the implication, friend.'

Sylver said, 'Sorry – naturally we suspect the animal who has most to gain from Brassnose being out of the competition.'

'Listen, weasels, I want to win, sure – but I want to win fair and round. It don't mean nothing to me to win by foul means. Up there in the ring is all that counts with me. There's no honour in winning any other way. I'm truly sorry about the Brassnose. I was looking forward to the fight.'

'I believe you,' said Sylver. 'If you hear anything, let us know, will you? We sort of have a stake in the outcome now.'

'I certainly will.'

They left the hall and made their way towards a courtyard in the east wing, where all visitors found a space to sleep and marked it out in the dust. Here it was lively and colourful: there were food stalls and water-sellers and other market traders. Here, too, the ex-outlaws came across an old acquaintance of theirs – an otter called Sleek, who was heavily into fabrics and fashions.

Sleek was now Princess Sibiline's personal designer, but he still moved among the common mammals. Today he was dressed in a burnt orange flowing robe (orange was his favourite colour). It was a fluid, loose-fitting garment inspired by more eastern climes and the light fabric drifted and wafted about his ottery self in gorgeous waves. On his head he wore an indigo-coloured turban; on his rear paws were sandals with burnt orange and indigo straps.

'Hey, Sleek!' called Scirf. 'How's the stitchin' business?'

The otter looked across and his face showed his pleasure at seeing the ex-outlaws. They had been in part responsible for his breaking away from his old set; they still lived in an underground river, terrified that their whereabouts would be discovered.

'Scirf, Sylver, Bryony, Alysoun, Luke!' cried the young otter. 'How simply wonderful to see you.' He floated over to the group and stood before them.

'You look as though you're doin' well enough,' said Scirf. 'Life at the castle suits you, eh?'

'I am the princess's favourite at the moment. She's so exciting. She likes everything I produce. I've got this beautiful textile coming from the far east of Welkin. It's being transported by mouse-caravan. The secret is in the dye, which comes from a clay found only in the Okaton basin . . .'

The weasels' eyes were beginning to glaze over as the otter waxed and elaborated on his favourite theme. They talked with him about this and that, and finally asked whether he had heard of any rogue brocks in the district.

The otter's brow creased into a little frown as he thought hard. 'I'm not sure about *rogue* badgers,' he said, 'but I did see two of the creatures the other morning. They came over the lake in the early mist and entered the castle before anyone was awake. That is, *I* was awake, but apart from a few dozy sentries I was the only one.'

'Do you know who they came to see?' asked Sylver.

'I saw them being met by Spinfer. He's the sheriff's stoatservant. They looked a scruffy pair of herberts, I can tell you. I heard Spinfer call them by name – Jerk? Lurk? No, wait a minute – *Herk*. Herk and Bare. That's what he called them.'

'Peltsnatchers,' said Scirf. 'I know 'em. Right pair of herberts, as you say, Sleek. When they're not robbing somebody's grandmother, they're stealin' corpses from gibbets, so that they can sell the hides to bootmakers.'

'Hmm,' Sylver murmured. 'So it looks as if we were right about Sheriff Falshed. He *is* behind this. Not much we can do about it, though, even if we could prove it. The prince is not likely to charge Falshed with anything. I suppose we'll just have to let things remain as they are for the moment.'

The ex-outlaws took their leave of Sleek and Sylver told the others he would see them later: he actually had a good reason for coming to Castle Rayn. When the boxing was first mentioned he had been against the idea of taking time out to attend the tournament, but then he had remembered that there was a very famous map-maker who resided at the castle. He was a polecat by the name of Polemy, one of the few mammals on Welkin who was friends with the birds of the air. Generally feather and fur went their separate ways, but Polemy had cultivated an understanding with flyers and their kind.

Sylver now went in search of Polemy. After questioning a few mammals he eventually tracked down the map-maker in a room in the north tower. This particular room had many windows, through which birds came to visit the polecat. There was a bell outside the room, which Sylver rang loudly.

'In! In!' called a shrill voice. 'It's open.'

Sylver opened the small door set into the larger one and entered a room full of sheets of paper. They were hanging everywhere, pinned to lines with clothes pegs. They criss-crossed the room like washing in the backstreets of weasel villages. On these sheets were squiggly lines in red, blue and various other colours. They waved gently in the breeze from the many windows. Beneath the charts, which were obviously maps with their ink drying, walked dozens of birds. They strolled around the room looking up at the charts with a discerning eye, sometimes stepping back and cocking their heads to one side, as if studying a particular section of the work before them.

'What can I do for you, weasel? Be quick. I'm a busy polecat.'

Sylver looked to where the voice was coming from and saw a lean, dark-coloured creature whose long, soft-looking fur showed a cream hue underneath when the breeze riffled it. He was sitting at a high desk, scratching away with a pen. Several other pens stood in pots of different coloured inks in front of him. Ink spilled over the edges of these pots, creating a rainbow which ran in rivulets down the desk top and into a pool on the floor beneath his stool.

'What is that thing on your face?' asked Sylver,

looking at a device made of wire and glass which clung to the map-maker's ears and nose like a shiny-eyed crab. 'It looks like a set of window panes.'

'These?' answered the polecat, amused, as he unhooked the implement. 'The scientific term for them is "goggles". I invented them. They're made of bottle bottoms and wire. They help me see better when I have detailed work which requires fine lines and a delicate touch.'

He put them back on his face. Sylver thought they looked very sinister and was not sure he could trust a creature who wore such a strange device. You could not tell what his eyes were doing behind those small round portholes.

'Well? You obviously wanted something or you would not be here. What is it?' demanded the map-maker.

'Ah, yes, sorry. I'm – I am Lord Sylver of Thistle Hall.'

'Heard of you. Used to be an outlaw. Then you were promoted to a lord.'

'That's right. Well, I'm about to go on a trip. My friends and I are planning to sail the Cobalt Sea. We need maps—'

'Charts,' corrected the polecat. 'The navy calls them charts.'

'What navy?'

'Oh, any navy. We animals don't have a navy, of course, but the humans had one. Charts, my dear weasel. They're called charts.'

'Right then. I would like to buy some of your charts.'

The polecat called Polemy went back to

scratching away at the sheet of linen-paper in front of him. 'Sorry, don't sell 'em to animals. They're works of art which are only for the birds. The birds treasure them as originals. They often frame my works and hang them. They're made precisely to order, you see, otherwise an artist like me would have no knowledge to work from.'

'I'm not sure I understand.'

The polecat stopped work again and peered at Sylver through his goggles, red ink dripping from his pen and running down his claws. 'Many birds migrate. They fly over the land and sea, memorizing the regions below their flight. They come to me and tell me where they've been and what the shapes of these lands and seas are like from the air. I turn those details into maps and charts. The migrators like to show their friends their journey and where they've been for the winter, or the summer, so they buy them to keep or give away as presents.'

'Don't you make copies?' enquired Sylver.

The polecat shuddered in the way that Sleek might have done if someone had suggested that he use brown sackcloth for one of his creations. 'Copies? I do not make *copies*. I've told you, these are works of art. But have a look around. Don't feel you're being pushed to go.' With that the polecat went back to his work, leaving Sylver somewhat adrift.

The weasel did indeed walk round and study some of the maps and charts which hung from the washing lines. They were just what he wanted. They showed the islands and coastlines of bigger land masses, with the sea and currents marked between. Indeed, the names marked on these 'works of art' were bird names. There was EGG-SHAPED ISLAND and NEST BAY and FEATHER SPIT and BEAK PENINSULA, but they would have been useful. Then suddenly, while he was wandering around the room, Sylver had an idea.

He went back to where the polecat was busy scratching away at his desk. 'Sorry, Polemy, I don't mean to bother you again, but don't you keep rough pieces of work – you know, first drafts of your main sketches and paintings?'

'What? Oh, those. Yes, yes of course, I have to have something to work from. They're all in those exercise books over there.'

Sylver went over to a stool where there were about a dozen exercise books with red covers. He opened one and found jottings and sketches of maps and charts on every page. They were not quite to scale and were of course a bit cruder than the works the polecat was producing for sale to the birds, but in every other respect they were the same.

Sylver returned to the desk and the polecat raised his eyes to the ceiling. 'I just wondered . . .' began Sylver, but Polemy interrupted him.

'You want to borrow my exercise books?'

'If it's at all possible.'

'Go ahead, go ahead. Take them. If it means I'll get rid of you for half an hour.'

'Well, I may be a bit longer than that.'

'Whatever. Bring them back when you like. Only leave me in peace.'

Sylver quietly gathered up the precious books of maps and charts and left the room.

Chapter Five

Prince Poynt did not of course know that Sylver and his band were still intent on finding the humans and restoring them to Welkin. The prince was one of those mammals who were unwisely complacent. He refused to take the threat of floods seriously and thought those who did were scaremongers. He told himself it did not matter to him that the coming generations would inherit a watery world. He could not care less, so long as he was comfortable and still in power. A few more lakes here and there did not matter. There was food on his table and honey dew in his cup, so surely all was right with the world.

So the ex-outlaws were careful whom they told about their coming expedition. The prince went in sublime ignorance of their plans. All *was* right with the world.

The boxing tournament began at seven in the evening.

Scirf had told Mawk that he had entered him in the contest against a hare called Mack-the-mauler. They had to drag Mawk, kicking and screaming, to his seat in the great hall. It was only then that Scirf told him it was all a joke.

'You're rotten, you are, Scirf,' hissed Mawk. 'One day I'm going to fix your wagon!'

There was a hubbub in the hall as they waited for the first bout. Naturally, the prince and his noblestoats were late and the competition had to be held up until they were in their seats. Once they were sitting down the noblestoats looked around and saw the ex-outlaw band three rows behind them. They hissed and booed, making nasty gestures with their paws. 'Weasels, weasels, weasels, weasels . . .' they chanted, trying to make Sylver and the others feel uncomfortable.

When the band remained in their seats, seemingly oblivious to the taunts, the noise soon died down and the first bout took place. This was between two young jack hares who were in their first season. The fight only lasted two minutes, after which one had to retire with a bleeding nose. The referee, a hare in his late summers, stopped the fight in favour of the green shorts and, though the yellow shorts protested, the decision was allowed to stand.

As the evening wore on, the bouts were contested by increasingly well-known and experienced hares. The amount each noblestoat bet on each fight rose accordingly. Most heavy purses were reserved for the main bout of the evening.

When the bell on the north tower sounded the hour of ten by the large water clock in the prince's courtyard, it was time for the final bout. Kipper came bouncing into the ring from the yellow side, shadow-boxing to keep his muscles toned and his feet light. Sheriff Falshed was looking smug and whispered something in the prince's ear. The prince clicked his teeth and rubbed his paws together. They both confidently expected an announcement that Bludger Brassnose could not appear due to unforeseen circumstances: Kipper would then win by default.

But then, from the back of the hall by the big doors, came sounds of a commotion. This spread through the audience like a ripple on a mill pond, until it reached the front rows. The prince turned and frowned. Sheriff Falshed also turned and his eyes rolled in panic.

Coming down the aisle, led by Wodehed, was Bludger Brassnose, looking a little battered but by no means out of the running. The big hare climbed into the ring unaided. The referee spoke to him, nodded, then went to the middle of the ring to make an announcement.

'Eyyyyeeee ammmm tolllld by the green shorrrrts that the fight willllll proceeeeed!' he cried.

A tumultuous applause greeted the news.

The two big boxing hares came to the centre of the circular ring and stood head to head. They glared into each other's eyes as boxers will when trying to intimidate one another. Then they went back to their respective sides and came out with paws swinging when the bell sounded. Kipper was a south-hand, which made him a difficult target for the Brassnose, whereas Bludger himself had a long reach and a wicked left hook. All in all they were well matched and therefore wary of one another.

The fight was not the magnificent spectacle which had been promised by gossip. These events never are. The public imagination builds them into something – a phenomenon – they can never achieve in a million years. It was a good hard contest and it ended rather unsatisfactorily in a draw. Boxing pundits would swear for years afterwards that had the Brassnose been on form he would have taken the Kipper for a long walk along a short pier, but such creatures will always 'what if?' a match, trying to change unchangeable history with afterwords.

Because it was a draw all wagers were null and void. The prince had not lost money, but neither had he won any. He stood up and turned to Falshed, saying quietly, 'A word with you in my quarters, if you please, High Sheriff.' The hapless sheriff followed the ermine out of the hall, visibly shaking. As he passed the ex-outlaws he threw them such a look of hatred it was a wonder they did not shrivel up and blow away.

When Wodehed joined the weasels they patted him on the shoulder with their paws.

'Well done, squire,' said Scirf. 'You managed to pull him together, did you?'

'My knowledge of healing plants helped a little, I think,' said the learned magician. 'I flatter myself that without them the Brassnose would still be lying on his back.'

Sylver said, 'I'm sure he would be.'

Later the Brassnose himself came to the weasels and thanked them for all their help. He told them that any time they wanted a favour which was in his power to grant, they would hardly need to ask.

The weasels left the castle that night, by late

57

ferry, not wishing to outstay their welcome. As the ferrystoat rowed them away from the castle they looked up to see the sheriff, hanging from the battlements by his ankles upside-down. He looked very miserable. They each gave him a little wave – a gesture he did not return or even acknowledge – and then turned their faces to the shore. Their big adventure was about to begin.

Their destination lay in the far north-west of Welkin, where the ships were said to be, some floating idle in a great harbour, some still on blocks in a dockyard. Sylver hoped they would find a usable craft, since the humans had taken many of them to sail away to Dorma Island.

No animal was *absolutely* clear why the humans had left Welkin. They had been gone now for many years: a long time in the lives of weasels, who counted their own span on earth by the number of seasons. Stories had been passed down from generation to generation and legend told of how one morning the humans had woken up all singing the same song. It had been an eerie tune, a haunting melody which had lodged itself in the human mind while they had been asleep.

Such enchanting music was brought by the fickle changing winds, from some dark corner of the world where natural magic came out of fissures in the earth like gas. This vapour was wafted hither and thither over the globe. For the most part this uncontrolled magic was dispersed by the elements, scattered by wind or diluted by heavy rains. Once in ten thousand years, however, it was so dense that it became part of the wind itself and was carried over land and sea, causing havoc wherever it passed.

So the adult humans had gone, swarming to the ports and harbours like lemmings, taking their children with them. Children, being of a different species to grown-ups, had not been so affected by the strange magic. Some of them had tried to break the spell of the wind, of the unearthly song, but as they were small creatures of limited strength, their efforts had been fruitless. They were dragged away by parents whose eyes were glazed, whose throats all moaned the same melody, whose minds had been hypnotized. One or two of the children had managed to leave clues behind, but that was all they were able to do.

Why such wild magic had visited the earth was part of the mystery of life. Humans had always threatened to destroy the very world that had given them birth, stripping the earth bare and killing all those creatures who were not useful to them. So perhaps the magic came to interrupt their crazy headlong rush towards disaster.

This particular mad wind had told the adult humans to make their way to an island where they would all fall instantly into a deep, eternal sleep, neither ageing nor changing in any way.

That night the weasels camped in an open field. They lit a huge fire and sang weasel songs until late. Scirf told stories in the old tongue while the others stared into the flames of the camp fire, with its crackling sticks and its logs spurting blue and orange flares. Once upon a time their ancestors had been afraid of fire, but now they looked to it for comfort, warmth and protection.

They were close to rat territory. In the morning they would have to be up and away early, for the fire would signal their whereabouts. For now, they were safe: rats still retained their primitive fear of fire; moreover, they never attacked in darkness – their strange marsh gods forbad it. The foul wizard Flaggatis would have urged them to attack, but even he had not been able to conquer the rats' terror of their feral gods.

Chapter Six

There was indeed a stirring in the unnamed marshes the following morning as Flaggatis's spies reported back to him that Lord Sylver and his weasels were on their way north-west and would brush his territory. Flaggatis had a hatred of the weasel band second only to the hatred of hedgerow birds for the cuckoo. These weasels had ruined his plans for domination of Welkin, just when they were within his grasp, and his sole aim in life at this point in time was to destroy them.

However, the ancient stoat wizard was also curious as to why the weasels would leave their safe homes in Halfmoon Wood to venture so close to a sworn enemy. He felt it was in his interest to have them followed. They could be destroyed later. He had at his command innumerable vast stinking hordes of demented rodents who would kill just to see the colour of another creature's blood. It would take but a word from him to have the rat tribes swarming over the countryside, their bullfrog-roarers whirling, their skull standards waving, their vicious hooks and sickles slicing the air in anticipation of a kill. (Flaggatis had of course sent out his hordes of deranged rats before now, without success, but he was ever the optimist.)

Sylver and his band soon became aware that they were being followed. These particular rats were good at swarming all over places, but they were not good at stalking. The weasels gave no indication that they had seen the rats. It was better to keep them in sight where they knew what they were doing. To turn on the rats and send them packing would only encourage Flaggatis to send out more sneaky patrols.

At around noon the weasels came across a corner of the swamp they would have to cross. This was bullfrog country, ruled by a massive frog called Glubba. In the normal way frogs are not dangerous to weasels: they are small, timid amphibians interested only in catching insects. In Glubba's kingdom, however, the frogs were so numerous that they posed a huge threat to wayfarers. They could teem over a mammal in their hundreds, suffocating, or even crushing their victim with the sheer weight of their numbers. They bred without hindrance here: they had driven out or destroyed all other creatures – fish, newts, toads – and few birds now visited this corner. Thus there were no creatures to eat the frog spawn or tadpoles: every single egg flourished, growing into yet another frog to swell the masses which already overran the swamp.

Sylver and the others entered the swamp under the glare of ten thousand frogs.

'What do you want?' boomed one, bigger than the others. 'What do you want here in the kingdom of frogs?'

'Are you King Glubba?' asked Sylver.

The frog let out an enormous croak, which

reverberated around the swamp. This was his equivalent of weasel tooth-clicking or human laughter. The big frog was expressing amusement. 'Me?' he said.

'Well, I had heard that King Glubba was the largest frog in the swamp – and you seem to fit that description.'

'Why do you wish to see King Glubba?'

'We need to pass through his kingdom and we have gifts of fly cakes for him in order to obtain safe passage.'

At this moment one of Scirf's fleas, those creatures of which he was so fond, crawled out of his bushy brow and onto the tip of his nose. Instantly the big frog's long tongue came lashing out of its mouth. It took the flea from the end of Scirf's nose with deadly accuracy. The frog swallowed and burped.

'Hey!' yelled Scirf.

But the frog merely said, 'A tasty morsel,' and turned away, telling the band to follow him.

With a stern look, Sylver warned Scirf not to complain further. The weasel leader then motioned his group to follow the large frog into the depths of the marshes. They had to keep to the dry paths through the swamp, while the big frog simply jumped from lily-pad to clump of bladderwort to reedy mat – anything which would support his weight. Eventually they all came to a place where the bulrushes were tall and stately. In the middle of this was a clearing in which sat a grotesque and hideous sight.

It was a frog of monstrous proportions.

King Glubba had expanded to twenty times the

size of a normal bullfrog. Moreover, his skin was stretched so tightly over his frame that it was almost transparent. The weasels could see his heart beating through the layers of shiny fat beneath. He really was a most fascinating, if repulsive, sight.

'WHO IS THIS WHO INVADES MY KINGDOM?' The words boomed out over the marsh reeds.

Sylver tried to study the king's expression, but his taut skin flattened his features. No-one could tell whether he was happy or sad, angry or pleased. His mouth ran like a thin trench across his face from ear to ear. Below this tight-lipped slit hung a bulbous chin, which swelled and flattened as the words were uttered.

Sylver made his reply. 'We have not come to invade your kingdom, but merely to pass through it. We wish to reach the harbour where the humans kept all their ships. In these haversacks on our backs are gifts for you, great king.'

'GIFTS?'

The weasels took off their backpacks and opened them up. One by one they took out packages of greaseproof paper and unwrapped them. Thousands of frogs edged closer for a good look as the fly cakes, with their runny red centres and greeny-yellow toppings, were revealed.

A general 'Ooooooooo . . .' drifted over the marshes as the appreciative frogs recognized the gifts.

'Fly cakes!' cried the frog who had brought them in. 'They're delicious fly cakes, O Bulbous One! Fit for the royal tongue, O Great Fat Potentate and Poobah of the swamps!'

'BRING ME ONE.'

Scirf took one of his cakes and tossed it high in the air. An enormous tongue, thick and long as a skipping rope, lashed out. The cake disappeared in an instant down the king's throat. There was a loud *burp!* which rushed like a gale through the reeds, flattening them and making them rustle.

'GOOD – VERY TASTY. A FEAST. WE MUST HAVE A FEAST!'

The other frogs seemed very excited at this announcement. They began hopping and jumping here and there, uncovering caches of food in the reeds, in the bulrushes, under pondweed, behind mudbanks. Soon the food began to pile up around the king, who squeaked in pleasure. He sat high and proud on a peat hag, his greedy eyes surveying the grub.

There were plates full of dragonfly wings dipped in syrup and baked to sweet bricks in the sun. There were bowls full of crispy dung-beetles coated in sugar. There were buckets full of writhing ragworms, their legs dripping with honey. On trenchers were balls of maggots laced with silverfish. Sandwiches of dusty moths garnished with chickweed formed one half-circle around the king; on the other side were open sandwiches of colourful butterflies. Heaped on dishes in the centre were crane-flies, horseflies, dead wasps and bees, green crickets with their legs set in neat rows, and cockroaches.

'EAT!' cried the king.

The frogs fell on the food and began eating with great gusto. Despite his great bulk the king was not slow to pile in either. The fly cakes were still mostly in their wrappings but Sylver did not think they would remain so for long. He had a feeling that the king was saving them for dessert. The weasels were not averse to a ragworm or two, but they were not going to fight for such morsels with thousands of frogs.

For a while the air was alive with the whip and lash of froggy tongues. They filled the space between the frogs like red party streamers. The beauty of being a frog, it seemed, was that you could eat off your neighbour's plate, or even *his* neighbour's plate, without leaving your seat. You simply turned your head and sent out that long lashing tongue to snatch away the last wasp or cricket. The weasels sat back and watched this gorging with distaste.

'What a greedy lot,' said Bryony. 'I've never seen such horrible manners.'

'Somethin' to do with them tongues,' muttered Scirf darkly. 'Them tongues ain't natural.'

When the banquet appeared to be finished the frog king called for his gifts from the weasels.

'Good grief, he's not going to eat any more after all that lot, is he?' said Alysoun. 'I don't believe it.'

But it seemed that the feasting before was just a practice run for the main event: the consumption of the fly cakes. The king announced that they were all for him. His subjects had eaten enough, he said, and their king should be left to enjoy the presents. The ring of frogs around the king widened with a disappointed muttering as they made way for the laying out of the gifts.

The bloated Glubba already looked fit to burst,

but Sylver could see the greed in his eyes as the weasels unwrapped the cakes. Those big froggy orbs glistened with pleasure at the sight of the food. A nasty dribbling oozed from the sides of the king's great mouth and dripped onto the swamp grasses. He began to tremble from nose-tip to tail-tip – a quivering that rippled through his taut body. His webbed feet kept curling and uncurling with anticipation.

'LET ME AT THEM. LEAVE ME TO EAT. I MUST EAT.'

The weasels stood back as the king's tongue began slashing this way and that in a frenzy of gluttony. Glubba could not swallow the food fast enough. He crammed it into his mouth, but it was so full it squelched out of the sides. He gobbled faster and faster, his cheeks bulging, his eyes glazed. Black ooze began to squeeze out of his nostrils and dropped to the floor in gobbets. He huffed and snorted and grunted, trying to take in air to breathe as he shovelling down the squashed dead flies.

The fly cakes rapidly disappeared, by ones, twos and threes. In the middle of it all the king was sick, but he still continued to eat until all the cakes were gone; then he sat there, gasping for air, his eyes starting from his head.

'That's disgusting,' whispered Bryony. 'I never saw such an exhibition of greed in my life.'

'You watch your tongue,' said a guard frog. 'That's our king you're talking about.'

But at that moment a whistling, hissing, squealing sound came from the mouth of the great king, like steam escaping from a boiling kettle. All eyes turned back to the royal visage. Ten thousand frogs and half a dozen weasels stared at King Glubba in amazement and horror.

Clearly all was not well with the monarch. He seemed disturbed. Bulges had begun to appear on his tightly stretched skin like small balloons. (You wanted to pinch them to make them pop.) A low wail was coming from the royal throat. His tongue suddenly flopped out and unrolled like a long thin scarlet carpet across the swamp. His eyes went huge and round and began to protrude. Pressure seemed to be building up within the royal personage.

'Watch out!' cried an elderly frog. 'He's going to explode!'

There was a general panic amongst the amphibians. They seemed to know what was going on. No doubt they had seen this sort of thing before with other king and queen frogs. They scattered in all directions, leaping for cover, down holes, into pools of stagnant water. Soon there were only one or two desperate frogs to be seen. The weasels were left stupefied, wondering whether to hide and, if so, where.

At that moment the king's eyes flew from his head like pebbles from a double slingshot. They rocketed over the swampland and buried themselves deeply into a bank of mud. The king's toes, on the end of those webbed feet, sprayed out in all directions. It was a miracle none of the weasels were hit by the deadly missiles. Finally the king exploded with the sound of thunder.

Bits of skin and bone flew everywhere, splattering down on the waters of the swamp, rattling through the bulrushes. For a while it rained bits of frog. Pieces of green skin were draped over the weasels' legs and backs. That great long tongue had wrapped itself like a constricting snake around Scirf. A webbed foot slapped Wodehed on the bottom as it went sailing past – the king's final parting shot before leaving for frog heaven.

Eventually all was still, except for the smaller bits still floating down like snake's scales.

'Yuk!' cried Bryony, wiping all the bits from her fur. 'That is disgusting.'

'Don't you know any other words?' grumbled Luke, trying to unravel the trussed and wriggling Scirf from the tongue wrapped around him. 'You keep saying it's disgusting.'

'Well, it *is* disgusting. I can't think of a better word.'

The other frogs did not return. They were all jammed into holes and crevices in the mud and saw no reason to vacate these comfortable positions. This left the weasels free passage through the swamps. They took it gladly. It had not been their intention to destroy the king of the frogs, but since he had done the job for himself, they saw no reason why they should not take advantage of the situation.

The moon was like a glowing swollen balloon on the horizon. The weasels trudged towards it, using its light to help them negotiate the paths through the swamp.

Chapter Seven

The weasels now felt reasonably safe. A small patrol of rats would not dare to enter Glubba's kingdom. It would take an army, probably under the direct leadership of Flaggatis himself, to cross the frog-infested quagmire.

Sylver's band approached the harbour on the Cobalt Sea with confidence. However, as they drew nearer to the entrance they saw that they were not alone. The docks were bustling with figures hurrying to and fro.

'What's this?' asked Sylver. 'A meeting place for statues?'

There were indeed statues of all kinds – chunks, gongs, puddings, blocks and stumpers; each one seemed busy. The weasels had never seen so many statues all in one place. Usually they were found wandering the countryside alone, looking for their First and Last Resting Places.

Scirf stopped a stumper on his way past. The wooden statue was carrying coils of rope on its shoulder. It looked in a purposeful mood.

'Where are you off to?' asked Scirf.

'To-my-ship,' replied the stumper, in the halting tones of one not used to speech. 'I-go-home.'

The outlaws could now see that a group of statues was loading a great barge with spare sails and ropes. Several stone statues were already on board. The barge was very low in the water – there seemed to be as many statue passengers as there would have been human passengers and stone weighs a great deal more than flesh.

'Where's home?' asked Scirf, not letting the stumper go until he had answered some more questions.

'Why, First-and-Last-Resting-Place-is-over-the-sea. My-wood –' he rapped his wooden knuckes on his wooden head '– it-comes-from-tree-not-found-on-Welkin. I-was-brung-here-from-faraway-place.'

'*Brought* here,' corrected Scirf, a stickler for good grammar in others. 'So, you're all going back to where you came from, are you?'

The stumper nodded slowly, then went on his way.

'So,' said Sylver, surveying all the activity going on around the harbour, 'these statues are sailing away, looking for their original homes. I hope they haven't taken all the best ships. We must look around and choose one for ourselves.'

The weasels threaded their way through the mob. It was a dangerous business, not because the statues were aggressive in any way, but because they were so clumsy. Gongs walked into blocks with resounding clangs. Puddings tripped over chunks and were in danger of shattering themselves. Stumpers tripped over their own feet – or roots, as they preferred to call them – being totally unused to walking at all. The weasels were in danger of being crushed by falling stone or crashing bronze.

'Keep to the edges of the warehouses,' Sylver ordered. 'I don't want to lose a weasel before we even set sail.'

They found that many of the serviceable ships had been taken by statues. Others were being made ready to sail. Many more were in a state of grave disrepair. One type the weasels particularly liked was a great windjammer, a ship which had been built for speed but was nevertheless a sturdy vessel. There were four of these ships lying side by side in dry dock.

Even the best of these had rot in the timbers, but the weasels decided it was nothing that could not be cut out and replaced. The sails were rotten, too, and mostly in ribbons. More would have to be found or made – similarly the ropes which made up the sheets, ratlines, buntlines and all the rest of the rigging. However, there was a nice spacious hold in the sleek craft, and some comfortable-looking cabins. Sylver decided that once they had repaired the ship, it would serve the weasels well for their voyage over the Cobalt Sea.

The windjammer was called *Scudding Cloud*, which seemed an appropriate name: with full sails set she would look just like a cloud scudding over the blue.

'She's in a bad way, though,' said Scirf. 'What're we goin' to do to get her shipshape?'

'I've been reading up about it,' Miniver the finger-weasel replied. 'We need some shipwrights – that's what the people who build and repair ships are called – to get her ready.'

'The trouble is,' said Sylver, sighing, 'there are no *people*, only animals. I'm not sure there are any skilled mammals who could repair a ship like this. It's never needed to be done before, so there won't be anyone with experience. We might have to make do with ordinary carpenters and black-smiths.'

'There's a bunch of carpenters I know from my old village,' said Scirf, who could always come up with someone. 'I'm sure they've got some black-smith friends. The work might not be brilliant, but I bet they can plug all the leaks good enough for one voyage. You want me to send for them?'

'How would you do that?' asked Wodehed.

'Attach a message to a carrier robin,' replied that redoubtable weasel. 'I'll tell them to carry some gifts for the new frog king in their back-packs, so they can get over the marshes, same as we did.'

'I should like to point out, my ingenious friend, that we have no carrier or even hunting robins with us.'

'Then we catch one and train it,' answered the imperturbable Scirf. 'I knows how to catch robin redbreasts. I seen it done hundreds of times. Come on, I'll show you.'

He explained to the other weasels that he needed some human gardening tools. They searched the area around the docks and found some houses. And behind one of these human dwellings, in a tool shed, they found a garden fork. Scirf needed Luke and Bryony's help to carry the fork to an old allotment where humans used to grow vegetables. Here they stuck the implement into the ground and, with sharp sticks, dug up the earth around it. Then Scirf suggested they stand back and watch.

Sure enough, only a few minutes passed before a robin with a bright red breast landed on the fork handle.

'There you are, never fails,' said Scirf. 'Somehow they're attracted to them fork things. Hi, robin. Stay there a minute. I want to talk to you.' He added something on the end of this sentence in a very strange chirping tongue which the other weasels did not understand.

'Can you speak robin dialect?' asked Alysoun, with some admiration in her voice. 'Where did you learn that?'

'Oh, here and there, while I was watching the rhubarb dung in me old job,' replied Scirf airily. 'Won't be a tick.'

The robin looked on warily as Scirf approached it. Scirf remained a good few feet away from the fork, so as not to pose any threat to the bird. Then he began to chirp and twitter nineteen to the dozen. The bird replied in kind, in a rather more sing-song tone. It was clear that the two creatures were having an animated conversation. Finally the robin flew off, but not before snatching a worm from the weasel diggings.

'Well, that's that then,' said Sylver, disappointed. 'I suppose it didn't like the idea of having a message tied to its leg.'

'Not a bit of it, squire,' Scirf replied. 'It's gone off to deliver my message by word of beak. One of my carpenter friends is good at robin dialect too. We used to be in the resistance together – rebels, we was – and we all learned to use robin-speak so's the stoats wouldn't know what we was saying if they overheard us exchanging secret information.'

'Resistance?' cried Bryony. 'What resistance?'

'That's what we called it, because we was resisting stoat rule. Well, I was only in it part time, 'cause I had my rhubarb dung to watch, but it was organized by a weasel called W.'

He pronounced the letter as a weasel kitten would say it.

'Wuh what?' asked Sylver.

'Just W. He didn't have no other names. Sometimes we used to call him Trespasser, but that was just a nickname due to his complete disregard for landowners and their property rights. Anyway, we used to spy on the stoats, study the supply routes their mouse-caravans took through the forest. Sometimes we would organize a raiding party and attack them. It was all exciting stuff. Only old W got killed and no-one else was quite bright enough to keep the organization together.'

'I would have thought you would be a natural successor to such a weasel,' said Sylver.

Scirf shuffled his claws modestly. 'Well, as to that, squire, I was bit young in them days. Hadn't got the sort of head on my shoulders that I've got now. Still, you don't forget strange dialects like the one used by robins. They stay with you. Anyway, that's the story. Now we've got to wait for the robin to come back. In the meantime I promised him we'd dig up more of the allotment. It's the worms he wants . . .'

They had dug up most of the allotment when a

cry went up from the direction of the harbour. The weasels, curious as ever, dropped their tools and went in the direction of the call. They found, on reaching the dock, that the barge full of statues was casting off. These creatures of wood, stone, plaster and bronze were on their way home. There was a simple look of contentment on their faces, which indicated extreme happiness. You never saw a statue jumping up and down in glee, or punching the air with its fist in triumph. They were on the whole a quiet and reserved bunch who rarely expressed excitement.

The quayside was crowded with other statues, bound for different climes. They were waving solemnly to the passengers on the great barge. Those on board waved back, their faces unsmiling. The lines were taken in, and the barge drifted slowly out into the middle of the harbour. Then the rusty-red sails were raised and the vessel strained and creaked, pushing forward with some effort through the tranquil waters.

The weasels could see that the craft was now even lower in the water. More passengers of stone and metal had boarded her. She was overcrowded with creatures who weighed a great deal. It was a wonder that some of the stone statues did not go crashing through the decks and put a hole in her bottom.

'I fear for them,' Bryony said. 'I do hope they make it, but I fear for them.'

Her fear was well-founded. It was all right while the barge was in the quiet waters of the harbour, but once she hit the open sea tragedy struck. The waves began to lap over its low gunwales. Lower and lower rode the craft in a mildly tossing briny.

There was a despairing groan from the crowd on the quay as they saw what was about to happen.

Gradually the barge sank. It had only made half a nautical mile from its moorings when it went down. Most of the statues on board went down with it. The stone statues remained standing on the deck as the water gradually rose up their bodies, past their noses, and finally covered them. The last tall statue gave the crowd a despairing wave before he went under.

The chunks were, of course, able to walk along the bottom of the harbour. They would eventually emerge from the shallows to stroll up onto the beach. The wooden stumpers, some of the blocks and a few of the hollow bronze gongs bobbed to the surface and floated away, carried out to sea by the currents. They would end up on some foreign shore as flotsam. The plaster statues would dissolve, after a time, in the salt water.

Where the boat had been was just swirling water full of bubbles as the pockets of air on board the barge continued to be filled with water.

The weasels had the feeling that this was not the first vessel to come to grief. No doubt there were many more at the bottom of the harbour.

'Well, let that be a lesson to us,' said Sylver. 'There'll be no statues when we set sail.'

The robin returned with a message that very evening. Six carpenters and two blacksmiths were on their way to the harbour. Scirf's message had included a warning about the frogs. At least there

77

would be no fat king to encounter – not for a while at least.

There was nothing much for the weasels to do except sit and wait. Some of them began learning how to make ropes. There was a rope-making machine in one of the long sheds alongside the dockyard. This was a wooden affair with cogs and wheels and hooks and spindles. Three strands of cord were attached to hooks and when a wheel was turned these were wound tightly into a long thin rope. Then three of these thin strands of rope could be similarly wound into a thicker rope.

There were many other things to learn, like knotting and splicing. Bowlines, sheepshanks, reef knots, sheepbends and all sorts of sea-mammal's knots would be needed during a voyage. Splicing was the art and science of joining two ropes together to make one by interweaving the three separate strands of each rope. End-splicing of a frayed rope would ensure that the rope did not fray or split.

Wodehed, Bryony, Alysoun and Luke busied themselves with this side of seamammalship. Some of their efforts were less than satisfactory, since their tiny claws had difficulty in managing the knots, but where they were defeated they came up with less precise alternatives.

Scirf decided he was ready to learn how to navigate. He took out some books from the port library and found that normal navigation required the use of brass instruments known as sextants and chronometers. Since he had neither of these, he turned to another form of navigation, which was practised in the South Seas. This was navigating by the stars, the sun and moon, the elements and, indeed, by all that is natural and common to the world on which we live. Such signs as:

Setting stars, rising stars
Waves, direction, size and shape
Winds, their direction and speed
Swells, their direction and strength
Rips, their position and type
Driftwood, the kind of tree
Coconuts and other floating seeds
Seaweed, the variety
Birds, species and whether land or sea bird
Clouds held by mountain peaks
Reflection of lagoons on cloud bases
Scents of sea and land
Fish, their types and numbers
Sound of reef
Underwater volcanoes
Colour of water
Temperature of water.

For this type of navigation he needed no charts: he had to learn the ways of nature, the rhythms of the earth, the ebb and flow of the ocean. This was much more to his liking. If there was one study he enjoyed it was that of nature's ways, be they the habits of dung beetles or paths across the sea.

Sylver kept going over the ship, noting all the parts that needed repair, familiarizing himself with the vessel. If he was to be captain of this craft, he would need to know it inside out and from top to bottom. So he made sure he knew every nook and cranny, and a few niches and crevices besides.

Mawk sneaked away each day to play holly-hockers with idle statues. Hollyhockers was a dicing game to which he had become almost addicted. He was forever dreaming of throwing double-jeopardies, widdershins, Molly Maguires and hurdy-gurdies. His nightmares consisted of throwing jabbyknockers one after the other, without a break, for two thousand throws. Mawk was selfish, lazy and incorrigible. Only the threat of death would have stopped him from playing hollyhockers every day, and everyone was too busy to remonstrate with the cowardly weasel. They were too engrossed in their own projects.

Chapter Eight

When the carpenters and blacksmiths arrived they went to work immediately. They did not even pause to discuss payment for the job. They said Scirf had explained why the weasels needed to reach Dorma Island and that was enough for them. If the humans had to be brought back to Welkin, so be it: they would fix scupper and quarterdeck to do it.

Having learnt all they needed to know about ropes, most of the others had turned to the sails. There were canvas royals to stitch and topmast gallants to repair, the materials having been discovered in the port warehouses. Needles flashed in the sun, flying back and forth: yards of sail were cut, shaped, hemmed, cross-stitched. While the hammering and sawing, clanging and banging went on aboard the ship, the other weasels produced enough sail to fill the various yardarms.

The weasel carpenters had made two *ballistae* – siege catapults that could propel huge rocks over large distances. Sylver was not sure whether he would need these great weapons of war, but it seemed a good idea to take some form of defence. There were also several large crossbows with bolts to match. These were human-made weapons, and seemed giant-sized to the weasels who had to wind them up. It took two of them to do this job, one on each handle, using all their strength.

The *Scudding Cloud* was beginning to look as spruce and sleek as it ever would, given the patchy nature of the weasels' work. Then Mawk came into the dockyard, leading a gang of ugly-looking pine martens. He looked dejected.

Sylver was at the top of one of the masts, fixing some lines. He called down, 'What's the problem, Mawk?'

The pine martens – about two dozen of them – began to march onto the ship. They peered about everywhere, their forelegs on their hips like humans standing akimbo. They had a proprietorial air about them.

Sylver slid down the rigging, just as one pine marten was poking around in a barrel. 'Hi! That's private property,' said Sylver. 'Who invited you lot on board my ship?'

Bryony, Alysoun and the others had stopped work and came amidships to see what the shouting was about.

A pine marten with a wooden leg, and a eye twisted out of skew, spoke for the others. 'Who said *you* could stay on board *my* ship is more the question, ain't it? I'd like you off before sundown, if you please. Me and my maties want to set sail with the tide.'

There was the ripe twang of the sea rover to the pine marten's accent, learned from listening to seagulls, no doubt. He was a nasty-looking character, a good deal taller than Sylver when he was up on his hind quarters. He sneered down at the weasel, watching the puzzlement on his face. Sylver, for his part, was having trouble knowing which eye to look into when he spoke. They changed positions so often it was difficult to tell which was the good one and which the bad.

Mawk crept away into the shadows of the quarterdeck.

'You seem to have it the wrong way round, friend,' Sylver said, determined not to be intimidated.

'Not at all, lubber. I just won this ship at a game of hollyhockers in the Red Admiral Inn. Ask yon quivering mess of jelly over there.' The pine marten pointed with his wooden leg at Mawk. 'He's the sad fish who lost it to me.'

Scirf went over to Mawk and stared hard into his face. 'You didn't do this. Tell me you didn't do this.'

Mawk blurted out, 'He put a black spot into my paw, just as I was about to throw a widdershins and win the game. It put me off. They told me it meant death. They said Blind Phew died of falling under mouse-coach wheels below the sign of the swinging butterfly, just after he got the black spot. It frightened me. I went and threw a jabbyknocker instead . . .'

'All this is beside the point,' said Sylver. 'Listen, you – I don't know what your name is . . .'

'Short Oneleg.'

'What?'

'That's me name, porpoise-face. They calls me Short Oneleg, 'cause I'm short a leg, see. You be Sylver, of the Halfmoon weasels. I heard o' you,

83

but it don't make no difference. This 'ere ship was won fair and square and it belongs to us, see. If you ain't off her boards by sundown, we'll come back with cutlasses gleamin' in the gloamin' and clear the decks with 'em.'

'Well listen, Short, the ship was not Mawk's to lose. It belongs to us all. You'll have to settle your debt some other way, with Mawk.'

There was a squawk of fear from the shadows of the quarterdeck. The pine martens began muttering in an ugly fashion and moved forward, as if they were going to settle matters here and now, but their leader, Short Oneleg, held them back.

'I gave you till sundown and that's how it stands. If you're here after that, you takes the consequences.'

With that, the pine martens left the ship and sauntered along the dockside, heading in the direction of the Red Admiral.

'What are we going to do?' cried Mawk, when they had gone. 'We'll have to let them have the ship and go and choose another one. They gave me the black spot. They said Blind Phew—'

'You oughter be keel-hauled,' said Scirf, glaring into his face. 'If I was captain I'd make sure you was run down and under the ship and scratched to pieces on barnacles.'

'Mawk,' said Sylver, 'there is no way we are going to give up this ship. Weasels, arm yourselves. You'll need plenty of pebbles for your slingshots. Bryony, Alysoun, Mawk, Luke – open the lock gates and let the water into the dock. I want us to be afloat like a real ship when that gang of cutthroats and thieves come back again. Jump to it. I'm a captain now.'

They jumped to it. Some of the carpenters went along to help with the lock gates, which were, of course, very large. Some wheels on top of the gates allowed them to open sluices first, in order to fill the dock. then, when the *Scudding Cloud* was afloat, they heaved open the huge gates. She was now ready to make her way into the harbour proper.

'Let's go, let's go,' cried Mawk in a panic. 'Let's set sail for Dorma.' He ran to the mooring lines to cast them off.

Sylver shook his head. 'We are not quite ready. We are underprovisioned, for a start. And the blacksmiths have not finished making cleats. And I'm not going to let a lot of bully pine martens force me to leave before time. We'll settle this here and now, before we leave.'

They remained where they were, alert and ready. On deck the weasel blacksmiths had got two braziers full of red-hot charcoal going. They were busy holding pieces of iron with tongs inside the braziers while one or two of the other weasels used bellows to make the charcoal white hot. They would remove the metal and begin hammering it, using an anvil as a flattening surface. Sparks rained like cascades of stars. The lump of red metal gradually took shape and became a cleat or an iron marlinspike or some other fitting or tool for the ship.

In the evening a blood-red sun went down. Shortly afterwards the gang of martens arrived on the dockside, armed with cutlasses. They were in an ugly mood: they waved their weapons and shouted insults to the weasels. Sylver kept his band calm. They lined the port side of the ship, their slingshots dangling from their claws, ready to repel boarders.

Now that the ship was afloat, however, it was difficult for the martens to board her. As the holds were empty, she rode high in the water, and the weasels looked down on the dockside from a height. Short Oneleg and his motley crew would have had to be great leapers to get on board and anyway, the weasels were there to stop them.

'This is not fair!' cried Short. 'You let us come on board and then we'll see who's the better.'

'You must have holes in your pelt to suggest that,' cried Sylver, clicking his teeth. 'Do you think we were born yesterday? This is not a game.'

There was some stamping of paws and gnashing of fangs on the quayside, then the leader of the martens called out, 'Give us Mawk then! We'll take it out on him. After all, I did win the ship fair and square. Give us the weasel and we'll call it quits.'

'What will you do with him?'

'We'll sell him as a slave. He's a useless lump of lard anyway. You won't miss him.'

'That's true.'

Mawk gave out a screech of indignation. 'You can't paw me over to them.'

Fortunately for Mawk, who was not in Sylver's best books, the leader of the ex-outlaws had another idea. 'Tell you what,' he called down to the martens, 'I have a proposition for you.'

'Let us aboard to discuss it,' replied the crafty Short.

'No – we'll meet on neutral ground. I'll come to the Red Admiral in half an hour. How's that?'

There was a little discussion amongst the martens, then Short Oneleg called up, 'Half an hour, then.'

'What's the idea?' asked Bryony of Sylver. 'What are you going to propose to them.'

Sylver stood on his hind legs and waved a paw at the ship and its vast array of rigging. 'Look at this windjammer,' he said. 'It's huge. We'll never be able to crew it night and day with the number of weasels we've got. A ship this size has to have several mammals ready at any one time to climb the rigging, reef the sails, let out the sheets – all that sort of thing. What if a sudden storm comes up, just when we're ready to drop from exhaustion? We need more crew. I'm going to propose to the pine martens that they help us crew the ship to Dorma and back. Once we return we will have no further use for it, and it becomes theirs.'

Luke said, 'You saw that lot! Once they get their paws on a ship of this size they'll turn it into a pirate vessel. No-one up and down the coast will be safe from them. They're a bunch of rogues.'

'It will take some time to reach Dorma Island. During that period we'll have the opportunity to turn them into decent mammal beings. By the time we return to these shores I hope they'll have other plans for the ship. They could go into trade, or carry cargo for merchants. There are plenty of honest uses for a ship of this type.'

'An' what about the humans – won't they want their ship back?' asked Scirf.

'The humans forfeited their right to such property when they abandoned Welkin,' replied Sylver firmly. 'This was a wreck before we turned it into a sound ship again. If the humans want windjammers they'll have to build more of their own.'

The weasels had never heard Sylver talk in this vein before and they were impressed.

'Well said,' cried Wodehed. 'We are on an equal pawing with the humans now. We all have to work together to make Welkin a fit place to live in once more. They can start by rebuilding the sea walls which they left to rot. Animals can handle the shipping side of things for a while.'

'My thinking exactly,' murmured Sylver. 'Now, Scirf and I will go down to the Red Admiral Inn. I'm taking Scirf because to a certain extent he speaks their language. He's more in touch with rogues than the rest of you. In the meantime, I suggest the rest of you start to clean the oil lamps in the hold. We'll need them on the voyage – and there are a dozen other jobs you can be doing – no groaning now. There's harder work ahead.'

Sylver and Scirf made their way through docklands to the Red Admiral Inn. The cobbled streets were poorly lit, mostly with light coming from behind greasy-looking windows of warehouses and other such buildings. What was going on behind those windows was anyone's guess, but it was probably not lawful. In the streets themselves dubious characters stood in doorways, or just within alleys, watching the two weasels go by. Stoats, foxes, martens, badgers and several other mammals loitered with intent, or sauntered down the street, keeping pace with the weasels.

Scirf suddenly stopped and said menacingly, 'There's somethink you ought to know about us two – we collects ears. Anybody comes near us, we cut off their ears and pin them to a sheet of cork to display 'em. You want to lose your ears, just step this way, gentlemammals!'

The streets suddenly cleared of dubious characters.

A short while after this the two weasels reached the Red Admiral. They could hear the sound of raucous teeth-clicking coming from within. Mugs were being crashed on table-tops. A mammal drunk on honey dew lay across the gutter under the sign of the swinging butterfly. He made a bridge over a dirty stream of slops and peelings from rotten vegetables.

'Well, this looks like the place,' said Scirf, 'an' a prettier establishment you're not likely to find anywhere else in this port.'

They entered the inn and immediately all activity stopped as mammals of all types stared at them.

'Customs and Excise spies,' growled the innkeeper, a stoat with a dirty apron. 'You're not welcome in the Red Admiral, gentlemammals. You'd best be away afore your throats are cut in a dozen places . . .'

A voice cried out from the other side of the tavern. 'They're not customs spies, blast ye! They're my guests. Send 'em over here, landlord. I'll vouch for 'em, fair and square.'

The innkeeper turned to stare at the owner of

the voice, who was indeed Short Oneleg. 'If you say they're all right,' he said, wiping his paws on his filthy apron, 'then I'll go along with ye, Short, but they're your responsibility, mind!'

'Stop yer jabber, stoat, and bring us another round of honey dew.'

Scirf and Sylver went to the table and sat down on the wooden benches. The martens stared meanly at them as they waited for the mugs of honey dew to arrive. With the pots in their paws, they slammed them down three times hard on the table top. BANG! BANG! BANG! and yelled, 'Eins, zwei, drei!' before quaffing the contents of the mugs in a single gulp.

Scirf and Sylver were clearly supposed to do the same. There were hard eyes on them as they swallowed down the raw, barely fermented honey dew. It was like drinking lamp oil. It burned Sylver's throat and made his eyes water. Finally he managed to pour the last drop down his throat. It had been the harshest, foulest drink he had ever had to swallow in his life.

Scirf slammed his pot down on the table-top, growling, 'Lovely drop of dew that! Fit for the belly of a king. Put feathers on the head of a bald eagle. Landlord,' he yelled, 'another round of your best dew for my mates, here. Let's get a few more jars down our necks before we talk business.'

Sylver screwed up his eyes and wondered whether he had done the right thing in bringing Scirf with him.

90

Chapter Nine

Prince Poynt had been up on the battlements, watching his sister drill her battalions of Jillazons, a fearsome female regiment which she had raised herself. They were much better at military movements than the prince's own troops – they had a better sense of rhythm. The prince did not begrudge his sister her success with the jills, but he was gloomy about his own ruffian soldiers, who could not keep in step to save their lives.

After a while he went back down to the throne room, where he was confronted by two scruffy-looking badgers. He regarded the two animals with distaste. Herk and Bare were really the pits when it came to soap and water. They both stank of grave-earth. His Royal Highness knew what grave-earth smelled like, since he spent so much time at his brother's graveside, whispering. No-one knew what the prince was whispering about but they knew there was some unholy secret associated with King Redfur's death. They did not want to know more. To be privy to that secret was to court death.

'So you saw the weasels at work in the port?'

'That we did, your sublime worshipfulness – and that's when we saw them doin' it,' answered

Herk, taking a foul-looking chokey out of his belt pouch and preparing to light it. 'We was sailin' round the north-west of Welkin, in a coast boat owned by a fishin' otter by the name of Grench, when we passed the harbour and saw them all at it.'

Prince Poynt waved a paw in front of his face to get rid of the stench of Herk's foul breath. 'Put that stinking thing away. You're not smoking in here. Now . . . building a ship?'

Herk reluctantly put his chokey back into his belt pouch. He was always miffed when other animals told him not to smoke. It annoyed him to have to curb his pleasures. He felt he had a right to enjoy himself. If others did not like the atmosphere around Herk and Bare they should get out of the room. However, he was inclined to make an exception of the prince. 'Yes, your overlordly magnificentship – a ship.'

'A simple "My liege" will do. But let us picture this. There were woodland weasels constructing a huge craft capable of sailing the Cobalt Sea? Is this what you're asking me to believe, you pair of shiftless gibbet thieves?'

'Not exactly constructin' it from scratch, so to speak,' said Bare. 'They was patchin' up the holes in an old one. They sent for carpenters and blacksmiths to do the skilled work. I heard tell it's called a windjammer.'

'What are they up to? What are they up to?' cried the prince. 'Fetch me Falshed, someone.'

'He's still hanging upside-down from the battlements,' replied the noblestoat Jessex. 'You haven't had him taken down yet, my prince.'

'Well, get him down now – and bring him here.'

Falshed was taken down and brought before the prince. The sheriff looked pathetically grateful for his freedom. He prostrated himself in front of the throne, as if he wanted to be stepped on like some old rug.

The prince grimaced at this show of rank grovelling. 'Get up, get up, Falshed. We have a problem here. Herk and Bare, two wandering badgers, have brought us some information regarding the weasels. It seems they are reconstructing a ship and intend sailing out over the Cobalt Sea. Why are they doing that? They are surely up to no good.'

The sheriff looked askance at the two badgers and was relieved to see from their expressions that this was nothing to do with their earlier business over Bludger Brassnose. 'My liege,' replied Falshed, his voice hoarse with being out in all weathers. 'It must be something to do with bringing the humans back to Welkin. You know they are obsessed with that idea, those woodland weasels.'

'How do they know where to look?' asked the prince.

'Oh, those sneaky creatures will have found out somehow.'

'Right then. You and these two badgers must stop them.' The prince turned to the badgers. 'I shall pay you well for assisting my sheriff here to capture the weasels.'

The eyes of the two badgers lit up at the mention of payment. Their recent exploits had not been to do with fishing, but with trying to capture walruses and seals for their valuable pelts. They had come a cropper on that one and had barely escaped with their lives.

'If you can't get to the port in time to prevent their ship from sailing,' the prince was informing Falshed, 'you have my permission to commandeer another vessel and follow them to sea in that. Don't come back without them. I shall try them as traitors and put them all to death. Even lords are not supposed to betray their prince.'

'Me? Go to sea?' cried Falshed. 'My liege, I'm no sailor. I get sick on a pond raft in mid-summer. I hate water. Please don't make me do this thing.'

Prince Poynt stuck a claw in each ermine ear. 'I'm not listening, Falshed. Stick your claws in your ears, Sib.'

'I'll do no such thing,' said Sibiline, staring at Bare's collar suspiciously. 'You, badger, what's that on your coat?'

Bare looked down at his collar, then had the good grace to look shamefaced towards Falshed, who had gone a ghastly colour which can only be compared with the grey-green hue of mould on a piece of ancient cheese.

Bare said, 'It's – it's a dragonfly, your princess-ship.'

'Don't call me that – it's too sibilant for a gentle-jill's tongue – there's too many s's for the word to flow prettily. Where did you get it? It looks remarkably like one I gave to someone who was a very dear friend at the time, but who no longer wears my favour . . .'

Falshed groaned as if he were about to be sick.

'I had it copied, your – your jillship. From one

which the sheriff keeps on his mantelpiece. I had to draw a copy first, for the sheriff would not let this particular dragonfly out of his sight – he seems to greatly treasure it for some reason.'

Sibiline's eyes went all misty. 'Oh – oh, does he? Is this true, Falshed? You – you have one of those carvings?'

'One of them? Why mine is the original. It is my most prized possession, princess. It is worth more than the whole world to me,' murmured Falshed.

Sibiline looked a little faint. 'Oh – oh – how charming. How perfectly gallant. I – I am sure whoever gave it to you finds you worthy of such a gift.'

Falshed's voice sounded hoarse with passion. 'Thank you, princess.'

'I'm still not listening!' cried Prince Poynt, breaking the drama of the moment, his words falling like heavy stones on pond ice. 'I saw your lips moving, Falshed. I'm not going to unblock my ears until you stop moving your mouth.'

When he was quite sure the sheriff had no more to say, the prince removed his claws. He glared at Falshed. 'Well, what are you standing about for? Off you go. Take your badgers with you.'

Falshed left the room, glancing at his two companions with great dislike. They were no badgers of his.

'Now,' said Prince Poynt, once they had gone, 'what about a bit of fun, noble jacks and jills? Has my sister any suggestions? A game of cricket? Shuttlecocks? Footie?'

Sibiline, who was now busy helping Sleek the otter make a new hat in the corner of the throne room, looked up. 'Oh, none of those, brother. They're all jack things. Let's do something the jills will enjoy too.' She looked up. 'I know, what about kite-flying? Let's fly some kites from the battlements?'

'Good idea, sis,' cried Prince Poynt, jumping up. 'Bagsy me the best kite.'

'We haven't made any yet. I'll go downstairs and fetch a few of the kitchen weasels.'

'Can they make kites?' asked Prince Poynt dubiously. 'I thought they could only scrape burnt fat off frying pans.'

'They *are* the kites,' replied Sibiline. 'You'll see, brother.'

Prince Poynt skipped out of the room with Pompom skipping after him. The pair of them went up to the battlements. So full of the joys of spring was the royal monarch it was difficult to tell which of them was the jester. Of course, no-one made this observation to the prince.

Some little while later Princess Sibiline appeared with several skinny kitchen weasels, who were more or less slaves. The weasels looked slightly unhappy. They had need to be. They were going to form the frames for the kites.

The princess had a bag full of silk kite-coverings which she had been stitching over the winter months. 'Here, try this one on – and you, this one – and the tall weasel there – put that on . . .'

The miserable kitchen weasels sorted out the kite-coverings between them. They pulled them on and stood in a star shape, back legs apart, front legs spread. Sibiline ran from one to the other, giving a tweak here, fastening a loose tail bit there.

Her winter creations were about to go on show. She sewed a good seam and was proud of her skill.

Prince Poynt waited impatiently for the first sacrifical weasel to be ready, so that he could launch it up above the battlements and gain some height before the other stoats tried theirs.

Sleek the otter had come to watch. Some of the kites were his creation, made of precious, gorgeously coloured fabrics from faraway exotic places. The tails were works of art in themselves – long flowing ribbons, some with crimped edges, others split into multi-coloured trails. One was made into little bows, all of different hues, which turned delicately in the wind like tiny propellers. another fanned out like the tail of a raptor, but in feathery sparkling silvers and golds. Another was so long and fluttery it lashed about like a live thing, flicking its fiery-red tip with a sound like a whip crack. These were the works of the great fashion designer otter and worthy of his name.

Sleek chatted nonchalantly to noblestoats and weasels alike, asking them their opinion of the designs. His role was adviser to the princess. She declared she did not know what she had done without him.

'What about this one?' he said. 'It's meant to suggest the lines of a flying dragon. Can you see it? Yes, of course you can. And that beautiful blue one over there. That's intended to melt into the summer sky. The frilly white bits around the edge represent cottony clouds of course.'

The first of the kitchen weasels, Jilinda, had the end of a ball of string tied round her waist. She then had to launch herself from the battlements. Forelimbs outstretched and back legs wide apart, she did what was expected of her, but her face showed her anxiety. If the kite had not been made to the correct specifications she would plummet down into the water below. She fluttered, dipped and then, to her delight, soared above the castle.

Suddenly she felt like a bird, swooping and diving over the lake, until the sharp jerk of the string reminded her that she was on a leash. It was a long leash, but she was still tied to the castle by that piece of string around her waist.

On the other end of the piece of string was Prince Poynt, delighted to be the first to launch his kite. 'Watch this!' he cried. 'I'm going to loop the loop with mine.'

Poor Jilinda went into a loop and came out in dizzying spirals. It was nice just to soar and watch the fields below sort themselves out into patterns, but doing aerobatics was something else. It made her feel quite ill and not a little insecure.

One by one other kites were launched. They climbed up into the sky, blotching the summer blue with splashes of colour. Even the kites themselves had to admit how pretty it all was. Having performed several somersaults and what have yous, each noblestoat set out to fly his kite the highest.

Up, up, up into the wide blue soared the skinny weasels. The higher they went the colder it became. From the castle walls they became mere specks in the heavens.

'Mine's the highest,' announced the prince,

though no-one could actually tell which kite was above the others. 'I win.'

'Well done, sire,' said Earl Takely. 'I think mine is second and betterer than anyone else's.'

'Rubbish,' snapped Jessex. 'Next to the prince I'm the bestest kite-flier.'

'You're both quite, quite wrong,' interrupted Sibiline. '*My* kite is the one immediately below my brother's.' Sibiline always felt that because she spoke more eloquently than the jack stoats her arguments were superior and therefore won her the day.

Thus a heated squabble took place in which there could be no winner, only stoats who thought they had won. They kept letting out their strings to make their kites go higher. But the kites were already mere coloured dots.

High up in the rarefied atmosphere the weasels were having trouble breathing: there was very little oxygen. Any higher and ice would begin to form on their fabric. They called to one another to keep their spirits up.

One: 'Don't worry, Jilinda, they'll soon get tired of this game – they haven't the attention span of a dodo.'

Two: 'I'm not worried, Ranter – at least, not much. My forelimbs are getting tired, though. I just want to close them, wrap them around my body.'

Three: 'You keep your forelimbs outstretched. If you don't watch it you'll go into free fall. It's a long way down there, you know. Even the castle looks like a snuff-box.'

Four: 'I've got my eyes closed. I'm not looking.

I *can't* look. I'll be sick if I do. The only consolation is, if I'm sick it'll be on that lot below.'

The last weasel in the group, and the only who had not contributed to this exchange, was little Xix, the chimney weasel. Down in the castle it was his job to climb up chimneys and sweep away the soot. It was a horrible job, made more horrible by the fact that he was terrified of heights.

Xix was wearing a pink and yellow covering which fluttered madly in the breezes, being just slightly too loose for his frame. Whenever his handler made him swoop like a hawk, his heart stopped in absolute terror. The wind riffled crazily through his cloth, his stomach dropped out, he could not breathe in the rushing air, and his limbs turned to jelly. It was a most terrible experience. All his nightmares were present with him on this flight into the unknown.

Still black with chimney soot, which would never ever come out of his fur, Xix's round white eyes told the whole story of those nightmares inside his head. Suddenly he spoke. 'It's no good. I can't stand it. I'm undoing my string. I want to die.'

A chorus of, 'No, no, don't be a fool, Xix,' did nothing to make the little weasel change his mind. He had had enough. There was a limit and he had passed it long ago. It was better to be dead on some sweet grassy knoll below, with the wind blowing through his pelt at ground level, than be subject to the whims of nothingness up here in the sky. He wanted something solid underneath him, even if he was not alive to appreciate it.

'I'm going to do it!'

To their horror the other weasels saw him lower his little claws to undo the knot at his waist. In doing so he started to drop like a brick down towards the stone castle immediately below. His long flowing tail went into a mad spiral. There was a long way to go and the knot was tight, yet he managed to undo it just a hundred feet above the castle bailey, into which he was about to plunge.

Jessex was standing silent and open mouthed, his string slack in his paw. The other stoats, Sleek and Pompom the weasel were equally dumbstruck as they watched little Xix hurtle down towards them. They could see that the chimney weasel was about to become a red blotch of fur and bone on the bailey floor. It was a horrible thing to have to witness, even for hardened stoats.

Then suddenly Xix opened his forelimbs again. He shot upwards like a glider on a thermal. It was a marvellous feeling, quite different to being tethered. He still hated the height, of course, but he felt more in control: he might glide down to earth in slow lazy circles, to land on his four feet if he wished. Free of the string he found he was able to dive and climb at will, going where he pleased.

And where he pleased to go was away from the castle, south-east towards Halfmoon Wood, where he knew he would find sanctuary. He was a bird. His bright tail trailed behind him like a glorious banner. He was escaping the clutches of Prince Poynt and the castle stoats. He zoomed above fields of green corn, watching his dark shadow flow along the ground.

'Goodbye, Castle Rayn!' yelled the sooty little aviator. 'Xix has left you for good!'

'Hey!' cried Prince Poynt from the battlements. 'Where's he going?'

'It looks very much like he's escaping,' said Sleek, trying to hide the amusement in his voice. 'And if you'll observe, the others appear to be doing the same.'

True enough, the greasy kitchen weasels still tethered to their strings had seen what had happened to Xix and were inclined to follow his lead. They all went into free fall, undoing their strings. Once loose, they went streaking off joyously towards the distant horizon like happy jays, blowing raspberries over their shoulders at the enraged prince and his noblestoats.

Of the stoats only Sibiline could see the funny side of things. She clicked her teeth and slapped her thigh. The prince stopped railing at the departing weasels and glowered at his sister. He did not know what to say to her, so he simply stamped away, with Pompom in his wake.

The princess was a complicated mixture of stoat snobbery and mammal understanding, which made her rather a puzzle to the prince. One minute she appeared to be all for the ruling classes and doing as she pleased, the next she was advocating the rights of weasels and the underclasses. The prince never knew where he was with Sibiline.

'Well,' she said to Sleek, 'there go our beautiful creations – like a flock of pretty silk birds flying south for the winter. Don't suppose we'll ever see them again. I shouldn't be surprised if those priceless fabrics are made into bedsheets for the poor.'

'We had our show,' said the otter, 'that's what counts. The world saw our new ideas, new fabrics, new colours – and they wept in frustration and joy.'

'Not as much as my brother is weeping,' cried Sibiline in amusement. 'He's got no-one to scrub the pans in the kitchens now.'

The two of them went into hysterical teeth-clicking, while the noblestoats – Jessex, Earl Takely and others – filed past them, brows raised, a disapproving look in their eyes.

Chapter Ten

After three mugs of the raw honey dew Sylver had had enough. Scirf and the pine martens were almost at the singing stage now. At least, thought the weasel leader, they are in a good mood. This had probably been Scirf's intention.

A forelimb was placed around Sylver's shoulders. This limb belonged to Short Oneleg, who was now becoming very friendly. Sylver felt uncomfortable – he didn't like false, drunken camaraderie. However, this time he did not complain.

Short spoke to him. 'Well, me old matey, what's this proposition of yourn?'

Now, a pine marten is at least twice as large as a weasel. It looks a bit like a small fox. It has that same sly look as a fox. However, it is a most agile animal and is sometimes known as a tree cat. Sylver thought that the martens would make excellent windjammer sailors, being able to run up and down the rigging without fear.

'The truth is,' said Sylver, 'we need you and your – your *maties*.'

'Eh?' cried Short, flattered by this remark. 'How's that, me salty old weasel? Need us for what?'

'Well, we wondered if your lot would come and crew the windjammer for us. It's a round-trip voyage. Once we've been to Dorma Island, we shall return to Welkin. Then the ship and all its fittings become yours. You won it fair and square at jabby-knockers, and it should rightfully be yours.'

Short peered at Sylver through narrowed eyes. 'Ours, you say? To keep? You won't go claiming ownership again, like today?'

'All we wish to do is get to Dorma and come home again. After that the windjammer belongs to you. What do you say? Do you think you could crew for us?'

Short considered this proposition for a minute before asking the inevitable question. 'Why d'you want to go to Dorma so badly? So far as I know, it's a magical island, where animals fall asleep not long after they set foot on it. Why d'you want to go there?'

'Treasure!' said Scirf, before Sylver could reply. 'Captain Murgatroyd's treasure. A whole chestful of brass farthings is buried there, me hearties, just ready for the takin'.'

At that moment a wren flew in through an open window and landed on Short Oneleg's shoulder. 'Brass farthings!' it said. 'Brass farthings! Brass farthings, with my picture on 'em!'

Short brushed the bird away impatiently, but his eyes were alight with passion. 'Captain Murgatroyd's treasure, you say?'

Sylver coughed. 'Er, yes. If you will help us find it, the ship is yours.'

Murgatroyd was an otter from olden times, now long dead. In the very year the animals took over

Welkin he went into piracy as if born to the work. He took one of the humans' ships and crewed it with otters of dubious character. Over the next decade he plundered the land up and down the coast of Welkin. He would cruise up a river, sack the villages on its shore, and sail down again ten times richer.

Any creature who posed a threat was instantly sunk by the merciless pirate. His preferred method of killing his enemies was to catapult them into the cliffside nests of seagulls and leave them to suffer a horrible death under a rain of sharp, savage beaks. King Redfur once hired some mercenary sailors to capture Murgatroyd, but the swashbuckling otter sent every last one of them to a watery death.

But one fine day the otter pirate set sail on the open sea for places unknown – and never returned.

'Captain Murgatroyd,' murmured the rest of the pine martens. 'Brass farthings.'

'Why,' said Short, 'I think we can accommodate our weasel friend here, maties. What say you?'

There was general agreement from the martens.

'That's settled then. Here's me claw on it.' Short took his forelimb from around Sylver's shoulder and offered it to shake. 'We'll need some rehearsal, mind,' he said. 'We're a bit rusty, so to speak.'

'Of course,' replied Sylver. 'We'll sail up and down the coast until you feel ready for the open sea. We're no sailors ourselves. I know the theory, but we need to be able to test it in practice.'

Short Oneleg shook his head impatiently. 'I

mean, with the drinking. We've got to get a few more jars down us. What say you? Ready for another three or five mugs of honey dew?'

To Scirf's disappointment, Sylver stood up. 'No, no, we must be going.' He reached into his purse and withdrew a pawful of coins. 'I'll leave a pile of groats on the table. Once you've spent that it will be the last honey dew you'll have until we get back from Dorma. I want no drunken martens on board *my* ship. When I turn it over to you, you can do what you like. Until then, this is last.'

Short looked as if he were going to swing a paw at Sylver's head: then his expression changed from anger to a greasy clacking of teeth in the matter of a second. 'Of course, Cap'n. You're in charge till then. We'll be on board the *Scudding Cloud* just after dawn.'

Sylver motioned to Scirf and the two weasels began to thread their way through the riotous mammals who now crowded the inn. The landlord and his serving jill were weaving in and out with frothing mugs of honey dew, which spilled onto heads without a complaint. Someone shattered a drinking mug against the wall, but no-one took any notice. There were half a dozen tuneless songs going in different parts of the room.

Just before they left the room Sylver shouted back to Short, 'By the way, what do you do? You personally, I mean. Are you the boatswain?'

'Me?' answered Short Oneleg, with a kind of a leer. 'I'm just the cook.'

'Well, we'll certainly need one of those,' Sylver said. 'I'll put you in charge of the galley then.'

Outside in the cobbled streets Sylver turned to Scirf and remonstrated with him. 'Why did you tell them there was treasure on the island?'

Scirf was unrepentant. ''S no good tellin' that rogue that we're going to Dorma to wake the humans. He wouldn't have nuffink to do with it. We had to give him some sort of incentive. Somethink to look forward to. This way he thinks he's going to do us out of the treasure.'

'I'm sure he's a scoundrel, that one. We'll have to keep a sharp eye on him.'

'Too true, squire. He'd steal your whiskers if he thought he could sell 'em somewhere else.'

The next morning, true to their word, the martens arrived on board. They really were an ugly-looking bunch. Many of them had bloodshot eyes and hung their heads. A few had obviously not slept at all the previous night. No doubt they had been carousing and wassailing into the small hours.

Sylver was determined to have no mercy on them. Their pain was self-inflicted and he had no pity with such creatures. 'Right, Short – you're to go down and join Luke in the galley. The two of you prepare breakfast for the whole crew. Fried thrushes' eggs and rashers of vole bacon will be fine.'

'Fried eggs,' repeated Short, looking a little queasy, 'fine – I can do that.' He went down the gangway to the galley, his legs unsteady.

'The rest of you,' ordered Sylver, 'on the dock-side. I want you all on the ropes. We have to pull the ship out of the dock and into the harbour before we can raise the sails. Snap to it! We haven't got all day. The tide changes soon.'

The weasels were not surprised by the gruffness in Sylver's tone. He had taken on the job of captain reluctantly, knowing that sea captains tended to be somewhat tyrannical. Tasks had to be carried out instantly, orders obeyed without question, especially in bad weather, or the whole ship was endangered. Sylver had looked at the rest of the crew and decided that he, as the woodland leader, had to take on the job. They were used to taking orders from him, though sometimes they argued. A ship's deck was no place to argue and he knew he had to change his character, drastically, if they were to survive without mutiny or going down in a storm. Even if he did not feel angry, he had to act the part, to gain their complete obedience. Although he would accept advice when he asked for it, all decisions were his. A captain could have no friends while at sea, he had told them when agreeing to be the captain, only subordinates. His was the overall responsibility and therefore he had to remain aloof from normal companionship, to keep his head clear and his decisions clean and sharp.

The martens knew no different. They probably thought Sylver had been a grouch all his life; in any case, they were used to lofty captains. These larger mammals jumped onto the dockside and took up ropes. They began to haul the floating vessel out of the dock and into the main harbour. They sang a song as they did so. This was not one of their drunken tavern songs, but a shanty which helped the rhythm of their work.

> 'Heave ho, Little Joe, we work for the Black Ball line.
> Work on, Big Bad John, we toil from nine till nine.
> Heave ho, Maggie Mo, we work for the White Star line.
> Slave on, Sailor Don, no sleep till the weather's fine.'

The weasels soon took up this chanting and found it did help to keep them all in time.

Finally they got the great ship out of the dock and into the harbour waters, where they all came on board again. The martens were then sent aloft to unfurl the sails. They were soon scrambling over the rigging. A few had helped the statues to test their ships on the water and the others had sailed for captains like Murgatroyd. These martens knew what they were doing. It was their experience which would cover Sylver's lack of nautical expertise.

Miniver had been appointed first mate. Lord Haukin had insisted she read about seamanship in the books in Thistle Hall library. Miniver had a very retentive brain – in this respect she was the best choice for the job. However, she had to stamp her authority on the rest of the crew and this was difficult because she was so small.

Miniver developed a stern expression, linked her forelimbs behind her back, and strode back and forth across the deck as she issued orders.

When someone grumbled about a task, she muttered something dark about being locked up for the rest of the voyage and fed on mouldy cheese. 'Anyone who disobeys orders will be chained in the fo'c'sle until his fur turns white,' she growled softly. 'The fo'c'sle's not a nice place in which to spend Christmases and birthdays.'

They therefore held their tongues and followed the orders issued by this pipsqueak weasel who knew the names of things on board. They scampered up and down the rigging, letting slip a sheet here, tying a bunt line there, familiarizing themselves with the tasks up above the deck.

The first few days of practice went very badly. This was mainly the fault of the weasels, who had to learn the names of the ropes and sails; they did not even know what 'reef' meant until Miniver explained it. Even Miniver herself was feeling her way: she put up sails and took them down by guesswork at first, until she learned about wind strengths and directions. Once or twice a look from a pine marten told her that she was doing quite the wrong thing and she reversed her decision.

Once or twice they nearly came to grief, but the *Scudding Cloud* was luckily a difficult vessel to capsize, and the pine martens were quick to put right any mistakes made by the weasels, though they grumbled about landlubbers and crab-watchers.

On one or two of these occasions, when the ship rolled heavily to one side or the other, there was a yell from the galley, and everyone knew that the soup of the day would have grit from the galley deck in with the carrots and potatoes.

The first time Mawk was sent aloft he managed only to climb ten feet off the deck. There he froze to the rigging, looking down in terror. He was supposed to be higher up – much higher up – on the royals. 'I'm not going! I'm not going! I'm not going!' His cries sounded the length and breadth of the vessel.

Scirf, his mentor, went to try to persuade him to climb higher, but before the ex-dung-watcher could reach the place where Mawk was clinging to the ropes, Sylver appeared.

'THAT WEASEL THERE! GET ALOFT, CURSE YOUR HIDE, OR I'LL HAVE YOU UNDER THE LASH!' he thundered.

Mawk blinked, shivered once, and began climbing upwards. He had never heard Sylver roar like that before. None of them had. It was not an experience they enjoyed. Sylver was usually so understanding of Mawk's cowardice. This was a new Sylver – one they would be seeing more of in the future.

Mawk summoned up enough courage to yell back down, 'If I fall, it'll be your fault, Sylver.'

'You fall and make a mess of my deck and I'll have your remains swept overboard with a stiff broom,' snapped Sylver, his heart sinking inside him even as he spoke the words. 'Don't ever answer back like that again while you're working. Just get up there and do the job. If you can't do it, go home to Halfmoon Wood. I've no time for slackers on board my ship.'

And so Mawk got on with it. He made it to the yardarms, inched out, his feet on the rope beneath, and helped to unfurl the sail. At first he trembled violently every time he looked down at the tiny deck below, but gradually he got used to the windy heights and his knees stopped knocking. He was able to work with his paws without being frozen with terror. It helped him to curse his captain.

Bryony and Alysoun had been appointed the helmsmammals and had to learn how to handle the rudder and steer the vessel. Normally one of them could do this job alone, but when stormy weather blew up it took both weasels to keep the ship on course. Once or twice, when too much sail had been raised and the wind slammed into the ship broadside, the two of them, clinging to the wheel as it spun out of control, were sent flying round with it, their tails streaming out behind them.

In the meantime, Scirf put his study of navigation into practice.

Gradually the crew got better and better at their work, until one day it seemed natural that the ship should have the right amount of sail aloft for the strength and direction of the wind. Bryony and Alysoun were now managing to keep the course true, using the edge of the wind to tack when necessary. Scirf had worked out a course for them across the Cobalt Sea, and was ready to put his talents into operation. Luke and Short Oneleg were now dishing up meals which were almost digestible.

Sylver spent most of his time in his cabin, apparently brooding. Perhaps he was having doubts and fears about his plan to bring the humans back to Welkin.

It has to be said that humans had not been the best of friends to weasels, stoats, martens and their kind, when they stalked Welkin's meadows and woods. The very people Sylver was planning to wake and bring back had hunted the animals with trap and snare, with bow and sling, hanging their pelts on gibbets. Humans had treated the carnivorous beasts as enemies, killing them whenever they could – not for meat, but simply because they were competitors for game animals. Now, Sylver was going to bring them back, perhaps at the cost of many weasel lives. It was not any easy task.

Yet the sea walls had to be rebuilt. If the animals of Welkin were to survive at all, the incursions of the sea needed to be stemmed. It was essential to bring back the humans, whatever their failings. So Sylver was left with little choice in the matter, though his heart was dark with misgivings.

Bryony, who had always been close to Sylver and knew his moods, came down to his cabin with a message from Miniver. She saw immediately how unhappy he was and set about trying to cheer him up. There was no other choice left for them, she assured him. The humans were necessary to the survival of all the species on Welkin.

Chapter Eleven

Flaggatis received intelligence reports that a ship named the *Scudding Cloud* was about to set sail, with the weasels on board. In his fort, set on stilts in the middle of the unnamed marshes, he cursed his rats. They had failed to report back to him in time. He had close to half a million rats under his command and they had not managed to get word to him that the weasels were renovating a ship. It was absurd. 'If you want something doing, you have to do it yourself,' he muttered.

'*Yesssshhhhh maaashhhhttter*,' cried the rat at his side, making him jump.

'Blast you, I'd forgotten you were there,' said Flaggatis. 'Why didn't I ever teach you creatures to speak properly. It's *master*, not *maaashhhhttter*.'

The rat had begun to open its mouth again and Flaggatis rapped its nose to silence it. 'I'm thinking,' he said. 'Never interrupt me while I'm thinking . . .' He knew that whatever he said the stupid rat would come out with the same two almost-words. The trouble with rats, he had found, was that they had eaten rubbish for so long their brains had turned to the same stuff. They had heads full of garbage. There was nothing he could do about that now except lose his patience from time to time. Not that this helped to improve their speech, but it made him feel better.

Flaggatis began to pace the floor again. It was the only exercise he got these days. The rats carried him on a litter, or he went by mouse-cart, if he had to go far. Flaggatis was a very old stoat: old and embittered. Ever since middle-age he had wanted to wrest the kingdom from the grasp of Prince Poynt and time was running out for him. The trouble was, Prince Poynt was relatively rich and could afford a standing army of stoats and a royal guard of ferrets. Flaggatis had to rely on rats, who were cheap – but very, very stupid.

Now, a dove had sold him some news that it had overheard while perched in the rafters of an inn called the Red Admiral. Some believed doves to be sweet-hearted angels, and ravens to be evil, grasping creatures, but in fact it was the other way around. You could not find a more honourable bird than a raven or a more treacherous creature than a dove. Doves would sell their own eggs to make an omelette if it meant more money to feather their nests. They looked so innocent, but in their puffed-out grey chests beat a mean heart.

This particular dove had told Flaggatis that, yes, the weasels were about to set sail for an island called Dorma. They were going because there was buried treasure on the island – the treasure of one Captain Murgatroyd.

'Money,' Flaggatis had said in a wistful voice. 'Money to buy *power*.'

'Speaking of which . . .' said the dove.

'Yes, yes.' Flaggatis had reached inside his long

116

flowing robes, which of late flowed even more freely since as he had grown older he had grown skinnier. 'Your payment, I know.' He had pulled out a cracked-leather purse, counted out thirty pieces of silver and given them to the dove.

He had watched as the dove took the silver and put it in a pouch around its neck. Then the bird had taken off into the blue sky. Flaggatis had immediately gone to the window and signalled to someone high above in the heavens. He continued to watch until he saw a dark shape curve out of the clouds and fall on the dove like a comet.

A savage claw struck the dove behind the head and the soft-grey shape fell out of the sky to land in the marshes below, dead as a stone. It fluttered there in the wind. Flaggatis was satisfied. He could not have allowed the dove to live. It would have sold its information elsewhere, to the enemies of Flaggatis. There was a hawk which lived nearby whose preferred diet was rats. Every so often Flaggatis trumped up some charge against a rat and had the others sacrifice him or her to the hawk. The hawk obviously appreciated this gesture and had become an assassin for the stoat wizard.

'Well, that's that,' Flaggatis had said, as the hawk robbed the dove of the silver pieces. 'So die all traitors, eh, Grersh?'

'*Yeesshhh maaahhhsster.*'

Flaggatis was now anxious to reach Murgatroyd's treasure before the weasels. He saw what he had to do: sink the weasel ship and then find Dorma himself.

An expedition was called for, but he could not

trust his rat generals: he would have to go himself. This was most inconvenient. His ancient bones ached with the damp, and a sailor's life can be very damp. There was nothing else for it, though. He had no choice.

He called his rat generals to his quarters. There were seven of them. They came in wearing their new admirals' hats, which were long, narrow affairs the shape of a canoe. From the sides of the canoe-shaped hats sprouted jays' feathers. This was to help them make the switch between general and admiral. Otherwise they were likely to shout 'Charge!' instead of 'Board!'

The 'admirals' were very proud of their head-gear. They had earned the right to such badges by being particularly barbarous in battle. A rat was promoted to general – and thus, admiral – only on presenting to Flaggatis a score of stoats' ears which had been chewed off at the roots.

'You generals are all now promoted to admirals, with effect from yesterday,' he told them. 'It's a sideways promotion, of course, but one of which you can all be proud. There's no extra pay, but there's a lot of status. Your new hats are a symbol of your sudden rise in station.'

The new rat admirals looked pleased. They turned their heads this way and that, very care-fully, and stared at each other, nodding in approval. Flaggatis could tell that the stupid creatures thought they looked very fine and grand in their new style headwear.

'*Thhhannnkkyoooo maaassshhhtter.*'

'This means you will have to go to sea.'

This did not bother the new rat admirals in the

least. They were a species known as 'ship rats'. Bigger and stronger than the local 'ditch rats', they were not afraid of the sea. It was like a second home to them. They had all arrived in Welkin aboard ships, after spending half their lives in the rafters of damp timbers. To have to go out onto the ocean again was somewhat refreshing. They liked the sea air.

And there was usually a lot of maggoty cheese to eat on board ship. There was not much cheese on Welkin, since the cows were not milked. The only cheese you could get came from vole- or mouse-milk, and the tiddly bit of cheese that produced was not worth the effort of chewing.

'*Wwwweeee goooowwww,*' cried the rat admirals. '*Yesshhhhh.*'

'Good, good,' cried Flaggatis. 'I shall go with you. You will have me carried to the port by litter. Once there we shall choose a craft and chase after these damnable weasels. We shall see who ends up with the treasure! They may find it first, they may even run their fingers through it, but we shall be the ones to spend it.'

One blustery day the windjammer *Scudding Cloud* was ready to set out for the open sea. Captain Sylver came up from his cabin at last to address the crew. He was sombre-faced and hollow-eyed. The first thing he did was borrow a hammer and nail from the ship's carpenter. Then he proceeded to nail a silver nutmeg to the mast. 'This silver nutmeg is for the creature who first spies Dorma Island,' he said. 'So if you see it, sing out loud and clear, and the silver nutmeg is yours. Anyone who calls falsely will, I'm afraid, receive ship's punishment.'

Bryony, who was standing at the front of the crew, blinked rapidly. 'Punished?' she said. 'How punished?'

'I have not devised the penalty yet,' replied Sylver, who believed such threats were important because of the naturally rebellious nature of the martens. 'Let's hope it won't be necessary.'

'Hang on a bit,' interrupted Short Oneleg, 'you're gettin' a little heavy, cap'n . . .'

'Listen, we are now about to go to sea. This voyage is my responsibility. The safety of those aboard and the success of the mission depends on me. If you want to choose another captain before we set sail, by all means do so. I shall be happy to step down. But if I go as your captain, then you will obey my orders without question, and those who fail me will have to be punished, whoever they are.'

The ex-outlaws stared at Sylver in silence. The martens? They did not know Sylver well enough to see that this was not his usual self, and they took it all on their whiskered noses. Most of the woodland weasels realized this was for the benefit of the rough-and-ready martens.

Mawk, however, took things at face value, as usual. 'Not much we can say to that, is there? I mean, who's going to take over the ship now? No, it looks like we're stuck with you, Sylver – Captain Sylver – like it or lump it.'

'Good,' said Sylver. 'Now, if I am not available, the navigator will be obeyed at all times regarding our course; the first mate is responsible for the running of the ship in good weather or foul; the galley is the strict province of Short Oneleg. If anyone has any grievances, they are to come directly to me, and I will try to settle the matter to the satisfaction of all.'

With that he turned on his heel and went up to the quarterdeck. 'First Mate Miniver!'

'Yes, captain.'

'You will make ready the ship, if you please. We will sail on the tide. I will see the navigator in my cabin. We shall work out a course to give to the helmsmammals. The rest of you, go about your tasks. I want no creature idle. Every mammal has work to do on board my ship.'

With that the captain went below. Scirf followed a little later. Luke went with Short Oneleg to the galley to prepare the next meal.

'He's a bit of tyrant, your head weasel, ain't he, matey?' said Short to Luke. 'I wouldn't like to cross *him* on a windy day.'

'He hasn't always been like that,' said Luke. 'It's this captain thing. He's taking it seriously.'

'Well, the sea's no jill to play pat-a-cake with. She can whip up a fury in a matter of seconds. It's good to have a captain on board that knows who's master. There can be only one master on a vessel and he knows it.'

'I hope you're right,' said Luke.

Chapter Twelve

The ship set sail with the tide in the early hours of the morning. After all the practice they had had up and down the coast the sails were raised without difficulty. Bryony and Alysoun took turns at the wheel and found the ship reasonably easy to steer in the following wind. Their watches were two hours on duty, four hours off. One of the martens was the third helmsmammal, having steered such a ship once before.

Scirf had difficulty in studying the stars in their courses, as the night was overcast, but he tried to work out their position by judging the direction of the swell. He was not totally confident of his navigational skills, but he was learning fast. He thought it would take at least two days to reach Dorma.

All went well until dawn broke above the curving horizon. Then the waves began to increase in strength. First, white horses began to appear on their crests. Then the deep sea darkened until it was almost black. Everyone came up on deck to stare at the signs of bad weather coming on. The sky was a gloomy brooding presence above them, growing blacker and uglier by the moment. A chill wind had sprung up from the north, sweeping across the surface of the sea and sending up spindrift, which soaked them all to the roots of their fur.

Before they left, the industrious Wodehed and Luke had stitched some oilskins together. These had been cut down from those fashioned for humans and left in a chest in the hold. The animals now put them on. It appeared they would have need of them in the next few hours.

Thunder began rolling across the sky like a beast growling deep in its throat – distant, but growing ever louder. It was as if a great black panther were running softly overhead, its satin-covered body blocking out the sun. Sheet lightning, silent as yet, lit up the heavens as if some distant god was opening and closing the door of a furnace. Those on board the *Scudding Cloud* felt cut off and vulnerable.

'I can't see any land anywhere,' said Mawk, with a violent shiver. 'There's nothing out there.'

The others were equally scared. They were woodland creatures, used to the comforting presence of friendly trees. If a storm like this blew up at home, they would simply hide in the hollow of an old oak, or find a nice cosy hole in the ground. Even out in the middle of a field abandoned birds' nests or old hare forms provided shelter.

But here, out on the ocean, there was simply nowhere to hide – no hills or tors; no forests or hedgerows; no thorny brakes, no gorse-covered heaths. There was only a great heaving mass of water on all sides. It was the emptiness more than the violence which terrified them.

As the storm came closer, the sea became

wilder. Soon the whole sky was alive with cracking lightning. The waves were like moving mountains. The same sparkling blue sea that usually lay several feet below the gunwales now washed over them and surged across the decks. Bryony and Alysoun fought to keep control of the wheel. Up above there was far too much sail for the ship to survive such gusts.

Miniver gave orders to shorten sail but it was time to call Sylver on deck. He had been exhausted when the voyage started and she had wanted him to get as much sleep as possible. But the situation was becoming serious and she needed someone to boost her confidence.

'What goes on?' said Captain Sylver, striding out onto the bridge. He stared at the burgeoning storm. Miniver could see from his expression that he was just as frightened as she was. 'Are they taking in sail, Miniver? Helmsmammals! Never mind our course – steer into the waves, if you please. We don't want one of those large rollers to catch us broadside.'

It seemed that the crew of martens were at least used to such weather, though they too appeared to be a little worried. They scrambled amongst the rigging, taking in sail, and tied down loose cargo on deck. It was a good thing for the weasels that these creatures knew what they were doing.

There was now some sense of urgency on board, with 'Aye, aye, sirs' going on all over the place as weasels and martens scampered to their posts. Determined sailors scrambled aloft, darting here and there over the rigging and edging out onto the yards along the footropes. It was dangerous work in foul weather.

One of the martens slipped and fell, but fortunately he landed on the canvas covering of a lifeboat, which broke his fall and saved his life. The others worked on, taking in sail just in time to avoid the ship capsizing.

The decks, too, were alive with scrambling figures in their oilskins. The rain came down in torrents and poured from their heads and backs, but they continued to work away at their given tasks. The diminutive Miniver strode about crying out orders, the deck rolling and heaving beneath her paws. She knew her duty now and she was resolute.

Through it all Captain Sylver stood by the wheel, his face set and his legs astride, his mere presence offering confidence.

Crosswinds began to build waves into heavy buffeting rollers which crashed down on the decks. Sometimes the ship's bows were buried under such a weight of water that they pointed to the bottom of the ocean. Then, just when the crew thought the ship would never come up again, they suddenly reared up, rising above the waves, only to be swamped again.

The brave crew ran along troughs, with walls of water on either side, wondering whether they were going to be engulfed. They rode high crests, fearful lest they should fall to their deaths down one of the steep slopes on either side. They crashed head-on through sharp curling waves, breaching apparently impenetrable walls.

The air was full of blinding spray. Sea salt stung

the eyes of those not quick enough to avoid it. It filled throats, making them thirsty and sore. Sometimes the waves would knock an animal clean off his feet and slam him down hard on the deck. Sometimes the wave crests formed whips of water which lashed their faces. They bore it all with fortitude, though their hearts despaired. There was not a mammal who did not believe they were all bound for a watery grave.

Despite their inexperience, somehow they managed to weather the storm. The raging winds and crashing waves passed over and around them. The ship lost a little of its rigging – a top-gallant yard came crashing down to the deck – but apart from these incidents the vessel remained intact and in good repair. The weasel black-smiths and carpenters had done a good job with the refurbishment.

When it was all over and the seas were calm once again, Captain Sylver called for the navigator. 'Where are we?' he asked. 'Do you know?'

Scirf studied one of the sketches in his notebook. He scratched his head as if in deep thought. Finally he had to admit to Sylver that he was lost. 'I've got no idea,' he said, 'but I've seen a couple of land-nesting birds flying in that direction.' He pointed with his paw. 'They've obviously been waiting for the storm to die down before they come out here to feed. I can *smell* land too. I'd stake my reputation that it's that way.'

'You're the navigator. We'll head that way.'

They cruised along with a fair amount of sail aloft, the wind having died down to a whisper. Short Oneleg came up from the galley with a tray full of vole sausages, which the crew were happy to tuck into – all except Bryony, who was a vegetarian. She was given kelp and told to like it or lump it. She did neither, but she ate it anyway; there was nothing else.

Short stared at the horizon. He had been below for most of the voyage. Now there was a frown on his features. 'It doesn't feel right,' he said, sniffing the air.

'What doesn't?' asked Sylver.

'Our direction. It just doesn't feel right.'

The harassed Scirf said, 'I'm doing my best. As far as I'm aware, we're all right.'

'You're the navigator,' sniffed Short, turning away, clearly disbelieving.

At eleven o'clock Mawk let out a yell that would have woken the dead. 'Dorma Island! Off the port bow!'

'That's the starboard, you ninny,' corrected Scirf.

'Whatever. I saw it first. The silver nutmeg is mine.'

Captain Sylver was still on deck. He stared at the cliffs looming out of the mist. They were not particularly tall, but they looked mysterious. Anything could lie behind those chalk cliffs. He was not going to award the silver nutmeg until he was sure it was the right island. If it was Dorma Island, they could count themselves extremely lucky. Neither he nor Scirf had expected to arrive so quickly at their destination.

'That can't be Dorma Island so soon,' growled Short Oneleg, coming up from the galley. 'Why, we're only a little way down the apple barrel and at least two sailors have to get scurvy before a ship gets to the place it's going. We're only part way there, to my way of thinkin'. What say you, maties?'

A murmur of agreement went up from the rest of the pine martens.

Sylver was inclined to be more optimistic, full apple barrel or no. They might well have been driven before the storm and miraculously hit their destination. It might be some other island, crawling with monsters, perhaps, but he did not think so. In any case it would be well to behave cautiously at first. There was only one way to find out and that was to take a party ashore.

'Mawk,' he said, 'you'll get your reward as soon as I verify your claim.'

Mawk protested, although there was little he could do but await the outcome of an expedition.

The ship was anchored well away from the actual shoreline, as they did not know the bottom.

'Right,' said Miniver. 'Party to go ashore.'

'Me . . . Me . . . Me,' cried all the pine martens, almost as a chorus. Now that they thought the treasure was close at paw they were beginning to look shifty-eyed again. Miniver chose Short and one other marten, just to make up numbers, but she left Bryony, Alysoun and Luke behind to prevent the rest of the martens from getting up to mischief. The other weasels went ashore, heavily armed: none of them had ever seen a live human but they knew them to be large, aggressive creatures.

Wodehed carried in his pouch the special herb, an antidote to Dorma's sleeping gas.

The rowing boat left the *Scudding Cloud* and headed towards a gap in the cliffs, where a beach could be made out through the mist. Captain Sylver went ashore too, of course. Now that land was close by he had begun to revert to his old self: a martinet was required only when the ship was at sea. He stood up on the bows of the rowing boat, watching the shore creep closer with every stroke.

The beach was piled high with weed, tangled driftwood and empty seashells. This flotsam and jetsam had been deposited beyond the normal high tide mark by the storm. Some seagulls, evil-looking birds, were already at work on the seaweed, rooting amongst it for food. There were some equally nasty-looking waders – godwits and dunlin.

Proceeding carefully in case he was overcome by sleeping gas, Sylver tried to question the birds. Seagulls and waders were unapproachable. They took to the air whenever he came near them, their yellow eyes staring narrowly at the trespassers. Others, such as the frigate birds, were positively dangerous, and would peck the eyes from your face as soon as look at you. It was best to steer clear of such birds altogether.

The dense mist drifted over the landscape: even if there had been a house or two they would not have seen it until they tripped over it. The party, led by Sylver, set off in single file, their slingshots at the ready; Short brought up the rear. A short distance from the beach they came across a statue, blundering around in the dunes, tripping over clumps of marram grass.

'Hey!' cried Sylver. 'Do you speak our language?'

The dull-faced statue, a block made from ivory, struggled to its feet and nodded slowly. 'Me-speak-you-language,' it said.

'Can you help us?' questioned Sylver. 'Can you name this place?' He wondered whether the statue was one of those which had set out on board a ship and had landed up here as a castaway.

'Yes.'

'Well, what is it, dunderhead?!' yelled Scirf, who was always a little impatient with the slow-wittedness of statues.

'This-is-beach,' replied the statue.

'Yes, but which beach?'

'Sandy-beach.'

Scirf was disgusted. 'You'll never get anything out of these clots,' he said. 'Anyway, you can't trust the answer. We'd be better to find out for ourselves, captain.'

Sylver was inclined to agree and continued over the dunes and into the grasslands beyond. The statue continued to trip over in the soft sand behind them. Miniver felt sorry for it, but she did not want to hold up the rest of the party while she tried to help.

The party found themselves brushing through tall grasses. Sylver told everyone to keep an eye out for adders. Scirf happily pointed out that there might be even more dangerous creatures in this foreign place. Crocodiles were not out of the question, he said; or lions. Sylver thanked his navigator for this piece of information, which set everyone's nerves jangling. Each pawfall was now tentative, and they made slow progress.

Then suddenly, at noon, they arrived on a hilltop. The mist cleared with the midday sun and the new land stretched out before them, revealing all its wonders. In the distance they could see a great lake, shining in the sunlight. In the middle of the lake was a castle. From the castle towers flew the flags of the lord of that region. They bore the crest of Prince Poynt.

'We're back in Welkin!' cried Scirf, disgusted with himself. 'We've come round in a circle!'

'I thought we was on Dorma a bit too soon,' grumbled Short Oneleg. 'We haven't even left yet, me hearties.'

'Back to the ship,' Captain Sylver ordered, sighing heavily. 'We leave on the evening tide.'

Chapter Thirteen

Clearly, distances on a map were misleading. Scirf – and Sylver – now realized it was going to take a long time to reach Dorma Island. Both now looked at the massive vessel they had refurbished and knew why it was so sturdy. It had to undergo many days – weeks – perhaps months at sea.

And the ocean was indeed a frightening place: it was vast, it was open, it was empty – at least, most of the time. On the third day out they saw a school of whales. Scirf knew what they were from the books he had been reading in Sylver's library at Thistle Hall. He had imagined that a whale would be about as big as one of Thistle Hall's rain barrels. It was not. It was as big as the hall itself.

'Look at them,' said Bryony, her eyes round in wonder as the weasels and martens crowded along the rail of the ship. 'I wonder if they talk.'

'You want to go down there and find out?' asked Short Oneleg, with some sarcasm.

They stared as a monster broke the surface, sending up a tall spout of spray from a hole on top of its body. Then a massive tail came out of the water, to crash down and soak the watchers with more spray. At about noon the whales dived and did not come up again near the boat. They were last seen travelling towards the horizon.

'Are all the fish going to be as big as that, Scirf?' asked Wodehed.

'Whales is not fish,' replied Scirf, scratching his fleas in a superior fashion. 'Whales is mammals.'

'You mean they're the same as us?' cried Mawk. 'Why don't they rule the world then?'

''Cos they 'aven't got any legs,' replied Scirf knowledgeably. 'You can't rule anywhere without legs.'

At that moment someone saw a huge squid off the port bow and everyone rushed forward to look at this new wonder.

'That's got lots of legs,' said Mawk. 'Why don't squids rule the world?'

'Because they're fish,' replied Scirf promptly. 'Fish never ruled anywhere with land on it. 'Course, they probably rule the ocean, because that's all water . . .'

At that moment a school of great white sharks came cruising by, with their small dull eyes, their mouths full of sharp teeth, their dark fins cutting the water. Every other fish in the vicinity seemed to melt away into the depths. The sharks turned this way and that, gracefully, but with deadly intent. There did not seem to be a fish which was not afraid of these predators.

'Then again,' added Scirf thoughtfully, 'maybe squids don't rule the ocean.'

After three days, too, the crew began to recognize that meals were not going to be banquets, or even very tasty. In the main they consisted of lots of hard biscuits and tough meat. The meat was salt-vole or salt-mouse – there was little difference between the two: they both tasted stringy and extremely salty. The biscuits stuck in the throat and had to be washed down with copious cupfuls of water. In order to avoid scurvy, Wodehed (the ship's physician) forced everyone to drink lime juice, which made their eyes smart and their throats raw.

'What's for dinner tonight?' asked Mawk gloomily as the crew sat at the long table.

Short Oneleg appeared with a steaming saucepan full of stew. 'Vole, with a dash of mouse in it,' he said, 'followed by your favourite afters, me hearty – hard tack.'

'I hate those biscuits,' cried Mawk. 'I hate everything you dish up.'

Short Oneleg squinted and placed the saucepan on the oak table, then carefully wiped his paws on the greasy dishrag he had been using to carry the hot pan, making them even dirtier. 'Are you sayin' there's somethin' wrong with me food, ye weaselly woodlubber, ye?' he asked in soft, menacing tones.

Mawk looked into the face of the three-legged pine marten, whose battered appearance told of many desperate fights in taverns across Welkin. There were scars beneath the fur and chunks missing from ears and tail which should have warned Mawk of the consequences of pursuing his complaint.

'I'm sayin',' said Mawk, 'that you wouldn't get a job in a top-class restaurant if your life depended on it.'

'Oh, is that what yer sayin'?' Again the tone was soft and menacing. 'Yer sayin' I'm a lousy cook.'

Scirf tried to save his friend from a clobbering. 'Lousy! Now there's a word to conjure with. I'm lousy, and proud of it. My lice are my companions . . .'

But Short was paying no attention to this interruption. He was looking intently into Mawk's eyes. He suddenly grabbed Mawk by the scruff of the neck and rammed his head down into the vole-and mouse-meat stew. Then he immediately lifted Mawk's head up, dripping gravy and bits of meat, and pushed it down into the water barrel at the side of the table. Finally he let the unfortunate Mawk come up for air.

Mawk stood up, gasping and spluttering.

'How did you like *that* meal, ye furry fardel, ye!' said the ship's cook, and went back to his galley.

Scirf and the others took a plateful of Short's stew. After the first spoonful Scirf looked up and said, 'Hmmmm, that's really tasty. It must be the new herb Short's put in it.'

'What herb?' asked Mawk, wiping his head on a towel. 'Where would he get a new herb in the middle of the ocean?'

'I believe it's called Mawkkopf. Yes indeed. It tastes strongly of Mawkkopf. I think we should ask him to dip your head in the stew more often. I've not tasted anything so delicious since we first left port.'

'Ha, ha,' remarked Mawk drily. 'I'm sure that's very funny. The trouble with mammals around here is that you offer the slightest hint of criticism and they take it as an insult.'

'I think,' replied his friend Scirf, 'these observations is all very well on land, where you can run away when things gets ugly, but out here on a ship, where the furthest you can run is from one end of the ship to the other, it's best to keep 'em to yourself.'

Mawk saw the wisdom of this remark and thereafter held his tongue at meal times, building up a store of resentment towards the ship's cook.

There were other aspects of life on board which were not to Mawk's liking. The crew had to sleep in the forecastle in hammocks made of old herring nets. They were covered in herring scales, and stank to high heaven. Mawk had washed his bed several times to get rid of the smell, but this attempt at laundering did no good at all. In the end, what with the swinging and all, Mawk preferred to sleep on the boards. The midnight watch trod all over him on their way to and from their own hammocks but he still preferred the floor.

Aloft in the rigging, Mawk, like many of the others, wished he were a squirrel. They climbed trees with great agility, and would have had no trouble crewing a windjammer. 'I hate it up there,' said Mawk. 'One day I'm going to slip on the pawrope of a yardarm and end up a splodge of strawberry jam on the deck below.'

There were many onerous tasks that sailors had to perform: scrubbing the deck, scraping the hull free of barnacles, sewing sails, and caulking the hold with pitch, among others. When they had free time the pine martens, who had never ventured out into the open sea but seemed to know all about it, taught them sailors' games.

'There's deck quoits. That's where we throw this ring of rope and try to get it over a marlin-spike. There's playing jigs on violins and dancing to 'em. There's drinking rum and singing drunken songs, though I prefers honey dew to rum.'

'Well, some of those sound rather nice,' said Bryony, 'but Sylver has decreed no drinking on this voyage.'

They were having this conversation on deck, on a sunny day with a fair wind, when a shout came from the crow's nest where Mawk was perched. Mawk pointed. 'Sail ho! Ship off the starboard bow!'

All those not on duty ran to the starboard rail and stared out over the choppy waters. There was indeed a ship. In fact it had no sail, but it did have a roof. It was long and slim, like a rat war canoe (only much larger, of course), greeny-black in colour, with a thatched roof which ran the length of the vessel.

Sylver came up on deck to view this newcomer. 'Stand by the catapults,' he said. 'But don't fire unless I give the order.'

He knew it was wise to be cautious, but there was no need to antagonize a perfectly friendly ship unnecessarily. Like all sea captains he was wary of another vessel. There were no flags to be seen; no mammal beneath that shady roof; no means of propulsion even – neither sails nor oars were visible. A strange craft indeed.

It was obvious that they had been spotted. The vessel turned very gently, as if it were carried along by the currents alone. It must have had a rudder and a tiller, though, for it steered purpose-fully for the *Scudding Cloud*. Under Sylver's instructions Miniver gave orders to shorten sail and the weasel ship slowed down.

They could now see that the roofed vessel was about 450 stoats long, 75 stoats wide and 45 stoats deep. 'Gopher wood,' murmured one of the pine martens on deck. 'I've seen that strange run of the grain before, those swirling knots, that unnatural colour. Yet I don't so much recognize it as *sense* it, feel it deep at the base of my tingling brain.'

'What?' asked Bryony, alarmed by the marten's bizarre tone. 'What was that?'

'I'll give you an example. A chalice was found once at the bottom of a well in a forest to the north of Welkin, near where I was raised. The cup had strange properties. It was full of red wine and could never be emptied, no matter how long you drank or how deep your thirst. That chalice was made of gopher wood. Now this ship. It makes you think . . .' The elderly pine marten, who normally said little, stared at the oncoming ship, his eyes deep and tragic.

'Where do you get all that from?' asked Bryony, looking up into the face of this sage.

'Oh, you know – gopher wood? It's the timber from which mystical objects are fashioned. Funny thing is, no-one seems to know which tree it comes from – what it looks like. No-one has ever seen a gopher tree.'

'Someone must have done,' replied Bryony, 'or you wouldn't get things made out of its wood.'

'As to that, why, who said such things were made by mammals, or even human beings?'

At first Bryony was not quite sure what the pine marten meant by this mysterious remark. Then a chill went down her spine as she realized what he was getting at. He meant that the objects fashioned from gopher wood had been made by creatures not of flesh and blood. He was speaking of supernatural beings – perhaps the shipwrights of the gods?

'Do you think they mean us harm?' she asked the marten.

The lean creature beside her sighed – a whisper of wind rustling dry corn – and shook his head. 'Who knows?'

As the craft drew ever closer, they could see that below the waterline the timbers were encrusted with barnacles and other shellfish. The planks of the hull were greeny-black with age, as if it had been resurrected from a grave of mud and slime. Yet it was whole and strong, able to plough through the water with ease.

'Can you see who is on the bridge?' asked Bryony. 'I'm not quite tall enough.'

The pine marten gasped, along with a number of other members of the crew. He murmured a prayer to some marten god, trying in vain to avert his eyes from the oncoming craft. He was transfixed, his gaze caught by some strange vision. 'A golden beast,' he said at last, 'like one of those statues in human courtyards. A golden beast with a dark flood of hair around its head . . .'

'A mane?' asked Bryony.

'Yes, a mane.'

'You mean, there's a real live lion on the bridge of that ship?'

'That's the creature I mean – a lion – and he looks as old and wise as I feel myself.'

A lion! thought Bryony. They were about to meet a lion.

Chapter Fourteen

The *Scudding Cloud* came up alongside and lines were thrown to lash the vessels together. The other craft was much lower down than the weasels' ship, which gave Sylver an excuse not to board her. He had very little wish to see his first lion close to, knowing as he did that the big cats were carnivores. Lord Haukin had made a study of lions and their kind, who had once roamed the lowest reaches of Welkin.

Sylver found he was staring down into the dark features of a great musty-maned beast, whose tawny fur, even at a distance, smelled strongly of sun on dry grass. Golden-flecked eyes looked back with a calm gaze. Sylver could read nothing in those eyes: neither friendliness nor hostility. They gave nothing away.

Sylver was alarmed by the size of the lion. He was a much larger beast than he had anticipated, even though he had been prepared for a greater cat. The picture books in his library at Thistle Hall had not done justice either to the whale or to this lion. They were both massive creatures by weasel standards and absolute lords of their own worlds.

'Who are you? Where are you from?' The voice was deep and vibrating. Its rich timbre made

Sylver's spine tingle. The words could have come from somewhere deep in the earth, where the furnaces of the world heated the gases. These gases now wafted over Sylver like a hot desert wind, making him want to choke.

Despite his apprehension and awe Sylver managed to keep his voice steady as he answered the great beast. 'We are weasels and come out of a land called Welkin.'

The lion paced restlessly backwards and forwards as he spoke. His muscles rippled underneath his fur as he walked on huge spreading paws. Sylver had never witnessed so much harnessed power before. Surely this lion creature was the strongest animal in the world? Why, one of his paws could cover Sylver's entire body. His fur was so thick you could have hidden an army of weasels in it.

'I asked you who you were. What is your name, weasel?'

'My name is Sylver. I am captain of the *Scudding Cloud*.'

'There are other creatures on board your ship?'

'Yes – more weasels and some pine martens – they crew for me.'

The lion's gaze travelled up towards the ship and he seemed to be studying the weasels and martens lining the rail.

While they had been talking, Sylver had heard heavy-sounding movements down below the deck of the lion's craft. He realized that there were other large beasts on board, probably like this one. They moved through darkness, for there were no portholes on this vessel. Sylver imagined their eyes penetrating the gloom below decks, as they paced back and forth. Some would be in black satin, others in yellow with black spots, others still wearing stripes. This ship was indeed full of greater cats.

Below were carnivores with huge claws, great teeth, strong jaws that could break the bones of a sturdy ox; with power that could bring down the fleet horse in flight. They had roamed a stranger, redder earth than weasels knew, where the smells were musky and strong; the world of the thorn bush and the dust storm.

As with all carnivores, there was the darkness of blood in those minds, too. Weasels had it, but it did not flow through their dreams in great rivers. These giant cats were a world apart from small country weasels and their kind.

'Why do you stare at me so?' asked the lion. 'Have you never seen one of my sort before?'

'Never,' confessed Sylver, peering down the long length of the craft, with its strange narrow roof. 'And I can hear and scent others like you below decks.'

The lion's eyes narrowed as he stared back. 'Yes,' he confessed at length, 'panthers, leopards, cheetahs and their kind. Would you like to go below and meet them?'

'No,' replied Sylver, rather too quickly. 'I prefer to remain here, in sight of my friends.'

'You do not trust me?' The rich timbre of the voice made the taut lines of the craft vibrate with its resonance.

'I have no reason to trust you,' replied the plucky weasel. 'I do not know you.'

The majestic head nodded in affirmation. 'True, true. Now tell me, where are you heading? I have been on these seas for a long time now . . . so long . . . so very long . . .' The lion's words trailed away, as if he were speaking in terms of eternity. then he seemed to jerk himself out of his reverie. 'Perhaps I can help guide you to your destination.'

'We are seeking an island called Dorma.'

The lids of the golden eyes closed for a moment, then opened again. 'I do not know of this place. Why do you wish to go there?'

Sylver realized now that he had spoken too hastily. These great predators would be searching for meat. Humans would make a reasonable prey for such a large animal. The weasel could not tell the lion he was going to a place where the humans were all asleep – his craft would make straight for such an island.

'We wish to make it our new home,' lied Sylver. 'Our real home – Welkin, as I told you – is run by the stoats. They treat us as second-class citizens. We are turned into serfs and slaves there. We seek a new world where we can be our own masters.'

If the lion did not believe this lie he gave no indication of it. He took in the words once again without a change of expression. His gaze did not flicker. He simply nodded that massive head again, slowly. 'I understand. The stoats rule. Is this the natural order of things, or has it come about by some change in circumstances?'

'Natural order?'

'We, the lions, were the natural rulers of the land from whence we set forth. There were stronger beasts, there were swifter, but we have

144

lordliness in our muscles and bones. We have nobility in our very form. Nature shaped us from a royal mould. We were born to our high station in life.'

'I see. No, the stoats set themselves up as the lords of Welkin when the humans left . . .'

'And the humans. Where did they go?'

Sylver swallowed quickly. 'No-one knows.' Then, to change the subject, or rather to turn it in another direction, he added, 'Did you have humans where you come from?'

'Oh yes, yes indeed,' said the lion. The beast's face was growing dimmer in the gloom of the evening, for they had been conversing for some time now. Lamps had been lit aboard the *Scudding Cloud* and were swinging from the yards. 'We had humans all right. There – there was a great flood . . .'

The lion hesitated for a moment, staring at the blood-red sun which was sinking below a distant horizon. It was as if he were thinking of a time long ago, which had all but faded from his memory. There were distant suns in his eyes, distant moons, faraway rains, long gone days of hunting the bush.

Sylver brought his host back to the present. 'There was a flood . . . ?'

'What?' The lion's head came up.

'You said there was a flood?'

'Oh – oh, yes. We had had no rain for several seasons – many years, in fact. The land was dry and parched, the river beds were dry. Then one day it started pouring, a deluge. Rivers of mud began to form across the plains, swirling,

145

gathering momentum, uprooting trees, sweeping all before them.

'At the same time a human – I forget his name – and his three sons and all their wives began building a boat. They gathered animals in, two by two, four by four, six by six, herding us into their vessel. Naturally the animals boarded the vessel, for they were very afraid of the day's darkness, of the thunder and lightning and the storm, of the constant rain. They feared they would drown if we did not obey this man, who said he had their welfare in mind.

'So there they were, carnivore and herbivore together – shivering in the darkness of this boat, listening to the raging of the storms. They were unconcerned by each other's presence. In the case of the herbivores, the greater fear of the planet's descent into the madness of wind and rain outweighed their fear of the predators. The carnivores in turn were too distressed to take notice of the proximity of their prey.

'The meat-eaters made friends with the herbivores – with the deer and the rabbits, the warthogs and the antelope, the buffalo and the zebra – and they learned to trust one another. They called each other by name. They discovered how much they had in common, being animals of the plains, and confessed how afraid they felt of the storm which threatened the small vessel, as it bobbed on the mighty waves.

'Then one day the storm clouds cleared away; the sun came out. The man – I wish I could remember his name – he sent some birds out to look for land. First a raven, then a dove. Finally the vessel landed, high up on a mountain slope, and was left there when the waters receded. The animals and birds were released back into the wilds, to do as they had always done.

'Many years later there was a second great flood. This time there were no humans around to direct things. We animals climbed up to the craft wedged in between two great rocks, and this time set forth ourselves to navigate the world. However, in this second instance, in our fear of the storm we forgot to load stores, and there was very little on board to eat.

'All went as before, until we predators lost our fear of thunder and lightning and looked about us for food . . .'

All the time the lion told this story his voice was getting lower and lower. In the gathering dusk Sylver could see his bright eyes shining in that face surrounded by the dark mane. There was something deeply sinister about this creature. The lion had some guilty secret, some horrible act had been commited, which was evident only in his tone. Sylver knew exactly what had happened when the floodwaters began to retreat and land began to appear again.

'. . . and we needed meat,' finished the lion.

'You – you ate the herbivores this time?'

'Yes, yes,' groaned the lion, a deep rumbling in his throat. 'We killed and ate the deer, the rabbits, the antelope. It was a terrible massacre: the screams of the dying were ugly to hear. They were trapped on the boat. Their speed was of no use to them here. Once upon a time they had been fleet of paw, perhaps still were, but in the confines of the boat this meant nothing. There was no place to run.

'But you have to understand – you *must* understand, being carnivores yourselves – that the lust for meat came upon us with a vengeance, impossible to ignore. We were left with no choice. They were helpless. They were at our mercy. Yet there was no mercy within us. A dark tide of red flowed through our minds.'

Sylver tried to imagine the scene, and even though he was a carnivore himself the picture was horrifying. 'So you slaughtered the other animals?'

The lion nodded his huge head and looked away.

Sylver shuddered. He asked no more questions now. He knew the history of those on board the strange ship. He might earlier have asked why they did not find some land, some continent suited to their needs, and settle down once more. Now he knew they could not, for they were tainted creatures, whose consciences kept them forever on the move. Hunting game on the plains, where the fit could run from their teeth and claws, was honourable – but to slaughter them in pens and coops – why that was another thing entirely. That was tantamount to murder.

Suddenly, Sylver knew why the lion – and those below the decks, who now paced restlessly, nervously, up and down the boards, their great paws padding on the planks – why they had stopped the *Scudding Cloud*. Here was a possible source of meat, this ship passing them on the ocean.

The lion lifted its head again to stare into Sylver's eyes, as if he knew what the weasel was thinking. 'You are a wise weasel, not to come on board at my invitation. Go on your way, weasel, and be thankful you are not cattle, deer, or even creatures as large as a fox, or we might have stormed your vessel despite the difference in height.

'We are growing hungrier by the hour. We shall cast off from your vessel and seek land some-where – we live by coastal raids nowadays – or we stop ships such as yours. Piracy on the high seas! It is one way to eat. It's been so long – so very long – since we began our never-ending, wearisome journey.'

Sylver did as he was bid. 'Cast off,' he ordered Miniver.

Miniver yelled out the order.

The lines were retrieved. The *Scudding Cloud* drifted away from the other craft, which fell behind the sailing vessel very quickly. The last they saw of the lion's ship was its silhouette against the setting sun.

Then it fell below the horizon, lost to their eyes.

Chapter Fifteen

Sheriff Falshed had at last arrived at the port. He was weary and bloodied, having had to fight his way through the kingdom of frogs. He had lost some of his best stoats in those swamps and was down to half a company of soldiers. But he had made it, accompanied by the two badgers, Herk and Bare. They tramped past the graveyard on the edge of town, looking forward to a good bath and a night at the local tavern.

Herk, smoking one of his foul chokies, cast a wistful look at the graves in the yard as they passed by. A local weasel was sitting on the gate to the yard, chewing on a piece of grass.

Bare called to the weasel, 'Any fresh bodies in the ground, youngster?'

Falshed turned in annoyance to reprimand the badgers. He was fed up with the pair of them. They were nasty characters, always out to make a quick groat, and their methods of earning money made Falshed shudder. In any case, this was not a time to be digging up newly buried corpses for their pelts.

The young weasel on the gate – a simpleton, by the look of him – was answering the badgers. 'New ones, yer rev'rence? Oh yerse. Several new ones.'

'What kind of mammal?' asked Herk eagerly. 'Any mink?'

'No minks, yer rev'rence – only a cartload of foreign weasels. They come up from the south. Got into a fight, they did, in the local inn. Got murdered by some pine martens. Vicious beggars, aye. Got murdered to death, they did.'

Hope sprang up in the sheriff's heart. If this was Sylver and his gang, slaughtered by the pine martens, why, there would be no need for Falshed to go to sea at all. He could go back to Prince Poynt and tell him that all was well: Sylver and the weasel band were all dead and buried.

'What were their names?' Falshed asked the youth sharply. 'Tell me their names.'

'Why, I did hear that it was One-eared Jake an' his motley crew what did the dirty deed,' said the simpleton, his eyes crossed and his bottom lip hanging down. 'Nasty bunch o' characters, yer rev'rence. They done been an' murdered many a good mammal in these parts, but no-ones can bring 'em to book.'

'Not the murderers' names, you fool. I'm not interested in them. I'm only interested in the victims.'

The young weasel looked astonished. 'Not int'rested in the murderers, yer rev'rence? Why, what's you here for then? I thought you'm come to arrest One-eared Jake and them others. Folks hereabouts always look to the law comin' from the south, being as we've got none here. Bain't you going to arrest them rogues, yer rev'rence?'

'Stop calling me "Your Reverence",' snapped

151

Falshed. 'I'm the High Sheriff, not some rotten bishop.'

Falshed realized that he and his men would have to put on a show for the local peasantry. It did not matter that the stoats were poor rulers, so long as they were seen to be trying their best. It was in out of the way places like this that revolution was fomented. It would do him no harm to gather up the pine martens and march them back to Castle Rayn.

'Shall I dig one of 'em up?' asked Herk. 'No sense in wastin' good weasel pelts.'

'Dig what up? Oh, the weasels. Not now, you moth-eaten badger.'

Falshed had been pondering on various options, staring at the ground as he did so, but when he looked up again the simpleton was gone from the gate. He had simply disappeared into the long grasses of an orchard beyond the graveyard. The sheriff was annoyed, but he decided he could assume the 'weasels from the south' were those from Halfmoon Wood. After all, how many weasel bands were there running about the countryside?

The sheriff felt decidedly heartened that he did not have to go bobbing about on a stormy ocean. He would arrest the pine marten gang as proof and march them back to Castle Rayn. Prince Poynt would be delighted. It would please the prince, too, that he could hang a few pine martens on the gibbet. Pine martens were not well-liked at the court of Prince Poynt.

'On to the local tavern!' ordered the sheriff. 'We have to arrest some pine martens.'

'What about the fresh bodies?' whined Bare. 'Can't we just have five minutes . . . ?'

Despite all his bad points, Falshed was rather prim and proper about death. He felt that it should be respected. He was rather afraid of it; if you did not treat it with good manners and propriety, he thought, it might visit you uninvited in the small hours of the morning. One did not desecrate graves, even those of enemies. He informed the badgers that if they touched one grain of dirt on the graves they would be subject to the law.

Now badgers are not small creatures. In fact they are rather large compared with a stoat. Many badgers, along with dogs and other such creatures, did not recognize Prince Poynt's rule over them. Herk and Bare did not like being told what to do by this pipsqueak of a sheriff. For the time being, though, it suited them to go along with Falshed's schemes. They swallowed hard, looked into each other's eyes with a promise, and followed behind the stoat soldiers as they marched on.

When the stoats reached the Red Admiral Inn it was growing dark. Lights began to wink on about the town as lamps were lit. Merry sounds came from the inn. Sheriff Falshed and his troops entered the place and immediately all merriment stopped. Pine martens, polecats, weasels and other mammals turned to stare at the stoat foot-soldiers in their dusty armour. Someone made a remark about 'white-bellies' – a nickname for stoat troops – and then the racket began again.

The innkeeper came over to Falshed. 'Why, it's our illustrious sheriff. To what do we owe the pleasure of this visit?' said the grovelling owner. 'Can I get you a mug of honey dew? Some mouse drumsticks? On the house, of course, but only for yourself. The troops have to pay. I would be a poor mammal if I let all the soldiers who came through here eat and drink for nothing, ha, ha.'

'I will have a mug of elderberry juice and some cold cuts of vole breast, if you please,' said Falshed, removing his new chain-mail gloves and slapping his thigh with one of them, the way he had seen the prince do with his velvet gloves. 'And be quick about it, landlord.'

The sheriff winced, water coming to his eyes. He bit his lip to prevent himself from crying out in pain. It was difficult to maintain a dignified pose, standing in the middle of the inn, surrounded by gawping yokels, but he managed it. The fact is, chain-mail gloves are not as soft as velvet ones. He had given himself a very nasty sting on the thigh.

The rest of the soldiers had plonked themselves down at tables and were ordering the serving jill about in their usual rough manner. They glared at the locals and asked them what they thought they were staring at. They snatched food from other mammals' trenchers without so much as a by-your-leave.

It was this kind of behaviour which had earned the soldiery a bad name. Falshed, to his credit, tried to stop it when he could, but much of the time he was so worried about his own affairs that he did not notice what his troops were up to.

Falshed sat at a table apart from his rowdy stoats. At that moment the door of the inn was flung open. In lumbered a pine marten on all fours, followed by several others. They looked a disreputable bunch, swaggering between the tables. Falshed recognized the leader immediately, for this nasty-looking character had only a stump where his right ear should have been. It looked as if it had been chewed away by a gang of wayward rats.

'Hi, you fellow,' cried Falshed, standing up, as the pine martens were passing the table where the badgers Herk and Bare sat. 'Come over here.'

One-eared Jake stopped halfway across the room. He feigned astonishment. 'Who – me?' he queried.

'Yes, you fellow,' replied Falshed imperiously. He almost slapped his thigh again with the chain-mail glove, but remembered just in time. 'I hear you're a dastardly murderer – and those mole's leavings with you, your henchmen.'

'WHAT?' roared the pine marten, his face darkening.

Falshed was rather taken aback by the violence of the question. 'Yes – that's what I heard.'

'Nobody talks to me like that,' cried One-eared Jake, 'and especially not a fancy-stoat from Castle Rayn.'

'I am the High Sheriff of all Welkin,' proclaimed Falshed.

'I don't care whether you're the stoat come to clean out the toilets on wharf five. No-one calls me a murderer. Right, into them, my jolly jacks,' he yelled. 'Give 'em a taste of waterfront justice.'

With that, the pine martens waded into the soldiery with claws, paws and teeth. The other tavern customers started cheering, seeing that the rude troops were being taught a lesson. One-eared Jake went straight for Falshed, who stood his ground and lashed out with his chain-mail glove, using it like a short whip.

For the next few minutes it was bedlam in the tavern. Fur flew everywhere. Teeth were sunk deep into legs and rumps. Claws were raking faces. Paws were punching the wind out of saggy bellies. Tables went over. Chairs were flung across the room. Bottles and glasses were smashed. Precious honey dew ended up in the sawdust on the floor.

The inkeeper yelled for order. 'Decorum, gentlemammals, decorum!'

No-one took a blind bit of notice.

The battle raged for at least twenty minutes, during which mirrors were broken, along with a few heads.

It was the serving jill who put an end to the brawl. 'ENOUGH!' she yelled. 'I'VE GOT TO CLEAN UP THIS MESS!'

Falshed was at that moment trying to bite Jake's left ear and wondering why his teeth kept clashing together. He realized too late that he was biting the missing ear. The pine marten was pummelling the stoat's chest, right on his burn mark.

'Nobody calls me a murderer,' repeated One-eared jake.

'You killed Lord Sylver and his weasels,' hissed Falshed. 'Do you not call that murder?'

'Who did I kill?'

'A bunch of no-good weasels from Halfmoon Wood. But that's not the point. As the law around here, I have to bring you to book. You will accompany me to Castle Rayn, where you will stand trial.'

'Who told you I killed these weasels?'

Falshed stared at his opponent. 'Why, another weasel. A young simpleton, swinging on the graveyard gate. He pointed out their graves to me.'

The pine marten snorted derisively. 'For a start, weasels don't bury their dead; they burn them on a bonfire at a kalkie, don't they? For another, I saw that weasel myself, just an hour ago, on the very same gate. He's not a simpleton, he's one of the carpenters this Sylver sent for to repair his windjammer ship. And for a finish, we never killed anyone, especially not these blasted weasels you keep going on about.'

Falshed blinked. 'A carpenter, you say?'

'Yes, from a village near Halfmoon Wood.'

Falshed's soldiery was sheepishly straightening out the room now, picking up overturned tables and chairs and helping the serving jill to pick up the pieces of broken mugs. They were being helped by the pine martens they had waded into just a few minutes previously.

The sheriff himself was beginning to see that he had been the victim of a foul plot. 'Sylver's still alive?'

'He and his crew set sail just a few days ago.'

Herk called from the corner of the room, 'Looks like you've been duped, sheriff.'

'Well and truly,' agreed Bare.

Worse still, from Falshed's point of view, he had not escaped going to sea. He would still have to find his own vessel and set out after the weasels.

157

It was this thought that annoyed him the most. 'Damn and blast!' he growled. 'Now I've got to chase them over the billows!'

One-eared Jake said, 'Will you be needing a crew, sheriff? Me and my jacks are willing to go to sea after these weasel characters. We've done some coastal sailing, which is all you can say for the pine martens who are crewing Sylver's ship – Short Oneleg and his motley crowd. We're as good as Short's mob, any day. How about it, sheriff?'

Falshed jumped at the chance to hire an experienced crew. 'You're hired,' he said. 'What do you do?'

'Well, me personally,' said One-eared Jake, 'I happen to be the cook. But my jacks here, they'll work in the rigging and do anything required of a good crew. Don't you worry, sheriff, we'll catch them weasels before they reach the treasure.'

Herk and Bare's ears pricked up on hearing this word. 'Treasure?' they repeated. 'What treasure?'

Jake clicked his teeth in amusement. 'Don't try to fool me – you know what treasure. Murgatroyd's treasure, that's what. Sylver and his bunch have gone looking for Dorma Island, where the brass farthin's is buried. But we can beat 'em to it, if we set sail right away.'

'Murgatroyd's treasure,' murmured Falshed. The sheriff's brain was working quickly. Unlike everyone else in the room, he was not taken in by this story. He guessed that Sylver had invented the tale in order to get the pine martens to crew his ship. He saw that he had to go along with it in order to do the same. 'Yes – yes, of course. And if you crew for me you can be sure to receive a good share of the – the brass farthings. Right then, let us go and find a ship. Let's get this voyage over with, before I change my mind and commit suicide instead – I mean, let's be on our way over the briny, quickly, so that we can all be stinking rich.'

A great cheer went up inside the tavern.

Falshed's stomach was turning flipflops at the thought of going to sea, but there was nothing for it but to put on a brave face.

Like Sylver, Falshed found that there were very few serviceable ships anywhere in the docks. The statues had taken all the best ones and sailed away in them. However, there was a fort on a small headland just north of the harbour and by chance one of Falshed's stoats wandered around the point. There, nestling in a tiny bay on the far side, lay a ship which was being refurbished by some statues.

'We'll take over this vessel,' Falshed informed the glum statues. 'You'll have to find another one.'

'But-we-found-this-one-first,' argued a block, as Falshed's stoats began swarming over the ship.

'My need is greater than yours,' replied Falshed, suppressing any feelings of guilt with the thought that, if he did not catch Sylver soon, the prince would be using his pelt as a windbreak.

The statues looked devastated by this news. Falshed saw that there were only about a dozen of them. 'Look,' he told them, his conscience getting the better of him despite himself, 'you can come with us, and if we pass the place where you want to go, we'll drop you off.'

At this news the statues brightened a little and

gave the sheriff's stoats a stone hand in finishing the repairs.

Falshed had thought to bring a few tradestoats with him. Carpenters and smithies set to work immediately, while others sewed sails and made cables. With so many stoats at his command the work was soon finished, and Falshed was called upon by the captain of the guard to inspect the finished vessel. The sheriff put on a new belt studded with brass drawing pins, decorated it with his best scabbard and sword, and sallied forth.

With much pomp and ceremony, drums drumming and fifes fifing, Falshed was taken over the ship by his captain. They began at the stern and worked their way to the bows. Here Falshed was struck by the unusual figurehead. It was double-faced, carved from oak, and somehow the two faces looked familiar.

'Who carved this?' he asked. 'Who's the artist?'

'No-carve,' answered one of the ship's statues – an ancient soldier whose head and right arm had been knocked off and who carried these two appendages tucked under his left arm. 'We-find-with-faces-on.'

'You found it like this? Amazing. Where did you get it then?'

'It-be-found-washed-up-on-beach.'

Falshed peered closely at the faces. 'Amazing work,' he said. 'They look so horribly lifelike. Those frowns and wrinkled lips, and sneers of cold command. I wonder who the sculptor was?'

At that moment the faces suddenly spoke, making Falshed jump. 'We weren't sculpted, you

160

idiot. We were imprisoned. Don't you recognize us?'

'Yes, you saw us enough times in Castle Storm – you've surely got a better memory than that.'

Recognition came to Falshed with the sound of the voices. 'Good grief! Rosencrass and Guildenswine!'

'At last the stoat's brain moves into action,' said Rosencrass, his face working in the wood.

Guildenswine added her postscript, 'Assuming there's a brain there.'

'Rosencrass and Guildenswine, well, well,' said Falshed, still a little overwhelmed, 'the ferret spies. How did you get here? If I remember rightly, you were trapped in a magical forest, for being tree-haters or bird-killers or something. How did you get here, to this harbour?'

It was Guildenswine who told him the story. 'As you say, we were trapped in the trunk of a tree by foul magic, and left there for eternity. However, a great storm came – a hurricane – which snapped our tree off at the base. The broken trunk fell into the raging river and we were swept away, until we reached the sea. The currents then took us round the coast. We were carried here, to this bay, and found ourselves washed up next to two vast and trunkless legs of stone with "Ozzy's shanks" written on their toes.'

Rosencrass took over the tale. 'The statues found us and shaped us into a figurehead. Until that point we could not speak, being still tree. But now we are statue we have our voices back again.'

One-eared Jake, standing to one side during the ship's inspection, now interrupted this unholy reunion. 'And very useful they will be, too,' he murmured.

'How's that?' asked Falshed, swinging round to face him.

'Why,' said Jake, 'they will see the rips and sand bars before we hit 'em, and be able to yell out a warning. They'll be able to guide us through dangerous waters – shallows and rocky headlands, and such. Most useful, they'll be. Talking figureheads. They'll help us no end, they will.'

'And what if we refuse to help?' cried Guildenswine. 'What if we say no.'

'Why, it's to your own advantage,' replied Jake, 'for if we founder on the rocks, you will be the first to go down to Duffy Jonah's locker.'

'Who's Duffy Jonah?' asked Rosencrass.

'He was a man who was swallered whole by a whale and throwed up again, onto a beach – but his private locker, containin' socks and underpants and a change of shirt, still lies on the ocean's floor.'

Rosencrass and Guildenswine thought about this for a while, then they indicated that they were in agreement. 'We'll watch for any danger,' they said, 'so long as we get a share of Murgatroyd's treasure.'

'How do you know about that?' cried Falshed. 'Does everybody know? It's supposed to be a secret.'

'Fancy asking that question,' the two spies replied. 'It's our job to know things.'

'What will wooden chunks do with treasure?' sneered Jake. 'You won't be able to spend it.'

'We'll buy ourselves a good magician and get

out of this horrible lump of wood,' came the reply.

Eventually the ship, by chance another wind-jammer, was ready to set sail. They cruised around the headland and past the harbour mouth, where rotting hulks and half-timbered ships were still anchored. The talking heads on the prow were hard at work at this point, yelling out instructions.

'Hard to port! Rotting hulk off to starboard!' said Guildenswine.

'Thank you, thank you,' replied the helmstoat, turning the wheel.

'Watch out, watch out, there's a floating log dead ahead!' said Rosencrass.

'Very grateful for the information,' the helmstoat said, altering the rudder.

'Keep to starboard, I can see sand down below!' said Guildenswine.

'Most grateful,' murmured the helmstoat, steering the ship out of danger.

For a while no instructions came from the figureheads, then suddenly there was great urgency.

'Oh, no! There's a horrible monster under our bows . . . turn to starboard, for your life turn to starboard!' cried Rosencrass.

Guildenswine yelled, 'No, to port, to port, or we shall all die! There are gigantic clashing rocks on this side.'

'To starboard!'

'To port!'

The helmstoat span the wheel back and forth in panic. The ship began to creak as if it were about to split in two, Guildenswine urging it to go one way, Rosencrass the other. Seagulls resting on the yardarms took to the skies in fright. Sailors rushed hither and thither, not knowing what to do. Falshed came up from below, responding to the alarm.

'To starboard,' screamed Rosencrass. 'Quickly!'

'To port,' shrieked Guildenswine. 'Now!'

'WHAT?' cried the helmstoat, spinning the wheel in confusion. 'Where? When? Now? Help! Help!'

There was silence for a while, then a set of sniggers came from the figurehead in front of him.

'Just kidding,' said Guildenswine. 'We got bored.'

Chapter Sixteen

The meeting with the lion had disturbed Sylver. It made him realize that dark acts did not just happen in Welkin. He had always imagined that, without a despot like Prince Poynt, everything in Welkin would be decent and wholesome. Clearly that was a very simple view of life: terrible events sometimes just happened, and there was little one could do about them.

He doubted whether the greater cats had set out on their voyage intending to eat everyone else on board; they were just made that way. When a fox found its way into a chicken coop, he might only be seeking a single bird to satisfy his hunger – but finding many more birds there, he often went berserk and massacred them all.

Sylver sat in his cabin and considered the gloomy subject of life and death.

'Steer to the left of the setting sun,' he heard Scirf call to the helmsmammal. 'When it gets dark, look for a star on the edge of the horizon directly in front of the ship's prow.'

A little later it did get dark and the moon came out. It shone through the porthole and created patterns from lights and shadows on the cabin floor. Sylver got out the notebooks of sea charts and ocean currents. He checked everything thoroughly, hoping he could rely on Scirf's navigation. It was not easy to find one's way across a watery desert with no landmarks – or, rather, seamarks.

'Land ho!' came a lazy cry from the crow's nest. 'Off the starboard bow!'

Sylver hurried up the gangway to the ship's rail, from where he could view this land.

The night was sultry and the ship was no longer being driven forward. She was simply drifting, despite being under full sail. Not even a breeze blew across the surface of the still ocean. They would have to make landfall whether they wished to or not. A strange fog seemed to cling to the shrouds, falling about the craft in wispy veils, to be inhaled by those standing on deck.

'What's going on up here? Why is everyone so idle?'

There was a sense of lethargy about the crew. They lounged over the rail, seemingly careless of whether or not the vessel was carried by the currents onto the beach. Even Miniver looked half asleep. It was her duty to wake the captain, should any strange event befall, and she had done nothing.

The warm, smoky fog which swirled about the ship may have had something to do with their languor. It had not managed to penetrate Sylver's cabin, and this probably accounted for the fact that he had not yet succumbed to its effects.

'Miniver?' said Sylver. 'Why is the ship just drifting, without any effort to steer her?'

His sharp words seemed to wake her from a

166

reverie, though he himself began to feel drowsy. 'Oh – Sylver – I – I – I'm not sure. I just sort of felt drowsy. All paws to the sails!' she called at last. 'Come on! Shake a leg! Let's take in the sails. Quickly now or we'll beach ourselves . . .'

The crew responded sluggishly to her urgent tone and reluctantly climbed the rigging. Before long the duty watch had the sails furled and tied to the yards. Then the sea anchor was thrown overboard to stop the ship from drifting even further inshore. They were near enough to hear the sound of drums coming from the island. It was a deep, throbbing beat, a threnody, a musical sound which is used at a funeral. Watch fires could be seen along the cliffs above the beaches. Clearly this was an inhabited island.

The mysterious fog now fell away from the craft and collected in a bank some way off the shore. The crew's heads began to clear. Wodehed muttered something about 'random sea magic' and Sylver assumed the magician was speaking about the soporific effects of this unusual vapour.

'We might do well to take on some more water here,' said Sylver. 'I realize it's dark, but we don't want to linger too long in these waters, with such strange clouds of mist around. Make ready a party to go ashore, Miniver. I shall be one of their number. We shall need something to carry water in, too. Empty gourds, if we have them.'

'Aye, aye, captain.'

The boat was made ready and Scirf, Mawk and Sylver were rowed ashore by two martens. As before, Sylver did not altogether trust the pine martens, so he made sure Bryony, Alysoun, Luke,

167

Miniver and Wodehed were all awake and armed before the rowing boat pulled away from the *Scudding Cloud*. The martens had simply got on with their work up until now, but there was something about Short Oneleg which made Sylver careful not to drop his guard.

When the party reached the beach Sylver left Mawk in charge of the boat. He led the others inland, each of them carrying two gourds. They followed paths up into the foothills, where they could see the fires burning. Beyond them rose a range of mountains which formed a ridge along the island's back.

Finally they came upon a village situated on a shelf of rock, surrounded by rainforest. When they got closer they saw that instead of huts the village consisted of a number of huge nests. These were made of twigs and straw bound together by a baked red clay. In the middle of the village stood a platform made of four rough posts supporting a litter. On top of the litter lay a strange-looking bird. A ring of fires surrounded this platform.

Other birds, equally strange, were stamping their feet, clacking their beaks and wailing in despair. The bird on the platform did not answer for the simple reason that he or she was obviously dead. The great beak hung open and the eyes were wide and staring. This was evidently some kind of funeral for a dead villager.

Suddenly, someone saw the party from the ship and gave out a yell. All heads turned towards the weasels and the martens.

'Hello, now we're for it,' whispered Scirf. 'They don't look none too friendly, them turkeys.'

168

Sylver could see why Scirf had called the creatures 'turkeys', for their bodies were round and turkey-shaped, but there the similarity ended. Their beaks were very large, with a hook on the end, quite unlike that of a turkey. They had small down-covered wings and tail, and their legs were short and stumpy, quite thick all the way down to the big feet.

'Intruders!' screeched a female voice. 'Spies from the blue-eyes! Kill them!'

The speaker was decorated with painted feathers, which sprouted from her tail like a colourful fountain. There was a long fluttering cloak covering those funny downy wings. It seemed to move and flow about her body as if it were alive. Over her head she wore a hideous mask made of grass formed into a cone, with dark eye-holes and a false beak. Around her thick ankles were sprays of seashells, which rattled as she walked. She really was quite grotesque.

Sylver guessed this bird was the shaman, the spiritual leader of the group, not the chief. 'Wait!' he replied sternly. 'We are not spies. We do not know these blue-eyes of which you speak. We come in peace from a great ship, which even now is anchored off the shores of your island. Many mammals await our return and will be coming here looking for us if we do not go back to them.' He paused for a moment to let this speech sink in, then he added, 'Where is your chief? I would speak with such a bird.'

The shaman threw some dust on a fire, which flared to brilliance with a *whumph*. In this bright light Sylver could see that the shaman's cloak was made of live moon moths, a ghostly white in hue and large of wingspan, which somehow clung together to make this fluttering, shimmering garment.

'Do not listen to these lies,' she shrieked. 'Kill them, spit them on a sharp stick, prise their eyes from their sockets.'

However, a plumper and more dignified bird had already left the flock to approach them. This creature wore a copper amulet around its throat which shone in the moonlight. It stopped once to turn and glare at the hysterical shaman, who under those baleful eyes halted her ranting. Her restless legs continued to rattle her seashells, but her beak had ceased to issue orders and threats to the villagers around her. Clearly the one with the amulet was the chief of the tribe.

The voice was female: 'Are you John Frums?' she asked. 'Have you come with more gifts at long last?' She stared hard at the gourds.

'*John Frums*,' murmured other members of the tribe, with longing in their voices. '*Gifts*.'

Even the shaman had overcome her hostility and moved closer to get a better look at these strangers.

'Why do you think we are these "John Frums"?' asked Sylver. 'Have you been brought gifts before now?'

'Our grandmothers and grandfathers were given presents by pale creatures who walked on two legs just as you do. These pale strangers brought with them many gifts of Jenny Hanivers. We were made powerful by possessing these gods. Our Jenny Hanivers protect us against evil, give us magical powers over our enemies, bring in the harvest and only occasionally let bad-smelling demons into our eggs.'

Sylver realized that he and Scirf, and the two martens, had been standing on their hind legs. He now came down on all fours to show the bird chief that he was not one of these legendary creatures. He suspected John Frums were actually humans and confirmed this with his next question: 'Did the gift-bearers have fur or were they hairless?'

'It is told that they had hair which sprouted from the tops of their heads like tufts of brown grass.'

'Then you are indeed quite wrong. We are weasels and pine martens, creatures of a very different ilk. See, we have fur all over our bodies. We are creatures of woodland and field. These objects in our paws are simply empty gourds, to fill with fresh water from one of your streams. I have no doubt that those of whom you speak are people. We refer to them as humans.'

'We call them John Frums,' said the dogged bird chief, 'for that is how they called themselves.'

A disappointed groan went through the birds when they learned that Sylver was not a John Frum, as they had hoped, and the shaman again began calling for heads to roll. The chief, however, approached nearer and opened her mouth. She went straight to Scirf and gripped his head in her hooked beak, but gently and, it seemed, by way of greeting. She did the same to the martens, then lastly to Sylver.

'Welcome,' she said, 'to the village of the brown-eyed dodos. Come, our funeral dirge is over. My son was killed today by the wizard of the blue-eyed dodos, a tribe of birds so despicable I have to spit every time I mention their name.' She did indeed hawk and spit a great gobbet at the feet of one of the pine martens, who shuffled back and wrinkled his nose. 'Lamentations have ceased, however, and the funeral celebrations now begin. You must feast with us on our fare of hard nuts and dry seeds. It is an unhappy thing you are not John Frums, but that is the fault of your parents, who laid the eggs from which you hatched, not you yourselves.'

Sylver followed the dodo into the ring of fires, within which a funeral feast had been laid out on large leaves. He did not point out to the chief that weasels and pine martens were not hatched from eggs: it was all becoming a little too complicated, and he simply wanted to find some fresh water so that they could leave the island to its strange wars between blue- and brown-eyed dodos.

The tribe's shaman had drifted away into the night, peeved at not being given the attention she felt she deserved. Scirf and the two martens sat down. They were immediately offered some unshelled nuts, which proved too tough for their teeth. They settled for the dry seeds.

'These seeds are almost as tough as the nuts,' complained Scirf. 'I nearly broke me front fangs on them longish kidney-shaped ones.'

Sylver was beginning to worry about Mawk. The doubting weasel would be getting anxious. It would not be out of character for Mawk to row back to the ship without them, worried that they had somehow got on board some other way.

Mawk was terrified they were going to leave him behind one day; he was convinced that nobody liked him.

'Chief,' Sylver said to the head dodo, as she cracked nuts expertly in her hooked beak, 'we really must be getting back to our ship. We came out looking for fresh water. If there is a stream nearby, where we can fill some gourds . . . ?'

'Oh no,' replied the chief emphatically. 'You have sat and eaten our fare. Now you must join us in battle against the blue-eyed dodos. It is the law. You have partaken of the seed. You are obligated to us now. We fight at dawn.'

'Fight?' said Scirf. 'What fight?'

'We didn't come here to battle with birds,' one of the two pine martens complained. 'I say we go back to the ship.'

They were suddenly surrounded by a number of brown-eyed dodos with long thin tubes in their beaks. They pointed the tubes at the mammals in a threatening manner.

Their chief frowned at what she saw as a display of cowardice. 'If you do not fight, you will die. I will order my birds to fire poisoned darts into your bodies. On the tip of each dart is enough sap from a goo-goo tree to kill a fully grown albatross in full flight. It takes but two minutes to die, but those two minutes will be desperate, excruciating agony. Your eyes will turn back to front in your heads, your tongues will become unhinged from their roots, your claws will burst at the joints, your nostrils will spout hot blood . . .'

'I think we get the general idea, chiefy,' said

Scirf gruffly. 'No need to paint us any more pictures.'

The chief gave each of them a brown disc made from the bark of a tree. 'You will wear these badges so that the blue-eyes know you fight for us.'

'Badges?' snarled one of the pine martens. 'We don't need no stinkin' badges.'

'Just the same, you will wear them. See – the sun begins to brighten the eastern sky. Soon I will avenge my son's death. You will each kill one blue-eyed dodo. If you do not, we will roast you over the fires until your belly swells and bursts. Now, make ready to march into the mountains.'

The weasels and the martens had no option but to follow the orders of the brown-eyed dodo chief.

Chapter Seventeen

Having no choice in the matter, the weasels and martens were herded with the tribe of brown-eyed dodos into the interior of the island. They marched towards some distant blue mountains, which lay encircled with cloud in the dawn's early light. These mountains had a mystical air, as they rose out of the lush greenery of the coastal forest. The morning mist could be seen drifting from their slopes and the glint of mountain tarns caught the eye from time to time.

Now that the multi-layered colours of the island had been revealed to them in the daylight, they could see that it was a beautiful land of forests, mountains and lakes.

'Are you two tribes the only inhabitants of the island?' asked Sylver of the chief.

'It is said there were once other tribes of birds, but they have since left their island home because of the war.'

'The war between the dodos?'

'So it is said.'

'It seems to me very foolish,' replied Sylver, 'that you should fight over the colour of your eyes.'

Scirf interrupted here. 'I was readin' once, in a

book, that creatures sort of alter over the course of many years in order to melt in with their surroundings. It's called camouflage. F'rinstance, if you gets mice livin' in a dark wood, they most probably develop dark coats. And mice livin' in amongst light-coloured rocks, they develop pale coats. It's protection against predators, so they won't be noticed so easily.'

'So?' murmured the chief.

'Well, it seems to me that you lot livin' in the forest have sort of got brown eyes through bein' amongst brown-trunked trees. And this other lot live in blue mountains, with blue lakes, and they've gone and got blue eyes because of it. Seems to me that you're fighting over nothin'. Seems to me that you probably all started out with the same colour eyes, squire.'

The chief shook her head. 'You speak strangely and I am no squire. I must tell you that it is not the colour of our eyes which matter most, but the stealing. Ever since time began the blue-eyes have been stealing our Jenny Hanivers. We must get them back – and take some of theirs to punish them for the theft in the first place.'

Sylver could see it all now. Wars throughout animal history had been caused in such a way. He did not know what these 'Jenny Hanivers' were, but these disputes were usually over land rights. One tribe would claim a piece of land which the other tribe believed was theirs and so they would go to war over it. If there were physical differences between the tribes, so much the better: no-one would have to wear a uniform to see who was who.

176

'Well,' said Scirf, 'I think you're all round the twist – you could have a good life here if you'd just accept each other as friends instead of killing each other off – but don't let me stop you.'

'The blue-eyes killed my son,' said the chief mournfully.

'Yes, I've been meanin' to ask you about that. How did they kill him? Did they send assassins in the night?'

'They murdered him with bad dreams. They had their Jenny Hanivers send a deadly dream on the night wind to make him ill. He complained of feeling sick one day, his feathers dropped out two by three, and then at last he grew so weak he died one night in his sleep. They are terrible murderers, those blue-eyes.'

Scirf coughed into his paw. 'He – he couldn't have just caught the croup and died of nat'ral causes – you know, old age and such – all by himself, I suppose?'

'This does not happen, weasel. Since we have had the Jenny Hanivers, we dodos are immortal. We have the power of everlasting life through our Jenny Hanivers. If we die it is because an enemy has hexed us. In the past few years we have lost many of our brown-eyed warriors. The blue-eyes see our senior warriors as a threat and as soon as they become elderly, they kill them by sending them bad dreams.'

'The victims complain of having bad dreams before they die?'

'Exactly! What other proof do you need of the murdering nature of those blue-eyes?'

Soon they were up in the mountains, creeping

177

through the blue rocks. The dodos all had blow-pipes in their mouths. Sylver and his group of mammals armed themselves with slingshots which they hoped they would not have to use. Finally they came across the village of the blue-eyed dodos, consisting of large nests very similar to those in the village down on the coast. However, this village looked deserted. There was not a bird to be seen.

'They knew we would come,' said the chief, in a disappointed voice. 'Now we cannot kill anyone.'

Sylver and the others were greatly relieved to hear this.

'Come,' said the chief to Sylver, 'you will help remove the Jenny Hanivers.'

Sylver, Scirf and the two martens were taken to what appeared to be a ceremonial circle of posts. Pinned to each post was a grotesque figure, like a flattened mask, with tiny arms, legs and tails. They were grey in colour and the eyes, noses and mouths were hollow black pits. The effigies stared out blindly at the mammals as if with evil intent. Sylver had never seen anything as revolting as these Jenny Hanivers in his whole life. Their hollow eyes seemed to follow him wherever he went. They looked mournful, like the solid faces of ghosts, and their open mouths cried out silently for attention.

One of the pine martens gave a startled cry and ran away to the edge of the village. There he stood, shaking from head to claw. The other marten stood transfixed with horror, unable to move or take his eyes from those ugly masks.

In the meantime the chief of the dodos walked from post to post, inspecting the Jenny Hanivers, as if searching for something in their grisly grey expressions. 'The sacred Jenny Hanivers,' she said. 'They are here to protect the tribe against its enemies.'

'Not doin' a very good job of it, are they, squire? Because here we are, attackin' the village.'

The chief ignored this common-sense logic. 'We shall steal them,' she said, 'and use their power against the makers themselves. With these and our own Jenny Hanivers, we shall be the greatest tribe that ever lived on the island.'

'What are they?' Sylver whispered to Scirf. 'Do you know?'

Scirf, more used to revolting things than the others, having held the post of rhubarb dung-watcher for many years and seen horror on horror crawl out from the fetid, steaming manure, was not quite so taken aback as his companions. He studied the sacred objects with a scholar's eye and recognized something he had read in a book about the pastimes of sailors while at sea.

There had been a paragraph about scrimshaw carving: making little figures from whalebone and whale ivory. There had been almost a whole chapter on mat-making from ropes. Then, right at the back of the book, there had been a sentence or two on making creatures from dried fish, mostly skate.

The seamen would leave a flat fish on the deck in the sun to dehydrate and shrink. Once the fish was dry, its skin became leathery. The artist would then take a sharp mariner's knife and carve hideous faces in the skate's hooded underside. Arms and legs would be formed out of the fins on either side of the body and at the base of the tail. They would shape it into a ghastly caricature of a human. The result was this frightening mask, which looked like a frozen phantom caught between the real and the imagined.

'Jenny Hanivers, yes,' said Scirf, stroking his whiskers. 'they're just fish, they are. Dried fish. Human sailors have carved them into these scary-lookin' faces with their sharp penknives. Nothin' to be worried about, squire. Just a load of old dead fish, that's all.'

The chief now came over to them. 'You will help gather the Jenny Hanivers. We must carry them back to our village in triumph. In the meantime, my warriors will wreck the nests of the blue-eyes.'

'Is that necessary – destroying the nests?' asked Sylver.

'Most necessary.'

The brown-eyed dodos enjoyed themselves, smashing up the nests of the blue-eyed dodos. It seemed to Sylver that an awful lot of work had gone into making those nests. Now the homes of the blue-eyes would have to be rebuilt.

'You don't seem to care that this tribe will have nowhere to sleep tonight,' he said to the chief.

'The ground is good enough for the likes of them,' she replied harshly. 'Let them sleep in the thorn bushes. Let them sleep on the sharp rocks. Let them sleep at the bottom of the nearest lake. What is that to us? We shall be comfortable in our own village.'

Once the Jenny Hanivers had been gathered in,

stacked, and made into convenient packages, the tribe set off again. They returned home the way they had come. Once down from the uplands they followed the same paths. They were wary in case they were attacked on the march. 'The blue-eyes are sneaky like that,' said the chief. 'They have no honour.'

Under the canopy of the rainforest the tribe felt more at ease. They told each other the blue-eyes would never dare come this close to the brown-eyes' village.

'It is not in their nature,' said the chief. 'They are cowardly creatures at heart.'

When the party arrived back at their own village the shaman came out to meet them. If she had been splendid during the night hours, she was even more colourful and bizarre in the daylight. Her bright feathers swept upwards from a band on her brow and fluttered in the morning breezes. Her pretty seashells rattled around her ankles. In her beak she held a fly whisk; she occasionally transferred this to one of her feet and then proceeded to flay persistent insects.

'Chief! Chief!' she cried, when she saw the tribe. 'They have been here!'

At first Sylver thought she meant mammals from his ship. He imagined that Mawk had returned to the ship and sent out a search party. But when he and the others stepped into the village, he saw that he was wrong.

It seemed that while the brown-eyes were wrecking the blue-eyes' village, the same had been happening in reverse. The blue-eyed dodos' village had been empty because they were out smashing the brown-eyes' village. The nests had been overturned, the twigs and straw kicked into the four winds, the clay which bound them together shattered.

'Where were you when all this was going on?' cried the distressed chief to her shaman. 'Did you not protect our home places, our beloved nests?'

'I – I was guarding the Jenny Hanivers.'

'So – you at least saved *them*.'

The shaman's claws shifted uncomfortably in the dust. 'Not exactly, O chief, O great one. I – I was savagely requested to stand to one side. The Jenny Hanivers were all stolen.'

The gloomy chief sat down in the dust. She seemed to be contemplating the claw marks of the blue-eyed tribe, still imprinted in the dirt of the village square. Nothing had come out of these two raids except more work. 'At least we have some Jenny Hanivers,' she muttered. 'At least we will have some protection.'

It seemed ludicrous to Scirf and Sylver that the gods which had failed to protect even the villagers who fashioned them, should be accepted by the wreckers as authentic.

Sylver said, 'It seems to me that you've got what you deserved.'

The chief's head came up with a jerk. 'Listen to me, you furry little monster. I think this is all your fault!'

'Yes, yes,' cried the delighted shaman. 'They have brought bad luck and disaster on the tribe. We should burn them at the stake. We should roast them until . . .'

'. . . their eyes pop,' finished Sylver.

At that moment Mawk and about thirty pine martens burst into the clearing, yelling and waving weapons in a threatening manner. They bared their teeth at the dodos, showing their sharp fangs, and swore terrible oaths. Wearing their sailors' kerchiefs of red or blue tied round their heads, they were armed with marlinspikes and other fearsome tools. Cries of, 'Let's do 'em,' and 'Let me at 'em,' filled the village. They looked like a blood-thirsty mob of demons, intent on savage murder.

The warrior dodos let out squawks of fright and ran away into the forest, leaving their chief and her shaman to face the music.

To Mawk's disgust, Scirf immediately ran over to him and hugged him.

'What a hero,' cried Scirf, 'you brought the rescue party!'

Mawk extricated himself from the enthusiastic Scirf. 'I just got worried, that's all.'

The chief of the dodos quailed. 'Now you will kill us all. This is the fault of the blue-eyes. They brought you here with the magic of our own Jenny Hanivers. You are all demons from the depths of the earth. This is why they stole them from us – to rob us of protection against such fiends as you.'

Sylver and Scirf had long since realized that all the magic and power on this island was put down to possession of Jenny Hanivers. Without those graven images the dodos would believe themselves to be powerless and mortal. They would no longer be able to kill enemies at a distance. In fact, they would be much better off without the things.

'Look, you overgrown yard bird,' Sylver cried, 'this gang of black-hearted pine martens would be more than happy to smash all your eggs and burn your nests, but I'm not going to let them. I feel sorry for you, so I'm going to make peace between you and the blue-eyes, once and for all.'

'And how are you going to do that?' asked the chief. 'There has been no peace between us for a hundred years.'

'I'm going to confiscate your Jenny Hanivers. Both tribes will surrender all those ugly effigies to me on the beach by midnight tonight. Without your symbols of power you will be harmless. You will have to live in peace. Send a messenger to the chief of the blue-eyes and his or her shaman and tell them to come down and bring all their Jenny Hanivers to the shore by the appointed time. Say that if they refuse they will be visited by a horde of mad demons with red and blue heads.'

Sylver let this sink in, then added, 'You know that in the past some of your eggs have been filled with a hot wind and foul smell, instead of hatchlings?'

'Yes, yes,' cried the shaman to her chief, 'this is true. Bad eggs, bad eggs.'

'If either you or the blue-eyes hold back one single Jenny Haniver then be assured that all your eggs will turn bad. We have the Jenny Hanivers now. The same will happen if you go to war with your blow-pipes. We will send bad dreams to make you fall sick and die. No-one is allowed to carry a weapon from now on, do you understand?

184

I shall tell the same thing to the chief of the blue-eyes when he or she gets here. In the meantime I suggest you collect all the blow-pipes and poisonous darts you have, make a pile in the middle of the village – and burn them.'

Chapter Eighteen

The blue-eyes sent their chief, but he was not in the mood to pass anything over to a bunch of motley mammals. In the meantime the brown-eyes' chief had recovered her composure and was also having second thoughts. She could see now that the ship's crew were not superanimal. The upshot of it all was that both chiefs steadfastly refused to be intimidated. They wanted to keep their Jenny Hanivers and their weapons, and defied Sylver and his crew to do their worst.

It was midday and the sun beat down hotly on the heads of all the opposing forces in the dirt square of the brown-eyes' village. Sylver stood confronting the two chiefs, who were backed by the whole tribe of the brown-eyes. It was animal nature that now the two tribes had a common enemy – Sylver and his crew – they stood firmly together as allies.

'You leave me no choice,' said Sylver severely. 'A lesson must be taught and learned here.'

The shaman of the brown-eyes sneered and did a little dance to show her contempt. She rocked from side to side, her seashell ornaments rattling noisily. Her great horny feet stirred the dust. The

186

dance was obviously supposed to be some form of gross insult.

The two chiefs told Sylver to take his mammals and depart before the blow-pipe darts started flying.

Sylver turned to Wodehed, who had come up from the ship with Mawk and the rest of the crew. 'Magic,' he said. 'Show them we mean business.'

Mawk groaned. Wodehed was the worst magician in the universe. His spells always went wrong somewhere. However, Wodehed himself was an imposing figure. He was portly and walked with a more dignified air than the other weasels. His brow was bushy white with age and his coat ran with silver hairs. Moreover, he knew the value of showmanship.

He stepped forward and glowered at the two chiefs, at the same time tripping up the shaman, who fell in a humiliating heap in the dust. He then proceeded to chant incantations, full of very dark and strange words, which startled the villagers into retreating a few paces. At the same time he took four magic stones from the pouch on his belt. 'I will show you,' he said to the two chiefs, 'how puny you dodos are next to us weasels. How far would you say it is from here in the foothills to the seashore?'

The blue-eyes' chief shrugged his feathery shoulders. 'A very long way.'

'Do you think I can throw a stone that far?'

'Of course not,' sneered the chief, 'you would have to be a god to throw that far.'

'Yet I *can* throw that far,' replied the confident magician. 'I can throw even further. I can make this stone reach our ship, which is anchored out in your lagoon.'

Mawk groaned again, but Scirf, ever the optimist, clicked his teeth in appreciation.

Wodehed spouted a few more incantations, looking up at the sun every so often, until finally he seemed ready for the great feat. The dodos began jeering at him, calling him a fake, and said they would chop off his claws if he failed. The pine martens shrugged and made designs in the dust with their tails, as if this was nothing whatsoever to do with them.

'Harken!' cried Wodehed, when the sun was directly overhead. 'There is a bell on the deck of our great ship. I shall make this bell ring four times, one after the other, by striking it with these magic stones.'

With that, he walked with great ceremony to the edge of the forest and stood just within its shadows. The ship's crew and the dodos then saw him raise his forelimb and throw four times. The missiles appeared not to reach even the height of the tops of the trees, before disappearing in the foliage, but Wodehed yelled in triumph each time he tossed a stone. 'Yes, yes, yes, yes!' he cried.

They waited. For the crew the suspense was agony. Seconds went by and nothing happened. The dodos cleared their throats, ready to ridicule the weasel magician. Then, miraculously, from the sea came the distant sound of a bell. Though faint, it was undisputably the clanging of a brass bell. Four times it rang – dong, dong, dong, dong – before falling silent again.

The audience was hushed, stunned into silence.

Wodehed was indeed a powerful magician in the eyes of the dodos. They shuffled backwards as this frowning, imposing figure returned to the square. He stared hard into their eyes, as if for two pine needles he would punish the villagers with some terrible spells. The young amongst them began whimpering. The elderly said they had never seen anything like it before in their lives. The strong quailed and the weak swooned.

'You will surrender your Jenny Hanivers,' boomed the impressive Wodehed, 'and your weapons. If you do not I shall raze your villages to the ground with magic fire, I shall smash your eggs with a nasty look, I shall cause your eyes to gum up and remain permanently closed.

'Remember, you are never out of range of my magic stones. I have the gift of far-sight. I see all things, I am aware of all things. I shall know what you are doing, even when I am on board my ship and sailing into the sun. If any dodo amongst you starts a war I shall kill that individual with a magic stone.'

This time the dodos did just as they were ordered. The blue-eyes' chief sent for his tribes' Jenny Hanivers and weapons. All were brought down to the brown-eyes' village, where the weapons were burned. The dodos were forced to shake wings with each other, brown-eye with blue-eye. Sylver suggested it might be a good idea if the two villages merged, to make one single nation of dodos, but added that this was up to them.

The crew then returned to the *Scudding Cloud*, carrying gourds full of fresh water. They also had the grotesque Jenny Hanivers with them. Alysoun and Bryony, who had missed all the fun, shuddered on being shown these objects. The two jills suggested they be thrown overboard, but Sylver, unable to judge whether they were works of art or not, decided to keep them. You had to be an expert in these matters, like Sleek the otter.

Sylver was totally ignorant about art, and he did not like the carvings, but Sleek might decide, on their return to Welkin, that the Jenny Hanivers were wonderful examples of craftsmanship. If the artifacts were destroyed now, and Sleek found out about it, they might be forced to regret it. Sleek might call him a philistine, as he had been known to do with some mammals. Sylver was not sure he knew what a philistine was, but the way Sleek used the term, it sounded barbaric.

And so they sailed away from the island of the dodos.

Of course, everyone on board – even Mawk-the-doubter – knew that Wodehed had not struck the ship's bell with the stones. It was rung four times *every* day at noon, signalling the change of watch. Wodehed had simply judged the time. That in itself was a feat, as well as thinking up the hoax in the first place.

For a while Wodehed had the status of a hero – until his next spell went wrong, of course, and he fell out of favour again.

The ship sped on, with Sylver poring over the books of charts and Scirf navigating by the sun and stars. The nights remained sultry and the days sweltering. The wind dropped and rose by the hour, an unreliable wind which was as hot and musty as dragon's breath. The sea seemed to thicken, with great areas of weed here and there, like islands floating just below the surface.

One morning they were becalmed when two vessels passed by them, one on either side. How these craft were able to propel themselves along without a wind was a mystery to Sylver and his crew. The *Scudding Cloud* had been drifting for hours, yet these other craft slipped easily through the water, as silent as phantoms.

On the ship which passed by to starboard was a single stoat. This strange, lean figure, gaunt and wasted, pointed to the tatters of his sails, which flew like mad banners from the masts and yards. Indeed, it seemed as if the ship were being pushed or pulled by some monster beneath its hull. This was the first stoat the weasels and martens had seen since leaving Welkin and he was surrounded by corpses of other shrivelled stoats with protruding, staring eyes.

Weasels and their kind tend to stand on their hind legs and sway and weave when startled by some peculiar sight – a willowy, serpentine movement. This they did as the strange ship passed by. The stick-like creature seemed to wave feebly to those on board the *Scudding Cloud*, though the gesture was as slight as the flick of a grass stalk in a breeze. Around the stoat's neck hung a dead pipistrelle bat on a piece of greasy string. This load seemed to pull him down with its weight. He let out a single rustling sentence from parched lips: 'Arrrgghh,' he croaked at the bobbing, weaving weasels and pine martens, 'more slimy, snakey things!'

Then he was gone in the spray and spume from his flying craft, away into the west.

On the other side, travelling in the other direction, sped a second vessel. This was a craft which seemed to have no real substance. It had ribs but no planks covering them – a skeleton with no covering. Its sails were so scant and thin you could see the sky through them. On board was a walrus with fur as pale as mountain snow, and eyes as pink as campion flowers. She was playing hollyhockers with a dark nebulous silhouette.

'Jabbyknocker!' cried the walrus gleefully, as the ship passed by them. 'I win again!'

The dark shape seem to shudder in fury at these words and the hollyhock seeds were picked up and shaken again.

At the last minute the walrus turned to glare at the martens and weasels. 'What are you lot looking at?' she snarled.

Then this ghastly ship sped away to the east.

The *Scudding Cloud* rocked in the bow waves of both these vessels and the crew shuddered as cold air swept over the whole craft from stem to stern.

'What was that?' cried Mawk, frightened out of his wits. 'Did you see them? What were they?'

No-one answered him. No-one on board was convinced that what they had seen was real. There were shimmering heat-waves on the water, which sometimes created strange mirages.

'But they both spoke,' insisted Mawk. 'You heard them!'

Still none of the crew was prepared to answer him, but he would not let the matter drop. He kept insisting that he had seen at least one real ship, though even he was not prepared to swear to the other.

That evening a blood-red sun stained the sky from horizon to horizon. They were indeed in some ghastly stretch of ocean, where gruesome sights were commonplace. Mawk was standing at the rail. Scirf approached Mawk from behind and gripped his forelimb in a firm claw. He then spoke in a compelling voice. 'There *was* a ship,' croaked he.

'Hold off! Unlimb me, grey-tailed loon!' cried Mawk.

Scirf released his forelimb and retreated to the far end of the ship, clicking his teeth in amusement.

Chapter Nineteen

Flaggatis arrived at the port just after Sheriff Falshed had set sail. Immediately the rat crew he had brought with him went on a drunken spree. They brawled their way through the normally quiet harbour town, almost destroying the Red Admiral Inn, smashing a seat outside the church which had been dedicated to a senior citizen, and locking their own captain in the stocks, the key of which had then been lost.

'Find an axe,' growled Flaggatis. 'If it had been anyone else, I'd leave him there, but we need Captain Bliggghtt.'

Captain Bliggghtt was a ship rat whose great-grandfather, also of the same name but with several more g's and t's in it, had eaten his way through breadfruit plants on a voyage back from somewhere west of Welkin. Knowledge of the sea had been passed on to the younger Bliggghtt by his forefather. Thus this Bliggghtt was supremely qualified to be captain of the ship pursuing the weasels. If anyone had asked the rat crew about Bliggghtt's appointment they would have pursed their lips and clacked their incisors in disapproval, but nobody did.

When he had sobered up his rats, and executed

one or two, Flaggatis laid down the law: 'There will be no more drinking or eating until a ship has been found. I don't want one of these windjammer things. I want a man-of-war . . .' There was a shuffling amongst his audience and Flaggatis said, 'Oh, all right, a *rat-of-war*. I want it to have fifty giant crossbows down each side of the deck, catapults fore and aft, and the makings of Greek fire.'

'*Wassshhhh Grikk fahhhhrr?*' asked Captain Bliggghtt.

'It's fire that can't be put out by water,' replied Flaggatis. 'In fact it's rather difficult to put it out at all. We shall send flaming arrows with shafts ablaze and dollops of the stuff from the catapults. Anyone who comes up against us will be sorry they ever looked a noble rat in the eye.'

There was a great cheer from his audience, as Flaggatis knew there would be. Rats actually disgusted him, but they were his only means to power. Without them he was just another lonely, broken old stoat wizard, of which there were dozens scattered here and there throughout Welkin. But he did have the rats in the palm of his paw, and if gaining the throne of Welkin meant he had to flatter them, he would do it without a murmur.

'I believe,' said Flaggatis slowly, 'that even the hated humans would be afraid of us once we have our Greek fire. Think of it – I can control elements of the weather. If I raise a great wind after we have set fire to other ships, they will go up like dry tinder.'

'*Theee haaartted hoooommmmannns!*' screeched the

195

rats, delighted at this picture being painted for them by their master.

When the humans were on Welkin there had been people called rat-catchers, with horrible rat-catching dogs called 'terriers'. The human rat-murderers were paid two groats for every rat tail they cut off and sent to the town burghers. At one time the guildhalls were bristling with sheaves of rat tails which hung from door jambs and window frames, such was the brutality of those two-legged fiends and their four-legged helpers.

One of the rats called out something which even Flaggatis struggled to translate into coherent language. What the rat had said was, 'If we catch any live humans, can we cut off their tails?'

'Humans don't have tails,' replied Flaggatis.

There was a strangled cry of disgust and horror from the rats. No tails? Why, everything had a tail, even if it was an almost-one like a rabbit's. How could any creation of nature have no tail? It did not bear thinking about. It revolted the mind. These humans were not animals; they were mutants from a strange place, probably from somewhere deep in the earth. They were as bad as adders, which were *all* tail.

'However,' Flaggatis promised his crew, 'if we do catch any you can cut off their noses!'

'*Tharrr nooowwsses!*' shrieked the delighted rats. '*Tharrr nooowwsses!*'

'But our main objective is the treasure which the weasels hope to find. We need that money. Money is power. Power is everything,' snarled Flaggatis. 'So now I want you to scour the port area for a good ship, a fast ship, but a ship bristling with weapons. Go to it, my lovely beauties. Find our sleek vessel and we shall be away, on the high seas.'

The rats scattered and ran about the port, searching for the craft Flaggatis required. They jumped on board vessels which were being renovated by statues. They pushed the statues overboard, sunk their boats, and generally went on a binge of wanton destruction. They hacked down masts, set fire to tar barrels, and drew beards and moustaches on the faces of the figureheads. Finally, Flaggatis had to stop them from scuttling so many craft, as they were clogging up the harbour with sunken vessels.

'We won't be able to get our own ship out, you fools,' he raged. 'Where's your common sense?'

But of course rats have no sense, let alone the common kind, and they carried on regardless. Flaggatis had to execute twenty or so of his own crew before he could pull them back into line. Their bodies were placed on gibbets throughout the town: they hung in their cages at the entrances to filthy alleys, sewers and all the favourite rat places.

Flaggatis then formed a shore patrol of bigger rats, promising them a greater share of the food, so that these rats could police the harbour area and keep the others in line. However, the first time he was carried out on a litter himself to see how things were going, he found his own shore patrol inside the local tavern, drunk on honey dew.

'What am I going to do with you all?' he

despaired. 'Heaven send me some other creature to assist me with my plans. Gypsy lurchers would serve me better than you lot!'

But heaven had no treacherous creature like the rat, except perhaps the dove, and there were too few doves around.

Eventually a suitable ship was found. It was a leaky vessel which needed extensive repairs, but Flaggatis was growing impatient.

'We'll set sail and do the repairs on the way. We don't need all that deck. We'll rip up a few boards and use them to plug the gaps where the water is seeping into the hull. Cannibalize, that's what we'll do. You're good at cannibalizing, my rat beauties, aren't you? You'd eat your own grand-mothers if you thought they tasted good, wouldn't you?'

'*Yesssshhhhh!*' screeched his delighted minions, enjoying the joke which was not a joke.

The vessel's name was *Christobel*. The rats changed this immediately to *Sssccccarrrggg*, the meaning of which was lost on all but themselves. Even Flaggatis had no idea what it meant and he did not bother to ask. The last time something like this had happened – the naming of a rat village – he had been physically ill when he learned what the word actually meant.

The rats built a chair in the crow's nest. Over the chair was a protective canvas roof and there were flaps which could be let down when the wind was particularly fierce. This little resting place high above the ship, where actually it was always windy, was to be the seat of Flaggatis. Up there he could get away from the fetid stink of rats and would be in a good position to survey the world he one day wished to own.

They set sail at midnight, the rats swarming all over the ship tying knots in ropes that did not need it, undoing lines that needed to remain tied, and tangling up lines which should have been freed. In general it was chaos, but somehow when there are so many rats they get it right in the end.

What happens is that one rat ties a knot in a line; another comes and undoes the knot; a third frees the rope from its anchor point and, finally, the fourth comes along and busies itself with tying the line to a cleet again. This fourth position is the correct one for sailing and is reached purely by accident. Similar lucky accidents were occurring all over the craft. All in all, the accidents balanced each other out and somehow the ship sailed out of the harbour.

The animals of the town had gathered on the harbour wall. When they were sure the ship was on its way they jeered and blew raspberries, and mingled in a few shouts of 'Good riddance' and 'Don't bother coming back' for good measure. Had it been left to the rats, the ship would have turned round and the crew would have laid waste to the town again. As it was, Flaggatis was not concerned with such petty goings on.

'Haul me up,' he said, sitting in the canvas loop of the hoist. 'Come on, snap to it!'

The ancient stoat wizard, whose bones were as brittle as sticks and whose skin was as loose as a mole's underwear, shot up the mast at an electrifying speed. 'STOP!' he yelled in fright. He came to an abrupt halt halfway up and swayed there in the canvas chair. 'Take – me – up – slowly.'

The rats began to pull on the hoist again, ever so gently, until Flaggatis was safely at the crow's nest.

From this position he could survey the whole ship, see what was coming on the horizon, and generally control his small world. In his paw was a megaphone. He used this instrument to communicate with his captain.

Captain Bliggghtt stood on the bridge, a fat ugly rat and a force to be reckoned with. He was surrounded by five admirals wearing wide hats. When they moved they had to perform a well-choreographed dance to prevent their hats from bumping into each other. Bliggghtt outranked these five individuals only when the ship was at sea. It was his intention never to step on land again. He was already contemplating how many keel-haulings and whippings he might safely dispense off his own bat.

The boss was right: power was everything. It felt good to be in charge.

'BLIGGGHTT – WHERE ARE WE GOING?' boomed a voice from the top of the mast.

'*Arrrraggghh*!' cried the rat captain, in a slight panic. He had given no thought to their heading. Getting the ship out of the harbour and into the sea lanes was enough for him. Its subsequent course was up to the gods.

'I THOUGHT SO. YOU HAVE NO IDEA, DO YOU, YOU MINDLESS IDIOT? SET SAIL FOR DORMA ISLAND. THAT'S IN THE DIRECTION OF THE WESTERN STAR YOU CAN SEE JUST ABOVE THE MIZZEN MAST. IF YOU DEVIATE FROM OUR COURSE BY A SINGLE STAR, I'LL

HAVE YOU GUTTED AND THROWN TO THE CRABS. DO
I MAKE MYSELF PLAIN?'

Bliggghtt evidently thought the message was plain enough. Sail in the correct proportions was ordered. The helmsrat was given a clip around the ear and the ship swung violently to starboard. Finally it was on course for the afore-mentioned star. The weather was fine, the prospects good.

By three o'clock in the morning they had run into the same storm which had hit the weasel ship. It was one of those nasty pieces of foul weather which hang around sea corners to make a nuisance of themselves. It ran full pelt into the rat ship without an excuse-me or a by-your-leave, making it shudder from mast tip to keel edge. The whole craft span in the water like a cork. It creaked and shuddered violently. Some of the crew were already making the lifeboats ready before the ship righted itself.

The rat crew had been busy hauling up their flag, which, needless to say, was a white skull and crossbones on a black background, rats having little originality when it comes to such things.

'GET ME DOWN!' came the voice from god.

Flaggatis was hastily lowered. His powers could not control weather like this. If a storm was already in full spate when it struck, he could not stop it.

First he ordered the lifeboats to be cut adrift. He did not want his crew deserting him while he weathered out the storm from his bunk. Then he went down to his cabin, to cower under the bedclothes. Like most stoats, and Falshed in

201

particular, he was not keen on a watery death. He left orders with Bliggghtt to remain on deck until the sea was calm.

The ship's captain did exactly as he was told. Bliggghtt had been in storms and they held no fears for him. Also he lacked any imagination and believed that, apart from death by flogging, he was immortal. His crew, unable to jump ship, decided they might as well carry out plan B and try to keep the vessel afloat. They rushed here, there and everywhere, obeying orders to the letter for once in their lives.

By eight o'clock in the morning the sea was calm once again. Flaggatis emerged from his hidey-hole and, after an unhealthy breakfast, ascended the mast to his high chair once again. It was full of seaweed and shells tossed up by the high waves. He emptied it, throwing the debris down on to the heads of those scrubbing the decks. They clicked their teeth, thinking it a great joke.

Flaggatis then ordered them to carry out drills. These were not safety drills, in the event the ship sank, but war practice. The rat marines, who operated the catapults and giant crossbows, had to run to their battle stations and fire off missiles as quickly and as accurately as they could.

At first it was the usual rat chaos. One rat even managed to get himself fired from his own catapult and hurtled out to sea. Flaggatis refused to turn the ship round to pick him up. The unfortunate rodent was last seen waving frantically, only head and shoulders above the surface.

The more they practised, the more accurate they became. By noon on the third day they were proficient. Flaggatis then sighted another vessel – a boat of quite a striking green. It was crewed by a domestic cat and a barn owl. These seemed to be the only two creatures aboard. Flaggatis regarded the green boat as a legitimate target: the rats sank it with the loss of only one crew member, who fell overboard in the excitement.

As before, Flaggatis refused to pick up the drowning rat. He was last seen being ducked by the enraged cat and owl. The owl then flew off. The cat climbed aboard the wreckage of its boat and caught the current to the east. It would live, of course: cats, with their nine lives, always do.

Chapter Twenty

The *Scudding Cloud* somehow found its way to the colder waters of the north, despite Scirf's best efforts at navigation. The ship wove its way between icebergs and came at length to an island which looked barren, vast and forbidding. They anchored in a wide horseshoe-shaped bay and studied the scene. There was little vegetation to be seen, apart from one tree, bare of leaves.

In the bay itself only the occasional bunch of sad-looking seals broke the stillness of the water. Once, those on board saw a polar bear, grumbling under his breath, drifting along the shoreline through the half-darkness. Large fish, probably salmon, broke the surface of the water, attracted by the clouds of midges which got in the weasels' and martens' fur, in their teeth, in their ears and noses, and in the stew dished up by Short and Luke.

"Bout the only bit of meat we get in our stew,' murmured Mawk – but not in the hearing of Short, of course.

On the bare and rugged wastes of the land itself a low hill soon rose into high mountains. Built into the rocky mountain face was a castle. Its architecture was nothing like that of the castles of Welkin.

From a distance it looked like the pipes of a church organ, its smooth, rounded towers, all of different heights, rising with the rock face. Here and there these showed a bulbous swelling, which might have formed a room. There was one single window in each tower, right at the top.

It was a most sinister-looking construction. The crew wondered who could have built such a castle and whether that person was still in residence.

'I say we sail away from here *right now*,' said Mawk. 'I say we leave this place to the walruses.'

'We'll stay one night here, but no-one is to go ashore,' ordered Sylver, to Mawk's dismay. 'There's some dirty weather out beyond the bay. We don't want to sail straight into another storm. We'll remain here until the sky clears.'

'We'll all be murdered in our beds,' cried Mawk.

By now, however, the pine martens were as used to Mawk's gloomy forebodings as the weasels. They rolled their eyes and hissed at him. Short Oneleg came clumping up from the galley and offered to protect Mawk with his soup ladle, a formidable weapon in the paws of the ship's cook. This caused great hilarity amongst the crew, who clicked their teeth in appreciation of the joke.

That night Miniver left a skeleton watch on deck; there seemed no need to post a full complement of twelve. It just so happened that it was Mawk's turn to remain awake. He was accompanied by a single pine marten known as Hup. While the rest of the ship slept the pair of them walked the decks restlessly, under the swinging frosted lamps, occasionally staring at the strange castle. No lights appeared in the castle after dusk fell. Mawk began to think he was being silly to think there was any danger. It was just another empty castle.

Sylver went to bed after a long discussion with Scirf and Miniver. The three of them had pored over the notebooks of charts and deliberated on natural navigation into the early hours. Scirf was convinced they were on the right course. He had been following the star paths faithfully, occasionally taking a fixed star as a point of reference. He had seen underwater streaks of light, which told him they were in a region of subsea volcanic activity. The shape and direction of the waves were right too.

'In that case this is the Frozen Coast,' said Sylver, looking at the charts, 'and we should be anchored here – ' he pointed to a curve on the map – 'in Scareman Bay.'

'Scareman Bay?' repeated Miniver. 'I don't like the sound of that.'

Scirf clicked his teeth. 'Why, what's that to us, Min?' he said to the finger-weasel. 'If they've got things to scare *men* away, then we don't need to worry, 'cos we're weasels.'

'That's true enough,' said Miniver. 'It's just the sound of the word I don't like.'

'Well, with any luck,' interrupted Sylver, 'we'll be on our way by dawn tomorrow. I suggest you follow the example of the rest of the crew and get some sleep, you two.'

So the three of them went and found little crevices in their own parts of the ship. They fluffed up their fur to keep out the cold and curled up into a shape very much like the round rope mats which decorated the decks. In this way they were able to get to sleep, despite the wintry chill.

Sylver woke with the sparkling light reflecting from ice-peaks on to his face. He stared out through his cabin's porthole and saw that a weak sun was quite high above the horizon. Mawk had forgotten to give him the early call he had requested. The ship was ominously silent, which meant everyone else had slept in as well.

Sylver growled an oath under his breath, rose and took a drink. Then he went up on deck, expecting to find Mawk and Hup fast asleep on duty. But the deck was deserted. Neither mammal was there. 'Wake up! Wake up!' he cried, ringing the bell.

There was movement below and within a few moments animals began pouring up onto the deck from below.

'What's the clamour all about?' cried Short Oneleg, who was always especially testy on being woken suddenly. 'Who's makin' that blasted racket?'

'I am,' said Sylver sternly, 'and that's "captain" to you, cook. I want everyone to search the ship from stem to stern. There are two mammals missing. Hup and Mawk are nowhere to be found up here. If they're asleep somewhere, I want them woken and brought before me.'

'Aye, aye, cap'n,' growled Short Oneleg. 'Anythin' ye say, cap'n.'

'Don't try me, cook, or you'll find yourself abandoned on this mammalforsaken shore.'

Thereafter Short wisely kept his counsel and assisted the others.

As for the search, Short came up short. So did everyone else. Hup and Mawk were nowhere to be seen and the rowing boat was gone. When Sylver studied the shoreline through a spyglass he could see the boat jammed between two large rocks. Moreover, there were prints in the frost, leading up towards the castle. There were no other pawprints besides those of the mammal pair. However, dotted about the beach were some strange marks which Sylver could not identify. It was as if someone had gone about with a stick, making holes.

'It seems that Mawk and Hup went willingly,' said Sylver. 'What could they be thinking of? Did they see something up at the castle which they felt they had to investigate? There's more to this than meets the eye . . .'

'I can't see Mawk just going off without wakin' someone,' said Scirf. 'That ain't like him at all. He wouldn't go ashore at a place like this unless he had a thousand weasels at his back, and two thousand in front.'

'It is very out of character,' agreed Miniver.

Short Oneleg felt the same way about Hup. He said that Hup, among a ruffian group of mariners, was usually cautious. 'He's a bit slowly-slowly, is Hup. He's not one for rushin' rashly into things.'

'Well, I could send out an armed search party right away,' said Sylver, 'and I would have done if there had been any other prints besides theirs. If they had been taken by force, then we could go out there and rescue them by force, but there's something weird going on here. We don't want to go jumping into a situation we know nothing about. I shall stand watch myself this evening, along with Short Oneleg, and we'll see what happens then.'

Scirf was upset by this. 'You're goin' to waste a whole day? What if somebody's frozen our Mawk into a block of ice up there? He might be dead when we find him.'

'I have the ship and the rest of the crew to think about, Scirf. I can't go endangering the whole mission because of two mammals. I want to rescue them, wherever they are, but I have to set about it with caution. You saw the prints. They went of their own accord. We have to find out why.'

That night Short Oneleg the cook and Captain Sylver remained on deck while all others went below. At midnight Sylver said to the pine marten, 'I want you to tie me to the mast, then go below yourself.'

'What?' cried the cook. 'What if something tries to get on board while you're all trussed up?'

'Nothing will, I'm sure of that.'

'You're the captain,' said Short, but his expression added, *For the time being.*

'Don't let me loose,' said Sylver, 'even if I order you to do so. Tell the others. No-one is to let me loose. You may untie the knots when the first rays of dawn creep up the sky. Until then I must remain secured to the mast. Is that understood?'

'Understood.' The cook lashed the captain to the mast then, stabbing an apple from the barrel with his knife on the way past, went below.

Sylver stared at the castle. He did not know what to expect, but he believed something must have persuaded the two missing mammals to leave the ship. He was convinced they went willingly. Sylver had asked the cook to tie him to the mast in order to resist the temptation to go ashore.

At midnight a needle of light shone from one of the windows of the castle. Sylver watched as it was directed down the escarpment of the mountain and across the beach. It struck the water and where it did so the sea sparkled like crushed diamonds. Like the stick of a blind man, the thin beam of light found its way across the waves to the ship, went up its side, and then over onto the deck. Finally it was shining directly into Sylver's eyes.

Sylver blinked. The light hurt his eyes. Somehow, from his eyes, it crept into his brain. There it seemed to wash the inside of his head. Within a few minutes he felt the desire to follow that beam of light to its source. He could not help himself. There was an urgent need inside him to go up to the castle.

At first he struggled with his bonds, thinking that he could break the rope. Then, after some time, he gave up and called out, 'Hi, cook! Come up here.'

No-one came.

'Listen, Short. I was wrong to give you that order some time ago. I want you to come up here and let me go.'

Still nothing. No-one stirred below deck. All remained peaceful, except for Wodehed's heavy breathing. Wodehed suffered from a blocked nose and his snores were very loud. Sylver listened hard for the creak of planks which would indicate that Short Oneleg was on his way up from below.

'Come on! Come on!' he cried impatiently. 'Someone come and let me loose.'

No-one came.

'I'll have the lot of you flogged!' fumed the weasel captain. 'How dare you disobey orders. Wodehed, Bryony, Alysoun, Luke, Miniver, Scirf – if one of you is not up here within five minutes I shall have you all clapped in irons, do you hear me?'

Obviously they did not, for still no-one came.

Sylver's desire to be free of the rope was by now very strong. He struggled until his sides hurt. Enraged, he screamed for assistance at the top of his voice, threatening his crew with some very imaginative punishments. Finally, after several hours, his voice broke into a sob and his head dropped. He was thoroughly exhausted. In the early hours he fell asleep.

The strange light left his face at about the same time. It had been switched off at its source. The next light to hit Sylver's face was daylight.

The ship's cook is often the first to wake, since he has to prepare breakfast. Short Oneleg was up at dawn. He went on deck to find Sylver still trussed but fast asleep. The weasel was almost doubled-up, with his head touching his hind feet. Short undid the knots and Sylver fell forwards in a heap, still snoozing. There he lay until mid-morning.

Scirf threw a bucketful of water over his captain.

'Wha— what? Who? What was that? I say – you ruffians! Did someone . . . ? I'm – I'm soaked.'

'Someone had to wake you,' said Scirf, 'and they was all too scared. You've been asleep since we all got up. What happened here last night?'

Sylver slowly came to his senses. He now
remembered the bright white light. It had hypnotized him. It had made him long to go up to the
castle. Now that the light was no longer in his eyes,
the desire had gone. He knew now what had
happened to Mawk and Hup.

Even as he was rubbing his forelimbs, where the
tight ropes had left marks, an idea was forming in
his head. It was the sort of idea that Scirf usually
came up with, so Sylver was quite pleased with
himself.

'Well?' demanded an agitated Scirf. 'Are you
goin' to let us in on your secret? In the meantime
poor ol' Mawk is in the clutches of some fiend.
Come on, captain; what happened?'

Sylver told the others what he had discovered
about the light from the castle.

'What are we goin' to do about it?' asked Scirf.
'We got to get up there and rescue Mawk an' Hup.'

'Or make whoever is trying to entice us from
our ship come down to the bay.'

Scirf blinked. 'How do we do that?'

'With mirrors,' replied Sylver. 'Come on, I'll
show you how it works.'

Chapter Twenty-One

That night Sylver ordered all the crew except for Scirf and himself to remain below deck. He and Scirf would be armed with mirrors taken from the captain's cabin. When the light came from the castle, they would hold the mirrors in front of their eyes and angle the light back again. Whoever was using this hypnotism would get a taste of their own medicine.

Dead on the appointed hour of midnight the light appeared and began moving down the hillside and across the bay towards the ship. Scirf and Sylver held up their mirrors. Sylver received the thin beam on his mirror and directed it towards the mirror held by Scirf. Scirf then directed the beam back to the window in the castle.

'*Now* we'll see who's responsible for kidnapping Mawk and Hup,' replied Sylver. 'Give them an hour or so to walk down to us and we'll have them in our grasp.'

'This is brilliant,' replied Scirf, 'in more ways than one.'

Sure enough, two hours later they heard a swimmer approaching the ship. The scrambling nets were already down and both weasels waited with their slingshots to see who would appear over the gunwales. They were a little surprised to see an exhausted Hup flop over the side. The pine marten lay on the deck, the freezing water draining from his fur.

'He made me do it,' he blurted, his breath coming out in clouds of mist. 'He made me stand in front of the window.'

Sylver was disappointed that he had not caught the originator of the mischief. But they did have Hup back and, once he had recovered from his swim, he was able to tell them what had happened to him at the castle.

'The light thing came and we had to go up there,' he said. 'When we got there the castle was surrounded by these strange wolves, protecting it, I think. They weren't *real* wolves. They were made of sticks and rags, with buckets for heads and brushes for tails. They looked *ghastly*, I can tell you.'

'*Scaremen*,' said Scirf, nodding. 'Not scare*crows*, but effigies of wolves to scare humans away.'

'That's it,' said Hup. 'You're right, they did look like scarecrows, only they were made into the figures of wolves. Yes, like you say, to scare away humans – or anyone really. There was magic there, 'cos the wolves were alive. They ran around and clattered the handles of their buckets like they were wolves' jaws. It was frightening.'

'But they didn't attack you,' interrupted Sylver; 'you were allowed into the castle?'

'That's it, we were let in. The owner of the castle is a knight in black armour, seven feet tall. His voice sounds hollow and weak. I think he must be dying of some dreadful wasting disease, because

214

he sounds very squeaky – and why would he wear the armour all the time? It must be most uncomfortable . . .'

'Go on,' encouraged Sylver. 'What else?'

'Well, at first I thought the knight must be just a hollow suit of armour – you know, like the statues from Welkin – but the voice was too good for that. I mean, you know how statues talk, in that halting, floundering way? This one didn't. Although his voice was weak he spoke well, without any stumbling over the words, and he sounded very learned.'

'In what way?' asked Bryony, her cheeks quivering with the cold. She and the other weasels were more ball-shaped than long and lean, as they hunched down into themselves, their fur on end.

'Why, when he saw us, he said, "So, we have a single brave little *Martes martes* and a quivering *Mustela nivalis*. Are you pair of sorry specimens from the ship in the bay? You are now my prisoners. You will be incarcerated in my grand castle until I am in possession of that fine vessel you own."'

'Hmmm,' said Luke. 'He used the Latin names for pine martens and weasels, did he? I don't think anyone's heard those since the humans left Welkin.'

'He also has this funny walk. He takes two steps to the front and one to the side. So when he crosses a room, it's in this strange, angular pattern. If he wants to go through a doorway he mutters to himself, working it all out beforehand, so that he passes through the doorway at precisely the right spot, while he's doing his two forward steps.

'Anyway, when I told him I didn't own the ship, that it was owned by you, Captain Sylver, he was enraged. He went around the room smashing things with his iron fist and threatening to throw Mawk and me to the wolves outside. He said they would tear us apart and scatter the bits over the mountains.

'Then, when you sent the light back, he said in that small voice of his, "Hmmm, a clever ploy, deflecting the beam of my hynoptic prism. You shall go down to your captain, pine marten, and tell him that if he wants to see this excuse for a weasel again he will hand his ship over to me." Then he stuck me in front of the window. The light hit me in the eyes. And here I am.'

Sylver looked up at the weird castle on the rock face. 'He wants the ship, does he?'

'He says he'll execute Mawk in a horrible manner if we don't give it to him. Mawk, as you can guess, is out of his head with fright.'

'Thank you, Hup. Now, what do we do about it? I suppose it's out of the question to attack the castle.'

'There's the scaremen to overcome before you reach the castle, and it's not easy to find your way into it, or around it. I've never seen anything like it before in my life. It's a labyrinth of corridors and rooms carved out of the sandstone cliff behind. But the knight keeps blocking and unblocking the passageways, almost by the hour. So you can go down a corridor, and then, a little later, you'll find it barricaded and the door at the end locked.'

'Ho, yes,' said Scirf. 'I get it.'

The crew all turned to Scirf. When he said 'Ho, yes,' you knew something profound was going to follow.

'Explain,' Sylver said, clapping his forelimbs around his chest for warmth.

'Well, I've heard about creatures like this before. It happened to a badger I once knew. He lived all on his own and his fears grew day by day, 'cos he had no-one to talk to about 'em. He convinced hisself that something was going to get into his sett and murder him in his sleep.

'So what he did was build lots of tunnels, so's he had lots of escape routes. But then he worried about all these exits, 'cos they were entrances too; if a murderer was going' to get in, it could use any one of the tunnels. So he blocked 'em all up, leaving only one. But then he worried that if this one was used by the murderer, there would be no escape.'

'I see what you mean,' said Sylver. 'He brooded and worried so much he was continually changing the structure of his sett. And you think that's what the knight is doing with his passageways?'

'Sounds like it to me.'

Sylver thought about the problem for a while, but he could see no alternative to attacking the castle. 'We have some large weapons on board, do we not?' he asked Wodehed, who suddenly found himself in charge of defending the ship.

'I – I think there's two large siege catapults stored below, captain. You remember you had them loaded before we left Welkin.'

'What size of rock will they fire?'

Wodehed, trying frantically to think of a good

217

example, said, 'Oh – I suppose – I think about the size of a baby bear.'

'The *ballistae*. Right, bring them up, dust them down, polish them, and get them ashore. You'll have to dismantle them first. They're too big to transport as they are. Once you get ashore . . .'

'. . . we'll mantle them again,' blurted Wodehed.

Sylver stared at Wodehed for some time before saying, 'You will *reassemble* them.' He then turned to the rest of the crew. 'We're going to give that black knight something to think about, so the rest of you make some fire brands of tar and straw and bring some barrel tops with you to use as shields.'

After giving his orders, Sylver went below.

Scirf, his misty breath sending plumes into the air, looked at Wodehed and shook his head. 'A – baby – *bear*?'

'Well, I couldn't think of anything else. You try to think of something about that size. It's not easy when you're under pressure.'

'*Mantle* them?'

'Well, Sylver knew what I meant.'

The martens brought the siege catapults up on deck. They were massive engines of war, mounted on platforms with wooden wheels. Ammunition for the catapults could be found lying around on the mountainside.

Leaving behind a skeleton crew, Sylver led the expedition to the castle. The weasels and martens fell in behind him, some of them harnessed to the siege catapults. Slowly they made their way up the shore and onto a gravel road which ran through the snowy foothills to the mountains beyond. Even before they were in the mountains, though, the ragtag wolves were upon them.

The creatures came in packs, converging from all corners of the barren landscape, as if they had received a message that enemy creatures were invading. They ran towards the party, their bucket handles clattering, their tails streaming out behind them in the wind.

Some of the wolves were obviously fashioned from old tables and chairs, and these clattered through the scree on their wooden legs, continually losing their footing on the slippery slopes. Others had been made from scratch, using timber of various shapes and sizes – even driftwood where nothing else would do. These, surprisingly, were more sure-footed.

The first wolf struck the lead marten and bowled him over, then battered him about with its bucket head. It was with some difficulty that his comrades beat off the wolf with sticks and stones.

'Light the firebrands!' ordered Sylver.

Tinder-boxes came out and the fire brands were lit. These made the packs of tatterdemalion wolves more wary. Being creatures of rag and straw, they had no desire to go up in flames. They began to circle the weasels and martens, snapping their bucket handles and growling deep inside their pans. They seemed prepared to follow and wait until the brands were exhausted, before moving in for the kill.

At first Sylver had not been too worried by the scaremen, for they had no real bite to their jaws. However, more and more began to pour out of the hills, as if the earth had opened up to let out a flood

219

of them. They were poor creatures to look at, since their frames showed beneath their rags, but their numbers were frightening.

'Halt!' ordered Sylver. 'Use one of the catapults!'

Scirf, in charge of the *ballistae*, had one of the catapults loaded with a large rock. The tension was increased by martens and weasels winching the ropes. When the wolves were in range Scirf pulled the trigger. The release mechanism went *twang* and the wooden arm rose up, sending the rock hurtling through the air to land in the middle of a pack. Bits of wood and iron flew everywhere as at least a dozen wolves were crushed or damaged in some way.

The other wolves let out a cry of rage, howling into the hills, and from the direction of the castle came a high-pitched squeal of anguish. There was the sound of a gong, which might have been a suit of armour beating its head against a stone wall. A moment later a shower of pebbles came flying through the air to fall around the expedition like hailstones. The weasels and martens used their barrel-top shields to protect their heads, the pebbles clattering on the wood.

'Sounds like our black knight is witnessing what is happening,' said Sylver, after waiting for a second attack which did not come. 'He doesn't like us damaging his pets, that's obvious. And it seems he has at least one catapult of his own, though he's filling its cup with small stones rather than large rocks. I wonder if he's getting Mawk to help him.'

'Oh, he'll be doing that all right,' said Hup. 'He's

pretty good at getting other creatures to work for him. I had to dust the library while I was there, and clean out all the fire grates. He threatened to stamp on me if I didn't, and there's not much a creature our size can do against a seven-foot iron man.'

The attackers proceeded towards the castle, hunched figures in the freezing wind. When they were within range Sylver had one of the catapults set up to send rocks crashing into the castle walls. The other was used to threaten the scaremen. These ragbag wolves continually circled the group as they laid siege to the castle, threatening to rush in and engage in close combat. But they remained wary of the catapult and kept their distance, howling hollowly.

The castle walls proved to be very strong, but the constant hammering from the stones must have made it very uncomfortable for those inside. Each time a rock struck, the whole structure juddered. chips of sandstone the size of fat stoats came flying from the battlements.

Every so often they saw the black knight appear at a window, shaking his fist at them. The catapult would then be aimed at that particular window. The knight would disappear from that part of the castle and a little later reappear somewhere else, whereupon the catapult would be swung round again. In the end it became a game, with the weasels trying to guess which window the knight would appear at next.

Chapter Twenty-Two

While the siege catapult pounded at the walls, Sylver sent some pine martens to look for a gateway into the castle. They found what at first looked like a gate, then saw that it was in fact a seat carved out of a rock facing the castle. In front of the seat, fashioned from the rock wall of the castle, was a roughly hewn set of organ keys, stops and foot pedals.

A lemming wearing earmuffs and thick gloves was on his knees in front of this extraordinary carving, sorting through some sheets of music. 'Staying for the show?' he said, looking up. 'You're very welcome . . .'

The martens declined, enquiring instead about the location of the main gate. The lemming stood up and pointed it out to them. They thanked him and went to inspect it.

They found it was fashioned of the same sandstone material as the rest of the castle. A *ballista* was brought up and a huge rock was fired at it. The gate cracked. A second missile broke it in two, dust billowing from the opening. The slabs of sandstone fell away and left the entrance to the castle open and unguarded.

'Into the breach, dear friends,' cried Scirf, his

cold-air cough spoiling the effect of the words, 'but don't jam up the openin' by going all at once.'

The weasels and martens filed through the gateway into the castle bailey. From here they spread out to search the interior. It was, as Hup had explained, a very difficult task, for they kept coming up against dead ends. Inside, the castle was a maze. Scirf, Bryony and Sylver found themselves on their own. They walked long passageways only to find that the door at the end was locked. If not, there was usually an empty room beyond, or yet another long passageway. Finally they resorted to yelling for Mawk, asking him for directions.

Mawk duly answered. 'Here, here,' he cried, but his voice seemed to come from the very air above their heads.

They kept asking him to describe his surroundings, but when he told them they were left none the wiser. Finally they stumbled upon the hapless weasel purely by accident in a room in one of the many towers. Like the rest of the castle the room was furnished with sandstone chairs, benches and tables. Mawk was chained to the wall, shivering, tears frozen to his cheeks.

'Thank Gawd you've come,' he sobbed, the relief shining through his tears. 'I thought you'd sail off without me.'

Scirf snorted. 'Would we do that? Now, where's the key to that lock?'

'The black knight threw it down the garderobe.'

'Down the loo? Typical. I always seem to end up climbing down loos. Where is it?'

Bryony said, 'You can't go swanning off down

garderobes, Scirf. We'll have to get him free some other way. The sandstone looks quite soft. If the three of us tug on his chain we can probably pull the spike from the wall.'

The three weasels, assisted by a frantic Mawk, tried to wrench the holding spike from the wall. It would not budge. They were still pulling when a sound came from the doorway. The weasels looked up to see an enormous figure entering the room.

'Is it safe?' he asked. 'Tell me.'

It was the knight of the castle, his dark armour gleaming in the light which shafted through the arrow loop windows. The visor of his helmet was closed; the crown sprouted a bunch of black feathers. The tips of these feathers were red where they had brushed the sandstone ceiling.

His walk, as Hup had described, was most peculiar: two steps forward, one step sideways, as he crossed the room to reach the weasels. For some reason he went for Scirf first.

'Safe?' asked Sylver. 'What do you mean, is it safe?'

The knight continued in his zigzag line as if he had not heard, still heading for Scirf. Scirf, however, was on to his game and shot behind a stone armchair just as the knight was about to grasp him. 'Check!' he cried.

This one word seemed to enrage the knight who, despite his funny walking pattern, moved very swiftly. He shot neatly forwards and sideways to grab Scirf, but the weasel was quicker, darting behind a bench.

'Check again, mate!'

'Stop using those words!' squealed the knight in a peculiar high-pitched voice. 'They irritate me.'

'Yes, and we know why, don't we?'

The other mammals were puzzled by this exchange. They had no idea why Scirf was saying 'check' and even less idea why it annoyed the black knight.

'You know what's the best game in the world?' said Scirf, dodging behind yet another piece of furniture to avoid the grasp of the metal hand. 'Hollyhockers.'

'What a loud of claptrap,' yelled the knight, stopping in his tracks. 'The best game is . . .'

'Yes?' cried Scirf, misty breath billowing around him. 'You was goin' to say?'

'Never mind,' squeaked the knight in fury. 'You just stand still for a minute.'

At that moment Luke entered the room and Scirf gave a yell of delight. 'Ho! Now we have a bishop. A monk is as good as a bishop any day. You have to move diagonally, Luke. Bryony, you're a queen, so you can move straight or diagonally. Sylver, you're the king, so you just move one pace any whichway. Mawk, you've already been taken, so you can't do anything. Am I gettin' close to the truth, Mr Black Knight?'

The knight stopped nipping forwards and sideways and seemed to stare at Scirf, though it was difficult to tell what he was doing behind the grill of his visor.

Scirf was triumphant. 'You're a chesspiece, ain'tcha?'

The knight staggered backwards one pace, then sideways two paces, out of Scirf's way. 'You guessed!' he exclaimed.

'Well, it weren't hard,' said the modest Scirf, 'if you know the game. I used to play it with the blacksmith when I was a dung-watcher, back in the old days. Pretty good at it, too. You come from one of them big outdoor sets, don'tya?'

'Your diction is appalling,' said the knight. 'And I wish you would not use such terrible grammar.'

'Take me as you find me,' Scirf said, 'or not at all. Now, what's the problem here, eh? You seem a nervous sort of knight to me, as if you're expectin' to be attacked at any time. Are the white chesspieces after you?'

'White *and* black,' squeaked the knight. 'They want to get me back again, but I've had enough of the game. I want to be on my own for a while. I'm fed up with playing war games. Unfortunately, the rest of the set don't see it that way. They say they are incomplete without me. They want me back on the board with them – but I won't go. I won't.'

'You're a big enough fellah,' replied Scirf; 'surely you can take care of yourself.'

'The spirit is big but the flesh is small,' said the black knight mysteriously.

Sylver interrupted with, 'Why do you want our ship?'

'Why, for an emergency. It was my intention to dig a tunnel from inside the castle to a cave on the beach. Then, if I felt my castle was no longer safe, I could run along the tunnel, come out on the beach, board the ship and sail away. I was going to moor the ship just offshore, ready for an emergency. I would have a crew permanently standing by, of course.'

'It would be rather a zigzag run, wouldn't it?'

'So long as the tunnel is wide enough that doesn't matter.'

'And where would you get your crew from?'

'I was going to offer you the job,' the knight squealed excitedly. 'You don't know what it's like, waiting for that army of black and white pawns to appear on the horizon, led by bishops, knights, kings and queens. They won't rest, you know, until they have me back in their ranks.

'Another knight will not do, of course. The set I belong to is unique. It was made in Missaglia by the famous armourer Pier Innocenzo da Faerno. Antonio Seroni was responsible for the clockwork which governs my steps. I am a masterpiece of engineering. There are only three others like me in the world – one black, two white.'

Sylver shook his head. 'I can understand why they want you back. Such a set is priceless when it is complete, but almost worthless if one piece is missing. But you're an individual too – you have the right to freedom – you don't have to go back if you don't want to, even if you are part of a set.'

'So you'll help me?' The knight was becoming hysterical.

'Sorry, we have a mission. We need our ship and we need the crew. You'll have to find some other way of protecting yourself. I agree with Scirf. You're a big knight: surely you can take care of yourself, even if they do come for you. Your makeshift wolves, your scaremen – they will help you.'

'You don't understand,' squeaked the knight. 'The wolves merely alert me to an approach. They're just an early-warning system. They can't hold back an attack by the rest of the chess set. The other pieces are the same size as me. They'll smash my wolves to bits if they attack.'

Just at that moment a howling sound came from the hills. The wolves! It was like a series of signals, being passed from one pack to the next. The knight executed a skipping square dance to the window and stared out. He gave a cry of dismay and turned quickly. Coinciding with the black knight's shout of alarm, the door flew open, and the rest of the weasels and martens came into the room.

'Hey-oop, captain. There's a whole bevy of metal lads and lassies comin' doon from the heights,' said one of the martens who, to judge by his accent, came from the north-east of Welkin. 'Blokes like this one here,' he pointed to the knight. 'They look like they mean business to me. Gan have a look, captain. See what ye think.'

Sylver went to the arrowloop window. Sure enough, the sun was gleaming on metal men and women, marching down from the high mountain passes: sixteen armed soldiers, four holy men, three knights in armour with lances and swords, two kings carrying sceptres and two queens bearing orbs in the palms of their right hands. They did indeed look purposeful as they came clanking towards the castle.

The knights were doing their squared walk. The bishops were moving like ships tacking, in zigzag lines, taking just as long as the knights to make forward progress. The kings came one tread at a time, with a stately pause between each step, during which they exchanged courtly chat. The queens, tall and confident, strode out magnificently. They were well ahead of the rest of the army, having no restrictions to their march across the board of the world.

'I must hide myself,' squealed the knight in a high-pitched voice. 'I must hide.' He left the room in some agitation.

The weasels and martens remained, crowded round the window.

'Well,' said Sylver, 'this is nothing to do with us. I suggest we go back to the ship and be on our way. If they find him, it's hard luck. I think an animal – even a human – is entitled to some individual freedom, but we can't fight his battles for him.'

'What about me?' cried Mawk. 'I'm still chained to the wall!'

The marten with the north-eastern accent stepped forward. He had brought a hammer and chisel with him. He struck at the links of the chain until they parted. Mawk still had to wear the manacles like bracelets, but these could be removed when they all got back to the ship. Sylver then led his crew from the room.

They found their way at last to an exit from the castle, leaving just as the metal army was entering. The giant chess set paid no attention to the mammals, but clanked on past them, into the recesses of the great castle.

As they walked away from the castle, monstrously loud music suddenly boomed out from the towers above. The whole building began vibrating with the resonant sound. Slowly the castle – indeed, the whole mountain – began to sink into the ground. It was bedlam.

The weasels and martens turned to see the lemming sitting on his rock seat, playing the sandstone organ keys, pushing and pulling organ stops, feet pumping away on the foot pedals. Like the mountain with its castle, he too was slowly disappearing, vanishing down into some mysterious pit.

He inclined his head when he realized they were staring at him. 'Toccata and Fugue in F,' he called to them gaily. 'Aren't you staying for the show?'

Even before the weasels and martens were a hundred metres from the castle gate, the chess set were dragging the black knight out of the disappearing gate. He was still protesting in his high, squeaky voice.

Scirf could not bear to leave the scene without having his say. Like all the ex-outlaws, he was a champion of the downtrodden and persecuted. With Sylver's permission and support he quietly excused himself and went back to confront the white king, who was now berating the wayward knight.

''Scuse me, squire,' said Scirf, shouting above the noise of the organ music. 'Sorry – I mean "your majesty" – we weasels think this individual has a right to his freedom. We know what it's like to be oppressed. We've had it back in Welkin, where we come from, with the so-called rulin' stoats. You should let him decide what he wants to do.'

The white king squealed back a heated reply. 'He does not have the right to decide. You obviously don't understand the situation. This is not the owner of the piece. The owner is in here with me. This is a thief!'

Scirf and the other weasels were puzzled. 'I don't understand. What do you mean, a thief?'

The king reached forward impatiently and threw open the visor to the knight's helmet. There, nestled inside, sitting in a metal chair a little too large for him, amidst clockwork levers and wheels, pulleys and wires, springs and rachets, sat a buck-toothed gerbil. His eyes glinted wildly on being exposed to the stares of the mammals. He reached frantically for the levers on either side of his chair, trying to force the mechanical knight through the surrounding metal army, but they pressed around him on all sides, hemming him in.

'It's mine, I tell you!' he squealed. 'I didn't steal it!'

'I'm afraid he did,' the white king told Scirf. 'Last time it was a black bishop, the time before that a white queen.'

'I inherited the castle from my dear departed granny, bless her cotton tail-warmers,' cried the gerbil, 'and her dying wish was that it should have a royal or a noble in residence. Don't you understand that, you rum-headed poltroons? I would like a king or queen, but I'll settle for a knight or a bishop. You can't make me give him back. You can't.'

The white king seemed to think otherwise. The castle had been empty for centuries, he said. It was just another lie from the mouth of the gerbil. 'We are hamsters and we have sold our tails in order to form this chess set. This gerbil, by no means typical of his kind, wishes to keep his tail *and* own one of our pieces. He's mad, poor fellow, and becoming more insane with every passing day.'

'Mad?' shrieked the gerbil. 'I'll show you how mad I am! I'm mad all right, you set of poppinjays.' With menace in his tiny eyes he began pulling levers and twisting wheels. The black knight's metal arms jerked up and began thrashing about, clanking against the sides of the other chesspieces. His feet kicked out and his head twisted wildly round and round, the black plumes flying.

'How dare you, you impudent gerbil!' cried one of the queens. 'You've scratched our bodice! We are far from amused!'

The other metal figures began striking back, flailing at the black knight, denting him in a dozen places.

Sylver led the weasels and martens quietly away. They could not help glancing back over their shoulders occasionally at the amazing fracas taking place in the dust in front of the great castle. In the background they could still see the lemming. Only his head and shoulders showed above the earth now, but his forelimbs and paws, leaping and flying over the keys, still pounded out the rich sonorous tones of 'Toccata and Fugue in F'. Slowly, slowly, he descended behind the fighting chesspieces, swaying and bobbing to the rhythm of his music.

'Who'd get mixed up with that lot?' said Scirf. 'Only a lunatic, that's for sure.'

The others murmured their agreement as they made their way down to the shore where the rowing boat awaited them. When they reached the ship, they turned to see that mountain and castle had gone. The grand music still poured out from the pit into which the mountain had disappeared. Then, to the delight of all those on board, the lemming's 'show' began. It was the aurora borealis, the northern lights, which lit up the sky with breathtaking splendour. There were pretty ribbons, beautiful curtains which hung from the heavens, great bursts of shimmering colour, all made of fantastic bright light.

'How wonderful!' cried Bryony, as the lemming's music rose to a crescendo. 'How lovely!'

The other weasels and martens agreed. They leaned over the rail of the ship and watched this magnificent show until it was spent. Then they went quietly below deck to contemplate the madness and the beauty in the quiet of the icy night.

Chapter Twenty-Three

It was a wet day at Castle Rayn as usual. The prince had been up at the window, looking out over the lake, where a land bridge was being constructed. The prince had found some creatures in the eastern angles of Fearsomeshire, had rounded most of them up and put them to work building a mud causeway from the mainland, across the lake, to the castle. Soon Castle Rayn would no longer be isolated, but would be joined to the mainland once more.

Grey clouds crowded in at the window of Prince Poynt's bedchamber, trying to nuzzle their way into the room. The prince glared at them, hoping this would intimidate them and cause a retreat.

The prince was at his exercises. He ate a lot, it was true, and he did not stint when it came to wassailing on honey dew. But he liked to think of himself as a lean, strong animal, so he did keep-fit exercises every morning from 9 a.m., when he got out of bed, until 9.05 a.m. These exercises consisted of opening the window and breathing deeply several times, before crawling back beneath the warm silk sheets of the four-poster bed.

At that moment a sergeant-at-arms came bursting into the prince's quarters.

'Well, what is it?' snapped the prince. 'Can't you see I'm at my exercises? How do you think I can inspect my troops unless I'm fit and furry? Spit it out, stoat, spit it out.'

'Yes, my liege. My liege, a messenger has arrived from Sheriff Falshed.'

The prince paused in mid-breath and closed the window against the depressing grey intruders. 'Message? From Falshed? Good, good. Where is it?'

'I haven't got the message on me, my liege. I – I thought it best you hear it from the messenger himself.'

'Oh, very well,' said Prince Poynt irritably. 'Go and fetch him.'

The sergeant-at-arms seemed about to say something else, then changed his mind and left the room. The prince fluffed up his white ermine coat with his claws and went to the roaring fire. He put a few more coals on until the room was stifling. Then he went to the doorway and carefully placed a cloth draught excluder in the shape of a sausage to cover the crack under the door. It had been moved by the sergeant when he came in.

A moment later the door flew open. The sausage went shooting across the room, startling the prince. And there stood an enormous seagull. This bird marched into the room. 'Whut? Eh? See you, Jimmy, ah've come wi' a message frae yon sheriff tae gie tae ye the noo, aye!'

The creature slammed the door hard behind him, making the corridor echo with the sound of the explosion. 'Aye, ye ken it's awfy hot in here!'

The prince's heart was beating fast. He was wondering whether this was actually an attempt on his life. Was this enormous bird – a herring gull by the look of him – an assassin sent by the enemies of the state? Had he come to sever his head from his body with that huge wicked beak? What was this language he was gabbling in? Some foreign tongue, no doubt.

At that moment, luckily for the prince, who had been about to scream and throw things, the Princess Sibiline came into the chamber from a side door leading to her room. 'What's going on?' she asked. 'What was that crashing sound?'

She regarded the seagull with some disfavour. The gull smelled of fish – reeked of it – and in the stifling atmosphere of the prince's room it was choking. His dirty feathers were smeared with seashore tar and were marking the floor.

'What on earth are you doing in here?' said Sibiline disapprovingly. 'Don't you know this is the bedchamber of the Prince of All Welkin? Go back to your digging in the mud for nasty cockle-shells, if you please.'

'Ah'm no likin' cockles, hen. Ah'm more a mussel bird, mahsel', ye understand. 'Course, ah dinna mind a wee plate o' winkles noo an' then, but ony on Saturdays.'

'It's the language of the devil,' cried Prince Poynt, with his claws over his ears. 'Don't listen, Sib. You'll probably change into a toad or something.'

'You're already a toad,' she snapped at her brother. 'Don't be so silly. The seagull is speaking in the dialect of the northern outer islands. You just have to listen hard to catch the cadence and the lilt.'

'What did he say, then?' asked the prince suspiciously. 'Tell me what he said.'

'He merely informed me that he does not like cockles.'

'Aye, that's about the size o' it, hen. Ah'm no a great lover o' shellfish in ony case. Ah much prefer some o' they honey cakes ye get at the baker's.'

The truth began to dawn on Prince Poynt. 'You mean to say that oaf Falshed has sent a whacking great seagull with a message, instead of a robin?'

'Aye, well, it may have escaped yer notice, me auld china, but there's no mony robins oot at sea. Ye tak' what ye can get an' ah'm it, so tae speak. an' if ah constantly get this feelin' ah'm no wanted here, yer likely tae get the heed across ye, an' then ah'm away, ye ken, wi'oot gieing ye the message.'

'What did he say? What did he say?' cried the prince, once again convinced that the bird's glaring yellow eye was sending him the signal that all was not well and that assassination might indeed follow quickly.

'He said he does not appreciate the welcome he's getting and if you continue to treat him in a hostile fashion he will be forced to butt you with his great head.'

'I knew it!' yelled the prince. 'He's come to kill me. Help, ho, guards! Assistance here! Your beloved prince is in mortal danger!' He waited for a few moments but no-one came.

Sibiline ignored her brother. 'What's the message, if you please, gull?'

'Crivvens, jings and help ma bob, that sheriff cu

237

telt me to say he's gannin' after they other coin. He says he's no but a few wee nautical miles ahind them. Now, if ye'll just gie me a few of they honey cakes ah'll be awa back tae mah wee butt 'n ben oot in the islands, ye ken. See, yon brither o' yours needs a wee kick up the shanksy if ye ask me.'

'I am just about to deliver it,' replied Sibiline. 'I did not understand just two words of your message. You spoke the words "cu" and "coin"?'

'One's the singular, the other's the plural o' the same word. A cu is one o' they hairy things, wi' four legs, pointy ears and lots o' teeth. They aye yap-yap-yap when they run up and doon the beach chasin' shadows, ye ken. In the auld days they would hae collars roond they necks.'

'Dogs? You mean dogs?'

'Aye, that's who ah mean.'

'But Falshed is not a dog, he's a stoat.'

'Aye weel, ye might be right, but tae seagulls every thing that scuttles on four legs is a cu.'

Sibiline called for the sergeant-at-arms and told him to take the seagull down to the bakery and provide him with as many honey cakes as he could eat and carry. Once this was done, the great bird had stomped out, chattering to a bewildered sergeant in a dialect which was music to the ears of the northern island animals, but incomprehensible to most of Welkin's brethren, apart from the splendidly clever Sibiline.

The princess confronted her shaken brother. 'What's the matter with you? How can you be such a wimp in front of strangers.'

'I thought he'd come to kill me, sis,' moaned the prince. 'He was a wicked-looking beggar.'

'Don't always go by appearances, Pointy,' she replied, melting a little when she saw how frightened her brother had been. 'Some of the nicest animals are horrible to look at. Our late uncle, for example—'

'Yes, yes, never mind all that,' snapped the prince, returning to his old testy self again. 'What did the creature say? Has Falshed captured the weasels yet?'

'No, but he's close behind them in a fast ship apparently. It shouldn't be long before Falshed brings Sylver's head back on a platter.'

'Yek!' said the prince. 'He can bring it to you then – I don't want it.'

'It's just a figure of speech, brother. I mean he will return with the weasels in chains. Now, why don't you go back to doing what you were doing before you were interrupted. I'm sure it was more important that the fate of a few woodland weasels.'

'My exercises,' said the prince proudly, 'but I'm finished now. Feel my muscles.' He held out a bent forelimb for his sister to feel his biceps.

She did so with an impatient, 'Yes, lovely. You're as strong as an ox, dear brother. But I have to get back to my "taste" class. Sleek the otter is advising us all on taste.'

Prince Poynt licked his lips. 'Oh, I could do with some of that. I haven't had breakfast yet. Tasting what?'

'No, no, you oaf – *good* taste. Tasteful furnishings, tasteful fabrics, tasteful table decorations.'

'Oh that,' replied the disappointed prince. 'I don't know what you see in all that stuff, Sib.

I mean, kings, princes and princesses have all got natural taste. Anything we choose is bound to be tasteful, because we're who we are. It's a sort of inbred, mystical thing. We can't help it. We're just brilliant at choosing things which go with things – colours which match and complement, things which aren't kitsch, things which critics admire, things which, even though they may appear cheap and garish to other eyes, *must* be inherently tasteful because we chose 'em.'

'Sleek doesn't see it that way. He says taste has to be learned. He says even if you have natural taste you can still refine it.'

'Oh, he does, does he? To talk to a prince or princess like that is tantamount to treason. How would he like his tasteful head lopped from his tasteful shoulders? – in a tasteful manner, of course.'

'You touch one hair on Sleek's tail, Pointy, and I'll never come and stroke your brow again, *especially* if you've got a horrible headache.'

Prince Poynt gave her a sulky look. 'Oh, all right, go to the blasted otter's taste class then. I'm going up on the battlements for a bit of fresh air. This place stinks of fish now. What was that guard thinking of, bringing the cod-eater in here? Vulgar, raffish bird . . .'

Sibiline left the room with a flourish.

'. . . all water creatures should be drowned at birth,' finished the prince with a hateful look at the door through which she had departed. 'Especially gulls and otters.'

'I heard that!' came a voice back, faintly.

Prince Poynt did not care. He made his way

through the winding stone passageways up to the battlements. As he passed guards and stoats-at-arms, they snapped to attention, rattling their breastplates. The prince never tired of being saluted by his soldiers. It was one of the good things in life, the way they slammed their hind legs together, whipped up a forelimb or gave him a smart 'present arms' with a weapon.

Then he remembered something. 'Why didn't you lot come to my aid when I called for you?' he roared down the corridors. 'I was in fear for my life. That's your job, you blasted skivers!'

Fortunately not one head turned his way. The guards continued to stand like statues. Had but one of them flinched, there would have been a summary execution. Prince Poynt humphed and narrowed his eyes. 'Just watch it, you lot,' he finished.

He stepped out onto the battlements with a sigh. It was one of his favourite places. From here he could see his whole kingdom, even if it was a bit watery now, even if the day was very grey, even if it was drizzling . . .

'WWWWHHAAAAEEEEIIIIIAAAHHHNNNAAAIIIEEE!'
The prince nearly fell through the crenelations to the lake far below. The noise had come from directly behind him and it was an unholy racket. It made the hair on his neck curl in a most unpleasant manner. It made his eyeballs start from his head. The noise was not only loud; it was screechingly loud.

He turned to see the enormous seagull marching up and down playing – that word may be taken with a pinch of salt – playing a swollen octopus by blowing through one of its legs and squeezing its body under a feathery wingpit. The creature beneath the seagull's wing was obviously in great pain. It continued to scream and shriek while the callous sea bird walked up and down the battlements, crushing the life out of the poor thing.

Then the seagull let it go. It gave out a last despairing whine, and dangled limply – obviously dead – from the seagull's strong grip.

'Ah've always wantit tae do that,' said the seagull. '*Sockie Island Abrave*, frae the battlements of a cu castle. How did ye like mah music, eh, me auld china?'

Prince Poynt caught hold of one word. 'M— m— music?'

'The pipes, ye daft cu. Did ye no enjoy the skirl o' the pipes? Did it no mak yer toes curl? Ah must confess it reaches right doon intae mah belly and plucks at mah short intestines, so it does. Naething like it on this earth!'

'Nothing like it indeed,' quavered the prince. 'Now would you please leave my house. I'm rather tired. I think I have a headache coming on. Sib? Sib?' he called. 'I've got one of my headaches. Would you please come up here?'

The seagull from the northern islands shrugged, tucked his bagpipes away somewhere in those voluminous feathers, and took to the air, flying directly towards the sea. The prince fell in a heap on the floor. He was still there, blubbering, an hour later when his sister came to find him. She comforted him, of course, as she always did, then left him in the care of Pompom, his weasel jester, who did his best to cheer the prince up with his inflated mouse's bladder on a stick.

But the prince screamed at him to take the thing away.

Chapter Twenty-Four

Having left all the chesspieces arguing with the black knight, Sylver and his crew collected the siege catapults and took them back to the ship. They were anxious to be away from the place. Once on board, Sylver gave the order to set sail. Soon the ship was on its way, ploughing through the cold seas. The crew went about their various tasks, or, if they had been on watch, went below to sleep.

Sylver remained on the bridge, watching the land fall away aft, wondering what would be the fate of the strange gerbil now that the chess set had caught up with him. Quite soon, though, the island dropped down below the horizon and Sylver turned his mind to other things.

'Miniver,' he said, 'take your reckoning from the navigator, Scirf. I believe he wants us to sail a little to the left of the setting sun. I am going below. Call me if I'm needed.'

'Yes, Sylver.'

'Very good, Miniver.'

Sylver had to maintain his distance from the crew. Although he missed socializing with the other weasels, he knew that a ship's captain needed to remain above all the bickering and petty squabbles which arise when mariners live together in such close, confined quarters. The captain had to sort out those quarrels and offer clear judgements if need be. He could not do that if he was embroiled in those quarrels.

That night he could hear his crew singing on deck with the pine martens.

'Yo ho ho and a jug of honey grog –
fifteen minks on a dead rat's chest . . .'

They sang songs and played jigs and hornpipes, making the deck planks rattle with their dancing. Sylver remained in his cabin, listening and sighing, but unable to join in the fun.

At about noon the following day Sylver heard a commotion on deck. A little later there was a polite knock on his cabin door.

'Who is it?' he asked.

'It's me, Miniver. And seaweasels Wodehed and Luke. We have a stowaway.'

A stowaway! That was unusual. Who would want to stow away on a ship that was heading out into unknown waters, looking blindly for an island full of humans? Most animals would avoid such a ship like the plague.

'Enter,' called Sylver.

Miniver opened the door and Wodehed and Luke came in holding a creature between them. The animal was protesting loudly at being subjected to 'inmammal treatment' and asking by what right he was in custody. Sylver stared at the belligerent figure before him. It was the gerbil from the castle.

'So,' said Sylver, 'you escaped from the rest of your chess set.'

'That lot?' said the gerbil. 'They couldn't catch a cold in winter.' He clicked his teeth as an amusing picture came to mind. 'They couldn't hold Narky . . .' Narky was obviously the gerbil's name.

'I challenged the white knight to a duel,' he went on. 'He was the only figure besides me who was in one piece after the scrap outside the castle walls. We decided to settle our differences on the tournament grounds, like real knights. The two of us fought with broadswords for a while. Then I had him on the ground and stood with my sword raised, ready to decapitate him . . .' The errant gerbil clicked his teeth again.

'Then what?' asked Sylver, interested in spite of himself.

'Then I slipped out of the secret trap door in the back of the black knight's helmet. The audience – the other bits of the chess set – were so horrified by what I was about to do to the white knight they failed to see me escape. I expect they're still standing there now, staring at a black knight about to behead a white knight. They probably don't realize that the brains of the suit of armour is here on board the *Scudding Cloud*.'

Sylver stared at the gerbil, who was gesticulating excitedly as he told his tale. 'How did you get on board?'

'I came down to the ship while you were still fiddling with your siege catapults. A friendly seal gave me a lift on his back. It was nothing to scramble up the anchor rope and through one of the portholes. And here I am.'

'What am I going to do with you?' asked Sylver.

'Throw me overboard?' replied the gerbil, flicking his tail this way and that. 'Keel-haul me? Give me fifty lashes of the cat? You're the captain. You can do what you like.'

'Don't be ridiculous. We don't punish animals unless they've done something very wrong and I expect you know that. So far all you've done is stow away on my ship.' He turned to Luke. 'Luke, I'm going to relieve you of your duties in the galley. This gerbil will take over as assistant cook until we can find a suitable sand spit to leave him on.'

'Yes, captain,' said Luke, more than a little glad to be out of the hot galley, with its dangerous boiling hot soups that tended to splash over the edge of the cooking pots if the ocean was even a little bit choppy. 'I'll inform Short that he has a new skivvy.'

'What?' cried the gerbil wildly, all amusement and bonhomie gone from his expression. He sat up on his hind legs, his little forelimbs gesticulating, his claws opening and closing with anxiety. '*Work?* I can't work. I've never worked. It isn't part of my make-up. I'm an – an aristocrat. We don't know how to work, you see. We're born to leisure, us nobs. I should just put me on a deckchair in a sunny corner of the ship and leave me to contemplate the nature of the waves, if I were you. I'd be more trouble than I'm worth. I'm ineffectual, I am.'

'You'll work in the galley and that's that,' replied Sylver, becoming a little irritated with this gerbil. 'I'm not having a mammal lying around

247

idle while the rest of the crew work hard. It would cause ill feeling. You'll report to Short Oneleg in the galley forthwith, and I want no more argument.'

'You don't know what you're saying,' objected the gerbil as they dragged him out. 'It's not that I don't want to work – I *can't* work. I don't know how to . . .'

Thankfully Wodehed slammed the door and the voice trailed off as they marched him along the gangway. Sylver heaved a sigh of relief. This Narky was a nuisance: he was almost tempted to turn the ship round and take him back to the island again, but he knew he would lose too much time.

The gerbil had the knack of annoying Sylver without even trying. His mere presence was enough to set Sylver's teeth on edge: he was one of those animals whose influence could transform a mild disagreement into a riot involving hundreds.

So uneasy was Sylver about the new member of the crew that he called Short Oneleg to his cabin the next day. 'How's your new assistant coming along?' he asked. 'Put him to work, have you?'

'Ah, there's a thing,' said Short, shifting his weight off his wooden pegleg. 'Ever since Narky's been on board he's been sick. Taken to his bed, he has, poor fellow.'

Sylver wrinkled his brow. 'Has Wodehed seen him?'

'Aye, cap'n, but he can't seem to find out what the malady is. 'Tis a mysterious illness, that's certain. The gerbil just lies there, starin' at the bulkhead. His eyes have the look of a dying animal, cap'n. I think he's just wasting away.'

Sylver had other ideas. He decided to go and see the gerbil for himself. He accompanied Short to a corner of the forecastle, where the cook had made a space for the gerbil to lie down. The stowaway was there now, his eyes staring blindly, his demeanour listless. Even when Sylver called his name he did not turn his head.

'Narky?' said Sylver. 'What's all this then?'

'I'm ill – seriously ill,' moaned the gerbil.

In another corner of the forecastle some martens were quietly playing hollyhockers with Mawk. They were speaking in hushed tones and casting sympathetic glances at the sick Narky. There was a sort of reverence paid to sick animals, especially when they were close by.

'Nonsense,' snapped Sylver. 'You were perfectly fit yesterday, when I saw you. How is that today you are at death's door? I think you're malingering, trying to get out of working in the galley. It won't do, you know.'

Narky seemed to make an effort to sit up, but then fell back weakly on his bunk. 'I – I want to work, captain. My body just won't let me.'

Sylver lost his temper. 'I want you up and working within five minutes. I shall leave Short in charge of you. If you don't get up, you'll be severely punished.'

With that, Sylver left what he was certain was a faking invalid and went back to his cabin. A few moments later there was a knock on the door. Sylver nodded to himself, thinking this must be a contrite gerbil, ready to apologize for his silly attempt to shirk his duties. 'Come in!' he said, less severely than he might have done ten minutes before.

The door opened and Mawk stood there. Behind him were some martens, who waited politely outside the cabin while Mawk went in. Mawk had only recently had the manacles removed from his forelimbs. He had worn them like bracelets for two days, waiting for the ship's blacksmith to see to them.

'Ahem,' said Mawk, clearing his throat. 'Thing is, Sylver – thing is, we believe you're being rather harsh on poor Narky. We think he's quite poorly. We think he should be left alone and allowed to rest—'

'What?' cried Sylver. 'Don't you know this creature is faking it? Mawk, sometimes I wonder about you. Go away and don't bother me any more.'

Mawk shrugged and quietly closed the door. There was an angry muttering of voices outside the cabin for a while, then the voices drifted away.

Sylver could not believe what was happening. It seemed that Narky not only had the power to arouse his own worst feelings; he could also manipulate other crew members.

Mawk had never been concerned before, when anyone else was ill. He was too selfish for that. He only seemed to care when he himself was unwell. Why should he bother about this strange gerbil who was clearly a fraud? Who had, moreover, captured him and put him in chains! Sylver had not forgotten that the gerbil was a master persuader and had drawn animals from the ship and up to his castle in the dead of night. Perhaps he still had that prism he had used to hypnotize them.

Sylver went to Scirf, who was with Bryony and Alysoun at the wheel. He told them what had happened and asked for their opinion.

'My advice is to throw the baggage overboard,' said Bryony, referring to the gerbil. 'He's just a waste of space.'

'Well, we can't do that, you know,' said Sylver, 'but I will put him off at the nearest island.'

'I knew that creature was a lay-about, soon as I set eyes on him,' Scirf said, with narrowed eyes. 'Can't stand skivers, meself. Mawk is such a pushover for sentiment. He probably thinks he's standing up as the champion of the underdog. Well, this time he's taking the wrong side.'

Armed with the knowledge that there were others on his side, Sylver visited the forecastle again. There he ordered two martens to get the gerbil up. Mawk tried to protest but Sylver told him he would spend the next three days in the crow's nest if he could not keep quiet. The martens stood one on either side of the gerbil, propping him up, his legs having apparently turned to jelly. When Sylver ordered the martens to let the gerbil go, the creature fell in a sprawling heap on the deck.

'It's my legs,' moaned the gerbil. 'There's no strength in them. My bones have gone all wobbly. My muscles won't work properly . . .'

'It's you who won't work,' cried an infuriated Sylver. 'Now get up and go to your duties.'

'I can't. I'm sick, I tell you. Have you no heart?

251

Look at me. Do I look like a well mammal? I can feel the illness coursing through my body. It's robbed me of all strength. You may do your worst punishment, captain, but I'm afraid I shall still not be able to work, even though I want to, desperately, to prove I'm not lying . . .'

Sylver began to relent. The creature *did* look a little lethargic, his fur dry and musty, his eyes milky. Perhaps he was telling the truth after all. Perhaps Sylver had jumped to conclusions too quickly. He decided he would give the gerbil a day or two to get over his sickness, then review the situation. He told Mawk to put the gerbil back to bed and inform him, the captain, of any developments.

A whole week went by and still the gerbil did not get up from his bunk. At first he had his meals brought to him in bed by Luke, but on being told that Wodehed could find nothing wrong with him, and that his appetite was not that of an ill creature, he began to eat less. Or so it seemed.

In fact, thick soups and titbits were brought to him by Mawk and other members of the crew. Not one of the martens would think of leaving a meal without taking a little piece of biscuit, or some stew, for Narky. The gerbil would sit up and hold forth gloomily about fatal illnesses; then he would settle back down and either sleep or talk.

Once again Sylver attempted to assert his authority by forbidding anyone to feed the gerbil. 'The next crew member who sneaks food into Narky's sick room will be put ashore and left there,' he warned.

No-one disobeyed this order, yet Narky still

seemed to flourish even though he did not get up for meals.

One day Sylver went down below to check on the Jenny Hanivers and found nothing but fish bones. They had all been gnawed away by the gerbil. Sylver was furious. He threatened all sorts of punishments, but none seemed effective. Somehow the gerbil always managed to gather enough sympathy to deflect the captain's wrath and continued to remain in bed.

Chapter Twenty-Five

Falshed was standing in his rubber boots at the bow of the ship, the invigorating wind blowing in his face. He had been told by the martens that rubber boots would weigh him down if he ever fell overboard but he did not care. He hated getting his feet wet and chose to risk the possibility of death rather than the probability of damp socks. What was more, he had been sick over the bows for about the fifth time that morning.

'Do you mind?' came the voice of Guildenswine from below. 'That was all over Rosencrass and me.'

Falshed looked down to see that he had been ill over the figureheads, with their double-ferret face. The ship's passengers, the statues, had been put off on a large island. The sheriff wondered whether he should have put the figureheads off at the same time. After all, Rosencrass and Guildenswine were in truth now statues – wooden statues, or stumpers.

'Can't make a lot of difference,' he murmured. 'The seagulls have already covered you with bird lime.'

'It makes a difference,' came back Rosencrass; 'believe me.'

The sea was like a millpond, but there was an underlying swell which made the vessel rock as gently as a kitten's cradle under the paw of a loving mother. To Falshed this constant rocking and swaying was as bad as a storm. He did not trust the deck beneath his feet. It moved. It sloped first one way and then the other. It was not natural.

'Why did I ever come on this voyage?' he groaned to One-eared Jake, who had come up from the galley to get some fresh air. 'I'm not made for a sailor's life.'

'You'll get used to it,' said the marten, slapping him on the back. 'Breathe deeply. Get some ozone in your lungs. You missed breakfast this morning, that's your trouble, cap'n. Nice plate of greasy vole's liver in your gut would chase away all that queasiness.'

Falshed closed his eyes and tried to banish the picture of fried vole's liver from his mind. His stomach began to churn and well up again. He blocked his throat with his tongue, hoping to keep down whatever wanted to come up. 'I don't think so, Jake, and I'd be grateful if you did not mention it again.'

He needed distractions, so he asked his companion, who was chewing on something quite vile, 'What are those fish which keep leaping through the bow wave.'

'Them's dolphins. They're not fish, strictly speakin', cap'n. They breathe air. That's why they play around on the surface of the sea, rather than swim in its depths.'

'I don't like them – they look hungry.'

'Lord bless you,' clicked Jake, slapping his thigh with his paw, 'they won't hurt you none. It's sharks you want to worry about. A great white shark would take a stoat like you in one swaller for a starter, before his main meal of the day. See, look, that black fin out there, cuttin' the water? That's a tiger shark. They're pretty vicious too. Along with barracuda they're just about the most ferocious fish going.'

Falshed stared at the dark fin and shuddered. He hated it on board the ship, but he knew he would not last five minutes in the water either. What he wanted was his nice solid castle under his four paws. Stone. Immovable stone. Stone buried in thick clay. That's what he wanted. But he wasn't going to get it.

Falshed had already had his share of adventures. By means of his seagull scouts he had managed to follow the weasel ship on its journey including sailing to the cold north. He had narrowly escaped being roasted alive by dodos, murdered by some hamsters who lived in dismembered chesspieces and, on top of that, had stopped at one island not visited by the *Scudding Cloud*.

Right in the centre of this island was a perfectly conical mountain. There were caves in the mountain which were said by the seagulls to contain diamonds. Diamond mines!

This had been too tempting for Herk and Bare, even though Falshed had forbidden anyone to step ashore. The two badgers should have taken warning from the glass bones and skulls which littered the shoreline. They should have been worried by the fine glass sand which flashed and sparkled in the sunlight. They should have wondered about the huge pebbles which lay amongst the glass skeletons, buried in the glass sand.

The gulls had warned Falshed and the crew that if any animal *did* go ashore they were not to look back at the ship. Of course, not only did the badgers disobey Falshed's order; they also looked back. On strange territory the urge to make sure your escape route is safe is overwhelming. You can't help but glance over your shoulder to gain comfort from the sight of your ship still at anchor in the bay.

Herk and Bare were instantly turned into pillars of glass. They were there in the morning, when the rest of the ship woke. The sun shone through their clear forms. Besides their glass skeletons, you could see every glass organ inside them: liver, heart, kidneys, lungs. Their chests, however, were stained dark brown on the inside, like the bowl of a smoker's ancient briar pipe. The old tar and nicotine was a thick sludge smeared on their precious breathing tubes and lungs.

If you ignored the filthy residue from old chokies, Herk and Bare looked much finer as cut-glass figures than they ever had in life. They might have adorned the courtyard of an emperor's palace with their splendid glassiness.

But not for long. Cave birds came from the direction of the mountain and dive-bombed them with stones. The pair, tragic looks frozen on their badger faces, were shattered before the eyes of Falshed and his crew, their glass bones falling out of their broken glass shells. Over time their skeletons would be ground down by the restless sea to become the shifting glittering sands which made up the beach.

'At least they won't be dug up by grave robbers,' said Falshed, viewing all this through a spy-glass, 'and I expect in time visitors will find this foreign shore and start collecting the sand in little bottles to take home as presents from Cone Island . . .'

He then remembered his precious dragonfly brooch, given him by Sibiline and stolen by Herk and Bare. The badgers had refused to give it up, insisting it was theirs. This must also have been turned to glass. Falshed let out a gasp of dismay: he had hoped to retrieve it before returning home. Now he had no idea what he would tell Sibiline.

The sheriff was still musing on the fate of his dragonfly carving when a shout rent the air.

'Sail ho!' cried a voice from the top of the mast.

'Boat coming this way!' cried the faces on the figurehead, almost as one. 'Looks like a warship.'

The sheriff looked upwards to see a marten pointing in the direction of the sun. Falshed squinted into the light, hoping that at last they had sighted the weasels. He was sure that Sylver was having the same problems with seasickness as he was, for why should woodland weasels be made of any stronger stuff than castle stoats?

'Can you see what it is?' Falshed cried to the sailor above.

'Strange lookin' craft,' came back the call. 'I count seventeen sails. Wait a bit. It's foundering.

Looks to me like the bowsprit keeps getting tangled with the rudder!'

'What? How can that be? They're at opposite ends of the boat, aren't they?'

'Well, that's what it looks like; and I should know, because I'm a mariner.'

'Can you see who is on board?'

The look-out peered hard at the oncoming vessel. 'Seems to me that there's a beaver on board, along with a bellcat and various trades-mammals – a bootblack and baker are two of them, but I'm not sure of the others. They're all armed to the teeth with harpoons.'

Jake said firmly, 'Better stand by to repel boarders, cap'n.'

The sheriff rang a bell. 'All paws on deck! All paws on deck! Take up battle stations!'

Martens and stoats began to pour out of the hatch onto the deck. They quickly took up positions behind catapults, or in the rigging, or along the rail. Falshed had trained his stoats well and the pine martens were already swarming over the rigging, making the ship ready for an encounter. Gradually they came up alongside the other ship.

The beaver waved a harpoon in greeting. 'Where are you bound?' he called. 'Are you hunting?'

'Hunting what?' replied Falshed warily. 'Whales?'

'No – no – the Snark. Are you hunting the Snark? Have you seen the beggar anywhere?'

'Stop waving that spear thing under my nose,' cried Rosencrass; 'it's making me go cross-eyed.'

'Be quiet, figurehead. Look, beaver, I – I don't

259

know what a Snark is,' confessed the sheriff, as the two vessels sped by one another.

The beaver seemed irritated. 'It looks like a Boojum, only it isn't one.'

Falshed did not want to admit that he did not know what a Boojum was either. 'No – no – we haven't seen one of those.'

'Well, if you do . . .' the beaver began to say, but at that moment there came the sound of beating wings from above. Everyone on both ships looked up, as a shadow passed over the sun and began to descend. Wind rippled through the creature's feathers as it hurtled down towards the two vessels. It was a bird, but such a bird as Falshed had never seen before in his entire life. It was dressed in clothes that might have been designed by Sleek the otter, they were so stylish. It had several sets of cruel-looking talons as well as a long, hooked, razor-sharp beak.

'The Jubjub bird!' yelled the alarmed beaver. The butcher, baker and other tradesmammals immediately left the deck and went below. Only the bellcat and the beaver remained on deck. A hideous noise came from the bird's throat. It was like the sound of a windmill's sails that have not been oiled for over a century. It brought tears to the eyes. It put one's teeth on edge. It made one wince.

The Jubjub bird came in low over the sea. On its first pass it managed to rip all the sails on Falshed's ship to ribbons. It did the same with the sails on the beaver's boat. Its claws were like sharp sickles, which cut through the canvas with ease.

Falshed had been unsettled by the suddenness

of the attack, but now he rallied his forces. They managed to get in several catapult shots at the attacking bird as it circled the two ships. One of these shots took out a few tail feathers and the Jubjub shrieked in fury. It flew in a long loop away from the vessels, then turned and came hurtling back just above the waves.

'Steady, crew,' said Falshed in a firm voice. 'Get it in your sights. Don't fire until you see the purple bits under its front wings . . .'

This time the Jubjub was met with a hail of missiles which deflected it from its course. It swerved off to starboard at an incredible speed, oaths and menacing threats leaving its throat in a series of broken squawks.

'How do we kill it?' asked Falshed.

'Search us,' cried the bellcat and the beaver. 'You're on your own.' and with this they went below, out of harm's way – provided the Jubjub didn't sink them outright.

'Charming,' snarled Falshed, as the bird wheeled for a second run. 'In that case, if it's up to me . . .' He went forward to the bows, where a giant crossbow stood. He pushed the stoat who was standing behind it out of the way and took aim with the weapon. Falshed had panicked many times in his life, had made many mistakes through worry or nerves, but for once he had a cool head on his shoulders. Perhaps it was because he was so far away from Prince Poynt's authority. The prince had a way of making those around him jittery.

The Jubjub bird stretched its huge wings wide and came sweeping in again, its claws working

261

like scissors. Its intention was plain: to strike the stoat ship on the bows, sink it, and snatch as many mammals from the sea as it could eat in one go. Behind Falshed one or two stoats and martens cried out in fear, believing they were about to die. Certainly none of them had any faith in the sheriff, who was something of a joke amongst them.

Falshed, however, stood as solid as a rock. His keen eye looked down the sights of the crossbow. Closer and closer came the terrible bird with the well-cut, trendy clothes. The bristling shape became larger and larger, until it was almost upon them. No-one else on board would have been able to stand there, like Falshed, without firing that crossbow, or running. But Falshed stood firm, unblinking, a single claw poised on the trigger. When the bird was but a ship's length from him, the sheriff fired. The great arrow flew straight and true. It struck the Jubjub bird in the heart.

'Good shot!' yelled Guildenswine.

There was a squawk that would have shattered glass mountains. The dreadful bird's wings folded up and the creature plummeted into the sea. A huge cloud of spray went up where it struck the surface. For a short while it floated there, obviously stone dead. Its head, on the long snaky neck, lolled and bobbed on the swell. Its wings spread out to form a raft of feathers. Its great legs, with the cruel claws, stood straight up. Then the creature sank below the surface, never to rise again. Only one or two loose tail feathers marked its watery grave.

A loud cheer went up from the stoats and martens.

From the other vessel, however, came a cry of despair. 'You've *killed* the Jubjub!'

Falshed turned to see the beaver back on deck, an appalled look on his face. '*Somebody* had to do it,' he said. 'You weren't much help, ducking down below. I didn't want to kill it. It gave me no choice.'

The bellcat was there now, with the butcher and baker. 'Lordy-lord, you're for it now,' said the bellcat. 'I wouldn't be in your shoes for a Snark's eye teeth.' He looked up at the sky. 'A storm's coming on,' he said. 'The spirits of sea and air are angry now, and the land ones aren't all that happy. You'd best be prepared for your punishment, stoat. You have killed their favourite son.'

The baker and butcher nodded in agreement, while the bootblack sucked on his teeth and shivered violently.

'What else was I supposed to do?' cried Falshed. 'It was going to sink us.'

'You should have let it,' replied the beaver. 'I would've done. Now you're for it. Nothing to do with us. We didn't do anything, did we?' he asked of his companions. 'We were merely out hunting the Snark. It's you lot who are in trouble.'

With that, the bellcat hoisted a new set of sails and the other boat was off, scudding across the surface of the ocean, heading swiftly for the horizon.

'Now you've done it,' One-eared Jake said severely to the sheriff. 'If it was up to me you'd have to wear the Jubjub bird around your neck like a weight, to atone for your sin.'

The cook and crew went below, leaving Falshed

263

alone on deck. The skies lowered, dark and ominous. Lightning flashed on the horizon and a deep rumble of thunder could be heard. A waterspout, whirling and twisting, came from out of the east and disappeared into the west.

Strange portents filled the atmosphere above the ship, as the vessel drifted at the mercy of the wind, its sails in shreds. There were signs that the world was shortly coming to an end. The lonely sheriff stood on the bridge, watching the sea change from blue to grey, and the waves grow fiercer with each moment.

At that moment a streak of forked lightning flashed out of the sky, followed by a crack of thunder. The lightning caught Falshed on the whiskers and sent a jolt through him which made him shudder from head to toe. In that instant he lit up, glowing like a beacon. Then the lightning had fizzled away, and he was left standing there, miraculously still alive.

'Hey!' he said, after a few seconds. 'Hey!' He felt funny, as if he had been picked up and shaken furiously, then put down again. But more than that – it was as if he had been energized by the lightning strike, given renewed strength. He felt *powerful*. The lightning, which had spared his life, had filled him with a potency he had never experienced before. Falshed felt as if he could do anything – anything at all. In him was the strength of thousands. 'I alone am blessed,' he told himself. 'I have been chosen by the gods!'

It did not occur to him that he was standing on a wooden deck in rubber boots. Welkinites did not know of such science. These insulators had helped to save his life, but to Falshed it was all magic, all the miracle of being chosen.

Funnily enough, he didn't feel seasick any more. He shook a clenched paw at the heavens. 'You can chuck what you like at me,' he railed. 'See if I care! I killed the Jubjub bird, and I'm glad, d'you hear, glad! And I'd do it again tomorrow if need be. I'd stuff an apple in its mouth and roast it for supper if it hadn't sunk to the bottom of the ocean, so there, you cretinous spooks!'

The wind howled as if in angry reply to this blasphemy. The waves grew higher and higher. The wind became stronger and stronger. It began raining as it had never rained before, coming down in sheets. Lightning flashed all around now and the thunder cracks were directly overhead. The world had darkened as if it were night and not the middle of the day.

Finally, when he had ceased ranting at the heavens, Falshed realized what a dangerous position they were in. Opening a deck locker he took out some oilskins and put them on. Then he sounded the bell to call the crew on deck. 'All paws!' he yelled, water running from his oilskins and sou'wester. 'To your stations! There's a storm brewing. I want crew up here *now*!'

The stoat crew came up through the hatchway, frightened looks on their faces.

'What a bunch of wimps,' snarled Falshed. 'You're all too superstitious. There's nothing going to happen to us, if we don't let it. A storm is a storm. It has to be beaten. Get up that rigging and fight, you oafs.'

The stoats went up the rigging. Falshed felt fully

and truly in command now, for the first time in his life. He was confident and sure of himself. The lightning had recharged his spirit with courage and fortitude. There were no insolent looks on the faces of his stoats as he shouted out his orders. They respected him. He was the master and they the servants. That was how it should be. That was how it had been ordained.

But what had happened to the martens? Were they still cowering below?

'Step aside, stoat,' said a voice from behind Falshed. 'Get away from that wheel.'

'Wha—?' Falshed turned to see that the martens were all armed and looked mean. 'What are you talking about?' he cried.

'Don't you know a mutiny when you see it?' asked One-eared Jake, clicking his teeth. 'We're taking over the ship. We're fed up with this wild wren chase. We've been hot and cold in angry turns and we don't seem to be any nearer to this treasure you promised. It's time to call it a day.'

'But I was just getting used to this job,' snarled Falshed. 'I was just getting the feel of it.'

'Well, now you can get the feel of being clapped in irons,' growled Jake. 'Take the lubber below, me hearties. Show him where the chains be held. This is my ship now. Any stoat who tries to resist will get what his master's got. You're either for me, or you're agin me. What's it to be, the rest of you stoats? D'ye bend, or d'ye stand and die?'

'Stoats! To me!' cried Falshed. 'We'll show you martens what *real* courage is, won't we, my brave-hearts?'

The stoat marines and sailors edged cautiously

forward, at the same time baring the blades of their weapons. This rather pathetic and uncertain move had a startling effect on the martens. They seemed incensed. Whistling and jeering and issuing terrible oaths, they rushed straight at the stoats. They sliced the air with the hissing blades of their cutlasses, threatening to disembowel the first stoat or ferret who took another step forward.

The stoats stopped in their tracks.

'Lay down your arms,' growled Jake.

There was a clattering and clanging as weapons were dropped on the deck.

'You rotten cowards!' cried Falshed. 'I'll have you all clapped in irons.'

'No,' said Jake, '*I'll* have *you* clapped in irons.'

'Is that the worst you can do?' sneered Falshed.

'No,' replied Jake quietly. 'I can make you walk the plank. You'll end up in the oggin with the sharks.'

Falshed swallowed his next jeer very quickly and allowed himself to be taken below. He was joined a little later by the rest of his stoats, who had remained loyal to him – that was at least some consolation to the sheriff.

They spent a miserable time in the airless, damp confines of the forecastle, with only the beetles and bugs for company and the sound of the storm for entertainment. It was even worse when the storm died and the sun came out: they knew it was a beautiful day above, and here they were, shut in the darkness of the hold.

They were left to rot there for several days, then suddenly, one morning – or perhaps it was evening: no-one knew – there came the sounds of a struggle on deck. Eventually the noise of battle ceased. Then the hatch opened and the sunlight poured in, hurting eyes which had spent over a week in darkness. The sunlight was followed by a bird, though he did not exactly pour in: he dropped like a brick. His left eye had a black patch over it and in his left claw was a cutlass.

'Who's down here?' the bird demanded. 'Come on, show yourselves!'

'We can't,' Falshed said. 'Ironically, we're chained to the bulkhead.'

'Where's the irony?' asked the bird.

'It's what the chains are made of,' cried Falshed, clicking his teeth. The bird was silent and eventually the sheriff added, 'I've spent three days down here since I first thought of that joke – you might have the courtesy to show some amusement.'

'Oh, it was a joke, was it? I thought it was some kind of trick answer.'

The bird, who said his name was Colin, eventually had the chains taken off and Falshed and his stoats were led up on deck. There they found that the martens were prisoners of a pirate crew made up of ptarmigan and red grouse. Near by, their ship, a coracle, flew the jolly roger.

Colin, the pirate chief, said to Falshed, 'Don't I know you?'

'I don't think so,' replied Falshed with dignity. 'I'm not in the habit of consorting with pirates.'

Colin strutted up and down the deck in a threatening and menacing manner. 'I wasn't always a pirate. I once lived in an area east of Castle Storm. You sure you aren't the ferret that killed Robbie, the red grouse?'

'Ferret?' snapped Falshed, the word distasteful to his tongue. 'Ferret? I'm a stoat.'

'So you say,' replied Colin, peering at him closely with his one good eye, 'but I'm just a mountain bird. I can't tell the difference between one murderer and another. You're all covered in fur, you all have those sharp little fangs, and you all think a lot of yourselves. You certainly do. Listen to me, weasel, or whatever you are, you're a prisoner, not a prince.'

'I am the prince's High Sheriff,' Falshed said haughtily. 'I had no paw in the death of this Robbie.'

One of the red grouse shouted out, 'Naw, he's not the one. Robbie was killed by a pair of ferrets called Rosencrass and Guildenswine.'

There was a gasp from somewhere under the bows.

Colin looked round, saying, 'Who's that? Who's there?'

'No-one,' replied Falshed, not wishing to lose his valuable figurehead. 'You probably heard a dolphin come up for breath. Did you know dolphins are not fish, but mammals? You're surrounded, you know. The ocean is full of us too! Whales too – porpoises – and walruses, sea lions, seals. You don't stand a chance, you birds. Us mammals are everywhere—'

'You be quiet,' snarled Colin, turning on him and showing him the edge of his cutlass. 'You can still swing from the yardarm if I've a notion to do away with you. What are you looking at our ship for? Never seen a coracle covered in apple skin before?'

269

Falshed was indeed staring at the other vessel. Now he recalled who Colin the ptarmigan and Robbie the red grouse were. Sylver and some of his band had come across them once before. 'I remember you – you chased me into the Forest of Lost Birds! You're on your way to Rood Island, aren't you?'

'We were,' grumbled Colin, 'until we were set upon by a ship full of rats, led by a maniac called Flaggatis – a ferret like yourself, but old and crumbly, falling to bits, he was, his joints coming apart and his skin all wrinkled. He smelled too – disgusting creature. They *all* smelled.'

'Rats?' breathed Falshed, overlooking the ferret insult this time. 'Flaggatis is on the ocean too?'

'Turned me into a pirate, he did. We have no stores left. The rats took 'em all. So now we have to resort to piracy on the high seas. Sometimes even on the low seas. Pirates can't be choosy. What have you got? We need food.'

'There are plenty of stores below. You may take what you need to get you to your island, Colin. But you must harm no-one and no part of this ship. If you promise that, then you can have what you require.'

'We could just take it,' replied the ptarmigan. 'But you're right, we're not really cut out to be pirates. We haven't the heart to plunder for pillage. Or is it sack for spoils when on the ocean? Anyway, you have my word; I agree. No-one will be harmed. Now, where are these stores?'

Falshed turned a hard eye on One-eared Jake. 'This traitor will show you to the hold. I'm not sure what I'm going to do with him yet.'

'The trouble is,' said Jake practically, 'you need me and my pine martens. Your stoats couldn't crew this ship alone to save their lives.'

Falshed knew this was true, of course, but he hated to admit it to Jake. 'I might just have you thrown into the sea, Jake. We'll see how loyal your martens remain to you after that.'

'They won't work for you, no matter what.'

It was left at that. The martens had been stripped of their weapons and the stoats re-armed. Falshed could not rid himself of the martens, but he decided to keep a keen eye on them in case they tried to mutiny again.

Once the birds' stores were replenished, they boarded their coracle again. They were just about to sail away, when Colin gave a startled shout and pointed at the ship's figurehead. 'Rosencrass and Guildenswine!' he screeched. 'I thought they were dead!'

'They are, good as,' replied Falshed. 'You gave your word remember – no-one and no part of my ship. Be assured they have suffered for their crime, being trapped in wood.'

Colin glowered, staring hard at the two ferrets locked inside the figurehead. 'I have given my word,' he said, 'and I must abide by it – but if I ever see you again, you two, I shall turn you into kindling and use you to warm my wingtips of a cold evening on Rood Island, you hear?'

The two ferrets wisely remained silent.

Chapter Twenty-Six

'Sail off the port bow,' came the cry from the crow's nest, followed by an equally urgent addition: 'And sail off the starboard bow too!'

Hearing the calls from within his cabin, Sylver came hurrying up on deck. Miniver was on the bridge with Scirf, while Bryony was at the wheel. Their eyes were on two craft, one of them a windjammer, the other a warship, approaching rapidly from two different directions.

Sylver took his spy-glass from his belt and trained it on the warship. 'Leaky old tub,' he murmured. 'Looks like it's falling to bits. Hold on, it's swarming with rats! What the . . . ? They're armed to the teeth! Now – that figure in the crow's nest – why, it's – it's *Flaggatis*. It's the wizard with his rat hordes. They've come after us, even out here! Unbelievable.'

'What about the other ship, captain?' asked Miniver. 'That's coming in rather fast too.'

Sylver swung the spy-glass round and stared at the oncoming windjammer. 'Sheriff Falshed! He's standing on the bridge. Yes – stoat marines, all bristling with weapons. Pine martens. He's copied us and crewed his windjammer with martens. Nothing original about Falshed, that's for sure. You can rely on him to follow rather than to lead. What's that in front . . . ?' Sylver peered hard through the spy-glass. 'Good grief, I can see Rosencrass and Guildenswine!'

'I thought they were dead,' said Miniver.

'No, they were locked in a tree. They still are, only the tree has been carved into a ship's figure-head. They're stuck on the prow of that vessel. I can see their mouths moving. They're talking to one another, or to Falshed. How extraordinary.'

Scirf said, 'I'm impressed, cap'n, but how do we get out of this? We might be able to fight off one of them, but not two at once. What do we do now?'

'Wodehed,' replied Sylver firmly. 'It's about time that old magician worked up a decent spell for us. Get him up here on deck. At the same time I want all paws standing by their battle stations. We may have to fight.'

Miniver summoned all hands on deck to mammal their battle stations.

Down below, the 'sick' gerbil, Narky, enquired weakly what was the matter.

'Battle stations,' replied Short Oneleg in a satis-fied tone, when he came back to grab his sharp butcher's chopper. 'We're being attacked by a horde of rats – and a ship full of stoat marines – two lots. Looks like we're in for a scrap. I ain't been in a battle like this since the Sea Wars off the Windies, with Ginger Cat and his blood-thirsty crew of cutthroats and murderers.'

The ship's cook approached the gerbil's bedside and offered him the edge of the chopper. 'Feel this.

Sharp enough? Will it slit a stoat's throat, is what I'm arskin? Out with it, Narky.'

'I – I believe so, cooky. Oh, heavens, do you think they'll win? The other side, I mean?'

'Well,' replied the marten with narrowed, determined eyes, 'if they do, it'll be over my corpse, and they'll be short o'mammals afterwards, because I'm goin' to take a few with me when I go. It'll be a bloody fight, that's for sure. Ye ought to get up and arm yourself, young Narky. Better to die with blade in paw than in bed with your seaboots off.'

'They – they won't hurt a sick gerbil . . .'

'Don't you believe it. Them rats have no souls. They don't care who they kill – or when. They'd just as soon ye was lyin' in your cot, helpless, so's they can stab you through the heart without no trouble at all. An' they'll do it, believe me. I seen rats throwin' baby birds out of their nests, just to find a place to sleep for the night. Ye'd best get one of my meat cleavers and come up and hack a few before ye die.' Short Oneleg then left the gerbil alone in the half-dark.

'Ooooohhhh noooo!' moaned Narky, shaking with fear. 'I don't want to die.'

Scirf was passing by the galley and looked in. 'None of us want to do that,' he replied, pausing to scratch his beloved fleas, 'but we have to prepare for it.'

'Look,' cried Narky wildly, 'I don't feel sick any more. I'll work, I really will. But afterwards. After the battle. I can't fight. I – I'm not allowed to. It's against my religion. You'll have to protect me. You'll do that, won't you, Scirf? You'll look after me?'

Scirf was disgusted with this whining, whingeing creature. 'Listen,' he said, 'if the rats don't get you, I will. I'll come back down 'ere and throttle you with me bare claws. Now, find yourself a weapon and come up on deck. At least look as if you're ready to fight.'

The gerbil was left whimpering into his sheets. Then a cunning look came into his eye. He tore a piece off one of the sheets and looked around the galley for something to tie it to. He found a kebab stick. 'I have my weapon,' he murmured, going to the porthole and waving the white flag. 'I wonder if I ought to write something on the galley door. That'll stop them from coming in and killing me without thinking . . .'

Up on deck, things were getting interesting. The two enemy ships were closing fast. Wodehed had been called upon to produce a spell. His pride was at stake. So many times before he had not produced the goods when it came to the crunch. Or, to be more accurate, he had produced the *wrong* goods. This was his opportunity to show his mettle. This was a war between wizards – Flaggatis and himself – and if he could get something going first, so much the better. 'I'm going to raise the Kraken!' he cried dramatically. 'Raise it from the deeps!'

Mawk, trembling a little from the violence of Wodehed's words, asked, 'You sure you know what you're doing?'

'Of course not!' said Wodehed excitedly, 'but it'll be fun finding out, won't it? No-one's got a better idea. I'll raise the Kraken from its thousand-year sleep, jaws dripping with slime and encrusted with barnacles, seaweed hanging like green hair from its monstrous body, eyes aflame with fury and mouth gaping with ten thousand razor-shell teeth, and we'll see if that doesn't stop a few hearts on those enemy ships.'

'What about *my* heart?' cried Mawk. 'How's that going to keep going?'

Scirf put his forelimb around Mawk's shoulders. 'Don't pretend you're a coward, Mawky – I know you better than that. You an' me, we've been to the icy wastes of the Otherworld and back. We'll stand together, me an' you, and fight to the death. As for this ol' monster, well, we'll just spit in its eye if it comes near us, won't we?'

'I'm not brave, I'm not!' cried Mawk, distressed.

Scirf clicked his teeth in an animal chuckle, clearly refusing to believe this was not a humorous act for the benefit of the martens looking on. 'You're a card, you are, Mawk. You're such a kidder,' said the ex-dung-watcher warmly. 'Right, now let's get up on the bridge, where the best fightin' will be had. They always try to take the bridge first . . .'

Mawk stared at the oncoming enemy ships. The rat ship was closest, being a good three hundred metres nearer than Falshed's windjammer. Its mainsail had a rat's skull painted on the canvas, with elongated fangs. Above this sail, in the crow's nest, sat Flaggatis, conjuring up a strong wind to drive his ship forward towards the *Scudding Cloud*.

The warship was alive with more rodents than there were fleas in Scirf's coat. As usual, they had painted their faces to make themselves look more ferocious in battle. There were red ochre rings around their eyes and white bars across their noses. They were a formidable bunch, with their spiked collars and amulets, some with strange, dark, ugly-looking vole-leather helmets. They hung from the rigging, from the gunwales, from the yardarms. Some had scimitars and cutlasses, with which they continually sliced the air with practice strokes. Others had knives and hooks, sickles and barbed spears. One meaty-looking fellow had a mace of nails. They swarmed over the craft, eager to be let loose on the weasels.

The rats on deck were stoking fires underneath vats of what looked like boiling tar. Others were making ready the weapons to catapult this tar at the weasel-windjammer. Still others were whirling bullfrogroarers about their heads, or rattling empty skulls together, or beating skin drums. The din was eerie and frightening. Even the martens looked apprehensive.

'Here comes the first dollop!' cried Sylver, as a catapult went *twang* on the deck of the rats' ship. 'Don't let any get on your fur, or you'll regret it.'

A flaming glob of hot tar came hurtling towards them. It roared over the deck and into the ocean on the other side, narrowly missing the mainsail. Where it struck the sea great spouts of steaming water flew up and sprayed the *Scudding Cloud* from end to end.

'That was close,' cried Bryony, now trying to change course in order to avoid the next shot.

The rats made some hasty adjustments under

directions from the crow's nest and the second catapult was fired. This time the gobbet of tar was more accurate and struck one of the royals. The sail went flying out over the briny like a comet trailing its tail. It had burnt up even before it hit the sea. Again there was a hiss of hot tar hitting the cold water and a spout of steam and spray.

A great cheer went up from the rat ship. This was cut short by an accident on board. A rat who was ladling flaming-hot tar into the catapult pan spun round excitedly. He wanted to see the damage to the weasel ship but, in his haste, he managed to send drops of burning tar flying in all directions, some landing on the feet of his comrades-in-arms.

There were screams of pain as rats with scorched toes leaped up and down, some even jumping overboard to cool their claws in the cool sea. These ship-jumpers were left behind in the wake; those on board were tossed down the hatch, where they would cause less confusion.

'First blood to us!' yelled Sylver. 'Self-inflicted!'

Now the rat ship was in range of the *Scudding Cloud*'s catapults. Bags of sand went arcing through the space between the ships. The weasels were more accurate than the rats and the bags landed plumb in the middle of the main deck, bowling the rats over like ninepins. One bag landed in the middle of a tar pot, burst, and thus smothered it, putting it out of action for the rest of the battle.

'Ready on the crossbows!' cried Sylver. 'Shoot!'

The giant crossbows were fired, sending their

flaming arrows skimming over the blue waters. They thudded into the walls of the rat ship and fire attacked its rotting timbers. Rats grabbed buckets of water and poured them over the sides of the ship to douse the flames.

'How's that spell coming along, Wodehed?' yelled Sylver. 'Are you nearly there?'

'Almost, almost,' cried Wodehed. 'Now you've interrupted me – I might have to start again.'

Falshed's ship had slowed almost to a halt now and was waiting further off, its sea anchor out. Sylver knew that the sheriff would probably keep out the way for a while: after all, which ship should he attack? He had no love of rats, nor they of him. If they both defeated the weasels, they would only set upon each other immediately afterwards.

The rats would probably fight both Falshed and Sylver at once, for rats go berserk and recognize no allies in the heat of battle. They are just as likely to kill friends who get in their way as enemy mariners and marines. Creatures go down like chopped celery.

Falshed had quite sensibly decided to hold off and see who emerged the victor. If the rats won, he would quietly sail away and report that he had destroyed Sylver on the high seas. If Sylver won, then the sheriff would engage him in combat, knowing that the weasels would already be exhausted and their ship damaged from the first fight. He could not lose either way.

'Watch out! Watch out!' came the cry, sweeping through the rigging of the *Scudding Cloud*. The rats had a secret weapon which, now close enough to the weasel ship, they unleashed. It was a ladder with a spike at the top. This dastardly contraption had been strapped to their main mast, but was now untied by Flaggatis. The ladder fell over the gap between the ships, the spike burying itself in the bridge of the *Scudding Cloud*.

''Ware rats, 'ware rats,' the cry went up.

The rodents now began swarming along the ladder towards the weasel vessel. This vanguard were the terrible berserkers everyone feared, high as kites on the smell of blood and tar. Mawk gave a screech of terror, but was rooted to the spot, unable to run because his legs had siezed up.

The doughty Scirf jumped forward onto the ladder, and ran out along it. There he stood, between the ships, ready to defend the *Scudding Cloud* on his own. The rats would have to pass him to board her and he looked determined to stay where he was. 'Come up behind me,' he called to his friend Mawk, 'and when I fall, you take my place!'

Mawk was so used to following Scirf's suggestions that he jumped up on the ladder without thinking. He soon realized his mistake, however, and would have turned and gone back, except that Alysoun had jumped up behind him. He could not move forward or back. He would have to stay there, as if he were some hero, to the bitter end.

Scirf glanced behind him and saw that Mawk and Alysoun were there. These three stood alone, defending the bridge against the might of the rat hordes. 'And how can weasel die better,' cried

Scirf gallantly, 'than facing fearful odds, for the woodlands of his parents and the forests of his gods?'

'Nice bit of poetry,' snarled Mawk, infuriated with both Scirf and himself, 'but we're going to be shark meat soon.'

Chapter Twenty-seven

For the next quarter of an hour a desperate struggle took place on the ladder. Scirf stood his ground, with the other two backing him up. The rats came rushing towards the bridge of the *Scudding Cloud*, skipping from rung to rung. Scirf's love of singlestick, practised in the glades of Halfmoon Wood under the tutorage of Lord Haukin, stood him in good stead. It had strengthened his sword limb and given him skill. One after the other rats fell screaming to plop into the waters below.

It was fortunate that, because the ladder was so narrow, the rats could only attack him one at a time. They came, big and small, desperate to be heroes of the hour. One huge fellow with a long, naked tail almost got the better of the weasel by using his sheer weight to barge past, but Mawk thrust under Scirf's right forelimb with his sword and stabbed the bold fellow in the shoulder, causing him to bellow in pain and retreat in haste. In so doing the big rat knocked several others off the ladder, into the foaming briny below, and thus assisted the weasels in their fight.

'Good one, Mawk,' praised Scirf. 'That great lump of lard nearly had me – but you saw him off.'

Missiles were continually streaking from the decks of one ship towards the other. There were balls of fire, which no-one knew how to put out, and great rocks which crashed through the decks. Arrows whizzed and skimmed through the air, striking the woodwork and sails. Bits of ship fell down, bits of ship were sent flying, bits of ship sank to the bottom of the ocean.

During this mêlée Wodehed had been working up his spell, chanting incantations and casting powders into a pan, which fizzed and sparkled and flared in various colours. Finally he gave a shout: 'IT IS DONE!' he cried.

His call was so loud and so urgent that the fighting ceased on all sides. Everyone stared at the wizard. Wodehed looked exhausted. All his energy had been spent on the task of raising the Kraken. He sank against the ship's rail, hanging there like a wet rag, staring at a spot in the ocean just beyond Flaggatis's ship, near to where Sheriff Falshed's craft was moored to its sea anchor.

After a few minutes' silence, in which nothing happened, Flaggatis screamed from his crow's nest, 'Get on with it – nothing's going to happen! That fool couldn't raise a cloud of dust with his foot.'

But Flaggatis was wrong.

The space between the rat ship and the stoat ship suddenly began to boil. Bubbles rose and burst on the surface. They were full of foul-smelling gas, trapped there, no doubt, since prehistoric times. The sea around became discoloured. Something was stirring the primeval mud deep down below, sending it up to the surface along with ancient bits of seashells, rotting weed and pieces of dead crab. The surface of the water was now swimming with decayed, stinking sea creatures trapped in the mud since time began.

'Something's happening down there!' cried Sylver. 'I think Wodehed has finally done it. Wodehed has raised the Kraken.'

The magician himself was looking slightly awed. Was it true? Had he at last worked a spell to perfection?

Yes, he had.

The Kraken rose roaring to the surface, all eyes and mouth. It was as large as a hundred ships. It was monstrous and slimy, with a great bulbous body covered in lumps and warts. There were seventeen heads on seventeen long serpentine necks, and each of the heads had seven mouths full of massed needle teeth. There were fins projecting from every part of its ugly torso, covered in spines which dripped with seaweed and speared fish.

There were eyes, big bulging eyes, in every part of its grotesque form, with spikes for eyelashes. Jets of water and steam hissed from holes along its flanks, sounding its fury. It was a hideous, awe-inspiring creature.

'Oh – my – Gawd!' cried Mawk. 'It's looking at me!'

'It's looking at *everyone*,' whispered Bryony.

'Don't move,' cried Wodehed in tremulous tones. 'It can't see. It's been under the mud so long it's gone blind. It can probably sense movement, though, in the air, in the water. And it can hear. Just keep still, don't talk, and it probably won't attack you.'

Even as he spoke one of the heads swung round in the direction of the voices. Mawk gulped and the head shot forward, closer to him, as if searching for the owner of that sound. Mawk-the-doubter, who doubted the wizardry of Wodehed no longer, hardly dared to breathe. He could hear his own heart pounding in his ears and was sure the Kraken could hear it too. It sounded so loud in this still atmosphere.

Perhaps to keep his spirits up, Rosencrass began whistling softly. His mate, Guildenswine, rebuked him sharply. 'Shut up!' she hissed. Seventeen monstrous heads swivelled on seventeen snaky necks, to stare at Falshed's ship. The sheriff was trembling from head to paw. Those near him saw him close his eyes and knew he was wishing himself a long way away from this place where horrible monsters dwelt.

In shouting out a warning, of course, Wodehed had revealed the same secrets to the other two ships, whose stoats, rats, ferrets and pine martens were trying to stand as still as death, but many trembled in their armour.

The rats in the water, however, were less fortunate. They had to keep swimming to stay afloat and their movements were detected. These unhappy creatures were picked from the sea, wriggling and screaming, by several Kraken heads working at once, as if the creature were plucking ripe damsons from a tree. *Crunch! Crunch!* Each rat was chewed quickly, bones, skin and all. Only the hairless tails were severed and spat from the creature's foul mouths. Several more crunches later, a few swallows, and most of the rats were gone for ever, down throat shafts to the bottom of the deep black pits.

The Kraken then began swimming in tight circles, vacuuming the water in front of it, siphoning it down its many throats and spurting it out again in jets. They could see what it was doing. It was dragging the immediate area for any swimming rats it might have missed. It found one, a fellow who had wisely been floating motionless on his back. His body was snatched by one of the mouths, soon to become a mushy-red paste. To the horror of the watchers his tail, naked of any hair, hung twitching out of the corner of the Kraken's mouth. It remained there, stuck on one of the pronged teeth, as a witness to the monster's greed.

The Kraken, its hunger still not satisfied, rolled on its back, revealing a ghastly fish-white under-side covered in barnacles, limpets, hermit crabs and other parasites. Ugly little rock creatures scuttled here and there, snatching at small stranded fish. Mudskippers slipped and slid from one slimy crevice to another. Moray eels worked their heads through holes, peering out with tiny malevolent eyes. Spider crabs ran deli-cately on spiny legs, looking for refuge from invisible predators. Sea snakes strangled them-selves, rolling and writhing around fleshy projections on the Kraken.

It was a world in its own right, the Kraken, harbouring thousands of other creatures which lived in the creases and hollows of its skin. There were bits of partly-digested fish, whose bony protuberances and spiny shells had worked their way up from the monster's many stomachs to its various necks, bulging and bursting through like ripe boils. There were fronds of green weed, flowing like hair from its skin.

Feverishly, while on its back, its many heads under the water looking for fish to eat, the three ships made ready to depart. They wanted to be away from this loathsome creature from the primeval mud before it rolled back up again. Mawk was quietly reprimanding Wodehed for raising such a disgusting animal from the ocean's depths in the first place, while Wodehed himself was feeling rather proud of his achievement.

Flaggatis was hastily calling up the winds to drive his ship away from the deadly monster. He did not seem to care whether he conjured storms and squalls, so long as it would drive his vessel away quickly.

Falshed had already ordered the sea anchor to be taken in and was raising sail.

Short Oneleg, on the *Scudding Cloud*, had hacked away the ladder which joined them to the rat ship. Miniver was quietly issuing instructions under the direction of Captain Sylver. Soon the three ships were ready to depart – in fact Falshed's craft was streaking away, running with the wind; there was already a good distance between it and the monster.

At that moment the Kraken decided to turn over again and rolled, heads up, to the surface. Sea water streamed down from its body, many fins and several necks. It heard rats, pine martens and weasels running everywhere. The rats, being the closest, were eaten first. All movement suddenly stopped again, the mammals caught in mid-stride. It was like a game of statues, except that this was no game; a matter of life and death.

Flaggatis's magic was working now: the winds were getting stronger, wheeling down from the north. There was a swirling in the air. Spray was being whipped up from the wavetops, which had turned a choppy white. In the midst of this impending storm, the Kraken was busy trying to hold its position in the currents, its senses tuned to movement. Most of its heads were now very high in the air, like flowers on the ends of thick stalks, looking to snatch wild seabirds flying overhead.

Finally a storm arrived from one direction and a squall from the other. Ships and sea monster were blown apart as even more formidable powers were brought into headlong collision. Nothing can withstand the force of nature when it runs into itself. The rat ship was hurled to the west, the monster dived once more to the ocean deeps, and the weasel ship was taken on the crest of a great roller surging eastwards.

Once more the weasels had escaped their arch enemies. Though they had to weather the high winds and waves, they were now getting used to the vagaries of the ocean. They set to as one mammal and pitched in to ride out the storm. In a few hours it was all over and they were free of both Flaggatis and Falshed.

'I had no idea we were being chased,' Sylver

said. 'We must keep a keen eye out for both ships in future. We can't rely on Wodehed's unpredictable magic. He's as likely to conjure up a rhubarb pie as a monster next time.'

Wodehed should have been miffed by this remark but he had to admit that there was some truth in it. Too many times, he had failed to produce the goods. This time he had been successful, but it might never happen again in a lifetime.

'Just the same,' said Sylver, coming over to the magician, 'we owe you our pelts this time. You did excellent work there, old friend, and I'm very grateful. What say we show our appreciation for Wodehed and his magic?'

The crew gave the magician three hearty cheers and Scirf thumped him on the back.

Wodehed clicked his teeth nervously. 'It wasn't difficult, really,' he replied modestly.

'It was more difficult than anything I had to do.' This was praise indeed from Sylver. Wodehed felt quite overwhelmed by it all.

Once the storm was over Scirf and Sylver inspected the ship for damage. When they reached the forecastle, they found a number of messages scrawled on the galley door:

I SURRENDER.
I ACTUALLY LIKE RATS A LOT.
I WAS KIDNAPPED BY SYLVER.
HURRAH FOR STOATS!

Around the edge of the doorway were white flags.

As the door opened a voice came from within the galley. 'Gerbils in here, gerbils in here! We're rats really, but in our country we call ourselves gerbils. I actually have some real rat blood in my veins – my great-grandfather was a rat on my mother's side. It's at times like these, when we're all fighting weasels, that rats should stick together, eh? Eh?'

Scirf stepped into the galley to find Narky hiding behind a thick mattress. When he saw Sylver come in behind Scirf, the gerbil groaned, as if in pain. 'I'm not well. I've got this headache . . .'

'You were well enough to write messages on the door,' said Sylver.

'Ah, yes – I wanted – I wanted to protect your galley from vandalism. You know what these rats can be like with private property. Smash anything, just for kicks, they will. I hoped to avert any tragedy like that. You should thank me for policing your galley during the fighting. Rats tried to get in the porthole but I fought them off, with valour.'

'Yet you invited them into the galley just a moment ago,' said Scirf, 'not knowing it was *us*,'

'I'm not well, I told you,' moaned the gerbil, lying down on the floor. 'I told you, I have this brain fever. It makes me say things I don't want to say. "Gerbils eat garbage." There, I didn't want to say that, but it just came out. "Narky is a twit." There, you see, I just can't help it. "Scirf is a flea-ridden son of a dung-beetle." Oh, heavens, there I go again – sorry, Scirf, I'm just speaking in tongues. I'm not very bright.'

'I'll give you some tongues, my lad,' said Sylver.

'How would you like a taste of the cat? That's got a few dozen tongues which will make you smart when they lash your back.'

'Have you no heart, captain? Can't you see I'm unwell, lying here, my mind running amok. My spirit is feverish too. I'm running a temperature, inside and out. Look, feel my head, it's like there's a raging bonfire inside.' The gerbil choked back a sob.

'One of these days,' Scirf warned, 'you really will be ill, and no-one will listen to you. You've heard the story of the weasel who cried "Human!" once too often in jest. No-one believed him when it really happened and he ended up on a gibbet.'

However nothing they said had any effect on the gerbil, so they left him to his wiles again. The pair went up on deck to fetch the ironsmiths and carpenters, setting them to work on the repairs. Then both went up on the bridge to discuss navigation. When they were back on course for Dorma, Sylver turned to Scirf and said, 'You know, I'd forgotten that story about the jack who cried "Human!"'

'Yes, well, there's a lot of truth in those old tales.'

'But we're actually out here looking for humans, trying to find them, to make them return.'

Scirf nodded, looking out over the sea for a while. 'I know what you're trying to say, Sylver, but it's like this: just because they was bad once doesn't mean they'll be bad again. This time humans and animals has got to get together to make a start on the right paw. This time we've got to learn to tackle problems together, instead of separately – or, even worse, one lot working against the other.

'We're doin' the right thing, captain. We've just got to hope they do the right thing, too.'

Chapter Twenty-Eight

Lord Haukin was deeply concerned. All was not well on Welkin. Reports coming in from outside Fearsomeshire, the county he ruled, claimed that the sea walls were deteriorating fast. There were floods everywhere. These were not life-threatening at the present, but it it would not be long before there was a serious breach in the dykes. Only the day before, a ferret who lived in an old boat on the west coast woke in the morning to find himself quite a long way inland. His rotten old tub had been carried there during the night and deposited on the side of a hill.

'Culver,' he said to his loyal servant and friend, 'we must do something.'

'We stoats and weasels can't do much with our small claws,' Culver replied. 'The creatures who could probably help us the most are the coypus. They're used to digging holes in the mud of river banks. They've got short forelegs with powerful claws which they use to dig with. We must round up all the coypus in Fearsomeshire and try to patch up some of those leaks. It'll only be a temporary job, it's true, but perhaps we can hold the sea back long enough – until Sylver returns with the humans.'

'Do we have any coypus?' enquired the absent-minded lord; 'I don't believe I've ever met one.'

'That's because you don't live on a river bank my lord,' explained Culver patiently. 'Perhaps we should go out and talk to one. These coypus, they're rodents really, from a far distant land called Soothmerica.'

'Good heavens, did they swim all the way here?'

'No, I believe the humans brought them here in ships.'

'Rodents, you say?' said the lord, inspecting his collection of bottles, which covered the study tables. 'But not hostile ones?'

'Oh, no, my lord. They're quite friendly.'

'How will I recognize one.'

'You can't miss 'em,' said Culver. 'They're often a metre long, from tip to tail . . .'

'Four times as long as a weasel? Dear me.'

' . . . their coats are yellow-brown with short white fur surrounding the mouth. They have a superficial likeness to the rat, my lord, but there the comparison ends, for they are more like otters than rats in their habits. The most striking thing about them is their front teeth, which are bright orange in colour – quite startlingly so.'

Lord Haukin furrowed his brow. 'Really, how extraordinary. I should like to meet one of these fellows. Is it possible?'

'It would mean an expedition to the eastern angles of the county.'

'Why, that's splendid,' cried Lord Haukin. 'I've been cooped up in this study with my precious bottles for too long. I love their beautiful green glass, but one can have too much of one's hobby.

Best to keep it special, by doing little and often, that's my motto.'

'Yes, my lord,' agreed Culver.

Lord Haukin continued, 'It's time I was out and about in my new county. Stoats and weasels here don't know what I look like. Old Lord Ragnar was a nasty piece of work. I expect they hate the stoat lords here because of him. I understand he would rather flog a weasel than give it work. I must correct the impression they have of stoats.'

'Lord Ragnar (may his name rot in the fastness of some obscure region north of nowhere),' snarled Culver, who was not normally given to such rancour, 'was the worst stoat ever to leave his poor mother's nest. He was singlepawedly responsible for the deaths of thousands of peasant weasels in this county. He turned them out of their hovels in mid-winter, simply to provide store rooms for game he had shot. Those weasels froze to death, or starved, in blistering ice storms, blinding blizzards, trying to claw their way into the castle walls.'

'Dear me, the castle would have been frozen solid in winter. Are you sure old Raggy did this sort of thing? I know he was a rough fellow, – always was at school. Used to knock us about a bit, did Raggy.'

'My lord, you yourself have said – when Lord Ragnar was alive – that they ought to have put him down at birth.'

'Have I? Good lord. It's this memory of mine. Now that the old chap has gone, he seems to have improved somewhat, in my mind. If you say he was as bad as that, then he must have been. Anyway, what was I saying . . . ?'

'You were saying it would be nice to get out and about in the county so that you can correct the bad impression the local Fearsomeshire serfs have of their lord.'

'Yes, yes. Get my staff, Culver. And a warm mouse-skin cloak, I suppose. The winds can be pretty fierce in the eastern angles. I understand they shout a lot there, to make themselves heard above the noise of the wind. When the wind drops, they still continue shouting. Most disconcerting.'

Culver did as he was bid. He knew exactly where to look for the staff and cloak, having put them away himself. Lord Haukin was always losing things and it was only Culver and the other servants at the Great Hall who knew where things were. Once Lord Haukin was ready, Culver put on his vole-skin boots and joined the lord in the coach yard.

They set off together down the long, winding, dusty road which led to the eastern angles. Each time the pair approached a village there would be startled activity. Weasel peasants would run hither and thither, fetching fern leaves to strew in their lord's path.

Lord Haukin disapproved of this pointless exercise. 'You there,' he called to one weasel, standing in the middle of the second village square. 'Yes, you, that fellow working the water pump on the mouse-trough. Come over here, will you?'

The poor weasel, dressed in a dirty leather cap and wide cracked leather belt, came trembling towards his stoat lord. 'I didn't do it, sire,' he burbled. 'It was the others – they made me do it. What've I done?'

'Don't take on so, fellow,' replied Lord Haukin. 'As far as I know you haven't done anything – anything wrong, that is. Who's that jill over there, with the weasel kitten in her forelimbs? Standing in the doorway of that hovel. Is that your mate?'

'Yes, sire, but she ain't done nothink wrong, neither.'

'No, I'm sure she hasn't. Look, take this.' Lord Haukin took a silver groat from his pouch. It was more than the weasel would earn in a year. He placed it in the weasel's claw. 'What I want you to do is run ahead of me and tell all the villages in our path that we are coming past, but we *don't* want them stopping their useful toil to cut ferns, just to give me a softer place to tread. D'you understand, fellow?'

'Yes, sire, you want ferns to be cut for a soft path.'

'No, no,' said Lord Haukin, beginning to get irritated, 'that's *not* what I want.'

'Dock leaves, then? Or some nice bird feathers?'

Culver interrupted. 'Listen, weasel, we don't want anything on the road – nothing at all – do you hear?' He tapped the peasant's skull with his claw. 'My lord does not like dead foliage littering the road. It's untidy. You're to tell them not to do it. Understand?'

'I think so,' said the unhappy serf. 'I won't get into trouble, telling them not to do it, will I? Lord Ragnar used to cut off weasels' heads if they didn't all come out and lay ferns and praise his name and throw blooms at him. He said if weasels didn't throw flower heads, he would throw some weasel heads . . .'

'Well, this lord is different. Can your jill do without you for a couple of days, while you preform this task?' asked Lord Haukin. 'She does not require your presence in the village in order to put food on the table and water in the glass?'

'Eh? Doesn't she?' asked the weasel, looking to Culver in panic. 'Why doesn't she?'

Culver said patiently, 'Can she feed your kittens without you being here?'

'Oh, yes, o' course.'

'Then off you go, but don't spend that silver groat all at once.'

The serf went trotting off, remarkably swiftly for such an undernourished creature.

After this villagers just turned out to give Lord Haukin a ragged cheer as he went past. The old lord did not know whether they meant it, but he could not stop it so he allowed it to continue. He also promised them that he would try to improve conditions in their villages, with better houses and more land for the tenant farmers. They looked at him incredulously. He could not blame them, after they had lived so long under the iron paw of Lord Ragnar.

Finally, after much walking, Lord Haukin and Culver arrived in the eastern angles. Here they began searching for coypus. After a day's roaming over marshes and along river banks, they finally found an elderly coypu patching up his home.

'Excuse me, sir,' said Lord Haukin, 'I believe you are a coypu.'

The old gentlemammal showed his orange-enamelled teeth to confirm this fact.

'The fact is,' continued Lord Haukin, 'we were expecting to find rather more of you. I was told there were dozens of coypu in this part of the country.'

'Gone, all gone,' cried the elderly coypu in a crude country accent.

'Gone where?'

'Prince Poynt's got 'em. Building a causeway, they are. Prince wants it finished before winter.'

'Ah, they're at Castle Rayn? What a pity. We've come all this way to ask them to help us, and we find they're at the castle. Well, thank you, sir, for the information. We'll have to be on our way rather quickly now, to the prince's castle.'

'Ar – good luck to ye.'

They left the coypu slapping mud on his riverbank home and made their way westwards again. When they arrived at the shores of the lake which surrounded Castle Rayn they found the coypus hard at work, building the earth bridge to the castle. The rodent in charge was a big burly jill, who greeted Lord Haukin with a hearty slap on the back which nearly sent his teeth flying from his mouth.

'Heard of you,' she said. 'You're the new lord in our county. Good news, of course. The last one, now he was a bad 'un, but no-one's said a thing against you.'

'Glad to hear it,' said Lord Haukin. 'But tell me, how long are you planning to work on this causeway? We desperately need your assistance to plug up a few sea walls. There are reports coming in from all over that the dykes are giving way.'

She told him she was committed to the work until it was finished. It appeared to be a long way from completion. They were building it of sticks, birch twigs and mud, ten centimetres wide – just wide enough to carry creatures like stoats and weasels. It was as yet only three centimetres long. By the time it was finished half the country would be covered in water. This was not a prospect which bothered coypus, but it worried Lord Haukin no end.

'The only way we could stop work now,' she said, 'would be if Prince Poynt let us go.'

Lord Haukin took a ferry across to the castle, with Culver by his side. The ferryweasel grumbled about the coypus putting him out of business. Once there was a bridge there would be no need for ferries.

'Not their fault,' said Culver. 'It's Prince Poynt who's ordered the building of the causeway.'

Once at the castle they paid the ferryweasel and requested an audience with Prince Poynt. Lord Haukin was not a favourite with the prince, so they waited more than an hour. (It was only when Sibiline discovered Lord Haukin waiting in the outer chamber that anything was done.) Culver was told to wait there while Lord Haukin was bustled into Prince Poynt's presence. Sibiline was there, and Pompom, the prince's jester, and Jessex, a noblestoat.

Pompom leapt up when he saw a visitor enter the room, eager to whop someone with his inflated mouse's bladder on a stick, but when he saw it was Lord Haukin he changed his mind. Lord Haukin was likely to give him a clip around the ear. Lord Haukin did not enjoy tomfoolery when visiting the prince.

'My liege!' cried Lord Haukin.

When Lord Haukin was not around, Prince Poynt often got to thinking he did not like the elderly stoat. Haukin was always censuring bad behaviour at the castle. The Thane of Fearsome-shire, late of Elleswhere, had too many morals and principles for the royal stoat. Haukin was a bit like a stern uncle, who only had to look at the prince to make him feel guilty. When Haukin was around there was no fun to be had in games like baiting kitchen weasels.

No, Prince Poynt had always preferred the company of stoats like Lord Ragnar. Raggy would as soon spike a kitchen weasel as not. The blustering old ruffian could quaff a gallon of honey dew at one sitting, begin an argument with a neighbouring knight, and end up stabbing someone (fortunately not always fatally) with his dinner fork. It was one reason why the prince did not allow knives at the banquet table. Too many of his knights would end up dead at the end of a meal.

However, today Lord Haukin looked really genial, as if he were quite pleased to see the prince.

'Yes, Lord Haukin? To what do we do owe the favour of this visit? What do you require of me?'

'What do you get when you take the "uff" out of buffoon?'

The prince squirmed uneasily in his white ermine fur and blinked rapidly. He had the distinct feeling he was being insulted, but he could not work out how. 'I beg your pardon?'

'Boon, my liege. I require a boon.'

The prince felt he was not being very bright, but why should Lord Haukin come to him for such a thing? 'You – you want me to give you a *bone*?'

Lord Haukin's voice became a little stiff. 'I said "boon", not "bone". A favour, my liege.'

'Oh, I thought you were talking posh, the way you do sometimes, Haukin. Yes, you do, you know. Boon. Oh, I get it now. Leave the "uff" out of buffoon.' He turned to his jester. 'You should think of good ones like that for me. I'd like to be first to say witty things like that.'

Pompom scowled, though not in the direction of the prince.

'So,' said the prince, making sure Jessex and Sibiline were near by in case he had to refuse Lord Haukin his request, 'what is it you want?'

'My liege, you have all those coypus working for you, building a causeway to the castle. An admirable scheme, I'm sure, and I'm glad to see you're working so hard for the common good. However, I should like to borrow the coypus for a while, if you would not mind them ceasing work on the bridge, just for a short period while they are with me.'

'Eh? What do you want them for?'

'I want them to assist in repairing the sea walls. There is sea water seeping through everywhere. If we don't make do and mend until the humans get here, there won't be any Welkin left. Only the humans can make a proper job of it, with blocks of stones and the like, but the coypus could block up those apple-sized holes which are appearing in the banks.'

The prince puffed himself up. 'No Welkin left? Oh, come now, Haukin. There'll always be some little bits, here and there.'

'At worst,' said Sibiline, 'we shall become an archipelago.'

The prince whispered into the ear of Jessex, 'What's that?'

'A group of islands, my liege,' murmured the noblestoat.

'Yes,' cried the prince loudly, 'we can do no worse than become a group of islands.'

'Prince Poynt, Princess Sibiline,' replied Lord Haukin patiently, 'whether you like it or not the humans will be coming home soon. Will you want to face them, knowing you have deliberately allowed the sea walls to crumble? What will they think of stoats when they find you did nothing in their absence to stem the flooding? I think they will be very disappointed in you, my liege.'

Prince Poynt turned to his sister and said nervously, 'He's trying to frighten me, isn't he?'

'He has a good argument there, brother,' said Sibiline, 'if it's true about the humans returning. But perhaps it isn't. So some weasels have set out in a ship to find the humans. It's by no means certain that the mission will be successful. And even if they do come back, I for one am not going to yield up my power just like that, to someone who abandoned it wilfully many years ago, leaving it to us animals to sort out their mess.'

'No – see, Haukin – we don't think it will happen.'

Lord Haukin looked severely into the eye of the quivering prince. Lord Haukin was Moses confronting Pharaoh. He was a stoat whose bushy eyebrows were awesome, when he wanted them to be, and those under his glare usually wilted. 'Oh, it will happen all right,' he said, 'I promise you that. The humans will be here soon. In which case I will wash my paws of you. When they come with their bows and arrows, their animal traps, their snares, I shall point to you, my liege, and say, "He is the stoat responsible for allowing the sea to eat away at our homeland. Take him and do with him what you will." "Oh, is he?" they will say. "Well, we'll see how he likes hanging by his back legs from a wire fence."'

'There he goes again, sis, trying to frighten me,' squealed the prince.

'Your brother, King Redfur,' went on Lord Haukin, 'would never have allowed such a thing to happen. He was not much of a king, but he did respect the land. He would never let the sea take half his kingdom from him without a fight.'

'Don't use my brother's name in vain!'

'I'm telling you truthfully what I believe would be his reaction to the crisis. King Redfur would have given me the coypus I require the moment I explained the problem to him. I would not have had to waste half a day persuading him that they were necessary. I always said you were not half the stoat your brother was, despite his gross failings.'

'There he goes, insulting me again.'

Sibiline shook her head. 'Let him have the coypus, for heaven's sake, brother, so things can

304

return to normality around here. He's right. We can't allow the sea to take half our assets, no matter what. The human thing we can deal with if it ever arises, but we must stop the sea from encroaching any further on our territory . . .'

The prince looked to Jessex, but received no encouragement there. Not many of the noble-stoats would gainsay Lord Haukin, whose brain power was renowned throughout the land; nor would they oppose the prince's sister, who never forgave anyone for anything and only dropped grudges once she had got her own back. Sibiline getting her own back was something to be feared.

'Well, what about my causeway?' cried the prince, recalling that he had sent Falshed to destroy the woodland weasels before they found the humans. 'I'm a prisoner in my own home.'

'Just as well, I should have thought,' said the wily Haukin, 'with the banshee about.'

'The what?'

'The Queen of Death. She has been seen in the forests hereabouts of late, looking for victims. One shriek from her lips and you dry up like a puffball, burst, and blow away in the wind . . .'

'You're just trying to—'

'GIVE ME THE BLASTED COYPUS,' thundered Lord Haukin, fed up with the game.

Prince Poynt went all meek. 'Oh, all right, but bring them back soon.'

Lord Haukin and Culver left the castle, armed with a parchment which ordered the coypus to obey the commands of the bearer. They took the ferry back across the lake and met with the burly jill coypu, who stopped work on the causeway immediately and ordered her gang of labourers to follow Culver. Culver split the wallers into several groups, each under a weasel from Fearsomeshire, and each group set out to repair a certain part of the sea wall. Of course, this was simply a short-term patch-up job, but Lord Haukin, was certain the humans would be back soon to do the task properly.

Chapter Twenty-Nine

In the Cobalt Sea the *Scudding Cloud* was entering a magical stretch of water known as the Spell-bound Straits. It was in these waters that enchanted islands, including Dorma Island, were located – the Island of Toad Ghosts; the Island of Skipping Creatures; the Isle of Upturned Trees, whose roots were the first of the plants to drink the scarce rain because they were on top of the tree, not at the bottom; the Land of Blazing Yellow Hares (hares who ran so fast their fur caught fire), and many, many more.

The weasels had indeed found the area in which Dorma Island lay, but there was a problem: the enchanted islands, unlike most pieces of land, did not stay in one place. They were all *floating* islands, which might be here one day and somewhere else the next. They drifted around in a dreamscape, their bases a living mass of seaweed on which soil had collected and trees had grown, forming each individual island. In the weed lived thousands of eels, which propelled the islands around.

In the Spellbound Straits there were also a number of fantastical ships of curious design to be found. Almost immediately upon entering these strange waters, which were a cold green in colour and very, very deep, the *Scudding Cloud* came across a strange craft. It had the appearance of a giant copper kettle, with handle, spout and a hole for the lid. Fixed to the handle of the kettle were sails made by bulrush leaves woven into mats. The kettle sailed leisurely past the *Scudding Cloud*, every so often belching smoke from the spout. There was obviously a fire in the bottom of the kettle, for the water around the craft was bubbling and steaming with the heat it was generating.

'Ahoy there!' cried Miniver, as the weird craft passed by. 'Anyone aboard?'

A moment later a head popped up, followed by several more heads, until the kettle's hole was jammed with lean heads.

'Did you hear what I said?' asked Miniver, as the kettle-craft slowed and turned to keep pace alongside the weasels' ship.

'Who are you?'

The heads all turned to look at one another, as if they were not certain themselves who they were. Then one of them elected itself spokesmammal. 'We're meerkats! Cousins to the mongoose! What are you?'

'We're weasels from the land of the Welkin, accompanied by a crew of pine martens.'

Another of the meerkats spoke in agitated tones. 'This is our kettle. We found it. You can't make us give it back.'

Sylver, who had been standing by Miniver all the while, now took over negotiations. 'We – we're not interested in your kettle – we—' He got no further.

308

'Not-interested-in-our-kettle?' repeated the astonished meerkat. 'Why, this is a very fine kettle – the best money can buy – why would you not be interested in it? It's probably an antique if you did but know it. Are you an expert in kettles? I think not. I have met kettle experts and they certainly don't look like weasels.'

'I'm not an expert in anything,' said Sylver, becoming slightly irritated. 'I simply—'

'Oh, we can see that. Not an expert in *anything*. That's quite obvious to us. I suppose you think you're clever, recognizing the kettle under its disguise as a ship. Well, it's not so clever, because we didn't bother to hide the spout, though it could be a teapot. How do you know it's not a teapot?'

'Teapots are not usually made of metal,' said Sylver through gritted teeth, realizing he would have to be patient if he wanted information out of these meerkats, whose heads were now bobbing up and down, producing a very comical effect. 'I can see it's a kettle and I acknowledge that it's a very good one.'

'I should think you jolly well would.'

'So,' said Sylver, 'where are you bound?'

'Ah,' cried one of the meerkats, 'I knew you'd trip yourself up soon. You'd like to know *that*, wouldn't you? Well, what if we don't want to tell you?'

'That's up to you,' replied Sylver, who was aware that his crew were clicking their teeth in great hilarity at this exchange. 'If you don't want to, then I respect your wishes.'

There followed a buzz of conversation between the meerkat heads, punctuated by some belches of smoke from the spout of the kettle, then one of them spoke again.

'We're sailing to Byzantium,' said the meerkat in a very serious tone. 'We've heard that it's a nice place. It's a fabulous city, you know, full of gold and jewels and learning – and equally important in the overall scheme of things. You – you wouldn't know in which direction it lies, would you?'

'Scirf,' cried Sylver, having something to bargain with at last, 'fetch me my charts.'

Scirf hurried away and returned with an exercise book. He and Sylver opened it together on the deck and whipped through the pages. 'Billingsgate, Brighton . . . ah, here, look – Byzantium. Yes, it's south-east of here, in the Meditation Sea. You can't miss it, so long as you head for a cloud that looks like a flying horse.'

'Grateful!'

'Grateful!'

'Grateful!'

The meerkats' heads popped up one after another and all spoke the same word.

Sylver said, 'Now, perhaps you can help me—'

'Stop looking at our kettle! Don't you know a watched kettle never boils the water around it? Did you never learn physics at school? How are we expected to get to Byzantium if you keep looking at our kettle and stopping it from boiling the water.'

'Why would you want the water to boil?'

'Physics, which you lot obviously never learned in school, says it's best. Don't you know a kettle travels faster through boiling water than through

310

cold water? Hot water is more buoyant than cold water, so the kettle sits higher in it, and skims over the surface. I should have thought that was obvious, even if you didn't do physics.'

'Is that true? I don't think that's true,' said Miniver. 'It sounds silly to me.'

'Who was your physics master? Ours was Charles Lutwige Dodgson. He's the best teacher there is!'

Sylver could not stop Miniver now; she was furious with the stupid meerkats. 'We were taught the principles of the universe by Lord Haukin, who is a very learned stoat – a philosopher – and I'm sure he would have told us about such things – if they were scientific facts.'

To her surprise the meerkats seemed to have heard of Lord Haukin. 'Oh, *him*. He discovered the three elements, didn't he? I quote: "The three elements that form the matter of the universe are bottle-glass, water and fire, for we see through bottle-glass darkly. Now abideth bottle-glass, water and fire, these three, but the greatest of these is bottle-glass." Oh, yes, we know Lord Haukin, all right.'

Lord Haukin certainly loved his old bottle collection, but Miniver was certain the meerkat had got it wrong. 'Lord Haukin never said that. He said, "*Earth*, fire and water".'

'Bottle-glass is symbolic of earth and presents a better picture in the mind's eye.'

'Never mind all that,' said Sylver. 'Could you please tell us where you last saw the Island of Dorma?'

'This way.'

'That way!'

'Over there.'

'Just here.'

The meerkats were all pointing in different directions. In fact their forelimbs looked like the pointers on a compass, and they were spread out like the petals of a marigold.

'This is hopeless,' said Sylver to his crew. 'We'll have to go on and hope to meet some animal with more sense.'

The *Scudding Cloud* sailed further into this imaginative sea. Here the water sparkled with many highlights. There were islands everywhere, mostly small with one or two palms, or simply a coral bar protruding above the surface. It was a pretty place, the sun was warm, the air was tranquil. Seabirds flew back and forth and fish broke through ripple rings to watch the weasels go by. Finally they saw two mammals sunbathing on a rock.

From a distance they seemed to be a strange species. Then, on seeing the boat, they did something quickly. It appeared that they had changed heads. It then became apparent that the two were actually a walrus and a cassowary. For some reason they had first been wearing each other's heads, but on the ship's approach, changed them over as easily as if they were hats.

When the *Scudding Cloud* drew level with them, Sylver stood on the bridge and called, 'Ahoy there!'

The two creatures, the bird and the sea mammal, affected looks of surprise. There was a guilty look on their faces as they addressed Sylver.

'Yes?' replied the walrus, licking his moustaches. 'What can we do for you?'

'We're looking for an island by the name of Dorma.'

'Ah,' cried the cassowary bird, 'I remember that. It floated by here just a few days ago. It went in that direction.' She pointed with her wing.

'Thank you,' Sylver replied, relieved to have some reliable information.

Scirf could not let the matter of the heads rest, however. 'What did you do, just a while back?' he asked the pair. 'Did I see you change heads?'

The walrus pretended to look very shocked. 'Who? Us? Certainly not. Don't you know it's illegal to change heads with anyone, even a close relative? It flies in the face of personal identity. Why, it would mean a walrus could find out what it was like to be – to be – a bird.'

'And vice versa,' said the cassowary, looking down at the rock while she spoke. 'She could find out what it was like to be a walrus – or a giraffe – or something. I hope you're not accusing us of anything like that. We're respectable creatures, we are.'

'Look, it's nothing to me what you do with your heads,' said Scirf. 'I was just curious, that's all.'

'You should watch that curiosity,' the cassowary said. 'It'll get you into deep trouble.'

Sylver ordered the ship to tack in the direction indicated by the cassowary. They sailed away, leaving the two ruffled creatures sitting on the rock. When they were quite some way from them, the walrus and the cassowary changed heads again. Then the astonished crew saw the walrus

313

flapping his flippers and trying to fly from the rock. He fell into the sea. The cassowary dived after him, using her wings to propel herself through the water.

'Fish!' she shrieked. 'I must have fish!'

It was the last the weasels ever saw of the pair.

'What a strange couple,' murmured Scirf. 'I wonder if we'll run into any more weird creatures . . . ?'

Even as he spoke a lobster came drifting high above the water, its right claw gripping a banana-tree leaf. The leaf was being carried along by the wind, like a loose kite, and the lobster was using the leaf for transport. She dangled there, above the ship's quarterdeck, then suddenly let go and landed with a clackety-clack on the boards.

Scirf walked towards the creature, intending to throw it into the sea, but the lobster raised its claws defensively.

'Stand back,' she said. 'Don't come any closer.'

'I'm not going to hurt you.'

'Ho, yes, the last human said that, and I ended up in some kind of cage on the ocean floor. Only escaped by using my sageful wit and sagacity. Keep away. I'll chop off your hands if you come any nearer. I mean it.' The lobster clacked her claws for effect.

'We're not humans,' said Scirf. 'We're weasels – and pine martens.'

'That's what they all say.'

'Wait,' said Sylver. 'Where did you last see these "humans"?'

The lobster pointed in the same direction the cassowary had indicated. 'That way. Now, if you'll excuse me, I intend to make my departure.'

She scuttled across the deck, through a rope hole in the gunwales, and plopped into the sea. Having had the cassowary bird's direction confirmed, Sylver was reasonably happy. The ship sailed on, further into the Spellbound Straits.

Chapter Thirty

Sylver had hoped to come across Dorma Island by chance. However, after much zigzagging between various islands he soon came to the conclusion that this would not work.

He felt sure that Dorma would be subject to currents which had set paths through the Cobalt Sea. He had to find somebody who knew which currents flowed when.

'We have to go ashore again,' he told his weary crew, 'to gather more information.'

They groaned, knowing that every time they stopped, they got into some sort of trouble.

The windjammer came to an island which was vast compared with others in the Spellbound Straits. Sylver decided to lead a party ashore and make enquiries. He left Miniver in charge of the ship, taking Mawk, Scirf, Bryony and Alysoun. He also insisted that Narky went with them, to get a bit of exercise.

'I'm sick,' complained the gerbil. 'I'm not well.'

'That's precisely why I'm taking you with me,' said Sylver firmly. 'Obviously sea life does not agree with you. You need a good long walk to get all the ailments out of your system.'

'Animals who're sick need to lie down and rest.'

'You haven't been out of your bed for at least a week, yet you don't have a temperature and your colour is fine. Time you shook off this so-called illness of yours. A good brisk march in the fresh air is what's needed.'

Narky started to whine again but Sylver would not listen to any of his moans. 'You're coming,' said the captain, 'and that's that.'

The party rowed ashore and moored the boat in a small inlet. From there they set off on foot, into the hinterland. It became apparent, as they proceeded inland, that they were on a civilized island. Crops had been grown in vast square fields.

They could see birds working out in the fields – finches mostly – pulling up weeds from between the rows with their beaks. These birds looked thin and wasted, as if they had not eaten for weeks. The weasels and the gerbil watched their activity for a while, with Sylver wondering if the birds would be able to answer questions in an intelligible tongue. So often birds spoke in an incomprehensible dialect.

Just as Sylver was about to call out to one of the birds, there was the sound of a horn in the distance. The birds all looked up in alarm, then took to the air. They settled in the hedgerows on either side of the fields, chattering angrily amongst themselves. Then there was a rumbling sound and the ground began to tremble under the weasels' feet.

A nearby bullfinch shouted, 'You'd better get out of the way, strangers – the muntjac are coming!'

317

Sylver and the others scrambled into the ditch which ran alongside the hedgerow just in time. Over the horizon came thousands of small deer. They appeared to be in a high level of excitement as they raced across the fields. A dust cloud accompanied them, billowing round their speeding forms. It was like a cattle stampede. The noise of their feet pounding on the earth got louder and louder.

Then the leaders were suddenly level with Sylver's crew, as the herd thundered past, squashing the crops beneath their hooves. It was like a sea of brown bodies flowing past. The dust flew up and choked the watchers. When it had settled, the muntjac deer were now gathering at the head of the beach, where their race ended.

The finches came down from the hedgerows and stared with disgusted expressions at their flattened crops.

'Another season of going hungry,' said one. 'I don't think I can stand it.'

'What happened here?' asked Sylver, emerging from the ditch. 'Why did they do that?'

The bullfinch who had warned Sylver's crew of the muntjac's approach came over to them. 'Happens every season,' he said bitterly. 'We plant the crops and, just when they're almost ripe, the muntjac come through and destroy it all. We'll salvage what seeds we can, but it's a crying shame ...'

'Have you tried talking to them? The muntjac, I mean,' Bryony asked. 'Perhaps they don't know what they're doing.'

'Oh, they know what they're doing, all right.'

Scirf, who was ever on the side of the

underdog – or, in this case, the underbird – decided to try to do something. He asked for Sylver's permission to go and speak to the muntjac, while Sylver was getting information out of the bullfinch.

Sylver nodded. 'See what you can do.'

Scirf took Bryony and Narky, leaving Alysoun and Mawk with Sylver.

The small deer were now milling around, discussing their charge across the fields. 'I knew Fletcher would win,' one was saying. 'She won last year. She's got feet with wings on them . . .'

'Speakin' of wings,' interrupted Scirf, causing the deers' heads to swivel in his direction, 'I don't suppose you noticed our feathered friends over there. They was your audience when you trampled down their crops just a minute ago.'

A muntjac who was a little more aggressive than the rest pushed forward and confronted the weasel. 'So?' he said. 'What about it?'

'Well, I was just wonderin', being a stranger to this island, why you would want to do such a thing. Here we have some perfectly innocent birds, plantin' their crops, nurturing them, watering them – then just when they're ready to harvest the grain, along comes a crowd of hooligans and destroys all their work. Now, as I said, I'm just a stranger, but it seems to me this is all a bit unnecessary.'

'Oh, does it?' said the muntjac. 'Well, stranger, I suggest you mind your own business.'

'Listen, you cloven-hoofed thug,' said Scirf, 'let's have a few manners, eh? We're merely enquiring.'

'We're of a curious nature, friend,' Narky said, wanting to get his few words in. 'It costs nothing to answer.'

The deer stared hard at the three mammals before him. They looked small but tough. The muntjac was not particularly afraid of weasels, or gerbils, but this bunch looked as if they could handle themselves in an argument.

'Not that it's any concern of yours,' the muntjac replied at last, 'and bearing in mind I don't have to answer any of your questions if I don't want to – I have about three thousand deer at my back if you want to make trouble – but we're running our annual race for a prize. We go from the edge of the mountain there to the sea, and whoever gets here first is allowed to graze in a very lush piece of bottom land, close to the river, which we call the Little Green Acre.'

'I see,' Bryony said. 'So you wait until the crops planted by the birds are almost ripe, then trample 'em in spite.'

The muntjac had the grace to look a little shame-faced when Bryony put it this way. 'Not at all. We were racing before the finches ever came here. It just so happens that our race coincides with the ripening of their crops. It's not our fault they chose to plant their corn and stuff on our racetrack.'

'Well, I imagine the birds looked around for the most suitable soil in which to plant their crops,' interrupted Scirf, 'and chose this valley because its features and climate were exactly right. You must have surprised them with your first race. After all, how do you expect newcomers to understand your culture?'

The muntjac said, 'It wasn't like that. At least, I suppose we did give them a shock, but this race is traditional. We've been doing it for many years. We're well within our rights, you know. If those finches think they can try to stop us exercising our traditional rights, then they'd better think again.'

Bryony stared about her at the level plain, with the tall, white-tipped mountain beyond, and the green verdant edges to the valley. She turned and looked back at the sea, fringed with golden sandy bays. The waters beyond the turquoise lagoon were a deep blue highlighted with glints from the sun's rays. 'This is a beautiful island you have here,' she said to the muntjac.

The deer all puffed out their chests in pride.

'Yes, it is, isn't it,' replied the leader of the muntjacs. 'We think so, anyway.'

'What a pity it is, then, that it's spoiled by a lack of harmony.'

The deer's lower jaw dropped. 'Lack of harmony?'

'Amongst the creatures who live here,' continued Bryony. 'I mean, what a shame you can't get on together. I expect there's a lot of sniping between you and the birds. I suspect you can't pass a hedgerow without being insulted in some way.'

'Oh, you're right there,' cried a female deer from the back. 'Why, you can't walk down a lane without being heckled in some way – those birds . . .'

I expect you give as good as you get, though.'

'Oh, too true,' replied the leader. 'Why should

we take a lot of beak? We're entitled to be here, just as much as they are. That's what I mean about our race. It's our given right. We've been doing it for—'

'I know,' sighed Bryony; 'for years.'

'Yes.'

'Well,' continued that redoubtable jill, 'where would be the harm in holding your race a couple of weeks later in the season? I mean, what's a few days when there's harmony at stake?'

The muntjac looked uncomfortable. 'Well, we've *always* had it at this time of year.'

'No reason not to change, is it? There was a time when you didn't have it at all – you haven't been running this race since the world began, have you? How was it decided to have it precisely at this point in the year? Maybe it just happened by accident.'

'The story is that one muntjac cried, "Race you for the best grass," and the others followed. They remembered it the next year and did it again, until it became a regular thing.'

'Well, there you are then. Pure accident. No reason to stick to a date just because of an accident. Just change the programme a bit and you can all live together happily, birds and deer.'

The deer frowned and began muttering amongst themselves about 'tradition' and 'deer culture'. They did not seem too pleased with the idea of changing the date of the race. Bryony could hear some more moderate voices amongst them – "Well, it would be cooler . . ." – but for the most part the herd did not want to change. It was as if by altering their programme they would somehow lose something valuable.

'They're just a rigid bunch of blind fools,' said Narky disgustedly. 'Come on, Scirf, let's get back to Sylver.'

'We *always* have it on this day,' the muntjac leader argued. 'It wouldn't feel right on another day.'

Bryony would not give up though. It seemed incomprehensible to her that the deer would rather let the birds go hungry than alter the date of their race. She did not believe anyone could be so uncompromising. 'It'll soon feel right, once you start doing it,' she said. 'Change always feels a bit funny at first, but as soon as you've got half a dozen races behind you, you'll forget you ever had it on this date. Just try it.'

'No, no, it wouldn't be right. You don't understand. You come from a different culture. You don't know how much this means to us, this race. The birds will have to find somewhere else to plant their crops. This is our race course.'

'Your "once a year" race course,' muttered Scirf.

Bryony said, 'Promise me one thing, then. In two weeks' time, have *another* race. See how it feels. See if it's really any different. Try it out and perhaps you'll find it will make no difference to your feelings for this particular date.'

The muntjac leader looked sceptical, but in the end he agreed to try a second race in two weeks. But he wondered about the prize for that race. There was only one Little Green Acre.

'Why not have yet another race, two weeks after that! The best of three.'

A muntjac in the middle of the herd jumped on this idea. 'I'll go along with that. I've always felt that one race is over a bit too quickly to decide a winner. The best of three would be a much better test of speed and stamina. It would eliminate all the elements of luck.'

There was a general murmur of approval, since many of the deer had been only just behind the winner when she crossed the finishing line. There were those who felt that, if they just tried a little bit harder, they might win a second race. And who knew, perhaps the third too, making them the overall winner? It was all over too quickly, this one-race business.

'Then,' said Bryony to the leader of the herd, 'you might find you can move this day's race to the end, after the other two, and kill two birds with one stone, so to speak – or rather help many birds with one move.'

'I don't know,' replied the muntjac. 'It might work . . .'

'Give it a try – that's all we ask,' Bryony urged. 'There's no harm going to come out of that, is there?'

Thus they left the deer with the seed of change planted in their minds. Bryony explained what had happened to the birds, who were very sceptical. The small muntjac deer had always been so inflexible, they said; they would not even listen to reason or arguments. The birds felt nothing would come out of Bryony's intervention.

But the weasels – and the gerbil – were hopeful, as ever, that some good would come out of it.

Chapter Thirty-One

Sylver learned from the birds that there was an old mole in the Land of the Giants, who was in tune with the rhythms of the world and knew the waterways of the islands.

'Over there,' said the chaffinch, pointing with her wing. 'That's where you'll find him.'

'What, in the highlands?' replied Sylver, staring at a range of hills in front of the big mountain.

The chaffinch clacked her beak in amusement. 'Highlands, yes. You know who made those hills?'

'The creator of the world, I imagine.'

'No, they weren't formed with the shaping of the earth, in prehistoric times. They were made by the old mole himself. You see, he is one of the giants. There's three of them: a giant cockchafer, a giant shrew and a giant mole. You have to get past the first two to reach the third, who is the one you want.

'Those are mole hills out there. New ones appear every so often; old ones fade away. Good luck, then. And watch out for Cyclops! He's the worst of the three.'

'Which one is that?' asked Scirf, but the bird had flown.

'Right,' said Sylver, 'let's be on our way, or

we'll never manage to finish this journey.'

'I'm not going!' cried Mawk and Narky in unison, competing for the cowardice medal of the year. 'I'm not going!'

'Stop messin' about, you two,' Scirf said. 'We can't afford to play games. We ain't got time for such things, have we, captain? Come on, packs on backs, let's hit the trail. How about a song while we march along? Do you know the one about the twenty mountain hikers, when they get lost in the mists and fall over the edge one by one?'

He began singing in a lusty voice, '*Oh, then there were nine, there were nine, there were nine – and no-one was really to blame – but one by one they dropped to their deaths – oh, ain't it a cryin' shame.*'

'If you think a horrible song like that is going to encourage me to join this party!' complained Narky, but Scirf was not listening. He was too busy singing.

'*. . . they broke their necks and drowned in becks – oh, ain't it a cryin' shame. They snapped their spines and cracked their skulls, and spilled their porridgey brains . . .*'

'I think that's enough, Scirf,' said Mawk, through gritted teeth, as he and Narky were helped on with their packs by Bryony and Sylver. 'I never liked that song anyway.'

'*. . . they plummeted down the fatal drops, screamin' all the way – oh, ain't it a crying shame, a cryin' shame, there wasn't a rick of hay? There wasn't a rick to break their fall – oh, there wasn't a rick of hay.*'

A sparrow seemed to agree with Mawk, for it warned Scirf as he passed by the hedge: 'I wouldn't go making that noise in the hills, if I were you. Cyclops can't stand noise. And if you sing like that the Cannibal will hear you and find out where you are. You have to creep about amongst those hills. Good luck. You'll need it. I've never heard of a mammal ever coming out alive, but I suppose there has to be a first time. Birds are all right. They can just up and fly away, see, but mammals have to run . . .'

'The Cannibal?' gulped Mawk. 'He eats his own kind?'

'Well, *she* would do, I've no doubt of that, but she earned the name because she eats raw flesh. Bye, bye.' With that the sparrow took off into the blue sky.

'I'm *definitely* not going,' cried the two cowards, in perfect harmony. 'Never, never, never.'

'They're a pair, ain't they just,' said an amused Scirf, clicking his teeth. 'Come on, Alysoun-the-fleet, we'll set the pace.'

And he strode out, Bryony close behind him and Alysoun overtaking them. There was no holding back Alysoun, once the pace was stepped up. Despite the sparrow's warning all three were soon singing the Mountain Hiker Song. Sylver took up the middle position, his mind on more serious matters than singing songs.

Mawk and Narky trailed along miserably at the rear, nervously looking around. As Bryony said, *'Like two that on the lonely road, do walk in fear and dread, because they know some frightful fiends are not that far ahead.'* She and Scirf clicked their teeth hilariously at this misquotation, while Mawk and Narky scowled their disapproval.

By noon they were in the hills, tramping silently

now. Even Scirf was not so daft as to try to attract attention to himself when there were flesh-eating giants about. In the middle of the afternoon they approached a bridge over a ravine. It was a hastily thrown-together affair, by the look of it, fashioned out of a tangle of weeds and rattan sticks.

Just as they were about to cross this flimsy-looking bridge, a giant cockchafer came running out of a cave and stood on the far side of the ravine. She was the size of ten weasels and had distinctive fan shaped antennae. Each of her six monstrous legs ended in sharp, knife-like tips. Her snarling roar boomed out over the chasm to greet the exploration party.

Clearly this creature was too heavy for the tanglewood bridge and had to wait for her victims to cross over.

'All right, time to turn back,' said Mawk. 'We tried, but this is obviously the Cannibal. Look at the skeletons around the mouth of her cave.'

True enough, the others could see the untidy heaps of bones scattered in the dust. Clinging to these piles were massive white grubs, which Scirf said were called 'rookworms'. They were the larvae of the cockchafer. They had huge swollen abdomens and brown heads bearing vicious-looking curved jaws. These were the brood of this giant insect.

'There's going to be more of 'em soon,' cried Narky, his eyes starting from his head, 'when that lot hatch.'

'I wonder if she ever lets them hatch,' replied Bryony, looking down at the bottom of the chasm. 'There's some more down there. They look partly-hatched to me; they're all halfway out of their larvae skins. I expect just as they are about to hatch, she pushes them over the edge of the cliff. She's the queen of the hills – she won't want her own children for rivals.'

'She kills her own young? What will she do to *us*? And why does she wait to do it?' asked Alysoun. 'Why not get rid of them before they hatch out?'

'Your guess is as good as mine.'

'I'm not well,' cried Narky. 'I feel ill. Someone make a stretcher. I need to be carried home.'

'I'll do it! I volunteer!' cried Mawk. 'Poor old Narky – I don't mind helping to carry him home.'

'No-one is going home,' Sylver stated flatly. 'We're going to wait until the cockchafer falls asleep, then sneak past her into the hills. Scirf, you take the first duty harassment. Keep her on the move, keep taunting her, make her furious, make her run up and down. I'll take over in an hour, then Bryony, and so on. We must make sure the cockchafer remains on the alert, while we take turns to rest. Once we exhaust her, she'll hopefully drop off into a deep sleep and we can be on our way.'

' YOU SIX-LEGGED FREAK!' yelled Scirf, taking up his duties immediately. 'YOUR MOTHER WAS BORN AT THE BUSINESS END OF A DRAIN!'

Whether the cockchafer understood the words or not, she certainly did not like the tone. She rushed at the edge of the cliff as if to launch herself off. Too late Sylver and the others remembered that cockchafer beetles can fly – they tap at window panes on summer nights. However, a rush of relief went through the mammals as they realized that this particular insect was too heavy to fly. All six of them had begun to run when the cockchafer looked like gliding over the ravine; now they came back to stare over at the insect, who was running up and down, bellowing in fury.

Scirf was amazed at the anger his insult had produced. 'I can think of better ones than that,' he said, 'with a bit of practice.'

While Scirf kept up a round of abuse, every word of which seemed to incense the cockchafer, the others got some sleep in a nearby cave. One by one they were roused to take over insult duties, until they had all been twice. Still the cockchafer looked just as awake as when they had started.

Then Bryony suggested lulling her to sleep with song. Scirf took a blade of grass between his paws and blew eerie music, while Bryony sang a lullaby which was used by weasel mothers and fathers to send their kittens to sleep on those long summer evenings when it stayed light until late.

After a while the cockchafer sank to her knees, then sprawled on the ground with her legs sticking out every whichway. Finally they heard her husky snores drifting over the chasm.

'That's it – let's go,' Sylver ordered his crew. 'One by one, over the bridge.'

Bryony went first, followed by Alysoun, Scirf, Mawk and Narky. Sylver brought up the rear. The bridge flexed dangerously as they crossed it, bending in the middle. However, it took the weight of a single weasel without collapsing. The face of the snoring beast lay right by the bridge on the other side. They had to be very careful not to touch the antennae as they went past. Bryony slipped past, then Scirf, then Mawk, then Alysoun.

At that moment loud squeals came from the cockchafer larvae outside the giant's cave: 'LOOK OUT, THEY'RE GETTING AWAY, MUM! WAKE UP! WAKE UP! YOUR DINNER'S ON THE RUN.'

'That's why she keeps them until they're almost born,' cried Bryony. 'They're her guard dogs!'

The cockchafer stirred, obviously roused by the cries of her larvae. She rose on her six legs and, though wobbly and tired, scuttled towards the weasels. Bryony, Mawk, Alysoun and Scirf ran past the brown-headed larvae, which snapped at their legs with savage jaws. Successfully through the white, ridged horrors, they scrambled up the cliff face beyond.

Sylver and Narky were still on the bridge. Narky had almost reached solid ground when the cockchafer approached. Sylver remained just on the bridge, out of reach of the foul creature. He urged Narky to join him, but the gerbil tried to make a run for the cliff. However, caught before he was halfway there, the gerbil employed his favourite form of defence: he lay down on the ground, looking frail and pretending to retch. The cockchafer looked down at him.

'I'm not well,' wailed Narky to the cockchafer. 'I feel sick. I think I've got some deadly disease. I would stay away from me, if I were you. I've probably got the plague.'

The cockchafer's antennae twitched as she stood, swaying with fatigue, over the moaning gerbil.

'That's right,' groaned Narky. 'I'm very ill. I'm

stuffed to the gills with germs. You'd probably give yourself all sorts of stomach problems if you ate me. Just leave me here to die with my boots on. Then you can feed me to your young.'

The cockchafer had other ideas. She snatched him up in her horrible jaws, swallowed once, and he was gone. It was done so quickly, in the blink of an eye, that the weasels hardly knew what had happened. It was as if the gerbil had vanished before their very eyes. They only realized the truth when the giant gave out a loud burp, and ambled back to the bridge.

'She's eaten Narky!' shrieked Mawk. 'There's nothing left of him!'

Sylver, never easily rattled, was also shocked. He quickly made his way back to the other side of the chasm. The cockchafer watched him go, then settled down for a snooze with her antennae resting on the bridge. She was not going to be caught out a second time! Any movement on that bridge and she would detect it through her sensitive feelers. Sylver was truly trapped.

'You'll have to go on without me,' he called. 'I can't get across.'

'Not a chance,' yelled Bryony. 'We'll think of something.'

She sat down with Alysoun, the shattered Mawk and the imperturbable Scirf to discuss what they were going to do next.

'I have an idea,' said Scirf. 'The other giant must be fairly close by – a shrew called Cyclops. Giants are usually solitary creatures. They don't like to be in a crowd. I'm willing to bet I could lead Cyclops back here and persuade him to fight the cockchafer. He'll probably eat her. Shrews eat anything. What do you think?'

'Well, I haven't a better plan, so let's get started straight away,' replied Bryony. 'Come on, Mawk, stop snivelling. It's very sad about Narky. I wish we could have helped him, but there's nothing we can do now. We'll give him a kalkie later. That's a great honour for a creature who's not a weasel. On your feet now, it's time for action.'

'I agree with the plan,' said Alysoun quietly. She did not often speak when schemes were being hatched, so they paid extra attention to what she said. 'I agree with it in every aspect but one. It should be *me*, not Scirf, who goes to Cyclops. I'm the swiftest runner in Halfmoon Wood.'

No-one could argue with her there.

Chapter Thirty-Two

If the giant cockchafer was frightening, Cyclops
the shrew was even more so. For a start he was
twice as big as the cockchafer and his mouth was
full of massive sharp teeth. When he saw Alysoun
his eyes lit up with delight. Only a timely run
beneath a rock saved the weasel from becoming a
shrew appetiser.

Cyclops approached the rock and cocked his
head to one side to favour his good eye, peering to
see if he could located the hiding weasel. His other
eye was a milky white and obviously quite
useless. Alysoun was terrified to see these enormous orbs, one sightless, the other sharp and
keen, filling the gap beneath the stone. A mouth
opened below the eyes. White teeth as large as
forest trees appeared.

'COME OUT, LITTLE WEASEL,' boomed the giant.
'COME AND PLAY HOLLYHOCKERS WITH CYCLOPS!'

'Push off,' she yelled. 'Get lost!'

Bryony, Scirf and Mawk were up in crags above,
having let Alysoun go down to the shrew's den
alone. They were horrified when they saw the size
of Cyclops. He was as large as twenty weasels
crammed together. The reputation of shrews is
legendary. They are notoriously bad-tempered –

they fear nothing on the whole planet and have been known to attack cats who have bothered them and come off best; they are ferocious and deadly fighters; and they tunnel.

This one started tunnelling now, under the rock.

'Get out of there, Alysoun!' yelled Bryony. 'He's trying to dig you out!'

'I can see that, but what am I supposed to do about it?'

'You'll have to make a run for it when you feel the time is right. Use the narrow gaps between rocks, so that he has to skirt them. It'll slow him down. Remember our original plan – lead him to the cockchafer.'

'I HEARD THAT,' said the shrew.

The giant creature was digging furiously now, showering tons of dirt behind him thus creating another small hill. He paused every so often to try and get his snout beneath the rock, snapping on air with his huge teeth. Finally Alysoun realized she would have to make a dash for it, or be chomped up by those massive jaws.

She waited until the shrew paused to see how far he'd got, then threw two large clawfuls of fine sand into Cyclops's big eye.

'I'M BLIND!' yelled the shrew, his one good eye stinging with the grit. 'YOU HURT ME!'

Alysoun shot out between the shrew's legs. She raced up the embankment towards her three friends, running as only Alysoun-the-fleet can run. Soon all four of them were fleeing back in the direction of the bridge.

The shrew quickly recovered and was after them. Bryony's tactics of using narrow gaps between rocks seemed to work. The shrew had to run around all the boulders, snapping at the tails of the weasels, who had never run so fast in their lives. When they reached the bridge, they dashed into the cockchafer's cave, the entrance being too small for the shrew.

'YOU'D BETTER COME OUT NOW,' cried Cyclops, his voice booming into the cave. 'I CAN WAIT HERE UNTIL YOU GET THIRSTY.'

'Why don't you go and eat that huge meal by the bridge – the cockchafer?' enquired Scirf.

'BECAUSE COCKCHAFERS ARE DRY, BRITTLE AND TASTELESS. IT'S LIKE EATING WOODSHAVINGS. THERE'S NOTHING THERE BUT CRISPY WINGS AND CRACKLY SHELL, AND LEGS THAT GET STUCK IN YOUR THROAT.'

And so that was that: the best-laid schemes of intelligent weasels as well as silly harvest mice gang aft a-gley.

The shrew settled down outside the cave.

Not far away the cockchafer was distracted by this great mammal sitting in front of her home. Sylver could see she was torn between protecting her territory and waiting for this morsel on the bridge. Just then the shrew began eating the rookworms, the larvae of the cockchafer, smacking his lips at these titbits which had been left lying around.

The cockchafer was incensed by this terrible behaviour and ran full pelt at the shrew. She shrieked her disapproval of his bad manners – eating her children indeed! She would have killed them herself, later, but that was different.

The cockchafer, about half the size of the shrew,

stood in front of her adversary and rattled her wings. To the weasels this sounded like sheets of slate being clattered together. She hissed and spat, her antennae quivering with anger. Her sharply pointed legs dug into the earth as she shook with fury before the intruder.

The shrew's one good eye narrowed on seeing the cockchafer rush at him. It narrowed even further when the cockchafer began her display of aggression. Finally he darted forward, there was a breakfasty crunch, and the cockchafer was nothing more but large crispy flakes on the cliff edge. With a nudge of his pointed nose the shrew pushed the remains over the side of the chasm. They fluttered down to the bottom of the chasm.

'And then there was one,' said Alysoun.

The shrew settled down again, watching both the cave exit and the bridge, with Sylver still on the far side. Soon it was nightfall. During the darkness there were movements under the ground, below the hills. The very earth shuddered and moved as in the beginning of the world. Old caves disappeared; new caves were revealed. Chasms closed and gorges were formed. Fortunately for the weasels, none of this movement occurred near them, or they would have been in desperate straits.

Dawn came and still the situation had not changed. The shrew remained at the cave entrance; Sylver was still on his side of the bridge; the other four weasels were inside the cave. Everyone, including the shrew, was getting frustrated.

'How about a game of hollyhockers?' called

Mawk, desperate to get out into the fresh air. 'If I win, you let us go. If you win, we'll come out and be eaten. What do you say?'

'NOT A CHANCE,' came the reply.

Scirf now began to think hard. He had recognized what kind of shrew they had here. There were four sorts of shrew back in Welkin – common shrews, water shrews, pygmy shrews and the white-toothed shrews. Despite its size, this one was a pygmy shrew.

Pygmy shrews on Welkin were well-known for their clear thinking. They were extremely good at getting immediately to the core of the problem, because they refused to be diverted by side issues. However, if presented with a circular problem, they worried over it until they were sick, some of them even expiring from the mental fatigue.

All Scirf had to do was think of some conundrums and present them to Cyclops, to see if he could cope with the tangled thought-patterns such things produced. 'Cyclops,' he called, 'did you know. . . ?'

'DID I KNOW WHAT?'

'Did you know that everything I say is a lie?'

'IS THAT SO? I COULDN'T CARE LE—' The shrew stopped in mid-sentence, having thought about what Scirf had said. 'WAIT A MINUTE. IF EVERY-THING YOU SAY IS A LIE, THEN YOU'RE LYING WHEN YOU SAY "EVERYTHING I SAY IS A LIE".'

The shrew had taken the bait. Now Scirf could urge the creature forward into a kind of madness. It was a cruel thing to do, but they had no choice: otherwise they would starve or be eaten by the shrew.

The shrew had a frown on his forehead above his long, bewhiskered nose. He thrashed his long, thick tail as he considered this second statement. 'SO IF YOU'RE LYING WHEN YOU SAY THAT, IT MUST BE THE TRUTH.'

'Correct!'

'AND IF IT'S THE TRUTH, THEN YOU MUST BE LYING.'

'Corrrrreeeccct!'

'BUT IF YOU'RE LYING, IT MUST BE THE TRUTH.'

'Abbbsssolutely!'

This circular argument began to eat away at the shrew's brain, as he used all his thinking reserves to try to puzzle a way out. He was wasting his time. There is no way out of this conundrum – as many creatures have found to their cost. One owl spent a whole lifetime on the problem, trying to find a chink in order to prise it apart.

'IF EVERYTHING YOU SAY IS A LIE, THEN *THAT* MUST BE A LIE – IN WHICH CASE NOT EVERYTHING YOU SAY IS A LIE . . .'

Cyclops's one good eye began to spin slowly in its socket, as he repeated the same sentence over and over again. By mid-morning he was beginning to foam at the mouth. His tail lashed the dust, his ears twitched, his body went into spasmodic convulsions, until at precisely one-thirty he let out a strangled cry and rolled over in the dust. His brain had seized up. It could cope no longer, and it ceased sending messages of any kind to the other organs in his body, so his heart stopped.

'Dead as a duck when it's dead,' said Scirf, strolling out of the cave into the sunlight. 'It's a shame, but it was either him or us.'

'Don't start on us with your riddles,' grumbled Mawk. 'I can't abide them either.'

Sylver now crossed the tangle-twig bridge and met them on their side of the chasm. 'Well done, you four,' he said. He looked at the remains of the cockchafer, down at the bottom of the chasm. 'Shame about Narky, but I knew he would try shamming illness once too often. This time it didn't work.'

'He was a character, all right,' acknowledged Bryony. 'Can't say I liked him, but I wouldn't have wished him an end as savage as the one he got. What now, brave captain?'

'Now we find the mole, wherever he is.'

They skirted the massive corpse of the giant shrew and made their way along the hill ridges and through the hill passes. Eventually they came to a massive cave, which they soon realized must be one of the entrances to the mole's underworld. Gathering brushwood to make firebrands, they were soon entering the cavern and penetrating the darkness beyond.

'I hate these places,' said Alysoun, peering into the great dark void ahead. 'You remember all those tunnels we went down when we were at Castle Storm? You're never quite sure what you're going to meet around the next corn—'

There was a trembling of the ground at that moment and they stopped and waited for it to pass.

Around the next corner they came face to face with a white snake. Bryony stopped short, a little startled, and since she was leading the party the other four bundled into the back of her.

"Ere, watch it!' cried Scirf. 'Give a bit of warning if you're goin' to call a halt.' Then he too saw the reptile and stared.

The snake was wrapped around a pillar of rock, which had been exposed by the mole's digging. He turned his head towards her and hissed in a strange accent, 'Are you bats? Won't you bring your friends in to see me? We cave-racers like bats.'

'No, we're not bats,' replied Bryony, a little put out. 'You can see we're not.'

'No I can't,' replied the dissapointed snake. 'I'm blind.'

'Oh, so sorry. I didn't mean anything . . .'

'It's all right,' replied the snake cheerfully. 'All cave-racers are blind. We're that way from birth. It doesn't mean very much to us. After all, we spend our lives in darkness, so what good would sight be to us? I'm very good at sensing certain things, so that makes up for it.'

Alysoun remarked, 'You didn't know we were weasels.'

The snake snapped, 'Can't get it right *all* the time.'

'And you wish we were bats, do you?' asked Scirf.

'Yes, I do. Bats form the major part of my diet. I've eaten all the bats we had in here, save one. I was hoping a new colony would come. Fascinating things, bats. They hang upside down, you know. All except Nibor, over there. He doesn't. He hates hanging upside down, don't you, Nibor?'

'Hate it,' confirmed a voice from above.

The weasels looked up and there was a bat,

standing on top of the same tall rock. It looked rather peculiar, hunched up on its perch, with its head the right way up. Somehow bats don't look right unless they are hanging upside down.

Bryony said, 'How peculiar!'

'Why?' Nibor said. 'Just because I don't like the blood rushing to my head? It makes your legs and feet ache, gripping on to the ceiling and hanging upside down. I prefer to stand upright, if you don't mind, whatever the others do.'

'Well, I mean it's peculiar that you are a bat and this creature here is a cave-racer who eats bats.'

'What's peculiar about it?'

Scirf said, 'Come off it – why doesn't he eat *you*.'

It was the white snake who replied. 'Because I know his name. How can you eat someone who's just introduced himself to you? He said, "How d'ye do, sir, my name's Nibor," just like that, before I could shoot out my head and get my jaws around him. Once we were acquainted, it was difficult to think of him as dinner, if you know what I mean.'

'First thing I do when entering a cave,' Nibor explained, 'is to introduce myself to the cave-racers. I don't know why they're called that, because they don't do any running around, not that I've seen. They're pretty lazy really, as snakes go. I mean, I've met pythons that are faster on their feet.

'Once they know who I am, I don't have any trouble. Of course, I don't fly too near them when I take off, because in their blindness they're not too choosy about what they snatch out of the air. So long as I observe a few safety rules, I'm fine.

The cave-racers usually hang around the pillars – stalactites and stalagmites and all that. I don't bother them and they don't bother me. Good neighbours.'

'You said *feet*: that's very interesting,' interrupted the cave-racer. 'In point of fact, we don't have any feet. It's precisely this feature which makes snakes so interesting. We're as good as any other creature at getting about, yet we don't have arms or legs. Don't you find that interesting?'

'Not particularly,' replied Bryony for the weasels. 'Should we?'

'Well, you would if you were disabled in some way. If you no longer had the use of your forelimbs and hind legs, you might find it very heartening to see snakes like me whizzing about, climbing trees, swimming across ponds, racing through the undergrowth, doing all sorts of athletic things. I've made up a rhyme to celebrate the many talents of snakes. Want to hear it? It's called *Hooray for Snakes* and it goes like this.'

Without waiting for a reply, the cave-racer launched into a piece of poetry:

'Snakes do not have arms or legs
yet snakes can move extremely fast
and when the jungle races start
snakes never come in last.

Snakes have colour, snakes are pretty,
snakes have patterns on their skins –
no elbows getting ugly bruises,
snakes don't have such things as shins.

343

Snakes do not have legs or arms
yet snakes can climb up lofty palms –
and though they don't wear boots and socks
snakes can also run up rocks.

Snakes are wriggly, snakes are writhy,
snakes can squeeze through gaps and holes –
snakes can slither under doorways,
snakes can climb up washing poles.

Snakes have got no arms or legs
but snakes can tie fantastic knots –
they twist and curl in different ways
and sometimes can't undo for days.

Snakes are peaceful, snakes aren't noisy,
snakes are good at quiet things –
no-one's heard a snake shout "Bother!"
no-one's heard a snake that sings.

Snakes have not got hands or feet
but snakes always look very neat –
they don't have gloves to lose in town,
nor socks which keep on falling down.

Snakes are long and snakes are short,
elastic, stretchy, good at sport –
snakes are bright and snakes are smart
and *certain* snakes are good at art.

Snakes do not have feet or hands
so snakes don't have to wear armbands –
for snakes can swim and snakes can dive,
and snakes are very much ALIVE!'

Chapter Thirty-Three

Once the rhyme had finished Sylver discovered from Nibor that the giant mole was further down the tunnel.

'What's his name?'

'He hasn't got a name,' replied Nibor. 'He's always been called the Gross and Ghastly Giant, or 3-G for short.'

'Have you ever met this 3-G?' asked Sylver.

'Not as such. I've *heard* him. You can hear him roaring down the tunnel, boasting about his huge teeth and claws and how he likes raw flesh for breakfast. He threatens to eat anything that dares venture further down this tunnel. I wouldn't go on if I were you. He sounds really ferocious.'

Mawk made a whining noise and stuffed his paw into his mouth to stop himself from shrieking.

'I hear he's good at plotting the course of the islands,' continued Sylver. 'He knows the ways of the currents and swells in this part of the ocean.'

'I heard that too,' replied Nibor, 'but whether it's true or not is anybody's guess. I don't suppose 3-G has been near the ocean in a long,

long time. If you should get the chance to speak to him, before he swallows you whole, then he *might* be able to give you the information you require.'

'Right, that's it. Nothing for it but to go on. Who's with me?' asked Sylver.

Bryony said, 'I am.'

Scirf said, 'Lead on.'

Alysoun said, 'I'm with you.'

Mawk said, 'I think somebody should stay here with the bat and the snake, just to make sure there's a safe retreat. I don't mind volunteering for that. After all, I haven't volunteered myself for very much lately. So I'll stay here, if that's all right with everyone else.'

'Right, that's it then,' Scirf said, putting his forelimb around Mawk's shoulders. 'It's unanimous. We're all goin' to confront the Gross and Ghastly Giant.'

Mawk found himself being dragged alongside Scirf, who refused to let his best friend be left behind.

'Don't want to miss all the fun,' Scirf whispered into Mawk's ear. 'I'm sure Sylver appreciates you volunteerin' and all that, but you'll kick yourself later if you ain't in at the kill.'

Mawk winced. 'I don't like that last word.'

When they were about three hundred metres further down the tunnel a voice suddenly boomed out: 'WHERE DO YOU THINK YOU'RE GOING?'

The five weasels stopped in their tracks. The owner of that voice must have been huge. It was twice as loud as the voice of the shrew. Then came the sound of footfalls thudding on the ground ahead. At first they seemed to be coming in the direction of the weasels.

'Run! Run!' cried Mawk, turning on his heel. He would have followed his own advice, had not Scirf had a claw hooked into his belt.

They listened for a while to the loud thumps of the giant's feet on the tunnel floor. It was strange, but they did not seem to get any closer. It was as if the giant were marking time, on the spot.

Something else struck Bryony as peculiar. 'The ground isn't vibrating,' she said. 'I mean, if something that big were running towards us, we would feel the floor shudder, wouldn't we?'

'I would have thought so,' replied Sylver. 'Very perceptive of you, Bryony. I suppose other creatures never waited around long enough to wonder about such things. Most would have run at the first sound of that loud voice.'

'A very sensible thing to do, if you ask me,' interrupted Mawk in a tight tone. 'It's not too late to follow their example . . .'

But Scirf had wandered on, holding his flaming brand aloft, the shadows dancing on the walls around him. The ex-dung-watcher's curiosity had been aroused now. Nothing on earth would make him leave until he had solved the puzzle which Bryony had uncovered with her sharp mind. 'Come on, you lot,' he called back. 'Let's find this whacking great mole and see what's what.'

The others followed him quickly – all except for Mawk, who followed him slowly.

'I HOPE YOU'RE RUNNING FOR YOUR LIVES!' came the voice again. 'OTHERWISE I'LL USE YOUR EYES

FOR SLINGSHOT PEBBLES AND YOUR NOSES FOR TARGETS.'

'He *hopes* we're running?' murmured Bryony. 'That means he doesn't know what we're doing.'

The voice continued as they went deeper into the great tunnel. Finally they came to a cavern; here the sound seemed to be coming from the ceiling. They stood in the centre of the cavern and the words of the giant mole were all around them. Still no great lumbering creature emerged from any of the other tunnels leading off the cavern. In fact these tunnels looked too small to accommodate a giant.

'Just a minute,' said Scirf. 'I thought I saw something over there . . .'

The weasel marched purposefully towards a corner of the cavern and peered behind a rock. Then he took a step back, as if he had seen something quite extraordinary. Mawk made mental preparations to run. He decided he could get away if the other four were behind him and being gobbled up first. It would give him time to escape the foul beast who lurked behind that boulder in the corner.

Suddenly Scirf said, 'Why – he's only a little squirt!'

Bryony and Alysoun and Sylver, and finally (and reluctantly) Mawk, went forward with their flaming torches and shone them over the creature cowering behind the rock. It was indeed a very ordinary-sized mole of tender years. The little fellow stared into the glare of the torches with narrowed eyes, for moles are almost blind. He trembled from the top of his head to the tip of his tail.

'What do you think you're playing at?' blazed Mawk. 'We – we might have done something nasty to you – making us think you were a giant!'

'I *am* a giant,' whined the mole; 'a very *small* giant.'

'Giants are, by the very meaning and nature of the word, BIG,' cried Mawk, the relief making him angry. 'You ought to be more careful how you use words.'

'Well, I come from a very long line of giants, a very old family. My mother was ten times bigger than me – and my grandmother twenty times. It just seems as if we've been getting smaller and smaller with each new generation. It's not my fault I've been born the same size as ordinary moles.'

'So there's not another giant mole around?' said Sylver. 'You are all there is?'

'I'm afraid so. You can kill me now if you like. I'm so miserable.'

Bryony said, 'Good heavens, we don't want to *kill* you. We're friendly weasels, we are. It was just that we were expecting some creature like the cockchafer or the shrew – or even bigger.'

Mawk said suspiciously, 'How did you do that voice? You even fooled a bat and a snake further up the tunnel. They've lived here all their lives and they think you're some sort of god!'

'Oh, that,' replied the mole proudly. 'Look, I sort of carved a loud speaker out of this soft rock with my claws. I've got very strong digging claws, see?' He held them up, then continued. 'See this hole here? When you speak into it, the sound goes up and round a sort of trumpet-shaped tunnel, which opens at the ceiling. Here, go on, try it? I don't mind. I've never had anyone to show it to before.'

Bryony stepped forward and said into the hole, 'MAWK, I'M GOING TO EAT YOUR LIVER!' The voice boomed out over the cavern and down the many tunnels which led from it.

Mawk visibly jumped at the sound of his name. Then he grimaced. 'Very funny, Bryony,' he said.

Sylver sat on a rock and stared at the mole. 'I still don't understand why you did all this?' he said. 'Surely you don't intend living in this cave all your life, just because your ancestors did before you? I mean, if you were a giant, it would be different. Giants have a sort of home territory – a place where others may find them. But even though you say you come from a family of giants, you're just an ordinary-sized mole. There's a whole world out there. Why not experience it?'

'I was scared,' admitted 3-G. 'There were two giants out there in the hills. I had to let them go on believing I was a massive mole who had created the hills, otherwise they would have come here and got me. And if I wanted to see the world I would have had to get past those two and they would have eaten me alive if they had known my real size.'

'We felt the earth shuddering last night. We thought it was you, moving around, making new hills,' said Bryony.

'Oh, that was just the old tunnels collapsing. Now that my grandma's gone, there's no-one

350

to maintain them. They just dry out and fall in on themselves. Good thing really, because those two giants further down might decide to use the tunnels one day, and come up here and get me.'

'Well, you don't need to worry any more – they're both dead – we killed 'em,' said Mawk, puffing out his chest.

'You-killed-them?' said 3-G, the mighty midget, aghast. 'You're giant-killers, are you? Which one of you is Jack?'

'Three of us are jacks,' replied Mawk, not understanding what this mole was talking about, 'and Bryony and Alysoun are jills.'

'Well I never! Three jacks and two jills. You could have two goes to get up the hill to fetch a pail of water, and still have one jack in reserve. Astonishing. Well, I'm glad I'm *not* a full-sized giant, with three Jack-the-giant-killers around. Three Jacks, eh? I suppose none of you eats any fat.'

'How did you do the footsteps?' asked Mawk, thoroughly taken with the mole's invention. 'Come on, show us.'

The mole picked up two fair-sized rocks and repeatedly thumped them together near the hole. His timing was perfect. They did indeed sound like footfalls on a cave floor.

'Brilliant!' cried Mawk.

Sylver said, 'Well, we're not actually here to admire your skills, 3-G. We're looking for an island called Dorma and we were told you could give us the information we require.'

'Me?'

351

'Well – the mole giant.'

'Yep, that's me all right.'

Sylver added, 'We were told you were in tune with the rhythms of the earth. Is that true?'

'Well, certainly my grandmother was – and, to a certain extent, my mother. You can't burrow under the earth all your life and not feel quite close to it: you get a sort of feel for the ebbs and flows of its tides. I dare say I have the same sort of thing in me, though I haven't ever put it into practice. I could try to listen to the movements of this great planet of ours, like my ancestors did. It's all to do with lunar pushes and pulls – the new moon and all that – and gravity. You need to be able to tune in to the rhythms of the earth.'

'Can you tell us about Dorma, then?'

'I might be able to, if I go down to the seashore. I can just allow my body to feel the winds, to empathize with them. I can dip my paw in the water and feel the sea, get some sort of sense of what the ocean currents are doing. It's not going to be easy, but maybe I can reawaken some skill for it.'

Sylver said, 'You've never done it before, have you?'

'No, but I sort of know it's in my bones. I must have got it from my mother and grandmother. It's a sort of forbidden knowledge, buried deep in my blood. Even now things are stirring deep inside me, just talking about it. Images are beginning to seep into my brain. I know the names of all the islands. My mother taught me them as a kind of litany. It's like learning your times tables.'

Bryony wrinkled her brow. 'What are they?'

'Never mind – if you don't know, it won't mean anything to you, even if I take the time to explain.'

Sylver said, 'So basically, if you come down to the sea with us, you may be able to help.'

'Of course – unless you're not telling me the truth about the other two giants.'

'We're tellin' the truth all right,' clicked Scirf, 'as you'll soon find out.'

They set off back to the ship, passing the bat and the cave-racer on the way. They had to lead their new companion by the paw. Out in the daylight he was as blind as a bat (in the same way as a bat would be as blind as a mole). On their way down from the hills they passed the body of the giant shrew. Scirf also described to 3-G what had happened to the cockchafer.

The mole sucked in his breath when he realized the devastation his new friends had wrought upon the tyrants of the highlands. 'I'm glad I'm not a proper giant, if that's what would have happened to me.'

'It wouldn't have happened to them either,' Sylver said, 'if they had not been so aggressive towards us. We were simply defending ourselves.'

'Don't forget, we needed your help,' Bryony reminded him. 'We could hardly have asked for that after we'd killed you, now could we?'

'That's true.'

The mole was somewhat mollified by these remarks. However, he was still in awe of the five weasels, even when he smelled the sea and knew they were speaking the truth. It was the first time the scent of ozone had wafted up his nostrils. He gave a contented sigh, which coincided with the yells of rage and despair from the others.

'What's the matter?' he said. 'Is something wrong?'

'Something wrong?' cried Sylver. 'I should say so. Our ship has gone!'

Chapter Thirty-Four

It was true! The five weasels stared down at the empty stretch of water in the bay. There was not a ship to be seen. Something terrible had happened.

'Let's go down to the shore and see what we can find,' said Sylver, trying not to betray his anxiety to the others. 'Perhaps there's someone there who can help us.'

3-G wondered what all the fuss was about, but he knew from the tone of their voices that this 'ship' was important to the weasels. He allowed himself to be led down to the seashore without questioning them any further.

'It's that Short Oneleg,' said Mawk. 'I bet he's to blame. I expect he organized a mutiny and took over the *Scudding Cloud* while we were up in the hills. I never did trust that pine marten. He had a greedy look about him. You only had to say "brass farthings" and his eyes lit up. All he wanted was Murgatroyd's treasure.'

'Treasure?' repeated the mole, a new brightness in his voice. 'What treasure?'

'Don't you start,' growled Scirf.

However, as they walked along the sands, Sylver found bits of wood and sail, which had recently been washed up. A hatch cover was found a little further on. Then a wooden chest, which had been in Sylver's cabin. There was other debris still floating in the water, too. It was obvious there had been a battle of some kind.

Sylver stared out towards the horizon, but could see no trace of a vessel. 'Well,' he said despairingly, 'it looks like we're stuck here – but what's happened to the rest of our crew?'

At that moment there came a shout from behind the dunes. Luke and Wodehed suddenly appeared out of the marram grass. Then Miniver. Finally they were followed by several pine martens, including the much-maligned Short Oneleg, who was having difficulty with his wooden limb in the soft, sinking sands.

Wodehed came up to the five weasels and the mole. 'Oh, I'm so glad to see you still alive. We thought you'd all been killed for sure. Where's Narky?'

Mawk hung his head before saying, 'I'm afraid he won't be coming back.'

'Oh, how sad,' said Wodehed.

Sylver asked, 'But what's happened here? Where is the ship?'

Short Oneleg stepped forward and peered with his single eye, like Cyclops before one of his vicious attacks. 'It was Sheriff Falshed,' he said dramatically. 'He come at us out of the sun. Swept into the bay and put several holes in our hull before we was able to get a shot back in reply, blast his eyes. We've been scuppered, cap'n. The *Scudding Cloud* lies at the bottom of the bay, an' that shark-bait sheriff is on his way back to Welkin in triumph.'

Sylver absorbed this news in disbelief. That they should have come so close to finding the humans, only to fail, was devastating. He could not imagine what they were going to do now. It did not look as if there was another ship on this particular island. They could perhaps build a sea-going raft, but that would take time and effort. By the time they finished it, much of Welkin would be swamped.

'He's really done for us this time, ain't he?' said Scirf, referring to Falshed. 'He's won.'

Sylver privately agreed, but he put a brave face on it. 'Let's build a fire and make some food for everyone, while we decide what's to be done. By the way, this is the local giant, 3-G,' he said, introducing the mole. 'He was going to help locate the position of Dorma.'

'A *small* giant,' added 3-G.

Weasels and pine martens murmured their names and welcomed the mole to their camp.

'Sorry about your trouble,' said 3-G. 'I might just have a go at finding out the information you require, just the same, in case the circumstances change.'

Sylver said he appreciated that and the mole wandered down to the shallows to dip in his paws.

While the camp fire was being built, the ship's cook came to see Sylver. 'Listen,' he said, 'this business about Murgatroyd's treasure . . .'

'It was a hoax,' replied Sylver. 'There was no treasure. I needed a crew.'

'So you lied to us?'

'I – I'm afraid so. It was for the common good.

357

If Welkin is taken by the sea, the pine martens will suffer the same as the weasels and stoats. I'm sorry I had to take you away from your homeland.'

Short Oneleg stood for a minute balanced on his three good pegs and then lifted one and waved it. 'Aw, forget it, cap'n. We sailed the seas well together, didn't we? I'm a bit miffed about the treasure, but you can't win 'em all, can you? The important thing now is to find a way of gettin' to Dorma.'

'I'm afraid that's going to prove impossible,' sighed Sylver. 'We're stuck here.'

Soon all the driftwood on the beach had been collected and there was a roaring fire. They gathered round this blaze, roasting crabs and shellfish. Others had gone to gather nuts and berries. Once their bellies were full, they could concentrate on the problems in paw. They certainly did not want to spend the rest of their lives on an island with muntjac deer and finches. Somehow they had to find enough wood to make a raft, to drift down the Spellbound Straits.

At about midnight the mole came back to the fireside. He had been digging in the sands and dipping his paws in the ocean. There was a thoughtful look on his face. 'Listen,' he said, 'all is not lost, my friends.'

'You've thought of a way to get us off here?' asked Sylver hopefully.

'Not that, no. But I have managed to discover the course of Dorma Island. I've been getting in tune with the rhythms of the earth and the currents of the sea. Dorma Island is only a week away from here.'

Sylver perked up. 'What? A week away? What does that mean?'

Now that it was night-time the mole's eyesight had improved. He could see better in the dark than in the light. He turned his back on the fire, picked up a twig, and began to draw things in the sand. 'Look, this is us,' he said, sketching the rough shape of an island. 'And these are various other islands which are floating near by. Here –' he drew another shape some way off – 'is Dorma – yes, the wind brings the sleepy scent of Dorma from that direction –' he pointed with the stick out to sea – 'and it is getting closer. The islands never collide, of course; they sort of sense each other's mass and drift away from each other, like jellyfish – but they sometimes pass quite close.'

Maddeningly, the mole paused for a while to clear his throat while the others waited on tenterhooks.

'So,' he said, continuing, 'I estimate that in one week Dorma will be in this position here. It's the closest it ever comes to this particular island.' He made a mark in the sand, which the weasels and pine martens studied closely.

'What does that mean?' asked Sylver. 'In terms of miles, that is?'

'Miles?' cried 3-G. 'Why, it's *metres*. Five hundred metres, give or take a centimetre or two.' He let this information sink in, waiting for Sylver's elated response.

Finally Sylver whispered, 'We could make a raft and reach it like that.'

Bryony said, 'I don't think so. We don't really

359

have the materials. Look at the driftwood . . .'

They looked and realized that the driftwood consisted of small twigs and bits of rattan. It was good for a fire, but one needed logs to make a raft.

'What about the bridge over the chasm?' said Scirf.

Again Bryony shook her head. 'If you remember, that too was made of reeds. And the debris from our ship has been taken away by the swift currents which sweep by the island. None of it has been washed up on the beach.'

'In that case,' said Sylver resolutely, 'we'll swim. We'll swim to Dorma Island!'

Scirf looked at the ocean. 'Five hundred metres? That's a long way for a weasel to swim.' And he was right; it was a long way.

'Through shark-infested waters,' added Mawk. This was true; the sea was full of sharks.

'And the monsoon season is coming before then,' said the prophetic mole.

'The monsoon season?' questioned Sylver. 'What's that?'

'It's a time of mountainous waves and massive swells. Sometimes there are great storms, which pound at the shores of the islands.'

'Difficult waters to swim through, eh?'

'I'm afraid so.'

Bryony sought to lighten the mood a bit. 'Never mind,' she said, 'we'll send Mawk first. If he doesn't come back, then we'll have a kalkie on the beach and forget all about it.'

Weasels, pine martens and mole clicked their teeth in amusement.

'Very funny,' replied Mawk. 'I don't think.'

'We'll just have to wait,' said Sylver. 'We've got a week. It'll pass slowly, but once the island's here, I for one am going to make the swim.'

'I'm with you, cap'n,' cried Short. 'I may only have three good legs but my bad un's made of wood, so if I don't manage to swim, I'll float there just the same.'

One by one the weasels and pine martens all confirmed that they too would be swimming across – even Mawk, though there was a kind of strangled note to his voice.

Only the mole declined the offer of a morning dip. 'I'm not sure moles can swim and I wouldn't be able to see which way I was going in any case.'

'We never expected you to do more than you have already,' Sylver told him. 'And we thank you for that.'

After which they all settled down to a nice evening by the fire, telling stories, singing songs, bonding friendships.

Chapter Thirty-Five

It was a smug and, it has to be said, a slightly awed
Sheriff Falshed who sailed back towards Welkin.
He was smug because he had at last dealt a final
deadly blow to his enemies. He was awed because
he had carried this out by himself, with no assistance from anyone else – except his marines and
crew, of course, but they were lowly creatures.
When the time came to tell the prince what he had
done, the prince would not ask for the names of
the lower ranks.

Falshed tried to feel a little humble, but he could
not manage it. He was too full of himself. Even the
lightning strike had taken a back seat in his mind
now. It was all to do with Falshed the hero,
winner, victor, the invincible High Sheriff of
Welkin.

However, he did promise that those stoats and
ferrets who had distinguished themselves in battle
would be rewarded. It depended on what the
prince gave. A whole county? A fiefdom? A castle
in the country? Once he knew what he had got,
Falshed could dish out captaincies and sergean-
cies left, right and centre.

Falshed's confidence knew no bounds. On the
return journey he encountered sea monsters,

vicious sea fairies, dragons and hostile tribes of mongooses. He sallied forth with blade in paw and swept them aside, rent them asunder. The terrible dragon Grendel's mother had his sword still sticking from her ribs. He was glorious in battle; he was magnanimous in peace.

Rosencrass and Guildenswine were given to the mongooses in exchange for supplies, to use as totem poles. They were split apart and placed one at either end of the mongooses' island. It was their job to predict the weather and sea conditions. If they got it wrong they were chastised by the mongoose witch doctor, who drove sharp nails into their wooden heads.

'Don't leave us here!' pleaded Rosencrass.

'Take us with you!' cried Guildenswine.

'Sorry,' replied Sheriff Falshed. 'I needed fresh water and strawberries for the return trip.'

'But we can't do it,' cried Rosencrass. 'We don't know how to foretell the weather.'

'No-one does,' came the sensible reply. 'All forecasters get it wrong. You're not expected to get it right. Animals love to moan about the weather. If you were able to predict it accurately then there would be nothing to complain about, would there? Animals who haven't got anything to complain about get depressed very quickly. You're helping them.'

Falshed continued his conquests. Territories were taken in the name of the prince and ceded to local despots who agreed to pay tribute. Mountains were rediscovered and renamed. A giant wolf was slaughtered, skinned, and the hide stored as a present for Sibiline.

By the time Falshed landed on the shores of Welkin, his stature had grown tenfold. His soldiers, marines and crew hailed him as a god. They would have followed him anywhere. He had brought them treasure galore: they were rich from the spoils of war. They sang songs about his exploits. They would hear no ill of their leader, who marched them to Castle Rayn.

'At last!' he said to himself. 'I have realized my real potential!'

Marching across Welkin, Falshed noticed that the flooding was infinitely worse than when he had left the country, but he felt no pricking of conscience.

Prince Poynt was holding court when Falshed arrived. The sheriff had sent word ahead that he was back on home soil and had been victorious. He was a little surprised, and somewhat irked, to find no welcoming committee to meet him, either on the shores of the lake or in the battlements, when he stepped off the boat. It was to be expected that a homecoming hero would be greeted with cheers, fanfares and garlands.

Instead, there was only Spinfer there to say hello. Spinfer was all dressed up in noble's robes and a noble's chain of office. Clearly Falshed's servant had risen in station since the sheriff had left for foreign shores.

'Spinfer?' said Falshed, removing his helmet and shaking the dust of travel from his cloak. 'How now?'

'Oh, this?' Spinfer looked down at himself with a smug clicking of his teeth. 'I'm the new Lord Chancellor. You'll hear all about it when you see the prince. He's waiting for you in the throne room.'

Without pausing to take a bath, Falshed went down to the throne room and strode into the court.

Heads turned as he marched into the room. Lord Elphet was there, and Earl Takely, Jessex, Wilisen and a number of other nobles. Prince Poynt, in his white ermine, was lounging on his throne. Sibiline sat on her throne, next to her brother. Pompom was dancing around, walloping stoats and weasels with his inflated mouse-bladder on its stick. The whole room fell silent as Sheriff Falshed walked up to the prince.

The sheriff bowed low, with an elegant flourish of his cloak, and said, 'My liege, I come to you in triumph.'

'Do you now,' sighed the prince, fiddling with his belt buckle. 'And what triumph would that be?'

'I have sunk the *Scudding Cloud*, the ship taken by Lord Sylver and his weasels. They are now cast-aways on some remote island in the Spellbound Straits, deep in the Cobalt Sea. We shall never see or hear from them again.'

'Really?' yawned the prince, inspecting his claws for dirt. 'How interesting.'

Falshed was beginning to feel that others knew something he did not. Nobles would not meet his eye. Spinfer was standing to one side in his chancellor's robes, looking as if he might burst out laughing any second. The prince was clearly bored.

Or perhaps not. Perhaps this was a game devised by the prince. Should he play along for a while? He did not feel like games. He had fought a long and hard campaign. He wanted the merit due to him. Now.

'My liege,' he said slowly. 'This is most unbecoming of you, to play with me in this way. I have done everything asked of me, and more. I have destroyed your enemies for you. Welkin is safe in the paws of the stoats, with you as their ruler. I think I deserve more than this . . .'

Suddenly, the prince's countenance turned from a look of boredom to one of fury. 'How dare you speak to me this way, you impudent stoat! Do you think I don't know what you've done? I've harboured a snake in my bosom all these years. A common thief!'

Falshed blinked. 'My liege?'

'Yes, a low, sneaking thief.' The prince produced a small ornament from behind his throne. It was a carving of an otter by a pool. It was true this had been in the prince's possession, until Falshed had pinched it one day. It was a moment of rashness which any stoat might have succumbed to and later regretted.

'Do you deny you stole this from my chambers?' cried the prince. 'Speak now, before I have you executed.'

'No, not executed, brother. Please,' intervened Sibiline, whose interest in Falshed had flared into something more than mild interest now that he stood before her. Falshed seemed changed. He looked more confident, more able, more *handsome*.

'Executed!' thundered the prince. 'Look! Look at his face. He can't deny it, because it's true. Spinfer – Lord Spinfer brought it to my attention,

Falshed. Your servant betrayed you. How do you like that?'

Falshed found Spinfer's eyes and his ex-servant had the grace to look down at the floor in shame.

His faithful stoatservant had betrayed him! A *faithless* stoatservant. How ignoble. How stoatish. Still, that was for another time. Now he had to deal with the prince. Sheriff Falshed stared at the ruler of all Welkin. He could not believe his ears. He, Falshed, had just given the prince his greatest moment in history and the prince was worried about an ornament that had been nicked from his chambers.

Pompom came trilling and dancing over to Falshed and batted him in the face with his inflated mouse-bladder.

Falshed instantly grabbed the jester by the scruff of his neck and heaved him across the floor. Pompom went screaming the length of the court, sliding over the marble on his bottom, to crash into some chairs at the far end. His mouse-bladder burst on contact with a sharp corner. The stick snapped. The jester burst into tears.

Falshed stood there covered in the white dust of the road he had marched along from the port to the castle. 'Don't ever do that again, Pompom, to *anyone*,' said Falshed.

There was not a stoat in the room now who would meet the sheriff's eyes. They all knew of the injustice that was being done to him; even Spinfer was aware of it. Certainly Sibiline, dewy-eyed with embarrassment, felt for him at that moment.

Falshed spoke to the prince in a very firm, low

voice. 'Have you lost your reason, sire? Are you completely mad?'

The prince's head came up with a jerk. His eyes widened. He seemed about to have a fit. 'What? What? What? You dare speak to me in that manner? I'll have you roasted until your eyes pop. I'll have you cut into pieces and the bits minced. I'll . . .'

There were gasps of dismay and horror throughout the room, but Falshed knew exactly what he was doing.

'My troops,' he continued in the same low voice, 'have crossed the river Bronn.'

'What? What does that mean?'

'It means they are waiting on the shores of the lake. You have here your imperial guard, which numbers but a hundred or so stoats. The rest of the army is with me. We have fought a spectacular campaign together. I can do no wrong in their eyes. On the way here they sang songs about me. The chorus went something like this:

'"Falshed he is a captain great
and a jolly fine ruler he would make.
Pointy doesn't know his head from his toe –
paws up those who think Poynt should go."

'You get my drift? My troops want me to usurp the throne.

'Now, I took little heed of this, on the march. I was then a loyal subject of my prince. I told them I was an honourable stoat and wanted no part in any rebellion. They were disappointed. One of my personal bodyguard – they volunteered for the job, by the way, and call themselves "Falshed's Immortals" – said to me before I took the ferry here, "If you don't come back crowned in glory, we will raze the castle to the ground." Do you understand what I'm saying to you? Or are you still the way I left you before my voyage – as thick as two short planks?'

The prince's eyes blazed. At that moment a soldier from the battlements came hurrying into the court.

'My prince, the whole army on the banks of the lake is calling for Sheriff Falshed. They say they want to see him. They say they do not like him being out of their sight for so long! They say they want him to come up to the east tower and show them the laurel-leaf crown that he must by now have been given by you, my liege, as reward for his great endeavours.'

Even in the deep recesses of the castle, the court could now clearly hear the shouts from the distant shores of the lake. Some of the nobles were looking worried and had edged their way across the floor towards Falshed. Others were shuffling towards the doorway, ready to make a quick exit. However, the prince's brow was still clouded. His new chancellor, Spinfer, whispered in his ear.

'Off with Falshed's head!' roared the prince a moment later. 'My sister's Jillazons will attack and destroy any force which tries to take the castle!'

Not a soul moved to take the sheriff into custody. The guards seemed to have disappeared. Nor did the princess make any effort to summon her regiment of jills. The prince looked perplexed and angry. 'Off with his head, I say!'

Falshed strode up to the throne. The prince cowered. Falshed took the monarch by the scruff of his royal neck and eased him from his seat. He then took the prince's place, sitting on the throne, his cloak draped about him.

Prince Poynt screamed, 'Get out of my chair, you beast.'

Falshed looked at Sibiline, who placed a gentle paw on his forelimb and nodded slowly. An unspoken agreement had been reached between them. Without the need for words they both knew what the future held.

'Your sister and I have agreed to rule the kingdom together,' said Falshed to the prince. 'And if you don't shut up, very quickly, you'll spend the next three weeks in the dungeon – which, as you well know, is flooded at the present time.'

'I – I – I . . .' stammered the prince.

'Do be sensible and shut up, Pointy,' said Sibiline. 'Go to the ramparts and tell the army that Falshed is at this moment being inaugurated as Lord Protector of Welkin. Tell them you have stepped down through ill health. You have retired. You have been put out to grass and will spend the rest of your remaining autumn years playing golf.'

'I will not,' said the prince sullenly, finally getting the message that it was all over for him. 'I don't like golf.' He left the room in undignified defeat, his head low, his tail trailing.

The nobles crowded round the throne, congratulating Falshed, swearing fealty to the Lord Protector. Lord Elphet went up to the battlements and passed on the news to the troops on the far shores of the lake. A mighty cheer went up. Later, Falshed went onto the battlements himself, bathed and oiled, clad in a magnificent raiment out of the prince's wardrobe. Sibiline, majestic and regal as ever, accompanied him, her paw on his forelimb. She was wearing the wolfskin coat her lord had given her as a 'new partnership gift'.

'Whatever happened to that silly carving I gave you?' asked Sibiline coyly. 'I expect you lost it straight away. The one of the emperor dragonfly.'

A flutter of panic went through Falshed before he remembered he was the chosen one: the lightning had struck him, had filled him with greatness. 'My dear,' he said silkily, 'it was torn from my tunic breast by Grendel's mother.'

Sibiline looked piqued, and pouted. 'Who's this Grendel? Was she a jealous female, vying for the affections of my Falshed.'

'Grendel is a fearsome monster, a thousand times larger than a weasel. His mother is even more fearsome, being ten times larger than Grendel. I fought valiantly to save the brooch, but the creature swallowed it down one of her many throats. I tried to retrieve it, but she was too monstrous even for me. My trusty blade was buried in her bosom when she fled.'

Sibiline leaned on him and stroked his shoulder. 'Oh, Falshy,' she murmured. 'I knew you would be true.'

The troops on the shore went wild and cheered and yelled. Falshed sent them whole carcasses of roast vole and barrels of honey dew. They feasted all night long. The newly appointed generals amongst them attended a banquet at the castle with their newly elevated lord. They asked him to lead them on more campaigns, to conquer more territory. He waved a paw, saying that the country needed straightening out first and there were to be a few tournaments and games for the troops before any new campaigns could be launched.

Spinfer had hurried to his chambers and packed his bags, but Falshed's Immortals caught him trying to board a ferry. He was dragged in front of Falshed.

'Spinfer, you betrayed me,' said Falshed.

'Yes,' replied the servant, 'you treated me like dirt for many years.'

'That's not true, Spinfer. I treated you like a servant, that was all. However, I remember you provided me with many good ideas and advice and I think you were rewarded for those. Do you know what's going to happen to you now?'

'No – and I don't care,' lied Spinfer. 'I had my moment of glory. I shall die happy.'

'I believe you will die in pain,' snapped Falshed, who wanted an abject Spinfer. 'I can provide a lot of that, you know, now that I'm ruler. Bucketfuls of the stuff.'

Falshed was rewarded with the faintest shadow of fear crossing Spinfer's face. He was satisfied. No need to destroy his former servant now. Spinfer had always been useful in the past, having a brain the size of a watermelon squashed into that small, neat skull of his.

'However, I am magnanimous in victory. You shall remain as Lord Chancellor, to advise me as you always have done, with wisdom and wit.'

Spinfer blinked, hardly able to believe his ears. 'Do you mean that, my lord?'

'Of course I mean it,' replied Falshed. 'But one whiff of betrayal, ever again, and your head will be rolling down the skittle alley on Friday nights. You understand me?'

'Never, never again, my lord. I have seen the true stoat which lies beneath the High Sheriff of Welkin. You have my undying loyalty. I am – your craven servant.' Spinfer bowed low.

'Thank you, Spinfer,' replied Falshed.

The new Lord Protector's triumph was complete.

Chapter Thirty-Six

The mole's predictions proved to be accurate. At the appointed time a new island hove into view over the horizon. It came steadily nearer and nearer to the muntjac island, until Sylver judged it was as close as it was going to get. In another day it would be drifting past and on its way to an unknown destination. The weasel leader made ready his faithful weasel band.

'We are at the point in our quest,' he said gravely, 'where we are about to land on Dorma Island. Wodehed has the ground herb necessary to filter out the sleep gas in a waterproof pouch. He will be the first ashore. He will stuff the herb up his own nostrils, then treat each of us as we reach the beach. Remember to breathe through your noses.'

'Sylver,' said Alysoun, 'why don't we put the herb in before we start the swim?'

'Perhaps Wodehed would like to answer that one.'

Wodehed stood up and cleared his throat. 'We don't know how it will react to the sea,' he explained. 'Salt water might destroy the herb's ability to filter out the perfume from the flowers. It's best to take no chances. You will just have to

374

hold your breath for a minute or two, when you scramble up the shingle to the high-tide mark.'

Sylver felt enough had been said now. His weasels had been ready for this last leg of the journey for days. Now they simply had to get on with it. They gathered at the water's edge, with Short Oneleg and the pine marten crew to bid them good luck. Sylver had decided, despite their willingness to do the swim, that the martens and the weasel craftsmen should stay behind. They would be picked up later, if the weasels' visit to Dorma was successful. If the weasels failed, then the martens and the carpenters and smithies would either have to make a home on the muntjac's island or hope for a passing vessel to pick them up.

'Break a hind leg, Scirf,' said Short to that redoubtable weasel.

'What? You want me to be like you, do you?'

Short clicked his teeth in merriment. 'No, no – it's just a way of wishing you well.'

'You could have said "good luck".'

'No, it's bad luck to say good luck.'

'You've lost me there, cooky,' sighed Scirf. 'But I'll take your word for it.'

There was a slight southerly breeze blowing. This would help the weasels to get ashore before they smelled the 'lotus' blooms. The onshore wind would also carry the perfume into the island's interior. Fortunately for the swimmers, the weather was fine. There was a rippling sea, shimmering in the early morning light. No ugly shark fins could be seen cutting through the water. The swim looked fairly straightforward, though it was a long way for small creatures such as weasels.

Overhead the sky was almost clear: only a few woolly clouds drifted like lazy sheep gently across blue. There was a zest in the air, more than just the scent of the ozone. It seemed to come from the spirits of the weasels themselves, who had been a long time in preparing for this event. They were ready. Their very souls sparkled in their mortal houses.

'Well,' said Wodehed, stepping forward to lead the swim, 'here we go.'

He entered the water. Although the sun was hot, there was a very cold current running between the islands. He shivered slightly, before beginning the usual four-leg weasel-paddle: nose high and out of the water, tail acting as a rudder, waterproof coat, wet and dark, below the surface of the water. Wodehed gradually forged his way through the surface ripples, which were in truth like waves to weasels.

One by one the others entered the sea. Some – Scirf, for one – plunged in and shook themselves warm, before swimming on. Some, like Luke and Mawk, tested the water gently with one claw, before getting in gradually, letting the cold sea creep up their bodies until they were submerged. Bryony went in backwards, splashing her body to get it wet before she actually made the dip complete.

Soon, all the weasels were in the water. Their noses were black dots scattered on the surface of the sea. Little droplets of salt water hung, glistening, from their whiskers. The pine martens watched them go. They were silent. It seemed a bit premature to cheer. It was possible that none of the weasels would make it to that far and distant shore.

Almost halfway across that great divide the weasels did indeed begin to tire. They were tense with watching for sharks or barracuda. Their little forelegs, going nineteen to the dozen at first, slowed to the rhythmic ticking of grandfather clocks. 'Keep going, keep going,' cried Sylver, trying to keep the salt water out of his mouth as he spoke. 'Not far to go, my brave band of weasels . . .'

But there was a long way to go – an awful long way. A kind of desperation set in. Miniver, the smallest of the weasels, was already having trouble. Scirf was alongside, encouraging her, but she was tiring fast. Soon she would slip into that chilled, exhausted state which long-distance swimmers experience, and perhaps drop down below the level of the waves.

'We're not going to make it,' choked Mawk, his limbs aching so badly he felt like crying. 'We've had it this time.'

For once no-one argued with the doubting weasel. They all knew how he was feeling, for they felt the same way. Cold water has a way of reaching right into the marrow of your bones, robbing you of energy, sapping you of strength. It was a courageous effort – a valiant effort – but it would not be long before each weasel was fatigued beyond endurance.

Just when the weakest of the weasels was about to give in, an ancient man-of-war ship hove in sight. It sped towards the weasels with great determination, its ragged sails billowing, its prow ploughing a neat furrow across the sea. The weasels watched in amazement as it cut through the waves, bearing down on the spot where they now trod water.

'Ah-haaaaa!' screeched a voice from high above in the crow's nest. 'The weasels! The weasels! I have them at last!'

It was the voice of Flaggatis, strapped in his makeshift throne at the top of the mast. His ancient face was full of malicious glee. He waved a forepaw in exultation, victory over the weasels now firmly in his grasp. He would teach them not to stand in the way of one of the cleverest stoats that ever lived!

Hanging over the rails, dangling from the rigging, dripping from the buntlines and swarming over the decks, were hundreds of marsh rats. Their faces were decorated with war paint: the eyes circled, the noses striped with white and red bars. They showed their horrible yellow teeth, they rolled the horrible whites of their eyes, they waved their horrible hairless tails. The marsh rats were ecstatic: they were about to slaughter the hated weasel enemy.

However, because of the constant running repairs which needed to be made to the rotten old vessel, the rats had left their scrambling nets hanging over the side, even though the vessel was running before the wind. Sylver shouted to his band to try and grab the netting as the ship sped past. Three of them – Bryony, Luke and Mawk – managed to do so.

'Get them!' shrieked Captain Bliggghtt.

'Kill them!' screeched Flaggatis.

378

Bryony, Luke and Mawk had all clung to the port side of the ship. It was thus towards this side that all the rats ran. They had drawn sharp sickles and iron hooks, a rat's favourite weapons, and scrambled excitedly for the port rail, each eagerly hoping to have a slice of weasel flesh. Even the helmsrat had left his steering wheel spinning idly, seeking to bury his hook in the skull of a helpless weasel.

'STOP!' screamed Flaggatis in a great panic. Only he could see what was about to happen. 'Go back, you fools, go back!'

But it was too late. They could not obey what they could not hear. Their own blood-thirsty screeching and squealing drowned out any orders from above. Their attention was solely on the weasels. They could not get to the ship's rail quickly enough, anxious to be in at the kill. Rats went swinging from the yardarms, and streaming down the rigging on the port side. The weight of the ship's entire rat contingent rushed to one central spot on the port side.

The ship slewed round as the rudder was left to find its own medium, leaving the starboard side exposed to the wind.

'You crazy idiots!' screamed Flaggatis, fear gripping his heart and squeezing it with cold fingers. 'Spread out, or we'll capsize . . .' These were true words and the last he ever spoke.

The weight of the rats, combined with the wind bearing down on the ship's flank, caused the vessel to roll over. Those on board not strapped down were tipped into the water. Into the sea plopped dozens, then hundreds of rats, yelling and bleating as they hurtled down, still clutching their sickles and iron hooks.

The craft continued to capsize. The masts struck the water and were soon submerged, as the vessel turned upside down. Some rats were trapped underneath in pockets of air. Others were flung clear. Some bobbed about quite near to the upturned ship and clung to it.

The three weasels had continued to hold onto the scrambling nets. They were pulled under the water as the ship rolled and finally came up on the opposite side. They continued to hang there, surrounded by drowning, struggling rats. These blood-thirsty rodents were no longer interested in burying sickle or hook in weasel flesh, but only concerned about saving themselves from a watery grave.

Then a hatch cover, loosened when the ship went over, drifted by amongst other flotsam. Bryony leaped from the ship to this 'raft' and called for the other two to join her. They did so, jumping for all they were worth. Luke landed in the hatch. Mawk had to be rescued from the water and dragged on. Once the three of them were aboard, they paddled away from the sinking ship towards their friends. Soon all eight weasels were on the hatch cover.

Happily there was no room for any rats, even if the weasels had been feeling charitable. The exhausted band sat watching dispassionately as the rodents struck out for the nearest shore, which was, of course, the beach on the muntjac's island. Rats are reasonably good swimmers over short distances and these marsh rats were better than most. They had spent their lives crossing rivers and water wastes. They were not about to let themselves be sucked under by the ship.

Crying out with the stresses and strains, the ship began to break up, parting at the seams. Timbers creaked and snapped. Joints groaned and parted. Lines stretched until they were too taut and then twanged apart. In the galley the ovens, still hot from cooking rat food, exploded and sent hissing, sizzling metal flying everywhere. Planks sprang apart, their rusty nails like bared teeth. Chains twisted and wrenched, pulling stanchions from their moorings, drawing staples from their beams.

There was nothing anyone could do to stop the ship from going under. It went bow first in the end. The front of the ship filled with water and dipped its head like a duck diving for bottom weed. The stern came up like a duck's bottom, to point at the sky. Masts, including the main mast, came lurching out of the water one last time as the vessel straightened on its descent to the bottom.

The drowned, dripping body of Flaggatis, still strapped to the crow's nest, reappeared just for a moment. A forelimb flapped loosely, back and forth, with the movement of the vessel. It was as if the mad Flaggatis were waving a last goodbye. Then the stoat magician, ruler of the marsh rats, went down to the depths with his ship. It was a fitting end.

Finally there was nothing except bubbles on the surface of the sea, with rats grabbing bits of wood to keep themselves afloat while they swam for the nearest shore.

Once they had recovered their strength, Sylver and the other weasels paddled towards the shores of Dorma Island. As they approached it, Wodehed passed around the magical herb and they stuffed the ground leaves up their nostrils. They were still able to breathe through the concoction, which strained the poisoned air going to their lungs.

'Oh, loog,' said Bryony, speaking as if she had a heavy cold, 'Mawg's gone to sleeb!'

Mawk had indeed dropped into a doze. He snored quietly, having been slow to stuff his nose. Now he had fallen under the influence of the heavy perfume drifting from the shore. It was lucky that the weasels had *not* waited until they were on the beach: they might well have succumbed even before they reached it.

But then again, as Scirf remarked, Mawk could fall asleep in a thunderstorm.

Chapter Thirty-Seven

They managed to block Mawk's nose with the herb, but his mouth fell open and he began breathing through that instead. So Scirf put his claws around Mawk's snout and held his mouth shut. After a while the last weasel woke up to find himself surrounded by a ring of faces.

'You all right?' asked Scirf.

'Yeb, thing so,' replied Mawk dreamily.

'Good. We must be on our way. Bryony and Alysoun have already been exploring ahead. There are some caves not far away. I have no doubt we'll find the humans there.'

'How cumb you don't speeg as if you have a code?' asked Mawk.

'I'm used to filters in my nose,' replied Scirf. 'I used to stuff grass up there when the rhubarb dung got too high in the hot summer. It comes with practice. Sylver's not too bad either.'

'You-just-have-to-speak-slowly-and-deliber-ately,' replied Sylver.

The weasels now studied the landscape around them. The beach was not wide – only about three metres of sand lay between sea and rainforest edge. The rainforest itself was lush. There were loquat trees with small reddish fruits. There were big-bellied baobabs, their trunks full of water. There were tamarinds and figs, thorn trees and bananas. Cedars, with their many green shelves, stood with high shoulders over cocoa shrubs and waxy-leaved oleanders.

One particular plant stood out from all the others, though. This prominent member of the local flora group had huge, trumpet-shaped flowers, cream in colour, hanging from twisted vine stems bearing large, dark-green leaves. Yellow stamens lolled like swollen tongues from the dark recesses of the trumpet bells. A kind of reddish-orangey dust coated the cream petals where the stamens touched their velvety softness.

It was obvious to the weasels that these were the blooms exuding the heavy fumes that induced sleep. The powerful scent even penetrated the nose-plugs of the weasels, but fortunately not sufficiently to affect them. These large flowers were surrounded by sleeping birds of all varieties, which seemed to have simply dropped from the sky as they flew over the great blossoms. No doubt there would be insects and spiders scattered there, too.

Sylver had been calling these sleep flowers 'lotus blossoms', but in truth no-one knew the name of the wondrous plant.

'Forward,' said Sylver. 'Find the path to the caves.'

However, just as they were about to move off, the weasels observed a strange phenomenon. Out of the jungle came hordes of shadows; judging by their shape they had obviously belonged to human beings at one time. Now, however, they were not attached to any creature. They simply drifted around like dark rags.

The shadows formed a line in front of the weasels, blocking their path. 'Go no further,' warned one. 'If you try to pass through us you will be flung into eternal darkness.' The shadows linked arms to form a line which could not be crossed without touching them.

'We'll see if you're telling the truth, my friend,' muttered Scirf, as he watched a migrating bird fly through the nightmarish chain of shadows.

True enough, the bird seem to vanish the instant it flew into the heart of the speaker.

Sylver said, 'What is this? Why won't you let us through?'

'We know what you're trying to do,' cried the leader. 'You wish to wake the humans! We are their shadows. We do not want them to be woken.'

'Why on earth not?' asked Bryony. 'Don't you want to go back to Welkin again?'

'Of course not,' replied another shadow. 'Now that our masters and mistresses are in a deep, magical sleep we are *free*. We can do as we wish, walk or run where we want. If they wake up, we shall have to do their bidding, copy their actions, follow them like slaves. I like my freedom. I will not give it up easily.'

The shadows were tall and menacing in the early morning sun. They formed an effective barrier against the weasels, like an army from the land of the dead.

The weasels could understand the shadows' point of view, but Sylver felt that they should obey the laws of the universe, set down by the one

Creator of the world. Every other thing or creature was subject to those laws; it was not right that the shadows should detach themselves from the heels of their owners and fly away like wild birds.

Sylver told them as much.

'We care nothing for the laws of the universe,' came the answer. 'We snap our fingers at any Creator.'

This was blasphemy, which should normally have been dealt with by a higher order in the spiritual world. However, Sylver had had an idea. The shadows might have been able to flout certain laws of the universe, but there were other natural laws that could be used to thwart them.

Since abandoning their owners the shadows had lost some of their reason. A shadow is only part of a whole and without the creature that casts it, the shadow loses the safe boundaries which make it feel secure. This produces a kind of hysterical madness of the spirit, which the shadows could not control. They did and said things which were completely out of character.

'In that case,' Sylver told the shadows, 'we shall stay here until you are virtually gone.'

'We don't go,' came the reply. 'I expect you think that the night-time will see us off. Wrong! We join with the night to become one blanket shadow. If you are not gone before nightfall we shall swallow your whole band and none of you will ever escape.'

'Never mind nightfall,' answered Sylver, thankful for the tip to be off the island before evening; 'noon is much closer.'

He and the other weasels settled down to await

386

the midday sun, which they knew would shorten the shadows. Here in the tropics the effect was even more marked than in Welkin: the sun moved directly overhead, and there was nothing but a dark patch lost in the tall grasses – the top of each shadow's head and shoulders. The weasels were able to step over the line without touching it. The shadows moaned in unison, knowing they had been outsmarted.

Sylver and the others now approached the caves. Each small weasel heart was pounding. It had been one thing to talk about confronting humans; quite another now that the time had come to do so. Traditionally wild animals avoid humans: it is in the nature of the beasts of the field to steer clear of potential danger. Humans are unpredictable creatures. They are unreasonable. They often act on impulse. In short, wild animals did not trust humans, nor would they ever, completely.

Sylver entered the first cave alone. A human lay across the cave mouth, just inside the overhang. It was huge, bigger than Sylver had ever imagined. His heart raced. He had seen pictures of humans in books, of course, but until now they had been mythical creatures. Here was his first live one, breathing softly in a deep sleep. Humans were creatures of legend no longer. They were real.

He moved further into the cave, still in the light from the entrance. There were more of them, male and female, with skins of different shades. There were dark-skinned humans and pale-skinned humans and some with tints in between. And they were big, strange-looking mammals, unlike any other creature on Welkin. Sylver saw the famous human 'hand' with its equally famous 'thumb'. And the feet which had been flattened into a right angle with the leg, so that these creatures could walk upright all the time. He shuddered.

Sylver went back to the others. He was still trembling. They crowded round him sympathetically.

'Are they really that ugly?' asked Bryony. 'Are they so fearsome-looking?'

'Fearsome-looking, yes. As to ugly, I expect they like each other's looks well enough. It's not for us to judge one of the Creator's creatures.'

'But you look so shaken!' said Mawk, scared he would be asked to go into the cave too.

'So would you be,' Bryony said. 'I'm not looking forward to seeing my first human either.'

'Well,' replied Sylver, 'everyone is going to have to. I didn't see any children in that cave. They're probably on their own, in a separate cave altogether. Let's search them all.'

The weasels went about their task in fear and trepidation, but eventually they found the children's cave. These smaller creatures were not quite as frightening as the adults. Wodehed took some more of the magical herb from his backpack and a few of the children were treated.

One by one these young people woke, to stare about them in amazement. Finally the last one sat up and rubbed its eyes, saying, 'I was having such a nice dream – we were all on our way home . . .'

The weasels had retreated outside the cave. The children came out now, blinking in the bright light. When they were able to see better, they noticed the weasels.

'Ooohhh look – little animals with belts and backpacks,' cried one child. 'Are we still sleeping? I must be dreaming. There's one with a hat. And one with a little sword . . .'

For the first time in their lives the weasels heard the delightful sound of children's laughter.

Sylver stepped forward bravely, for the humans towered above him, even though they were children, their shoulders up in the clouds, their bright eyes like stars in the heavens. They moved awkwardly, but with confidence. Sylver knew he could outrun them, if he wished, but he was still very wary.

'Human children!' he said dramatically. 'I am looking for the girl called Alice and the boy called Tom.'

'It speaks!' squealed the little girl. 'I heard it talk!'

There was a hubbub amongst the children now. Sylver waited patiently for this to die down, before repeating his request. Eventually two children came forward. Sylver explained that he was the leader of a band of weasels, that he and the other members had been searching for the clues hinted at in Alice's diary found in the Thistle Hall library. They had been through many hardships in order to seek out the humans, wake them, and hopefully persuade them to return to Welkin.

'You found my clue at Thunder Oak!' cried Alice. 'How wonderful!'

'And mine at Castle Storm,' said the boy called Tom.

'What I would like you to do now, you children, is to wake your parents. Who is the leader of the adults?'

'Why, King Andrew, of course, for the northern peoples – and Queen Cheryl for the southern peoples.'

'I must speak with these two rulers and tell them how important it is that they return to Welkin. We need Tom and Alice, but in the meantime will the rest of you children begin to cut down the blooms from which the sleeping gas comes? Use sticks to swipe off the heads. They'll grow again later, but we need to rid the air of these vapours.'

The children did as they were asked, being children, who found adventure in these games.

Tom and Alice were given some of the herb and sent into the caves where the adults slept. Eventually two adult humans, a man and a woman, stumbled out into the sunlight. Alice and Tom came after them. Judging by their clothes and their imperious looks these two were obviously the king of the north and the queen of the south. They sat down on the grass to recover their wits. They appeared to be a little angry at being woken.

'My name is Sylver,' said the leader of the weasels, 'and these are Alysoun, Bryony, Scirf, Mawk-the-doubter, Luke, who is our holy weasel, Wodehed, our magician, and Miniver, the finger-weasel. There were more of us, but tragically some have been killed in our efforts to find your hiding place.'

The king started and looked quickly at the

queen. 'What's this?' he boomed. 'Talking animals?'

'These are the Spellbound Straits, Andrew,' she replied, 'you must expect magic in the air.'

Sylver was still in awe of these two great beasts, but he stood his ground and continued with his speech. 'We do not live in the Spellbound Straits, but are from Welkin . . .'

'Go away,' said the queen coldly. 'My head aches.'

Alice intervened with, 'But Your Majesties, the weasels came all the way from Welkin to wake us. Our old country is being flooded by the sea. The dykes are breaking down.'

The king rubbed his face hard and stood up. He stared about him. 'I have been asleep for a very long time,' he muttered. 'What's all this nonsense about sea walls? We came here to hide ourselves away. What of Welkin?'

Sylver said patiently, 'Sire, I realize we asked no permission to wake you, but surely you must still have some affection for the land which gave you birth. If you, and the queen, and your subjects do not come back with us to Welkin, it will soon be a few islands with waterways between. Already much flooding has taken place. The dykes are crumbling.'

'And what is this to you?' said the queen irritably. 'Can't you just find a bit of dry ground and leave us in peace?'

'My warreners used to hang such weasels as you from their wire gibbets,' said the king. 'Are we to listen to such creatures? Why am I even talking to you?'

Sylver's heart was sinking. He had known this would not be easy. The humans had left Welkin for a reason. They would not just jump up and go back again on the word of a weasel. 'I beg you will listen at least,' he said, 'even if you decide you cannot do as we ask.'

The king sighed in annoyance, but did not stop Sylver from continuing.

'It is this way. Remember those green meadows, with rich bottom land where the wildflowers grew? Remember the woodlands, with their oaks, planes, hornbeams and beeches? What about the brook that tumbled through rocky heather country and the river that wound its way to the sea? Do you not recall the grand castles on their mounds, and the little villages scattered about them, and the market towns and the spires of the churches which pierced the sky?'

The queen's eyes had been growing a little misty as Sylver went on. Strangely, it was she who showed some signs of melting, while the king remained very frosty. 'I remember them,' she murmured. 'I remember regretting leaving them behind.'

'Well, they will all be gone for ever, if you do not return to Welkin, Your Majesty.'

There was a long period of silence before the king asked, 'And what, exactly, will we find if we return?'

Bryony came forward now. 'It is this way. After you left, the animals felt they had a right to take over your lands and your buildings. You had abandoned them, so we felt you had tossed away your right to ownership. Our society re-formed much on the same lines as yours.

'It took many years of chaos before that happened, but eventually the stoats took over the management of the country, with the other animals doing their bidding. Someone had to be in charge and we were happy to leave that to the stoats. But the stoats eventually grew arrogant and believed they were superior to the rest of us. They became the ruling class and we their servants.

'Few repairs, if any, have been carried out on the sea walls since you left. They fell into disrepair without us realizing it. Unlike you humans, animals do not have the necessary engineering skills to rebuild the walls to stem the flood.'

'You want us to come back and repair the dykes, then leave again?' laughed the king humourlessly. 'You must be lunar weasels, mad as the moon.'

'Not leave again,' said Bryony. 'Stay and work with us. Many animals want to return to the wild. Some do not. We can surely work out a compromise between us? There will be those who say you have forfeited the right to live in your own houses. I was one of those. However, we will all have to make sacrifices, you and us, if you come home again. But I'll tell you this: the land is not the same without you, despite the fact that we feared and hated you. Humans are needed as much as any other creature. There is an empty place, which can only be filled by you.'

'Impossible,' said the king. 'We came here to escape our own follies, and stay here we will.'

'Surely you have punished yourselves enough,' said Bryony. 'You have carried out a penance.'

The king sighed. 'I loved the land of Welkin – to feel the tread of my sole upon its soil . . .' But then his voice grew firm and the tone strong again. 'But it cannot be.'

At that moment Sylver, Bryony and the other weasels felt a sense of failure. It seemed that nothing could change the king's mind and the moment had passed when the queen was ready to agree. They were resolved to stay. The weasels looked at each other in utter despair. No-one could force the humans to return. It seemed now that nothing would change the minds of those rigid ex-rulers of Welkin – except . . .

The children. The children came to the rescue.

Having finished cutting off all the flower heads, they came running up to the king and queen. They implored the royal couple to let them go back to their life in the villages and towns of Welkin. They cried that their world had been stolen from them by the adults, and that they had been made to leave the land they loved to follow them, though any strife was no fault of theirs, for they were but children.

While the children were pleading with the monarchs some of the other humans began to emerge from the cave, the wind having blown away the last vestiges of the lotus-flower vapour. Some of them had heard a little of what had passed between the children and their rulers.

An argument began to ensue: some of the humans wanted to go home; others were dead set against it. After they had got over their initial surprise at finding that talking weasels had come to fetch them back to Welkin, many of the humans were willing to listen to what these small creatures of woodland and meadow had to say about the matter.

'Some of us were not interested in becoming rulers,' Sylver explained to the newly woken. 'The dogs, wolves and badgers could easily have taken over, but they preferred to remain outside the struggle. The truth is, weasels, stoats, polecats, pine martens, ferrets and their kind developed intellectual powers faster than other creatures, and soon the conflict was confined to us alone, while other, stronger creatures let us get on with it.'

'The reason we left Welkin in the first place,' said King Andrew, 'was because we spent our time continually at war with one another. Queen Cheryl here and I were always at each other's throats, striving to take each other's territory. There seemed no end to the bloodshed. We could never agree on any compromise. In the end we were visited by a strange wind which brought a tune on its lips. It was a simple melody and people could not get it out of their heads.

'It drove us mad with its insistence – we could no longer think straight. It bewitched us in some way and we found ourselves setting sail to this island. I think we were forced to leave Welkin because of the chaos and destruction we were causing, both to our own kind and to the natural world at large. Some superior being felt that it was better for us to spend eternity in peaceful sleep than to remain in Welkin, causing havoc.'

'A change of king or queen would have made no difference at the time,' continued Queen Cheryl. 'We were so steeped in our ways it was impossible to break the pattern. Now, however, we have spent many years cooling our heels in these caves. I, for one, feel we could work together, humans and animals, for a more peaceful and harmonious society.

'Every conflict seems to be caused by the desire for *power*,' she added. 'We must curb those who seek to wield power; then perhaps we can manage to get along together. We don't have to love each other – we simply need to tolerate each other's differences and try to *understand* one another . . .'

Thus they talked, with the weasels contributing their views on the subject, of course, well into the afternoon. The arguments flew back and forth. Some of the humans felt they had slept for long enough; others felt they should remain in the caves. The queen now sided with those who wished to return, the king with those who wished to stay.

Sylver noticed that the rebellious shadows had crept back, had come to heel, as it were, and were now attached to the humans. They grew longer as the day stretched into evening. They had been tamed again, and were once more the silhouettes and mimics of their owners. It occurred to Sylver that the shadows were enjoying their return to their rightful places in the scheme of things. They were having fun, copying their owners' actions, outgrowing them as the evening sun stretched their forms, fading, then springing back to life when the full moon came out.

The weasels and the humans talked right through the night. The king and queen told the weasels that the 'lotus' fumes had not immediately affected them. Humans, being larger and stronger creatures than weasels, had been able to stay awake longer. It had given them time to beach their ships, raise them up on logs, and find caves in which to lay their heads.

It was Queen Cheryl who brought matters to a head. 'Well, here we are arguing about whether we should or should not go home, but there's no reason why all of us need go. I shall return. Those who wish to come with me are welcome to, whether they are my former subjects or not.'

'If that is the case,' replied the king, 'go one, go all. The half who remain here will be forever wondering if they did the right thing. I suppose that once the sea walls are repaired those who wish to return to Dorma may do so. However –' He pulled in his chin – 'I suspect that once I see those green fields and hills, I shall be as eager as any to wander through them and stare at the butterflies and birds.' He sighed. 'I do miss them, I must admit. I miss them a lot.'

The queen said, 'I shall send some people out to look at our ships. They will probably need some repairs. We will soon be on our way back to Welkin, thanks to these wild creatures from our homeland.'

'And to our children,' the king reminded her; 'the weasels would never have found us without the clues left by Alice and Tom.'

Sylver said, 'We must call in at the muntjac's island over there. We've left some pine martens behind. We have to pick them up on our way home. Also . . .'

'Yes?' said the queen.

'Also we promised them a ship, for helping us find you.'

'Animals wanting a ship?' mused King Andrew. 'Who'd have thought it? Well, if it's been promised them, then they shall have it. They shall have the choice of my navy. How's that, weasel Sylver?'

'That's excellent, Your Majesty,' replied Sylver, relieved. 'Only – only it's *Lord* Sylver, of Thistle Hall in County Elleswhere.'

'Why,' cried out an indignant human, 'that's *my* county. That's *my* home.'

This was a dangerous moment for all. It was difficult for the humans, who had owned everything on Welkin when they left. Here were some upstarts, some small weaselly creatures, who seemed to be claiming to be their equals. It was not an easy thing to accept. Animals had been animals and subject to the rule of the human.

'For my part,' said Sylver, 'the hall can go back to the original owner. I intend to live in Halfmoon Wood. But I cannot speak for all the animals. Each contested property will have to be negotiated. In many cases animals will not mind returning to the wild, or sharing the house with the original owner – even the king and queen might have to share their castles – but I'm afraid you humans must not assume you have the right to march back in and reclaim those places you abandoned so long ago.'

The king and queen, and indeed their subjects, looked a little stunned by this speech. Yet the long sleep on Dorma had done something for the humans: it had given them a new insight.

There was a pause, then the original owner of Thistle Hall said, 'Looks like it's time we humans shared a few things with the animals, doesn't it? I hope you haven't changed the decor in the study. I was rather fond of the tree-scene tapestry in there.'

'I'm afraid we have,' replied Sylver. 'The last occupant was Lord Haukin, a venerable and very intelligent stoat. He moved the tapestry from the east wall to the west wall. I think you'll find the light is better on that side of the room.'

There was another long silence, then the lord replied, 'Jolly good – should have thought of that myself.'

The king added, 'Well, Chalsford, the lords of Thistle Hall were never famous for their brains. Excellent horsemen and brilliant managers of the land, but not too bright otherwise. Good to have had a resident lord with a bit more scrambled egg in his noddle, eh?'

There was general laughter and teeth clicking all round.

The journey back to Welkin was almost as eventful as the journey out, with sea monsters and storms, but the humans seemed to take all these incidents in their stride. The weasels were amazed how capable they were at handling the ships; for their part, the humans were astonished by the weasels' ability to sense a change in the weather. Each had their own skills to offer and were delighted with the success of the other. Together they accomplished the voyage home with ease.

Chapter Thirty-eight

The Lord Protector of all Welkin heard that ships had landed in the far north. Then birds brought horrible rumours that they carried the weasels he had left in far distant islands (the birds said nothing of the humans at this point, being masters of the nasty surprise). Falshed's confidence began to wane with this news. He sent for Sibiline's brother, to offer him half the throne of Welkin in exchange for some good ideas about slaughtering weasels.

'So!' cried Prince Poynt, having been brought up from the basement. 'You are forced to return me to my divine and rightful position as ruler of this kingdom!'

Falshed glared at the prince. 'If you don't hold your tongue, Poynt, I shall have you sent back where you came from. We have a crisis on our hands. The weasels have returned. If they bring news of the humans they will be heroes in some quarters of Welkin and there will be rebellion.'

Even Prince Poynt, thick as he was, could foresee the problems the weasels' return might cause. 'We must raise an army,' he said quickly. '*Three* armies. Sib will lead the famous stoat Jillazons, marching northwards up the west coast.

I shall take my ferrets up the central plain. You, Lord Protector, will take your stoats up the eastern side of the country. We shall converge at a point just south of the unnamed marshes, and there trap the weasels in the head and horns of the stag beetle—'

'Stag beetle? What stag beetle?' asked Sibiline, losing the thread here.

'It's a strategy invented by your dead brother Redfur, a battle movement which is now considered one of the most devastating of all attacks,' explained Falshed. 'The prince's army is the head of the beetle, while yours and mine are the horns. The enemy soldiers gather for the onslaught of the one army they can see, the head of the beetle. Their columns are arranged to deal with a frontal attack while, unknown to their leader, the horns of the beetle are closing in on their flanks.'

'Exactly so,' murmured the prince. 'My brother was a brilliant warrior.'

Falshed was deep in thought: the prince would be useful to him until the battle was over; then he would have that spoilt royal stoat thrown back in the basement again. Or, better still, banish him with the surviving weasels to some remote island. Yes, that would be best: get rid of him altogether. Otherwise Falshed would have to watch his back for the rest of his life. But he actually said, 'And you are quite brilliant, my prince, for remembering his tactics and strategies.'

Thank you, Falshed, thought the prince, but don't think this flattery is going to save you when the time comes. I'm going to have you dragged behind a team of wild voles – water voles – who will eventually be allowed to head for the river, where they will submerge, taking you with them, thus ridding me of an upstart and rapscallion of the worst order.

These were the prince's thoughts, but he actually said, 'We work well together, Lord Protector. When we rule side by side, with our sister, we shall be the envy of the world.'

How nice, thought Sibiline, watching her two favourite stoats. How nice that my brother and my jackfriend are getting on so well together at last. It will be a cosy little threesome. There's nothing like solving problems for bringing families and friends closer together. 'It's nice to see that although you are rivals, you two, you can pull together when the need arises,' she said.

The armies were made ready for the march northwards. In the meantime reliable information had finally reached Castle Rayn that the humans were accompanying the weasels. This news did not daunt any of the stoat rulers in the least.

'We shall smash both the rebels and the humans and rid ourselves of the threat once and for all,' said Prince Poynt. 'Our swords will taste the blood of the Upright Ones. Our lances will prick their eyes. Our spears will fall on them as the ungentle rain from heaven falls upon the earth beneath.'

'I say, that last sentence was rather good,' Falshed said admiringly. 'Where did you get it?'

'Oh, from some book or other,' replied Poynt airily. 'I can read, you know . . .'

At that moment a messenger arrived in the

throne room to say that Lord Haukin had arrived. He was stepping off the ferry at that very moment. The Lord Protector, the prince, the princess and all the noblestoats of the castle waited for him.

Lord Haukin was not a popular figure amongst his peers. He was too studious in times of peace and too good a general in times of war. They were envious. They did not see how a stoat could be both sporty and bookish. It did not seem right. It flouted the rules. The sporty ones should be able to bully the bookish ones. Somehow Lord Haukin spoiled their fun.

'What is this I hear?' thundered the elderly stoat, sweeping into the court. 'You have gathered together every soldier in the kingdom . . . not to say peasant weasels from their fields . . .'

'We need *someone* to carry the luggage,' grumbled Prince Poynt. 'You can't expect my soldiers to look after the baggage train.'

'You must stop this nonsense at once,' ordered Lord Haukin. 'We need the humans to help us save Welkin from the floods. Sylver and his weasels have done a tremendous service to our country. Disband your troops instantly, or you will have me to contend with. I have my own soldiers waiting on the shore of the lake. If you do not stop this foolishness I shall order them to attack the castle at once.'

'You will do nothing of the kind,' snapped Prince Poynt. 'Guards! Throw this traitor into the basement! I want him executed three days after we set out on our march. Hang his pelt from the flagpole of the north tower. I want it to be the first thing I see as I march back in triumph from the wars.'

The royal ferrets moved in and secured the prisoner.

'You will regret this,' fumed Lord Haukin. 'My stoat army . . .'

The prince clacked his teeth. 'Your stoats? They were Lord Ragnar's stoats before you took them over. I'll tell them of your treachery towards Lord Ragnar. I remember you said Raggy went on ahead in the battle against the rats. But you didn't say he trusted you would support him with your troops! And you deliberately held back – yes –' the prince's eyes glimmered as he developed his untruths – 'yes – you allowed him to die unsupported in the claws of his enemies, so that you could take over Fearsomeshire after his death. You're disloyal, you betray your own kind, you are a foul murderer.'

'That's not true. Lord Ragnar overreached himself. He charged on ahead without thinking. I called to Lord Ragnar to return, told him to exercise caution, but he was always rash and headstrong. He took no notice of me.'

'That's the way I heard it too,' said Falshed, who did not like these court intrigues to get out of paw. 'Lord Haukin tried to save Lord Ragnar.'

'Well, you heard it wrong,' snapped Prince Poynt. 'Away with the traitor. Send word that the captain of Lord Haukin's troops is now a general. Promote everyone in his army. Take a chest full of golden groats and hand them out. Then separate Haukin's soldiers, mix them in with our own troops. We'll see how loyal they remain to their lord after that.'

It was a very clever move and one worthy of the sibling of the dead King Redfur.

'Brother,' said Sibiline, who was also uneasy about his extreme behaviour, 'we must not descend into chaos and lawlessness. In any case –' she quickly reverted to a more practical argument when she saw the fierce look in Poynt's eyes – 'you will have no-one left in the castle to do the execution. Why not just send Lord Haukin back to Fearsomeshire? He can do us no harm if we have his troops amongst our own.'

The prince looked around him quickly, then pointed to Pompom, the weasel jester. 'You – you will remain behind and execute Lord Haukin.'

Pompom almost jumped out of his skin. 'Me? I – I – yes, my liege, my prince. How – how shall I do it? Shall I beat him to death with my inflated mouse-bladder on the end of a stick?' Pompom was hoping to make a joke of it; he felt quite unequal to the horrible task.

'You will burn out his heart with a red-hot poker.'

'Yekk,' said a soldier standing nearby.

Pompom's fur stood on end and he looked faint. 'Yes, my liege,' he said in a small, still voice. 'I hear and obey.'

'Now we must be off,' cried the prince. 'I shall go to the armour room and get into my metal togs. I had this new suit of armour made by the blacksmith Spingleberg of Gattsmere – it's inlaid with gold and silver emblems of the moon and stars. It's never been worn in anger before. I shall look magnificent – I shall look like a stoat god. Falshed – you can borrow my old one.'

'But that one's gone rusty.'

'Touch of rust won't hurt you, stoat. Oil the joints with a bit of spit – that always helps. Come on, let's get cracking. I can't wait to get my claws on a weapon, can you? We'll smash them to bits. We'll send them spinning back into the sea. War is glorious, you know. My brother Redfur always said so.'

So the three armies gathered together. Lord Haukin's troops were promoted, bribed and split up, finding themselves in the ranks of three separate armies. Even those loyal to Haukin could do nothing about it. Finally the three armies began to march northwards. Eventually, the weasels were sighted, leading the humans along a valley.

Seen from a great height, the humans did not look so formidable. True, they were wedged in a narrow valley and it was difficult to assess their numbers, but the prince's eyes were full of blood and battlelight. He saw what he wished to see: a motley group of shuffling bipeds. Prince Poynt looked down on their heads and narrow shoulders far below and gained heart. He rallied his troops with a fiery speech, then went charging off in front, like a wolf descending on the fold.

The prince was running so fast in his shiny new armour that he could not stop when he hit the front rank of the weasels. They had not been expecting any attack, but had the foresight to break ranks. With his Royal Guard he thus breached the first line of the enemy. He then found himself confronting creatures who were taller than the tallest bunch of hedgerow thistles; they towered over stoats and weasels alike. Seeing a human from beneath, instead of from above, was an entirely different matter. The prince halted and gulped.

'What is this?' cried the king of the humans, accompanied by a queen. 'Is this supposed to be your idea of a welcoming party, ermine?'

Prince Poynt stumbled backwards and stared up in awe at this ugly, gargantuan animal called a human being. Never in his life before had he been so impressed. For several minutes he just stared. Thoughts whirled through his brain – ideas of subduing this king and queen of the humans. But the more he stared up into the broad, flat faces of these giants, the more impossible he knew his ideas to be. These were creatures with cunning and sagacity which far outstripped his own. These were great heavy beasts with grasping hands.

Instead of thrusting with his sword at the monstrous foot before him, the prince found himself unbuckling his armour and laying it on the ground. First he unsheathed his sword and stuck it point first in the turf. The same with his royal dagger. These were followed by the buckler and the foreleg and rearleg pieces. The last thing to leave his body was the magnificent breastplate and backplate, the cuirass fashioned by Spingleberg of Gattsmere, which he placed by the helmet with the oily-black raven's plume sprouting from its peak.

When he had finished, the queen said, 'Isn't your coat out of season, stoat?'

In that moment a wave rippled from Poynt's nose to the tip of his tail and the fur on his back changed from pure white to ordinary brown. Then, slowly, the muscular, blunt-nosed stoat went down on one knee. 'My lord,' said the prince to the human king and queen, 'you have my ever-lasting loyalty.'

'Glad to hear it,' said the queen, 'but get off your knees, stoat. In future let no Welkinian bow to another. We are all the Creator's creatures here.'

The other two armies had also now descended from the hills and witnessed this exchange between Prince Poynt and the humans. They saw the prince change from royal ermine to common stoat. They too were suitably awed by the mere presence of the humans. Quietly, Sibiline and Falshed both ordered their armies to remove their armour and lay down their weapons.

Soon everyone was heading south – weasel and stoat together with humans and other animals – marching peacefully out of the valley which was to have run with blood. Instead, it was strewn with glittering swords, shields, pikes, halberds and other arms and armour. Here they would lie, to sink into the mire on rainy days, to rust, to be forgotten.

As he approached Castle Rayn Prince Poynt was horrified to see a brown pelt hanging from the flagpole. 'Oh, Lord,' he said to Falshed and Sibiline, 'Pompom's gone and executed Lord Haukin. The weasels will be up in arms about this! What can we do?'

The other two stoats had no suggestions for the prince.

When they disembarked from the ferry boats onto the battlements, the prince kept his eyes averted from the flagpole. He waited for the screams of anguish from Sylver and his band.

'Hey,' cried Scirf at last, 'who – who's hung a doormat up there?'

Prince Poynt looked up to see a tatty old doormat, from the entrance to the dungeons, dangling from the flagpole. He had a momentary flash of anger at Pompom for not obeying his orders – it was difficult to break his old habits all at once – and then felt a flood of relief wash through his stoatly body. He put a comradely arm around Scirf's shoulder, noticing that his new friend's pelt was not in much better condition than the doormat of which they were speaking. 'Pompom did it,' he said. 'It's a sort of – joke.'

'All Pompom's jokes are *sort-of*,' replied Scirf. 'I must ask him to explain this one to me sometime.'

When they went down the spiral staircase, they found Pompom and Lord Haukin in the banquet room, making free with the prince's larder. Pompom jumped up and started to run, until he saw that Prince Poynt had lost his winter coat, was accompanied by weasels and humans, and was not looking angry.

Still the court jester hid behind Lord Haukin, who had a few choice words to say to the prince, before greeting the humans and informing them, in a brisk and businesslike manner, of the latest state of the dykes and sea walls.

It was all very satisfactory, as they say, in the end.

It was not long before the humans began to get

to work on the sea walls. They took their great ox-carts to the mountains and brought back great boulders which they jammed and wedged into the gaps in the dykes. They used huge oak and beech trunks to hold some of the blocks in place, hammering them point first into the ground to reinforce the earthworks. Then tons of clay were dug and rammed into place with adze and shovel. The weasels could only stand and watch in awe as these massive engineering projects took place.

Over the next few months, too, animal and human learned to live together. Of course, there was not universal harmony – there never has been – but justice was beginning to hold sway. Negotiation, rather than violence, was the order of the day. Everyone at least tried to temper any rush of blood to the head and think first before acting.

And the strange thing was, though magic did not leave the land at once, it began to wane bit by bit. The moment a human foot stepped onto Welkin soil, the statues froze and moved no more. They had become proper statues again, of metal, wood, stone and plaster. Some were left where they were, but others were brought back and placed in courtyards and town squares. Of course, many had found their way home to their First and Last Resting Place.

Seven months later Halfmoon Wood was a tranquil place, where weasels had once more gone back to living in weasel caves. They found holes under rocks, or in trees, or on the river bank. Here they made their homes, lining them with soft moss or hay. Sylver and his band had returned to the old ways, enjoying living close to the earth, with its own particular scents, sights and sounds.

They had a kalkie, not to a dead comrade, but to a dead life. There was a new life to be had, in forest and field. Every jack and jill in the land was now free to roam as he or she wished.

Most were happy to romp among the daisies, but there was one weasel who was not satisfied with simple, earthly pleasures, and needed to feel useful. This was, of course, Scirf, who had joined the band of outlaw weasels when there was a need for such creatures in the land.

Scirf took a job as a nightwatchmammal, and very good at it he was too.

FROM 'THE HISTORY OF WELKIN'

Once the humans had repaired the sea walls they began to return to their villages and towns, their manors and castles. They were changed creatures however and where there were weasels or stoats in residence, they came to some agreement, building a smaller, more suitable house for the animals at the bottom of the garden, or converting a shed for their use. Some of the town and village weasels found, like the animals of Halfmoon Wood, that it was preferable to return to the old ways. Others however were so attuned to a comfortable life in a house they took up the offer and stayed on, often as close neighbours to the humans.

Lord Haukin went back to live in Thistle Hall, the old owner being an elderly and rather lonely human who had spoken with Lord Haukin during the course of the sea wall restoration, and found him an intelligent companion. I, Culver, accompanied my old master of course, and found myself with enough free time to pen this History of Welkin, for posterity.

Prince Poynt remained as ruler of the stoats, and lived in an abandoned wooden fort on a hill overlooking Fearsomeshire. He still tried to boss weasels around, but they laughed and clawed their noses at him. His only companion, apart from his guards, was Pompom the jester weasel. The pair spent gloomy hours together inside the fort, recalling the good old days – of skittles with live scullery jacks as pins, and cricket with chamber jills for stumps. Occasionally Pompom would make the prince an apple-pie bed, just to remind the stoat ruler that his days of lording it over weasels had really gone.

Sibiline and Falshed left Castle Rayn for warmer climes. They went to live on a small island just off the southern coast of Welkin called the Isle of Blakk. They were joined by the otter, Sleek, and together they started a fashion industry, producing designer garments for wealthy stoats and weasels.

Sleek wrote to Scirf and asked him if he would like a job as their chief salesmammal, but Scirf declined. He told them he was more your pedlar type of salesmammal. Indeed he soon quit his job as a nightwatchmammal and began travelling with his wares on his back, carrying outrageous tales as well as saucepans from village to town, a familiar figure over the whole of Welkin.

Finally, there was Spinfer, the stoatservant who had been Falshed's ideas-mammal when the sheriff was at the height of his civil service career. It was rumoured that Spinfer went into human politics and was the brains behind one or two surprising political coups, though of course the humans who employed him kept him hidden in some back room somewhere. It is certain he lived in comfort, all his needs met, spinning out his intrigues and weaving his conspiracies, to the very end of his life.

From the pen of –
CULVER THE WEASEL

ABOUT THE AUTHOR

Garry Kilworth was born in York but, as the son of an Air Force family, was educated at more than twenty schools. He himself joined the RAF at the age of fifteen and was stationed all over the world, from Singapore to Cyprus, before leaving to continue his education and begin a career in business, which also enabled him to travel widely.

He became a full-time writer when his two young children left home and has written many novels for both adults and younger readers – mostly on science fiction, fantasy and historical themes. He has won several awards for his work, including the World Fantasy Award in 1992, and the Lancashire Book Award in 1995 for *The Electric Kid*.

His previous titles for Transworld Publishers include *Thunder Oak* and *Castle Storm*, the first and second titles in the Welkin Weasels trilogy, *The Electric Kid* and *Cybercats*; and *House of Tribes* and *A Midsummer's Nightmare* for Bantam Press/Corgi Books.

Garry Kilworth lives in a country cottage in Essex which has a large woodland garden teeming with wildlife, including foxes, doves, squirrels and grass snakes.

THE WELKIN WEASELS
Book 1: Thunder Oak

by Garry Kilworth

Long ago, before Sylver the weasel was born, the humans all left Welkin. Now life for a weasel – under the heavy paw of the vicious stoat rulers – is pretty miserable (unless you happen to be a weasel who *likes* living in a hovel and toiling all hours for the benefit of the stoats).

It's certainly not enough for Sylver. Or for his small band of outlaws, both jacks and jills. But slingshots and darts can only do so much against heavily-armed stoats and life as an outlaw has a fairly limited future (probably a painful one, too). That's when Sylver comes up with his plan – a heroic plan that could destroy the stoats' reign of power for ever. He will find the humans and bring them back to Welkin! And the first step is to follow up a clue from the past – a clue that lies in a place known as *Thunder Oak* . . .

ISBN 0 552 54546 5

Now available from all good book stores.

THE WELKIN WEASELS
Book 2: Castle Storm

by Garry Kilworth

Rats! Hundreds and thousands of rats are pouring down from the northern marshes in Welkin to seize power from the stoat rulers. Sylver – the leader of a band of outlaw weasels – has no love for the vicious stoats but, with Welkin itself under threat, must offer a helping paw.

But stoat treachery serves only to speed him on his way on his real quest: to find the humans who mysteriously abandoned Welkin many years ago. With his small company of jacks and jills, he journeys south, through myriad adventures, to the dreys of the squirrel knights who live beneath the shadow of an ancient castle – *Castle Storm*.

The second title in a dramatic and marvellously inventive trilogy, *The Welkin Weasels*.

ISBN 0 552 54574 3

Now available from all good book stores.

All Transworld titles are available by post from:

Book Service By Post, PO Box 29, Douglas, Isle of Man, IM99 1BQ

Credit cards accepted. Please telephone 01624 675137,
fax 01624 670923, Internet http://www.bookpost.co.uk
or e-mail: bookshop@enterprise.net for details

Free postage and packing in the UK. Overseas customers:
allow £1 per book (paperbacks) and £3 per book (hardbacks)